Praise for Karen Brooks

"Gleefully bawdy, delightfully irreverent, this vibrant novel not only invokes empathy for the struggles of women in Chaucer's times, it resonates with women's experiences today."

—Darry Fraser, bestselling Australian author, on *The Good Wife of Bath*

"Historian and novelist Brooks shows her research and imaginative chops in a luscious and astonishingly affecting chronicle of family scandal, political unrest, and redemptive hope in 1660s London."

—*Publishers Weekly* on *The Chocolate Maker's Wife*

"Brooks masterfully deploys surprising plot twists, deftly pacing the opening of closets to reveal hidden diaries and family skeletons. . . . A charming and smart historical novel from a master storyteller."

—*Kirkus Reviews* on *The Chocolate Maker's Wife*

"Sensual, seductive, bold. . . . A rich indulgence."

—*Booklist* on *The Chocolate Maker's Wife*

"The latest from Australian author Brooks is an excellent option for reading groups that enjoy multigenerational tales and historical fiction. . . . Your late middle English vocabulary will be sumptuously rewarded."

—*Library Journal* on *The Chocolate Maker's Wife*

"Meticulously researched and historically compelling . . . this fast-paced novel is a dramatic spy thriller that shines a spotlight on the inner workings of Elizabethan England."

—*Books + Publishing* on *The Locksmith's Daughter*

THE
GOOD
WIFE
OF
BATH

Also by Karen Brooks

The Lady Brewer of London
The Locksmith's Daughter
The Chocolate Maker's Wife

THE
GOOD
WIFE
OF
BATH

A (MOSTLY)
TRUE STORY

KAREN BROOKS

WILLIAM MORROW
An Imprint of HarperCollinsPublishers

P.S.™ is a trademark of HarperCollins Publishers.

HarperCollins books may be purchased for educational, business, or sales promotional use. For information, please email the Special Markets Department at SPsales@harpercollins.com.

Originally published in Australia in 2021 by Harlequin.

FIRST U.S. EDITION

Library of Congress Cataloging-in-Publication Data has been applied for.

ISBN 978-0-06-314283-1

22 23 24 25 26   LSC   10 9 8 7 6 5 4 3 2 1

This book is for my beloved friend, Kerry Doyle—the best of them.
She's a "good" woman as well as "wife" in all the wonderful, multiple,
contradictory, and complex meanings of that word.
It's also a salute to all the wives and women throughout time who've
been forced, for whatever reason, to endure; who've been abused and
neglected and punished for their strengths and their weaknesses.
May your voices be heard as well.

By God, if women had but written stories
Like those the clergy kept in oratories,
More had been written of men's wickedness
Than all the sons of Adam could redress.

—The Wife of Bath's Prologue, *The Canterbury Tales*
by Geoffrey Chaucer, translated by Neville Coghill

◆

The wisest man in the world is one who doesn't care who's in charge.
— Attributed to Ptolemy

CONTENTS

PROLOGUE

———— ✦ ————

WHO PAINTED THE LION?

The Swanne, Southwark
The Year of Our Lord 1406
In the seventh year of the reign of Henry IV

*M*y father would oft remark that the day I was born, the heavens erupted in protest. Great clods of ice rained upon poor unsuspecting folk, and the winds were so bitter and cold, those who could remained indoors. Any sod who couldn't, risked death in the fields along with the shivering, miserable beasts. He didn't tell me to arouse my guilt, but to remind me to hold up my head and stand proud. I may have been born the daughter of a peasant, but it wasn't every day a lass could say she made her mark upon the world.

I came into being on the 21st of April 1352, a day henceforth known as "Black Saturday" and not because the woman who'd carried me the last nine months died moments before I arrived, casting a ghastly pall over what should have been a celebration.

The story I grew up with was that my mother's fate was very nearly my own as, even in death, her womb refused to expel me.

It wasn't until the midwife, seeing the rippling of her stomach as if some devil-sent spawn was writhing within, understood the Grim Reaper had not yet departed the room. He was awaiting another soul to carry forth. Wishing him gone, she snatched his sacred scythe from his gnarly hand and ripped open my mother's body and, amidst blood and swollen entrails, pulled me forth like a sacrificial offering of old.

My father, hearing the screams of dismay and fear, forwent the sacred rules of the birthing chamber and burst through the door. Determining that the shade of blue coloring my flesh, while it looked fine upon a noblewoman's mantle, was no color for a babe to be wearing, hoisted me off the bloodied rushes where the midwife had dropped me and, ordering her to cut the umbilicus, swung me by my ankles, slapping my flesh until it turned a much happier puce.

Only then did I bawl—loud, long, and lusty.

The midwife promptly fainted; my father gathered me to his chest, laughing and crying while I hollered noisily, competing with the raging storms outside.

It was decided then and there (or maybe this is something I invented later) that though I was born under the sign of Taurus, I was a child of Mars—a fighter who stared death in the face and scared him witless. Papa declared, and the midwife—who came to at my screams—concurred: the moment I burst into life, the Reaper picked up his robes and fled the room. He even forgot his scythe.

But Mars was not alone when he blessed me with the blood and spirit of a warrior. Oh no. For while Papa, unaware Mama had died as he tried to soften my cries and sought for something in which to swaddle me, Venus, Mars's wanton bride, peered over his shoulder. Because she liked what she saw, she leaned forward and placed the sweetest of kisses upon my puckered brow. Not finished, she turned me over and pressed one each upon my peach-like buttocks as well. In doing this, the goddess of love and ruler over all Taureans thrice blessed me with her own deep desires. Desires that lay dormant for many years until they gushed forth, destroying all in their path.

God was preoccupied tending to my mother's swiftly departed soul and Papa's grief. His distraction allowed the pagan gods to claim me—Mars and Venus, Ares and Aphrodite—Roman or Greek, I'm partial to both.

Christened Eleanor, it was the name I wore for many years before fate forced me to change it. But I'm getting ahead of myself, something I'm inclined to do and pray you'll forgive me.

The years went by and the Wheel of Fortune turned until it forced God—who I swear until then barely acknowledged my presence, for He never heard my prayers—to notice me.

Before my monthly courses began to flow, my father passed from this earthly realm leaving me in the care of the woman who had elevated him beyond his wildest dreams. The Lady Clarice, a formerly wealthy landowner whose entire family and many servants died during the Botch, hired my father, by then an itinerant brogger who brokered wool for a living, as steward of her neglected sheep and fallow lands. Papa proved worthy of my lady's faith, increasing her holdings and the quality of her flock. Eternally grateful, or so she said, she made my father promises that, upon his death, she failed to keep. Foremost was that she would care for me if he died—unless you count being taken into service at the manor as caring. I was ten years of age.

Before handing me over to the housekeeper, Mistress Bertha, my lady imparted some words of wisdom. She told me I'd but one gift, the most valuable thing a woman could own. Misunderstanding her meaning, I waited eagerly for what she was about to bestow. Turns out, I was already in possession of it. My lady was referring to my queynte—my cunt. But, she made sure to emphasize, it was only of worth if it was untouched, pure and virginal. Then, it was an opportunity—something to be used to one day better my situation by marrying well. I was ordered to protect my maidenhead as the Crusaders did the walls of Jerusalem (though, one presumes, with more success).

From here on, said Lady Clarice, my body would be under siege—from the attentions of men and, much worse, the naturally lascivious thoughts a woman possessed and which I admit were already beginning to take up a great deal of space in my head. According to Father Roman, the village priest, women were the gateway of the devil, insatiable beasts who devoured hapless men with their longings. I recall looking at May, my rather plain and plump friend and fellow-maid, thinking the only kind of man she'd devour would be the cooked kind. Regardless, we women were all cast in the same lustful role, high born, low born, and anywhere in the middle. Even me, only recently thrust from childhood.

Rather than God, it was the man I thought of as The Poet who saved me from falling victim to my naturally lewd nature. At least, that's how others tell it—especially The Poet. In fact, he's always taken credit for my story.

I call him The Poet because that was how he was first introduced to me. Later, I came to know him as someone possessed of many guises: a wondrous spinner of tales, a wine-merchant's son, a Londoner, John of Gaunt's lackey, a diplomat, a watcher, a cuckold, even an accused rapist. Eventually, I would come to know him in a very different way.

Regardless, he was the man who took my tale from me and became its custodian. I want to believe he meant well in committing me to verse, that he sought to rewrite my history in a way that gave me mastery over it. Mayhap, he did that. He also protected me from my sins—not the lustful kind. Despite what you may think, bodily desire doesn't make the angels cower. Rather, in writing my tale, The Poet sought to shield me from the consequences of my darker deeds by distracting those who would call me to account. For, while folk are titillated and shocked by his portrait, they don't see *me*. In retrospect, it was a clever maneuver. I never thanked him properly. Perhaps this is what this is—a delayed thank-you as well as a setting to rights of sorts. I confess, there are some versions of me he crafted I quite like and may yet keep. We'll see.

Alas, he's gone, and I'll never really know exactly why he portrayed me the way he did, with boundless avarice, unchecked lust, vulgarity, overweening pride, and more besides.

The Poet equipped me with every sin.

Betraying my trust in him, using my secret fears and desires, he exposed my weaknesses—my strengths too—and turned them into something for others' amusement. Oh, amused they were—and still are, for I hear them discussing the wanton Alyson, the Wife of Bath, and her many flaws. Mind you, they're a little afeared as well, and I don't mind that so much. Either way, he's dead (may God assoil him), and it's time for me to wrest my tale back and tell it in my own way. As it really happened. And, when my story is complete, you can judge for yourself whose version you prefer: the loud, much-married, lusty woman dressed in scarlet who traveled the world in order to pray at all the important shrines yet learned nothing of humility, questioned divinity, boasted of her conquests and deceits, and demanded mastery over men. Or the imperfect child who grew into an imperfect woman—experienced, foolish, and clever too—oft at the same time. Thrice broken, twice betrayed, once murdered, and once a murderer, who mended herself time after time and rose to live again in stories and in truth—mostly.

All this despite five bloody husbands.

All this, despite the damn Poet.

PART ONE

The Marriage Debt

1364 to 1386
No sooner than one husband's dead and gone
Some other Christian man shall take me on.

—The Wife of Bath's Prologue, *The Canterbury Tales* by
Geoffrey Chaucer, translated by Neville Coghill

———◆———

The man is not under the lordship of the woman, but
the woman is under the lordship of the man.
[Another writer has added in the margins: "Not always."]

—From the thirteenth-century regulations of the poulterers of
Paris, edited by GB Depping, *Réglemens sur les arts et métiers de*
Paris rédigés au 13e siécle et connus sous le nom du Livre des métiers
d'Étienne Boileau, 1837

The Tale of Husband the First, Fulk Bigod

1364 to 1369
Wedding's no sin, so far as I can learn
Better it is to marry than to burn.

—The Wife of Bath's Prologue, *The Canterbury Tales* by
Geoffrey Chaucer, translated by Neville Coghill

ONE

I stared in dismay at the old man standing in the middle of the room who, as the steward announced me in the coldest of tones, looked as out of place as a whore in a priory. On second thoughts, knowing some of the local sisters, mayhap not. What on God's good earth was that pariah, Master Fulk Bigod, doing here at Noke Manor, let alone in her ladyship's solar? His reputation as a peculiar loner who grunted rather than spoke followed him like the stench of his person. A farmer and wool grower, he lived on the outskirts of the village. With four wives already in the grave, it was said he bullied folk until they sold him their daughters or their sheep. Papa never had time for him—not that he was alone in that respect. The man was despised and mostly avoided. By everyone. By me.

Until now.

Dear Lord, was this to be my punishment? Was this how I was to pay for my sin? I was going to be sent away and made to work for this man. It was said no servant he hired remained long. They fled the coop once they saw what roosted there. God help me. Though what was I doing requesting aid from the Almighty? It was a priest who got me into this mess in the first place. A mess that saw me locked away in my bedroom and now, days later, dragged before my betters.

I worried my lip as I regarded those who filled the room. There was my good lady mistress, her friend The Poet, the new steward Master Merriman, a number of servants—friends—who could scarce meet my eyes, and bloody, stinking Fulk Bigod.

Papa in heaven, help me.

Ever since *it* happened, I'd been kept in solitude and ordered to contemplate the shame my actions had brought upon my lady and my dead father. I was told to pray for forgiveness and my everlasting soul. Shocked by how swiftly my fortunes had undergone a change, as if the Fates had suddenly given Fortuna's wheel a random spin, I didn't comply. Not straight away.

When I was first confined to my room and Master Merriman latched the door, warning me I'd remain there until the lady decided how to salvage the situation, I banged on the wood and shouted myself hoarse. When no one appeared to release or console me, and the celebrations outside continued as if nothing momentous had occurred, I did indeed drop to my knees and pray to the Heavenly Father—for a few minutes, then I grew bored. It's hard to stay focused when there's no reply. May as well talk to oneself. I crossed myself, leaped up, and pushed open the shutters to see what I was missing out on.

Beyond the manor house, the sun cast a mellow glow over the May Day celebrations that were in full swing. The Queen of the May, Mariot Breaksper, the baker's daughter, had been crowned. She looked mighty fine in her green kirtle, her golden hair unbound and a garland of flowers planted upon her head. Twirling around the maypole, holding the brightly colored ribbons I'd helped attach, were my friends, their heads adorned with the greenery we'd woken early to cut from the nearby woods. There was clapping, stomping, and much laughter, all accompanied by flutes, viols, pipes, and drums. Fires were lit and, as the afternoon wore on and the smell of roasting meat carried into the attic to taunt me, I wished I was among it all. With a great sigh, I rested my elbows on the sill, my chin on my palms.

Movement in the courtyard below caught my attention. There was a gathering of horses and men and, in their midst, my lady herself. She looked regal in her blue gown, with a particularly lovely circlet of blooms atop her wimple. As I watched, she turned to converse with one of the riders. More soberly dressed than the others, having divested himself of his costume, was The Poet. He'd become a regular visitor over the last few years, and though I'd never really caught his name I always welcomed his presence. A relative of Lady Clarice's—a distant cousin or such—he was employed as a lawyer's clerk at Gray's Inn in London while studying for the bar, or so I'd heard. Thought to be clever, it wasn't his learning I anticipated—it was the stories he brought whenever he came, stories that transported all who heard them with their vivid descriptions of maidens in distress, knights on quests, lascivious friars, righteous monks, foolish millers, vain prioresses, gods, goddesses, and mortals misbehaving or enacting deeds of marvelous courage. Whatever the tale, The Poet knew how to hold an audience captive.

Only the night before, on May Day Eve, The Poet had delighted us with the story of Cupid and Psyche. The beautiful young woman, Psyche, was to be married to a monster in order to protect the city. But when her wedding night came, the monster, who insisted they remain in the dark so his bride could not see him, was gentle and passionate. Asked to trust him and to never, ever attempt to look at him, the silly chit listened to her jealous sisters who, beset with envy at how their sister lived and how she described her lusty husband, persuaded her to break the vow. One night, Psyche held up a lantern so she could see who was sarding her. It was no monster. Taken aback by her husband's beauty, she tipped the lamp and spilled some wax, which burned the beautiful winged god to whom she was really married. He fled, and she then spent years atoning in an effort to find him again. Everyone clapped and cheered when it was finished and called for more. All I could think was how the stupid girl almost lost a grand opportunity. Imagine, being married to a god! Who cares what he looked like? I would have happily remained in the dark if I was given endless coin to spend, a beautiful house in which to dwell, lavish clothes, and food aplenty. Never mind a deity to swive me.

The Poet was talking earnestly to Lady Clarice from atop his horse. I'd been looking forward to hearing more of his tales that evening. Now, as a witness to my shame, I was glad it appeared he was departing. I leaned as far out of the casement as I was able, but couldn't hear what was being said. The Poet nodded and touched his chest as if taking an oath. Lady Clarice passed him a purse, which he tucked into his tunic. I began to wonder if he would ever weave a story about me and what I'd done. It would be a good 'un. I forced a chuckle when all I really wanted to do was weep.

The Poet kicked his horse and, as he signaled for his squire to follow, looked straight to where I was watching and saluted me.

I leaped away from the window lest I incur more of my lady's anger. She'd been in a white-hot rage when she ordered Master Merriman to lock me away. With a deep sigh I sank onto the bed and thought about the reason I was banned from the celebrations.

Father Layamon.

He'd arrived at the manor a few weeks earlier and caused quite the stir among the household. Father Layamon had come to assist our priest, Father Roman. Rumor had it that Father Layamon was the bishop's bastard son. Not only was having him at Noke Manor a huge honor for my lady and Father Roman, but his presence brought great prestige to the village. Not that I or the other maids cared about any of that.

Young, tall, and ridiculously handsome with his jet-black hair, long lashes, twinkling dark eyes, and soft pillow lips, Father Layamon was like the heroes of The Poet's tales. I could have admired him all day—and listened to him. Alas, Father Layamon of the honey pipes was rendered mute during mass, doomed to assist boring old Father Roman, who delivered Latin like a series of insults. In less time than it took to say two Pater Nosters, that windbag of a priest had warned the young Father to keep his distance from all the maids, especially me.

'Twas my hair that made me the target of Father Roman's injunction. Red was the color of passion, blood, and whoredom. According to our priest, I'd been conceived when my mother should have abstained, and was therefore doomed. "As St. Jerome wrote," the priest would thunder, "flame-haired women are hell-bound."

Anyone with half a mind knew the worst thing to say to a young man—or woman for that matter, especially one with Venus as her ruler—was to forbid them to keep company. Cook should have known better when she urged me to keep my eyes off the young priest and eat my pottage. But how could I fasten my eyes upon gray gruel when there was a delicious alternative to feast on at the high table? And what about Father Roman? Why, he was drooling over the lad as if he was the goose Cook fattened for the Epiphany feast.

Cook's words—and the bloated Father's—fell on the deafest of ears. Ever since my courses began a few months back, I'd taken a particular interest in men. Actually, it would be more accurate to say I was interested in the effect I had on them. Previously ignored as a rude girl with too much to say for herself, suddenly men of all ages and ranks sought to catch my attention, exchange words, and, mostly, to fumble and steal kisses. Washing my face and neck carefully each morning, brushing my clothes and tying my apron so it accentuated my newly acquired waist, I would spend more time than ever ensuring my cap lay just so upon my locks, and my laces were undone enough to hint at growing bosoms. My face was nothing extraordinary, I was practical enough to admit that. I was in possession of big eyes, an even bigger mouth (so Father Roman kept telling me) with full lips and large teeth that had a generous gap between the front ones. Angry freckles scattered across the bridge of my nose and in other places besides. I did possess a set of dimples that were the envy of the stablehand's little sister and I made good use of those.

When I first came into Lady Clarice's service, there were those among the servants and villeins who remembered my mother and would say they saw little of her in me. They would remark what a beauty she was, breaking off mid-sentence when they realized they were talking about Melisine de Compton. With pinking cheeks, they'd drift away or change the subject. Not because they feared they'd offended my sensibilities. Nay. It was because, coming from a good home with a good name, it was felt my mother had lowered herself when she married my father, Wace Cornfed, a brogger. That was before the pestilence struck. I oft wondered if people would think differently about her choice now, since the world had transformed so. Well, because of that and other things, mostly Papa's hard work, luck, and the benefice of Lady Clarice and the fact there were no more de Comptons around—except me, I guess—Wace Cornfed had risen in the world. Not much, but, as Papa said, you took what opportunities you could and made them better.

Unless your name was Eleanor Cornfed, in which case you trampled all over them until they were nothing but a pile of shitty dirt.

You've probably guessed by now what happened. I lay with Layamon. It would be funny if it wasn't so serious.

For weeks, Layamon had been meeting me in the shadowy depths of the church, darkened hallways, and even the stables. The fact he singled me out from all the other, much lovelier options about the manor fair turned my head. It gave me boasting rights I'd never owned before and a shipload of envious glances. We'd kissed, oh, aye, we'd done that many a time and I'd been delirious, flooded with hot, liquid sensations that burned my loins. I'd never felt that way before, even when that grizzled but handsome knight, Sir Roland, hoisted me off my feet and kissed me deeply. After I'd overcome the shock of his tongue slipping into my mouth, I'd been more amazed that he could lift me when he only had one arm, as if I were made of straw. Mind you, he'd dropped me right quick when his wife found us, walloping him so hard across the face I thought his neck would break. Then she'd kicked me in the arse, ruddy cow. I'd a bruised rump for days. But Layamon, his kisses were different—*he* was different. I melted into his arms—both of them—and he pulled me against him as if he would solder us together the way the blacksmith did iron.

He was forbidden fruit and, when I was with him, it was Paradise.

Over the days, I managed to resist his increasing demands to plough my field, to storm my heavenly gates. Even I, the brogger's lass, a servant, knew not to surrender my maidenhead to just anyone. Lady Clarice's words were lodged in my mind.

But Father Layamon wasn't just anyone, was he?

When he appeared from under the heavy boughs of a willow as I was picking gillyflowers to make myself a garland on May Day morning, I felt giddy. He dropped to his knees, calling me his princess. Overcome as he pressed his face into my tunic, his breath hot against my queynte, which was, I confess, becoming rapidly heated as well, it wasn't until he drew me down on the soft grass and lay atop me, pressing kisses against my mouth, my neck, and my breasts, which he rapidly freed from my shift, that I began to feel uneasy. Why, anyone could come upon us. I asked him to stop. When he didn't, I asked again. When he began to lift my skirts and his robe at the same time, exposing his fleshy prod, my quiet asking became loud demands.

Instead of heeding me, he threw my skirts over my head, using his arm to press them into my mouth so my voice was muffled. I could feel his engorged prick poking my thigh. Kneeling upon my legs and slapping them hard to keep them open, he was about to batter down my postern gate when we were discovered. Lady Clarice, The Poet, Father Roman, monks from the nearby abbey, some more respectable of the villagers, such as the reeve, the ale-conner, and the sheriff, heard my cries and, diverting their walk, came upon us.

There were gasps, much laughter, and then shouting. Father Roman pulled Layamon away, taking care to cover his cock, leaving me to fight my way from underneath my linens. I sat up to see people gathered in a semicircle staring, pointing, smirking, and chattering. Layamon was being struck about the shoulders and head. I landed one swift kick to his exposed skin-plums, enjoying the cry he expelled. Sadly, I'd no time to fully enjoy his pain as I was wrenched away by Master Merriman. Immediately, my lady began to strike *me* across the neck and cheek using the rod she oft carried when she walked. Leaving Layamon aside, Father Roman also began to add blows, using words instead of birch.

"Filthy whore, temptress, how dare you! Try and force a son of God into sin? The devil take your soul, you corrupter of innocence, you foul weed in God's garden, you traitor of the tree."

Cue the chorus.

"You dirty little slut! You foolish wench. What would your mother say? What would your father?" cried other voices.

I learned a harsh lesson that day. Didn't matter that Layamon was primed and caught in prize position, it was all my fault.

I tried to defend myself, protest, but Layamon added accusations, stabbing a trembling finger in my direction and forcing tears, the spawn-cursed coward. Calling me a doxy, a meretrix, he began to describe how I lifted my skirts and begged him to take me. Unable to resist, he was simply doing what his weak flesh demanded. All the time he was blathering, Lady Clarice wouldn't stop hitting me. My attempts to offer the truth were reduced to squeals and, very soon, weeping. It was only when The Poet stepped forward and said something that my lady ceased to wield her rod. Layamon and Father Roman both fell silent.

Amidst tears and loud sniffles, I tried to fix my clothes. I remember little more beyond asking God to curse Layamon so his balls shriveled and his maypole shrank and dropped off.

Then I was shut away. It wasn't the first time I'd been punished in that manner. God's teeth, trouble was my middle name, or that's what Mistress Bertha always said, whether it was stealing kisses, bread, eggs, skiving off for an afternoon, or making up stories about my past. If I hadn't been so good at spinning and weaving, she'd threaten, the twinkle never really leaving her eye, I'd be out on my plump ass. But I hadn't done anything wrong this time, not really—well, apart from lying half-naked with a man. His pike hadn't breached my defenses, though not from want of trying. Why would no one listen? I was innocent—ish—in all this. God's boils, Layamon better be suffering. If his hairy nuggins weren't being roasted over hot coals right this moment, I wanted to know why.

But as the days went by, and no one came (except the other maids, Joyce and May, to bring me bread and water, and they knew nothing), I wondered if it was because I was caught with a man of God that was the problem. Even so, priests lay with women (and men) all the time, and while they couldn't exactly marry them, everyone knew many kept wives in all but name. Layamon was the bishop's son and it was said Father Harold from St. Michael's Within the Walls in Bath had a veritable herd of children with Goody Miriam.

I found the answers to some of my questions the day I was led into the solar.

I've already described who was present. The Poet was behind a large desk, a huge piece of parchment in front of him and writing implements all lined up like soldiers about to go into battle. He regarded me with something akin to wariness on his face. Was he afraid I was going to pounce and seek out his spindle? Not likely. For a start, he was old. Why, he'd be twenty-five if he was a day and, apart from his soft brown eyes and voice like burnt butter, he was ugly.

Then I saw Fulk Bigod. The fact he was there caught me by surprise. While everyone knew who he was, including me, we'd never exchanged a word. I often saw him standing on the edge of the Green on market days, or waiting by his horse. Drinking ale over near the well, or loitering near the manor gates, he'd watch as we maids did our daily chores. He'd been on the edge of the Green when we first danced around the maypole and played games on May Day morning. We'd nudge each other, laughing and nodding toward him, the man with no friends, knowing his mission to find servants, another wife, would fail. Ever since his last wife died a few years ago, the story was he'd been desperate to remarry. But the villagers kept their daughters away and refused his increasing offers in exchange for another bride. Silly old fool. I'd dismissed him from my mind then, just as I always did, but the tiny teeth gnawing away at my peace told me this time was different. My heart began to quicken. Nausea gathered in the pit of my stomach, rising to catch in my breast. I touched my tunic. It was cleaner than it had been only an hour earlier. My gown had been brushed and I'd been brought washing water and a fresh shift. A new scarf was found for my hair. My hand stroked it.

"Master Bigod," said Lady Clarice, rising to her feet and addressing the farmer. "It's been a long time since you graced these halls. I believe you know everyone, with one exception." Fulk Bigod did what he always did. Grunted.

Lady Clarice turned in my direction. "Allow me to introduce you to Mistress Eleanor Cornfed."

Never before had she called me "Mistress." I liked it not.

Master Bigod gave a small bow. I wish he hadn't. It fanned the flames of his odor. I took a step back and screwed up my nose.

"Eleanor," said Lady Clarice, stepping wide of Master Bigod and coming to my side. "Allow me to introduce Master Fulk Bigod." I lowered my head as I'd been taught. "Now," continued my lady. "Do you have anything to say before we proceed?"

"My lady?" My voice was small, dry. I cleared my throat. "I don't understand. Proceed with what?"

"Today, all things considered, is your lucky day, Eleanor." Lady Clarice gave me a small push in the back, sending me closer to Master Bigod.

"Lucky, how?" I resisted the urge to press my nose into my arm.

"Today, my dear, you plight your troth to a husband."

"A husband?" My ears began to ring. "Me?"

"In less than an hour, we'll meet at the church door and there, before Father Roman and Father Layamon, you will marry."

"Who?" I asked, my voice a whisper. I already knew the answer.

"Master Fulk Bigod."

Cold enfolded my body, color drained from my face, and with a sharp scream I tumbled dramatically to the floor.

Made not a whit of difference.

Before the bells rang for sext that day, the plans Lady Clarice, The Poet, and Fulk Bigod had made while I'd been locked away in the manor tower like a princess in a fairytale, came to pass.

I, the wanton Eleanor Cornfed, became Mistress Eleanor Bigod—wife to the most despised and dirty man in Bath. I married the monster.

Fulk was three score years and one.

I was twelve.

TWO

Bigod Farm
The Year of Our Lord 1364
In the thirty-eighth year of the reign of Edward III

*B*y mid-afternoon I was on my way to Bigod Farm, which lay between Bath-atte-Mere and the town of Bath. Two of Lady Clarice's groomsmen, Ben and Dodo, accompanied us, as did The Poet. A grubby young woman, who'd hovered by the church door as vows were exchanged, trotted behind our small party. Older than me, she was a sorry sight, with greasy auburn hair that hung below her cap, a filthy apron and skirts coated in dried mud. Her face was hard to make out, it was so grimed with dirt. I hadn't spied her before and wondered who she was. Mayhap, she'd never seen a wedding and been drawn by the pealing bells. For certes, some of the villagers were, lining by the road out of the village, mouths agape when they saw who was leaving and why.

"I never," said old Goody Edith, pulling on the one tooth in her head. "That makes five for Bigod now."

"Wonder how long this one will last," said Goody Grisilda, chewing her tongue.

"Hopefully longer than the last," added Goody Edith.

"Always knew that Cornfed lass would find her level," muttered Widow Henrietta.

"Can't get much lower," replied Master Rohan the cobbler, sending the women into gales of laughter.

Not even a withering look quieted them. I heard references to "that poor bishop's boy," "whore," and many more words besides, and knew that whatever reason was given for this hasty marriage, it wouldn't be the truth. I met The Poet's eyes and with a slight shock understood what I'd earlier thought was wariness, was in fact pity.

I didn't want anyone's pity, least of all his—the man who, I learned as I changed out of my old tunic and into the one my lady provided for the wedding, brokered this God-be-damned arrangement.

Forced me into marriage with a great lump of farting man-dung. Farting man-dung that owned a lot of land and sheep, apparently. Mistress Bertha babbled as she helped dress me. Said how Master Bigod had been given a sum of money to marry me, promised sheep as well. So, my husband (the word made me shudder) was not above a bit of bribery.

I glared at his broad back. Hopefully, he'd disperish before I had to swive him; fall off his horse and never rise. Funny how the word "swive" held "wive" in its grasp. Yet it also had the power to transform a woman. If the swiving is successful, wife becomes mother. Was that what Fulk Bigod wanted? For me to give him children? I repressed a shiver and rubbed the heels of my hands into my eyes. Damn if I'd bawl. I took a deep, shuddering breath, sat up straight.

Of a sudden, Papa's voice came to me. "You have to create opportunities where you can. No matter what life hurls at you, child, catch it. If it's shit, turn it into fertilizer. If it's insults, throw them back. Grip opportunity with both hands and ride it like a wild colt until you've tamed it. You've come from nothing, and unless you make something of yourself with what you're offered, it's to nothing you'll return."

Papa had made something of himself. The Botch had helped, killing so many folk the gentry had no choice but to accept workers they wouldn't usually consider hiring. Papa said the disease turned society on its head, making the rich beholden to the poor for a time. Could I make something of this? Turn the shit I'd been given into something productive? As we drew away from Noke Manor and the only life I could really remember, this seemed impossible.

I tried to recall what Mistress Bertha had said. As she helped me dress for the wedding, she'd tucked and pulled, twisting me this way and that. She didn't intend to hurt; she was rough so she didn't cry. Nervous, I babbled the entire time.

"There are people in the village saying he killed his wives and servants," I said. "If not deliberately, then through neglect. None stay. Some last only a day."

Mistress Bertha stopped what she was doing and put her hands on her hips. "Rubbish," she said, and spun me the other way. "Fulk Bigod may be many things, but he's not a murderer or a tyrant. It's just nasty idle gossip. Though I'll go as far to say the man's an enigma."

"An enigma?"

"Mystery."

"One wrapped in sheep dung," I mumbled.

Mistress Bertha slapped me on the ass. "You'll need to learn to curb that tongue, girl, or it will land you in more trouble."

"How can I be in *more* trouble?" I buried my face in my hands. "Why do I have to marry *anyone*? We didn't do anything, I swear."

"It matters not what you *did*," said Mistress Bertha, wrapping me in her arms, stroking my hair. The tears flowed then, and not just mine. "It's what you were *perceived* to be doing. Hush now," she said as I began to protest. "It's not all bad. Think of it this way: Fulk Bigod is a man of moderate means, but he's also old. At worst, you'll have a short period of pain followed by a lifetime of comfort. It's up to you."

Her words reminded me of Papa's.

As the sun sank beyond the horizon and the sky began to transform into a palette of blush, violet, and gold, I dwelled on those words, even as I latched onto the swaying backs of The Poet and my husband a few paces ahead. We rode in silence, well past the next village now, following the stream along a track better suited to feet than beasts. There was a thick wood to one side, a drystone wall encasing parts of it before it opened onto green hillocks dotted with creamy sheep. A lone shepherd and two panting dogs sat beneath a huge oak. It wasn't until they leaped to their feet as we drew closer, acknowledging Master Bigod, that I understood these were his lands I was admiring.

After a time, we rounded a bend and there, in a narrow valley not far from a chuckling creek, was a long, low building, whitewashed with a thatched roof. Smoke poured out of a hole somewhere in the middle. Shutters were open to allow air into the house. Two wooden doors at either end were ajar; the furthest one had chickens pecking around the threshold. Coming through the other door was a large sow followed by some piglets.

"God's boils, Alyson," bellowed Master Bigod, spinning on his mount to glare over his shoulder. "You forgot to lock up the fecking pigs!" It was the most I'd ever heard him say.

I jumped as he continued to shout, wondering why he was hurling such invective when it slowly dawned, it wasn't me he was abusing, but someone else. I looked around only to see the filthy drab from outside the church. Had she been there the entire way? Well back from the last horse, she'd frozen in her tracks.

With a growl, Master Bigod kicked his horse to quickly cover the final distance to the house.

I waited until the girl caught up with me. "May God give you good day." I tried not to stare. Up close, she was a wretched creature. She must be a serving girl or farm maid. They hadn't all left. For certes, she looked right hedge-born. Lady Clarice would never have allowed her servants or villeins to appear in such a way.

Instead of answering me, the girl picked up her pace, lifting her skirts to expose bare and grimy ankles in worn clogs, and stormed past. She shot me a look of such loathing, it was as if I'd been struck.

Indignant, sick of being unjustly treated, frightened of what lay ahead, I kicked the donkey and followed her. "Now, just you wait a minute . . ." What was her name? "Alyson," I barked. "You can't go treating me like that. Don't you know who I am?"

The distance between us was growing. The louder I called, the faster she walked, her back to me, her shoulders up around her ears.

An unnatural anger possessed me. The stubborn donkey was incapable of speed. I halted and slipped off its back and ran. I grabbed the girl by the shoulder and forced her to turn around, nearly making us both lose balance.

We faced each other, panting. We were of a height. She was frowning, I was glaring.

"I don't know who taught you manners, girl, but I won't accept being treated like that by you or anyone else. I saw you at the church. Your master wed *me*. You will show the respect I deserve!"

I sounded just like Mistress Bertha or even, I tried to persuade myself, Lady Clarice. I drew myself up, raised my chin and gave her the look I'd been told could freeze the millpond. In summer.

The girl stared brazenly, then muttered something, her lip curling in a sneer.

"What did you say?" I leaned closer so I might hear her forced apology.

"I said," she repeated slowly, "he's not my master." There was no remorse.

I began to suspect I'd been right all along. She was a by-blow, a tinker's get, or someone who'd fled their lord's lands to avoid paying chevage and was searching for work. A wave of pity swept me. Times were tough enough, especially for a woman on her own.

"Well, if he's not your master, then who is he to you?" I folded my arms and gave her a stern but benign look.

Her lips twisted as her eyes met mine. They were the color of slate. "He's my pa," she said.

My eyes widened, my mouth dropped open.

"Which, if I'm not mistaken," she continued, "makes you me mam."

THREE

Bigod Farm
The Year of Our Lord 1364
In the thirty-eighth year of the reign of Edward III

I was still in shock when The Poet, Ben, and Dodo departed a short time later. They weren't offered refreshment, or invited into the house. After untying my burlap and greeting two young men who appeared from indoors—one to lead the donkey away and the other to take my belongings—there was naught for the others to do. They loitered, trying to strike up conversations, but when no invitation was forthcoming, they'd no choice but to leave. The Poet took my hand and muttered some kind of consolation or words of hope, I knew not which. I didn't say anything. I was too stunned with the idea I was wife *and* mother—and mother to a dirty doxy some years older at that—to really note they were going until it was too late. When I saw the eddies of dirt being kicked up by their horses and their silhouettes disappearing up the track, I followed, waving and calling, but it did no good. They were gone.

I was all alone with my present. With my future.

I turned to face it. My husband and his daughter stood outside the doorway that only a short time ago had framed pigs.

If I'd thought Master Bigod and his daughter filthy, it was nothing compared to what I gazed upon. Not even the rich palette of the setting sun cast it in a favorable light. Animal ordure as well as piles of rotting vegetable scraps lay all over the yard. Nothing could hide the holes in the thatched roof, the splintered window and door frames, nor the weeds and flowers choking the walls and the nearby sheds, bursting through the wattle and daub, springing from the roof; nor could one ignore the green vines holding the shutters captive. There was an overgrown herb garden to the left of the main house and I could see an old tub and a few bushes over which some washed linen had been flung. Chickens pecked the dirt around a rusty wheel, a cow was tethered to the nearby shed, chewing its cud, while a milking pail rolled back and forth. Trees cast welcome shade over one side of the house and in these birds fluttered and chirruped. At least someone was happy.

Beyond the house was more pasture with neat drystone walls enclosing a large flock of sheep. They ambled over the ground, tugging at the plentiful grass, lifting their heads to watch as first Master Bigod's horse, then the donkey, were released into their field. The beasts bobbed straight over to a wooden trough and drank deeply. There were laden fruit trees and a scrappy vegetable garden. I could see evidence of kale, onions, beet, and herbs besides. I wondered who was responsible for that, and the neatness of the drystone walls, which, unlike the house, were in good repair. It was such a contradiction.

"What are you waiting for, wife, come, come inside," said Master Bigod. His voice was deep and gravelly, as if dry from lack of use. His words were accompanied by a smile. Much to my surprise, he had a nice one, despite having so few teeth. But so did the ale-conner and he was well known for beating his wife and taking bribes from the brewers.

Slapping me on the back as if I were a friend rather than his new bride, I almost tripped over the doorstep as he moved aside for me to pass.

"Alyson tells me she introduced herself," he said, following so closely I could feel his hot breath on the back of my neck.

"She did." I wondered what else the sullen girl had said and when. There was no sign of her. Master Bigod dragged a stool closer to the central fire, striking its wooden top. A cloud of dust rose. He used his sleeve to swipe it clean. "Here, sit, sit and let's have a bridal ale to celebrate. It's not every day I get to bring a wife home . . . well, not lately anyhow. Alyson!" he bellowed, looking about. "Get some ale."

Walking slowly to the stool, I tried not to think about the other women he'd brought here, nor their fates. Instead, I took in my surroundings. It was fairly dark, even though weak light struggled through the windows. The smoldering fire made the air quite smoky and left a haze sitting beneath the broad rafters. I coughed a few times. Noke Manor had a chimney in the Great Hall, so I wasn't accustomed to fighting for my breath indoors. I wondered what it would be like in winter with everything closed up.

Nevertheless, the style of the house was not unfamiliar, as it was very like some in the village, only longer and wider and not so well kept. I'd seen worse. Compared to the outside, an effort had been made indoors. One vast room, the house was divided by the fire in the center; a screen down one end concealed a kitchen. I could hear the sound of mazers clanging and a bung being removed from a barrel. Closer to the screen, there was a trestle table, stools, a bench, and even a sideboard upon which a few utensils rested—cups and spoons mainly. Some chipped jugs. A mean-looking weaving hung from one wall, its picture unclear in the poor light. Sconces with unlit candles were screwed into the smoke-stained walls. Above the central hearth hung a huge pot, some gridirons, smaller pots, ladles, an iron fork, and trivets. A chest sat beneath one window, and the ginger cat atop it paused in its grooming to stare at me with wide yellow eyes. Master Bigod waved toward it. "Don't mind King Claude. He thinks he owns the place."

King Claude. Well, I liked cats and would make sure to pay fealty soon.

It was just as well I was fond of animals, because the other end of the room had a compact dirt floor scattered with beds of hay. On one, a large sow reclined, piglets suckling sleepily at her teats, while two goats chewed contentedly next to her. Against the far wall, more chickens roosted. Together, they accounted for the smell and the shit.

Unable to stay still, my husband was pacing, clearly as nervous as I was, even though he'd been married many times before. He was the master of this domain. A domain that, as his wife, I would be excepted to manage. Oh, how I wished I'd asked more questions about how to keep house, how to be a wife, of Mistress Bertha, Lady Clarice, of anyone at the manor, even The Poet.

What should I do? What should I say?

My heart began to somersault and beads of sweat broke out along my forehead and between my breasts. Hot tears welled. I wouldn't cry, I wouldn't.

Just then, Alyson reappeared, a bunch of wooden mazers balanced under one arm, while in her other hand she carried a large jug. She thumped them all on the table and began to pour haphazardly, her face set in a deep, resentful frown. It was a wonder any of the ale went into the cups.

"Oy, you pair," Master Bigod called to no one in particular. The two young men I'd seen earlier reappeared. "Come and meet your mistress and share a drink. Oh, and find Hereward and Wake, would you?"

Squinting into the shadows, I could see there was another floor above the one we currently occupied. The bedroom must be there. Dear God up in Heaven, I hoped so. Mind you, the sow might not be so bad to curl up next to . . . she likely smelled better.

A volley of barks distracted me as two huge hounds burst in, followed by the young men.

"Hereward, Wake," cried Master Bigod, dropping to one knee and enfolding his arms around the two hairy mutts. The dogs, brown, long-legged things with wiry fur and big, slavering jaws, clearly adored him, putting their paws on his shoulders and licking his face and ears. Mayhap, that sufficed for a wash. Master Bigod chuckled and ruffled their heads. Standing, he pointed at me.

"Meet your new mistress," he said.

The hounds almost knocked me off my stool. Their great black noses nudged my legs, before they licked me with their velvet tongues. Their wagging tails struck my thighs, my arms. I didn't know where to put my hands, how to stop them, how to enfold them and kiss them back. Why, these dogs were adorable. Such affection, such obedience too, I thought as Master Bigod shouted a command and they immediately dropped to their haunches.

Not everyone earned such admiration. Nor had it returned with such ease. "Which one is Hereward and which Wake?" I asked.

It was the daughter, Alyson, who answered. She nodded at the smaller of the two dogs. "That's Hereward, and her brother is Wake."

"Blasted nuisances, the pair of them," growled Master Bigod, his hand chucking Hereward beneath her chin, belying his words. She tried to lick him. "Never mind them," said Master Bigod. "Let's raise a toast to the new Mistress Bigod." Lifting his mazer, he waited until the two men, Alyson, and I hefted ours. "Welcome to our home, Eleanor." His eyes flickered and he gulped nervously.

"Welcome," said the two young men and, along with their master, drank deeply. Alyson turned away, a sour look upon her face. She didn't drink, but I did. I was parched. Much to my astonishment, the ale was delicious. Much nicer than what the manor's brewer, Goody Allsop, made. I said as much.

Master Bigod wiped the back of his hand across his mouth. "Aye. Isolde taught Alyson how to brew, didn't she, may God assoil her. Isolde was my second wife. My girl does a mighty fine job of it."

I raised my cup in her direction. "You do. You could sell this and make a fortune."

For a mere moment, Alyson met my eyes and there was no resentment, only surprise at the praise, before it was replaced by a hard, suspicious look. Then, her father waved his arm, almost striking her. "Don't you go putting foolish notions in her head, wife. Who'd buy our ale out here? Anyhow, Alyson's been busy keeping house." He looked about, smiling again, then his face transformed. "Only, now she don't have to anymore. That's what you be here for, ain't it, wife?"

"I . . . I . . ."

"But . . . Pa," protested Alyson. "That's my job. I look after the house."

"Not anymore you don't," began Master Bigod, his face growing red. "Not on your own. Don't worry. You'll do as the mistress bids or we'll find something else for you."

Alyson jumped to her feet. "I don't want to do anything else. I've always done this. Always. I like looking after things." Her arm swept the room. "I like looking after you and the boys. She . . ." she spat. "She has no right to take that away. She's no right to be here."

Damn if my eyes didn't burn. I buried my face in the mazer.

Master Bigod forced a chuckle. "There, there." He flapped a hand, indicating she should sit. "No need to make a fuss. Come on, Alyson love. Sit down. Have a drink to my new bride. A bride who has every right to be here. Who knows? Mayhap, one day soon, we'll find you a husband and then—"

"I don't want a husband!" screamed Alyson. I almost dropped my mazer. Hereward and Wake whined, Wake lowering himself onto the floor. "I never want one. I don't want her here either, lazy little gap-toothed slut. Only reason she's here's because she's a sinner what swived a priest and no one else'd have her. Why'd you take her, Pa? Spoil everything. Couldn't you have left well enough alone? Left *her* alone?" She stood, her feet apart, hands on hips, eyes blazing. "Why don't you go back to your manor and la de da ways, eh? I don't need you or your help. Pa doesn't need you either, so why don't you just piss off?"

"Now, now." Master Bigod rose and reached out, whether to thump her or offer comfort wasn't clear. "No need to speak to your new ma like that."

"*Ma?*" screeched Alyson. "Why, she's younger than me. A child. A spoiled, stupid, ugly hog-child. She belongs in the sty." Fighting back tears, the look of betrayal on Alyson's face wrenched my heart. I turned to offer solace, anything, but she slapped my hand away and, with a great sob, turned on her heel and ran out into the evening.

The four of us sat unmoving, not speaking as the sound of her boots grew fainter and fainter.

The croak of frogs could just be heard, the house creaked, and a shutter whined before the cow bellowed, breaking the spell. I knew how it felt.

Master Bigod slowly sank back down on the stool, hitched up his breeches, and cleared his throat. He gave a crooked smile.

"All in all, I'd say that went very well, wouldn't you, wife?"

FOUR

Bigod Farm
The Year of Our Lord 1364
In the thirty-eighth year of the reign of Edward III

𝒲oken by the loudest of shrieks, I sat bolt upright, my hand clutching the bedclothes. I blinked, looked about, wondering momentarily where on God's good earth I was, before I remembered.

Then I saw him.

Directly across from the bed, at the top of the ladder, was a large rooster.

It locked eyes with me, its bold comb quivering as it lifted its beak to release another screech. Before it could, King Claude, who unbeknownst to me had been curled on the end of the bed, leaped. It was enough to send the bird flapping and squawking off his perch and out of sight. King Claude sauntered over to the doorway, really an opening in the wall against which a ladder leaned, before turning slowly and, with an elegant jump, returning to the bed. He completed a few circles then settled, raising his head to take my thanks, which I duly gave, along with a cautious pat on the head. I could hear the rooster scuttling about in the rushes below, clucking his indignation.

I slowly lay back down as the morning light revealed the room with its wide low beams and whitewashed walls, upon which hung a small cross and two sconces. A window had been cut into the wall to my right and I recalled leaving the shutters open as the smell of paint had been strong. Through the window I could see the day dawning. The air was moist, it had rained overnight, but it still carried the pungent odor of the refuse that surrounded the house. It really was intolerable. How like my lady I sounded. I wondered if she'd given me another thought. Had she asked The Poet how I fared? Had anyone? I wondered how long I might wait before I returned to Noke Manor for a visit. Would I even be welcome?

Trying not to think about that, I regarded the ends of the great wooden bed. I moved my feet, enjoying the feel of the soft covering, being careful not to disturb the cat, noting that the mattress was much more comfortable than my straw-filled one at Noke Manor. The sheets were clean, the coverlet appeared new. Altogether, a real effort had been made to prepare this room and, indeed, the house for my arrival. This was so contrary to what I'd expected, I still wasn't certain what to make of it. To my left was a cloth-covered chair, upon which yesterday's clothes were draped. I suppose I should rise and don them . . . Instead, I remained and thought about what happened yestereve after Alyson stormed out of the house.

It had been most uncomfortable, then Master Bigod set about being host. First, he sent one of the men, whose name I learned was Theo, to see if Alyson was alright.

"She'll likely be down by the stream, near that tree where the coneys have a warren." He gave Theo a pointed look.

Downing his mazer, Theo left immediately.

"Alyson oft goes there, 'specially after her mama died. She used to love casting stones into the brook, tickling the fish and such." I was struck by both Master Bigod's knowledge of his daughter's pastimes and his consideration. Dear God, if I'd behaved like Alyson, not only Cook, but Master Merriman, Mistress Bertha, *and* my father (if he'd been alive) would have dragged me back by the ears—that was, when they weren't yelling in them. Master Bigod didn't even appear cross, just resigned.

Maybe this was something Alyson did on a regular basis? Nay. She was out of sorts for one reason and one reason only: me. I wasn't used to that, either. The other maids had been my gossips, my friends. Never expecting to find someone close to my own age here, let alone a daughter, I wondered if I could make a friend of her. A mother, I could never be. How can one be maternal to someone older than themselves? And dirtier, I added ungenerously, smoothing my clean tunic over my knees.

Next, Master Bigod sent the other man, Beton, out to collect more firewood. With a polite bow, he left. He bore a very strong resemblance to Theo, both being in possession of unruly brown hair and pale blue eyes. Theo was much taller than Beton, who was of middling height, but with very broad shoulders. Neither spoke much, but like the hounds, were obedient. Yet they didn't seem afraid of Master Bigod . . . on the contrary . . .

Master Bigod went to the kitchen, returning moments later. The dogs followed and, from the way they sat with straight backs and eager snouts, it was evident they expected to be rewarded.

"I'm guessing you're hungry, wife," said Master Bigod gruffly, and set down a lump of hard cheese and a loaf of bread on the table. After detaching a knife from his belt, he began to slice.

"Thank you." I took what he passed me. I was famished. I was also confused. Thus far, the man mocked by the villagers and said to be at best a bully and at worst a murderer, had shown me nothing but consideration. The lack of cleanliness of his person and outside the house aside, he was trying very hard. Was this an act that, like the masked mummers, would be exposed when the curtain was drawn? I glanced up toward the loft bedroom. Or would he wait until we were alone?

Nibbling at the bread, which was coarse but surprisingly tasty, as was the cheese, I observed him as he absently fed the dogs bits of his meal, his eyes straying to the door.

Beton finished stoking the fire and, standing in the shadows, waited until Master Bigod not only beckoned him to join us, but insisted he help himself. Beton didn't wait for a second invitation, but used his knife to cut himself a generous slab of bread and cheese.

"We usually have butter too," said Master Bigod, his mouth full. "Alyson churns it regular like, but she was too busy sweeping out the house and preparing it for you, wife, and then coming to witness our marriage, to get that done."

"We all were," said Beton, spraying some crumbs. "Trying to get it nice for you, like the master wanted. We've been doing all sorts—cutting, polishing, hammering, even painting and washing."

The two men beamed. Washing? Not themselves.

I found a smile. "Ah, well, I'm grateful." I glanced about. "It's . . . um . . . er . . . very nice."

As the shadows grew longer and evening wrapped its velvet arms about the house, the flames of the hearth throwing dancing shadows against the walls, Master Bigod rose and lit the candles, bringing one to the table.

Unasked, Beton began to close the shutters and then went outside and led the donkey back into the other part of the house. It pootled in and then dropped onto what was clearly its bed. The remainder of the chickens went to their roosts, which were on wooden shelves off the ground, their quiet clucks pleasant.

When Theo returned, breathless from running, he had another drink, gathered up some bread and cheese in a cloth and, after a brief and quiet exchange with Master Bigod, doffed his cap and left again. At a nod from Master Bigod, Beton closed the door. Almost immediately, the smoke, which had been swirling outside, began to congregate around the hearth, spreading about the room.

"Alyson has decided to stay down by the stream tonight," explained Master Bigod. "There's a little hut she can sleep in. Theo will keep an eye on her." He sat down across from me. "Forgive her, wife. This has been a shock. I didn't know she'd followed me to the village till after we were wed."

I shrugged. Who was I to complain? If Alyson was shocked, it didn't hold a rushlight to what I was feeling. A wave of empathy for the angry young woman engulfed me. She was right, I'd no business being here, being married. But what choice did I have? I was but a girl, a commoner too, and thus beholden over and over to the whims of my betters. Unbidden, a tremor racked my body.

"Are you warm enough?" asked Master Bigod, concern etched on his features. "Would you like more to eat?" He topped up my mazer. The ale was going to my head. It was stronger than the small ale I was accustomed to drinking.

"I am, Master Bigod. Thank you." Hot. Cold. I was all and everything.

"You can call me husband," he said. "Or Fulk, if you prefer. I might be your master in God's eyes and the church's, but under this roof, you also be my mistress."

What a strange thing to say. Papa was the only person I knew who thought that while a man might be considered above a woman in every regard according to God and the law, only a foolish one cared who was in charge.

"A woman might be a man's helpmeet, but far better we meet in the middle and help each other," he would say.

"Is that what you and Mamma did?" I'd ask.

"As best we could," he'd answer.

Master Bigod asked Beton to play some music and the young man went to a pallet bed on the other side of the hearth and rummaged about, extracting a flute. Soon the room was filled with the plaintive notes of his pipe. Hereward and Wake sat up, their large heads tilting first one way and then the other. It was funny and I wasn't the only one amused.

My husband watched them, his eyes sparkling, his mouth curved in a warm arc. For the first time, I had the chance to really look at him, to see beyond the dirt and the rumors. There was no one to whisper in my ears this night and cast aspersions.

I studied him as Father Roman did his psalter. I really only knew Fulk Bigod by the reputation others had given him. Taller than The Poet but shorter than my father, he was lean, spare in the body except for the beginnings of a paunch, which not even his tunic could disguise. His arms were long and sinewy, his fingers, as they drummed on the tabletop in time to the tune, were knobbly and large. A farmer's hands, the backs speckled with spots and corded with veins. The skin was dry, like parchment. His legs, stretched out and crossed at the ankles, were well shaped. His face, hollow in the cheeks, was riven by deep wrinkles. His mouth was upturned and more generous in repose, his eyes deeply hooded. Yet, as he raised them to meet mine, surprisingly pale in color. Almost colorless, like rain on glass. They were hard to read in a face that told a hundred stories, none of them the kind to lift the spirit—or so I'd thought.

Had the man been read wrong? After all, he'd shown me nothing but kindness. I knew he was a freeman, a loner who made a living raising sheep and selling their wool; he leased lands from the monks at Bath Abbey and cared for their flocks as well. But what about his other wives? What about the daughter no one knew about? What about the vanishing servants?

"You needn't worry."

He caught me unawares. The entire time I'd been studying him, he'd been appraising me. My cheeks burned. "Worry? About what?" The quiver in my voice belied my words.

"'Bout doing your wifely duty. I can see by the expression on your face it is concerning you. But you need not dwell on that. Not tonight. Not till you're ready."

"Oh," I said. At the back of mind, I *had* been preparing myself for a bedding. I'd been imagining how long I could hold my breath, shut my eyes. Whether it would hurt. How I could tolerate his old hands touching me, that mouth kissing me . . . I'd tried not to let it come to the forefront lest I pick up my tunic and, like Alyson, run away as fast as I could. Though, unlike Alyson, I'd nowhere to hunker down.

"I want a son," he continued quietly. "But I'll not risk a demon-child by taking you against your will, wife. All I ask is that you don't wait too long. I not be getting any younger."

Or cleaner, I thought.

He was waiting. "Ah. Er. Thank you . . . husband."

He grunted and drank some more. The fire crackled, the music played on and the tightness that had kept my back stiff, my neck held just so, began to abate. I hadn't realized how coiled I was, like a tumbler before they leap and cavort.

I stared at the fire, then at my husband again. "May I ask you a question?"

"I'll not stop you."

"Why do you need a son? Cannot Alyson be your heir? It's not unheard of, you know, a woman inheriting."

"Aye, I know. And I have sons, wife." He gestured to Beton.

"Beton is your son?"

"Aye, and Theo. There were others too, but they left to seek their fortune in the city or to soldier for the King. Some are dead, some . . ." He shrugged. "I don't know."

"I'm . . . I'm so sorry." Sweet Jesu! The man bred like a coney.

He bowed his head. "My problem is, they're not *my* sons—or my daughter—in God's eyes. They're sons of my heart."

"I'm not sure I understand, sir."

Master Bigod gave a sad smile. "Not many do, wife. But the truth of the matter is, while they're not children from my loins, they are blood all the same and I love them like they're my own. And while I'll make sure to do right by them when I die, I've always wanted a child I had a hand in making, if you get my meaning. A son, if, God be praised, He blesses me so. A daughter I won't complain about. Not too much anyway." He winked.

I was so taken aback, it was a long moment before I responded. Why, this was an act of great kindness, raising another man's child. Children. But if they weren't his blood, then whose were they? Did he have brothers? Sisters? How many Bigods were there? Where were they? I wanted to ask but sensed I would learn in time.

"My father," I began, "never complained about having a daughter. Cook at Noke Manor always said that made him a rare breed."

"Been called many things in my time, many true, many not, but never a rare breed." His smile broadened.

He stroked Wake's ears and I couldn't help but think of all the things I knew he had been called. I began to wonder how many were false.

"Anyhow, breeding's not the only reason I brought you here."

"Oh?"

He nodded toward the door. "Alyson needs a friend. Someone

near her own age. It's not right, her being here day in day out with only me and the lads for company. You'll be good for her." He drank the last of his ale, stifling a belch. "And I know she'll be good for you."

Of that, I wasn't so certain.

We retired soon after. Me, upstairs to the loft and its huge comfortable bed and fresh linen, with herbs strewn over the wooden floor, clean water in the basin, and my burlap atop the chest in the corner. My husband, Beton, and the dogs took the pallets between the fire and the other animals.

I heard their quiet whispers, the contented noises of the creatures, the hushing sound as the ceramic fire-cover was placed over the smoldering flames, before falling into a deep sleep.

Voices and the shutters being opened broke my reverie and sent me from bed. Using the water in the jug, and a stained but clean cloth, I washed my neck, face, and hands and donned my shift. My burlap still lay unpacked—not that it held much. Sitting on the end of the bed, I undid my plaits and tidied my hair before redoing them and, as a married woman should, tucking them beneath my cap. The last thing I did was tie my apron then, with a deep breath, I descended the ladder.

"Greetings, wife," said Master Bigod. Sunlight streamed through the open windows, the fire was crackling, and the animals had been let out into the yard. A basket of eggs sat on the table, fresh baked bread, and a lump of very white butter as well. Alyson had evidently returned and been busy. My mouth began to water.

Before I could take a seat, let alone help myself, in swept Alyson carrying a basket on her hip. "Oh," she said, stopping in her tracks. "You're still here."

"Alyson—" Master Bigod raised a warning hand.

"Nay, husband," I said. "It's alright." It was anything but alright, but I made up my mind there and then I wouldn't let this chit intimidate me. Mayhap, the villagers had it wrong—it wasn't Fulk Bigod who was a bully but his daughter. Being the former steward's girl and having certain privileges within the manor, I'd sometimes been a target for malice among the other servants. At first, I'd give as good as I got, but I slowly learned that sometimes the way to vanquish a bully was not by being a bigger one, but by trying to befriend them. It didn't always work, and when it didn't, I just gave the offender a bloodied lip. Don't mess with a daughter whose father came from peasant stock. While part of me wanted to slap that smirk off Alyson's filthy face, the more reasonable part of me—the godly part, some might say—thought to try and make her an ally.

I gave a small curtsey. She read something in my face, because as I approached, she took a couple of quick steps back, thrusting the basket between us. When she saw I wasn't going to attack, she resumed her casual but hostile pose.

"Truth be told, I thought you'd be gone before cock crowed," she said.

"Truth be told, so did I. Instead, the King exiled him from my domain." I nodded toward Claude.

There was a guffaw behind me.

Alyson tried to stare me down. I stood my ground.

Closing the small distance between us, she hissed, "You know nothing about running a house, looking after Pa and the boys."

I glanced over my shoulder; the men were pretending not to listen. "You're right. I don't. But then, I'm only twelve years old."

"Twelve?" Alyson shot a disbelieving look. "I've six years on you. You sure you're only twelve? You look older."

"So I'm told."

"You act older too, all uppity."

"Aye, been told that too."

Was that a grin Alyson swallowed?

"You had fancy clothes." Alyson jerked her arm toward my tunic and apron. "People say you carry the favor of Lady Clarice. She bore witness at your wedding, even though you're a slut."

If carrying my lady's favor landed me here, she was welcome to it. "Mayhap. But I was, still am, a servant." I omitted the slut part. "You're right, I don't know the first thing about running a house." I hesitated. "I was hoping you'd teach me."

"Teach *you*?" Alyson's mouth dropped open.

"Aye."

"What?"

"What my tasks are, how I can help. I just want to do the right thing by you." I turned to include the others. Sensing something afoot, Hereward and Wake trotted over, thrusting their faces at me and Alyson, demanding petting.

"Is that so?" said Alyson, ruffling Wake's head while I scratched Hereward's. A sly look crossed her features. "Some of the work is dirty."

"I'm not afraid of a little dirt."

"It's hard."

"Nor hard work neither."

Putting the basket down on the table, Alyson made up her mind. She broke off some bread and ripped a piece of meat from a haunch. She shoved them in my hands. Over her shoulder, I could see Master Bigod grinning fit to split his face. I took the offering, trying to ignore the grime of her fingers.

"That's my girls," he said.

"Well, eat up," said Alyson. "If you're serious 'bout wanting to learn, I'll show you. But you have to promise to do exactly as I say." The aggressive note returned and she frowned, daring me to back away from my commitment. I didn't like where this was going, but I'd baited the hook, thrown in the line, I had to take whatever I caught.

"I will."

Alyson gave me, then her father, a smug look. After that, we ate in silence while the men discussed chores. There were sheepfolds to move, trees to prune, and sheep to milk and check. The shepherds would meet with them at sext to discuss the flock, while Master Bigod had appointments in the afternoon, first with the monks, then with some merchants interested in buying wool. Before the men left, three others arrived, help Master Bigod hired over the season.

They left without introductions. Master Bigod nodded to me and whispered something in his daughter's ear before leaving.

I felt strangely bereft when he left. Bereft and more than a little anxious about being alone with Alyson.

Rising, she picked up the utensils and took them to the kitchen.

Gathering up the jug and empty mazers, I followed. The kitchen consisted of little but a bench, some sharp knives, other tools for dissecting meat, sacks of grain and legumes, a quern for grinding corn, vials of herbs, and a pile of wood. Above the bench hung rabbit and lamb carcasses, a decent-sized hock, and bunches of dried flowers. Already, flies had settled on the rabbit. Maggots crawled across the surface. My face must have given away my disgust, for Alyson snickered. "Better get used to it." She strolled out.

"Shouldn't we fetch water and wash the mazers and such?" I called.

"*We* won't be fetching water. I will."

"Oh. What should I do?"

A wicked grin appeared. "You're going to clean." She indicated the far end of the main room. "All that shit. And, after you've done that, you can go outside and shovel up the cow, donkey, chicken, and other shit as well. Papa wanted it done before you arrived. Since you're so eager to learn what it takes to run this house, you can do what I didn't have time for."

She stood, arms folded, waiting for me to defy her.

I wanted to shout and rail and tell her she could clean the shit since she already smelled like she'd rolled in it. But I didn't. Sweet Mother Mary, I bit my tongue, smiled, and said, "Then tell me where the shovel is, and I'll make a start."

My only satisfaction was seeing the look of astonishment on that scummy, toady face. A face I swore that, one day, I'd make eat shit, if it was the last thing I did.

FIVE

Bigod Farm
The Year of Our Lord 1364
In the thirty-eighth year of the reign of Edward III

I spent each and every day thereafter trying to win Alyson's regard by allowing her to order me about as if I was her servant. Though there were some tasks I'd never undertaken (threshing grain, baking bread, brewing ale, and preserving meat, for instance), nothing was beyond my abilities—not that you'd know from the way Alyson bossed me about, speaking as if I was a child. My attempts were never good enough. Plain wrong, unfinished, had to be redone, tasted terrible, better tipped out, too bitter, too sweet, poorly constructed, too much, too little. On it went. I took her criticisms without complaint, my insides like a simmering pot all the while. In retrospect, pandering to her whims was the worst thing I could have done—it didn't earn me anything but more contempt.

Not that the men ever saw this, as her manner altered the moment they came home.

Before none they'd stomp wearily inside and sit down to a bowl of pottage and some coarse brown maslin bread. One day Alyson even roasted a lamb Master Bigod had found dead in the field. It was delicious. We ate well, including the hounds and King Claude. The pigs and chickens not only had food scraps, but the draff left from making ale. Overall, Master Bigod kept a good table and we never wanted—not for meat, fish, eels, cheese, fruit, or nuts, nor the bread Alyson made each day.

The only thing I surpassed her in was spinning. She could card, but then so could a tinker's monkey. What she lacked was my deftness with the spindle, and was confounded as to how I could roam about outside or even in the house, one hand stirring a pot or shooing King Claude off the table, the distaff tucked under one arm as I worked the spindle. Little did she know it was a craft I'd mastered from the cradle.

When I finished turning a sack of wool into fine thread, I asked if there was any way we could weave it. Astonished I knew how to work a loom, as he only knew male weavers in Bath, Master Bigod determined to acquire one. The following day, he returned home with an old one in need of repair.

Out in the barn, I examined it. Possessed of a strong upper beam, it needed a new tension bar below. I explained what had to be added or replaced, and Beton cut some rods that could be used for the heddle and batten, as well as to tie thread and create the warp. Theo, wanting to be part of something so exciting, carved me a shuttle. Once these were complete and the loom working, it was simply a matter of carrying it inside and setting it near the hearth so I could take advantage of the light and thread it.

When I began to weave, quickly catching the rhythm once I'd overcome the initial problems of a foreign loom, Alyson was dumbfounded. She could mend clothes as well as any goodwife, and her spinning was slowly improving, but weaving was an altogether different proposition. When Papa and I first arrived at Noke Manor, he'd convinced my lady there was a market for cloth to be plundered. English cloth, he claimed, made from Cotswold wool, was a product he believed would one day compete with the fine material being produced in Flanders and Brabant. He persuaded my lady to hire a weaver or two and train some servants in the craft. I was among them. At first I'd resented it, but after I became skilled, I found it relaxing.

The evening I commenced weaving at Bigod Farm, they all sat around passing comments and admiring the pattern that emerged. Even Alyson forgot to snipe. Delighted with their attention I preened, suggesting I weave cloth so they might have new clothes. Fulk smiled warmly, pleased his wife was so clever. Theo and Beton began talking about how they'd wear their fine threads to church, encouraging Alyson to add her wishes. Part of her wanted to throw my offer back, while the other longed for something fresh, something pretty. I discreetly studied her reactions, trying not to show my joy in the men's praise or resentment at her lack of it. Slowly it dawned on me that here sat someone who'd never allowed herself to want much. Mayhap, because, in the past, it had been lost to her. At that moment I began to see Alyson in a kinder light.

I occupied those first few weeks not only cleaning away the shit and refuse from around the house, making it look and smell almost respectable, but managed to persuade my husband to hire men to repair the thatch and walls and rehang the doors. I'd quickly discovered that far from appearances, which suggested a man of very modest means, my husband, as Mistress Bertha had intimated, was reasonably well off for a freeman. For certes, he kept a locked box inside the chest in the bedroom from which he extracted coins to pay the help. Though I couldn't open it, I did weigh it in my hands and it was very, very heavy. Did Lady Clarice and The Poet know when they married me to this man? A man who still hadn't tried, thank God, to exercise his conjugal rights.

Three weeks later, the outside of the house was transformed. The inside had been prinked as well. I'd replaced the rushes with fresh ones and found some rosemary, lavender, and rose petals to scatter through them. The house and its surrounds may have improved, but the same couldn't be said for me. I smelled like the shit I'd spent days clearing (and still did daily, after all, the animals were like eager parishioners, generous with their offerings). I also began to resemble the family of which I was now a part. My hair was lank beneath the stained cap. My apron and tunic, despite my efforts to beat them clean each night and air my linen shift, had become so dirty, it was hard to distinguish between them. The only positive thing to come out of this was I could no longer smell my husband, Alyson, or the men.

When Alyson said I should accompany her to market the Wednesday after I arrived, I made an excuse not to go. I didn't want to be seen. Likewise, when Master Bigod offered to take me to visit the manor when he'd business to conduct, I declined. While what had led to me being evicted from the manor and catapulted into this new life still rankled, it wasn't the only reason. Call me childish for not wanting to face Lady Clarice (though I doubted she'd deign to see me), much worse was the thought I might see May, Joan, Cook, Mistress Bertha, Master Merriman, and Father Roman. Or Layamon. I knew the servants would press me to tell them what Master Bigod was like. They'd be expecting me to add to the terrible tales about his uncleanliness, his bullying, the dead wives and disappearing servants. God forgive me, I wasn't ready yet to defend him—but nor did I want to embellish stories I now doubted. Was I a coward? Was I disloyal? Aye, both those things. But I was also so very young. I hadn't yet learned the power that can come from telling the truth and standing by it. Nor did I want my friends to guess the lengths I was prepared to go to in order to make a friend of Alyson—a woman who, to May, Joan, and the others, was beneath their notice. Was I not her mistress?

Aye. But I was also her stepmother. How could I admit to that?

What finally caused a shift in my relationship with Alyson was the shit.

Things reached boiling point the week after I was finally satisfied the yard was clean and tidy. I'd dragged fallen branches from the brook, used some old barrels that were rotting at the back of the barn, a rusty wheel, and other bits to form a makeshift fence—just enough to deter the donkey (whose name was Pilgrim, after the person Master Bigod bought it from), the sow and piglets, and any sheep that escaped, so they were confined to the rear of the house. The only exception was a rough path which directed them into the house or barn. I determined to persuade Master Bigod to relocate all the animals (Hereward, Wake, and King Claude excepted) there one day soon. My idea was, if the animals were going to shit, then it was going to be where I could control it. So far, it was working.

I was admiring how golden the compacted dirt was, having enjoyed a good drenching from the rain the last two days before drying in the sun when, out of the corner of my eye, I caught Hereward and Wake chasing Pilgrim. Confounded by the fence, the donkey veered at the last minute and, instead of taking the path into the house, fled into the relative safety of the barn. The hounds, startled by Pilgrim's maneuver, pulled up short and began barking. I ignored them, that was until they went quiet. Turning to see why, I was horrified to find them rolling in the pile of shit I'd made, a huge mound Theo and Beton were meant to have spread over the fields.

"You filthy bastards!" I yelled, half-laughing, half-wanting to weep as I ran toward them, brandishing the besom above my head. "Stop that!" Both dogs leaped up, shook themselves, their tongues lolling and then, thinking a game was on, ran straight at me. They knocked me off my feet and began licking my face and, God's ass, rubbing their shit-covered fur all over me.

I was shouting at them to cease, pulling their ruffs, when I heard someone screaming. Not at the dogs, but me.

"What are you doing? Leave them alone, you bitch!"

Before I knew it, Alyson flung herself on top of me. Snatching the broom out of my hand, she threw it aside, and began slapping me. Hard.

Stunned at first, it took two blows to my cheek and a couple to my chest before I reacted.

That was it. A red veil descended, and the loudest of bellows erupted. It was enough to give Alyson pause as she sat upon my torso, straddling me.

I did what I'd wanted to do ever since she'd first spoken to me. I hit her back. First slamming my forehead into hers, I pummeled her arms, her shoulders, slapped her spiteful, ratty face.

Fists flew, screeches followed. We tugged and pulled each other's clothes, trying to find a grip, rolling around, kicking, biting, scratching. I grabbed a hold of her greasy hair and yanked. She yelped. Reaching around, she caught hold of an ear and began to twist it. I yelled in pain. The dogs, wanting to join in, flung themselves on us. Alyson and I came apart and tumbled to one side and into the shit the hounds had begun to spread.

Horrified I'd landed in the stinking, rain-soft dung, I tried to lever myself up, but Alyson had other ideas. She picked up a handful and smeared it all over my tunic and then drew back her filthy hand and slapped me hard, streaking my cheek. My mouth filled with blood as I bit my tongue.

I let out a yowl of rage. It was so long and loud even the dogs gave pause. I was disgusted by what was on my clothing, in my hair, and on my face. White-hot fury filled me. I lunged and, before she could duck, twined her greasy hair through my fingers and around my fist and, using strength I didn't know I possessed, swiped her feet out from under her at the same time as I pushed her face deep into the shit pile. I held her there as she kicked the earth and scrabbled with her hands.

Aye. I made her eat shit.

When I was certain she'd gained a mouthful, I let her go, leaping away, eyes fixed on her, my chest heaving and heart beating faster than a soldier's drums. I raised my fists like a pugilist, ready for another bout.

She lay face first in the muck, unmoving.

I was just starting to get worried when she stirred. Ever so slowly, she lifted herself onto her elbows. The dogs, perhaps sensing something, also retreated, taking refuge in my stinking skirts.

Already, I was beginning to regret what I'd done. I wondered how I'd explain this to Master Bigod, Theo, Beton. The thought of what Alyson would do to get her revenge made the heat of our encounter turn to frost in my veins.

She turned and blinked. Her face was coated in dark brown muck. Her hair was plastered to her forehead, to the sides of her face. Her mouth . . . oh dear God. I wanted to be sick just looking at her. The smell was already in my nostrils; the cause of that stench was quite literally filling hers. She spun to one side and spat, spat again, then

retched a few times, loudly. She held a finger against first one side of
her nose, then the other, and blew out sharply.

Gorge rose in me. Gorge and a deep, deep fear. I rested one hand
against Hereward's head. She whined. I almost did too.

Then, Alyson did what I never, ever expected. She took one look
at me, and began to laugh.

She rose unsteadily, fell back down before trying again; until she
stood straight. She studied the state of her clothes, lifted the heavy
strands of hair from her shoulders, then regarded me and laughed
harder.

Her laughter was so bubbly, something I never thought to hear,
that I began to giggle. She staggered toward me, doubled over with
mirth, and threw an arm about my shoulders, whether to keep herself upright or drag me into the dirt again, I wasn't sure. But when
she simply continued to laugh uproariously, tears pouring down her
cheeks, I joined her.

How long we stood there, I'm uncertain. By the time we'd drained
the merriment from our bodies, things had altered between us.

"You, step-mamma," she said, hiccoughing, "stink."

"So do you, my child."

For some reason we found this hilarious and began laughing
again.

———·———

Hours later, after we'd taken the dogs to the brook and washed them,
stripped off every last stitch of clothing and scrubbed it and the worst
from ourselves, we returned stark naked to the house. There, we
boiled water, filled a tub, and cast handfuls of herbs and petals into
it. Then, we helped each other wash the last of the stench from our
bodies, paying careful attention to our nails, ears, between our toes,
passing the soap to and fro, pointing out where we'd missed. We
even washed and brushed each other's hair.

The water only needed changing three times, but by the time we'd
finished, we were cleaner than a churched mother.

Sitting in front of the hearth, we shared an ale and studied each other anew. Apart from her cut and swollen lip where I'd punched her, and the lump on her forehead which matched the one on mine, Alyson's face wasn't the least bit ratty or toady. On the contrary it was a very nice face with plump cheeks, large eyes, and even creamy teeth set in a generous mouth above a small chin. Her skin was also very white and, like mine, had a smattering of freckles, something all the dirt had hidden. Her hair was the most glorious shade of auburn, like the leaves as they turned in autumn. It was also quite long and curly. Her eyes, a dark shade of blue, were intelligent and warmer than I would have ever thought from the glacial stares she'd given me.

"You pack a mean punch for a mother," she said.

"You pack a mean one for a daughter," I replied.

We giggled. This had been going on all afternoon.

"You look better smeared in shit than no mother I've ever seen," she said.

"You make eating shit look tastier than any daughter I've ever known."

That started us off again and it was how Master Bigod and the men found us a short time later.

"What's going on here?" asked Master Bigod, coming into the house and staring, Theo and Beton right behind him. Hereward and Wake bounded over, almost tripping him up as he joined us. "What's so funny? How come the dogs look so . . . clean? How come you both . . ." He paused and took in the swollen lips, the scratches, the rather prominent lump on Alyson's forehead. He thought better than to pass comment. ". . . Do as well? Are we expecting the King?"

"Nay, Papa," smiled Alyson. Sweet Jesu, she was a girl transformed. I prayed with all my might this alteration might be a lasting one, not a fleeting thing born of our furious, revolting tussle. I prayed the cleansing we'd undertaken together was of more than just our bodies. As if reading my thoughts, Alyson met my eyes and nodded, her smile widening. "We—Eleanor and I—just decided that since we were cleaning the house, it was time to look to our persons as well."

Clever girl. The fight was to be our secret.

"Why, the resemblance between you both is quite striking," added Master Bigod, looking from one of us to the other. "You could be sisters."

I stared at Alyson in bewilderment, as she did me. Strange to think only a few hours ago, I would have been appalled by such a comparison. Not any longer. We shared a long, slow smile.

Before any more could be said about that, and not one to miss an opportunity, I stood. "We thought you, Beton, and Theo might also like to partake of washing. Look, husband, the water is still there and we have more warming on the fire." I pointed to the brimming tub, the water not too gray as it had been changed before we'd finished with it.

Hands in the air, Master Bigod began to back away. "I don't need a bath. I had one afore Yuletide and not due another for a few months yet."

Theo and Beton began to skulk toward the door.

Damn. So much for thinking that upon seeing and smelling us, the men would be keen.

"Papa," said Alyson, raising a warning finger, before, quick as a flash, she bolted to the first door and closed it. Then, she raced to the second. "None of you—" she pointed to the men one by one, "are leaving this house until you've bathed. Properly. That means taking off all your clothes and getting in that tub. Now, who's first?"

There were furious objections and any number of excuses as we helped the men remove their clothes, me modestly averting my gaze when they took off their shifts and braes. (I confess, I did peep when Master Bigod undid the cord on his and stepped out of them. He may have been a humble farmer but there was nothing humble about his plough, if you get my meaning.)

Together, Alyson and I boiled more water, helped the men wash their hair and backs, and scurried to and fro fetching clean shifts, breeches, shirts, and hose. Master Bigod complained that the only other set he had was his Sunday best, but as Alyson pointed out, what did that matter when he so rarely went to church anyhow. I silently vowed that I would weave enough cloth to make all the men extra sets of clothes.

We sat by the hearth that night, the hounds and Claude curled about us, the other beasts snoring and snuffling, and drank, ate, and told stories through the thick smoke. Beton played his pipe, Theo beat a drum. Outside, the rain fell and thunder growled in the distance, causing Hereward and Wake's ears to twitch, but not to disturb them enough that they raised their weary heads. Nor did I as the rain lashed the roof when I went to bed, my husband, at my insistence, sleeping beside me. He didn't touch me, but I found his presence a great comfort and, with his fresh odor in my nostrils, slept more soundly than I remembered in a long, long time.

SIX

Bigod Farm
The Year of Our Lord 1364
In the thirty-eighth year of the reign of Edward III

Call it the will of God, the hand of Fate, the Wheel of Fortune turning in my favor, whatever you choose, but a few days later, while we were still basking in the goodwill produced by shit, soap, and water, we had not one but two unexpected visitors.

The first was our neighbor, Master Turbet Gerrish.

I'd heard Master Gerrish's name a great deal since I arrived. Not only had he supplied my husband with the broken loom, but his lands abutted ours. The men would oft meet to discuss sheepfolds, repairs to drystone walls, storm damage, and who was to blame when sheep or lambs were unaccounted for.

When he appeared at the house bright and early one summer morning, before the men had left for the fields, Master Bigod invited him to join us, albeit with some reluctance. His squire and another man remained outside with the horses. At the time, I put my husband's aloofness down to his dislike of people in general, which just went to show how much more I'd yet to learn about him.

Master Gerrish reminded me of the gentry and bishops who occasionally graced Noke Manor. It wasn't just his practiced manners, but his fine clothing as well. It looked so out of place at Bigod Farm. Despite the efforts we'd made, before Master Gerrish with his fancy embroidered paltock, parti-colored hose, and leather boots, we looked like peasants. Back then, I didn't understand this was how we were meant to feel.

Gorgeously attired for a freeman, Master Gerrish strode into the house as if he owned it. On seeing me rising from the table, he demanded an introduction and, taking his time, took my hand and kissed it, then proceeded to shower me with compliments. I was overwhelmed, and for many reasons. It was partly his scent, which hovered about him as bees do flowers. It was exotic, wild, and very, very strong. It made me want to discreetly sniff my person and sprinkle myself with rosewater (I didn't). I was initially lost for words because it was the first time I'd met someone of his rank as a wife. I was shown a level of respect I'd only ever seen offered to Lady Clarice, the clergy, and sometimes Papa. I liked it. A lot.

Oh, alright I admit it. My head was turned. I was only twelve. It didn't take much.

Keeping a hold of my hand, Master Gerrish examined the house appreciatively, his eyebrows arched. He waved a beringed hand in the air.

"And I suppose you're the . . . *woman* responsible for this wondrous transformation?"

The child in me responded.

Alyson made a noise deep in her throat.

"Oh, not me alone," I said swiftly. I wouldn't risk our newfound accord for anyone, not even for this stranger who called me a woman. "Alyson had already done a great deal before I arrived. Since then, we've been working together to make some improvements."

"*Some?* Why it's positively . . . altered." Master Gerrish squeezed my fingers then released them. "You've done very well for yourself, haven't you, Bigod?" he said with an exaggerated wink at my husband, who scowled and plonked himself on the bench. "Found yourself a proper, obedient, and very young wife. Someone you can train. I like that."

Alyson rolled her eyes. I resisted the urge to sit on my haunches and bark.

"And I have to say, Mistress Bigod—" he cast another appreciative eye over me, "you're not what I expected, not at all."

Without thinking, I was about to ask what he did expect, when my husband intervened.

"What brings you here, Gerrish?"

"Ah, well," said Master Gerrish, taking the proffered place on the bench, forcing Theo to slide along. He grasped the mazer of small ale Alyson passed him and drank before answering. "Apart from wanting to meet your lady wife, something I've been remiss about doing, though with good reason, as I've been in London. That's why I'm here. I thought you'd like to know what's happening in Calais now that it's operating as the Staple port for the wool trade."

"I would," said Master Bigod. "But it won't change my position, Gerrish. If we can't resolve our problems honestly then we're as bad as those we accuse of fleecing us."

Master Gerrish laughed and faced me. "You've married an honest man, Mistress Bigod, for better or worse."

I didn't see how being honest could ever be worse, but kept my peace. Rising, my husband touched Master Gerrish's arm and gestured to the door. "How about we take this conversation outside? The women don't need to be bothered with this."

Goddamn his patched hose. This is precisely what I *did* want to be bothered with. As a brogger's daughter, I knew all about the Wool Staple, how it had been moved from Bruges, then to a number of ports and places in Britain before being established at Calais last year and thus back onto English territory. How the King made certain all the wool our country exported went through the one port, where subsidies were paid and the sacks were measured and weighed before they went onward to international buyers. Its purpose was to prevent alien merchants from cheating English buyers or wool growers. There was an uproar when it became evident the only ones doing the cheating (or the main ones) were the twenty-six English merchants based in Calais who not only charged excessive fees—even to their own—but bought land there and demanded exorbitant rents, basically manipulating the market by forcing small producers out so those remaining profited at everyone else's expense. Master Merriman had been furious, claiming it an outrage.

Apart from owning a large flock and leasing good pasture as well as a few acres to grow crops, I was still to learn Master Bigod's level of involvement in the wool trade, exactly how many sheep he ran and what sort of coin he earned. If he was interested in the Staple and what was going on, then he must be exporting some wool as well.

I watched the two men talking outside. They were out of earshot, but the tone of their conversation and their facial expressions were clear. My husband was sour and angry, a contrast to Master Gerrish, who was a great deal . . . lighter. Slightly younger than Master Bigod, he appeared to have an altogether different disposition. I said as much to Alyson.

"Don't be fooled by appearances," she said, standing beside me, arms folded. "His smile is like the sun on an overcast day—it shines all too briefly, giving a false impression of warmth. Come on." She nudged me in the ribs. "Let's make a start on the barn."

Yesterday I'd managed to persuade her we should shift the animals out of the house altogether. Enjoying her newfound freshness as well as our equanimity, Alyson had been swift to agree. I wanted to make sure we acted quickly, lest she change her mind.

Nonetheless, I looked back at the men as we went out the door. Master Gerrish waved and smiled. Master Bigod grunted. If Master Gerrish's grin was insincere, there was no denying it came in an attractive, if somewhat over-scented package.

I don't know when the men departed, or the boys, just that Alyson and I worked hard all morning preparing the barn. We moved the brewing equipment to one side, swept the stables and, of course, shoveled more shit, and brought in some new hay.

The bells for sext tolled faintly in the distance as we moved the hens' nesting boxes out of the house, many of them clucking as they tottered after us, the rooster scratching at the dirt, pecking and following to see what we were about. We'd have to ask Master Bigod to repair the barn doors, but they weren't in bad condition for something that had been neglected so long. We created an area for Pilgrim, and one for the sow and her piglets as well. The goats could be partitioned near the door and the geese we'd corral with the ducks and hens at night.

When we broke for some bread and ale, I almost fell off the bale when Alyson suggested we go to the brook to bathe and wash off the sweat and dirt of our labors—and the fleas, she added. What? Two baths in as many days. I readily agreed, the memory of Master Gerrish's heady perfume still in my nostrils. I too would be glad to get rid of the wretched fleas and any lice that may have burrowed into our hair since the last wash.

An hour later, we were walking back to the house, and I was thinking how relieved I was that the resentment Alyson had borne me appeared to have evaporated. All it had taken was some shit. Papa would laugh. What was it he always said to me? If you're given shit, turn it into fertilizer. Hopefully, this is exactly what I'd done.

We heard the jangle of harness and the sound of voices. Alyson stopped. "Don't tell me Master Gerrish is back."

I shielded my eyes with my hand. "They're riding mules, not horses." Whoever it was, I was grateful they hadn't arrived earlier when we were covered in muck and straw.

"Well, the devil take my soul," I muttered as they drew closer. A favorite curse of Cook's.

"Can you make out who it is?" asked Alyson, squinting.

It was The Poet. Fear prickled my spine, made my innards liquid as I wondered what brought him here. Was there to be more trouble over what happened with Layamon?

Deep down, what worried me most was that he'd come to take me away. I may have only been at Bigod Farm a short while, but already I'd grown accustomed not just to the way things were, but my new position. Here, I wasn't a servant, but able to make decisions and have others do my bidding. To my surprise, I wasn't ready to relinquish the little authority I had. Nor put at risk the burgeoning friendship with Alyson.

Little did I know that, though unremarkable at the time, both our visitors that day had roles to play in my future.

SEVEN

Bigod Farm
The Year of Our Lord 1364
In the thirty-eighth year of the reign of Edward III

*T*he Poet and his squire trotted up the track, heads swiveling like hawks as they took in the changes. Ambivalence warred within me. I couldn't forget the part The Poet had played in my marriage—a man I barely knew influencing my fate.

I lifted my skirts and strode to meet them, Alyson on my heels. The men drew their mules up outside the house.

"God give you good day, Mistress Bigod," said The Poet in that mellifluous voice of his. "You too, Mistress Alyson."

Wait. What? He *knew* Alyson.

"And you too Master Geoffrey," said Alyson, dipping a curtsey.

Master Geoffrey?

"And God's good day to you, Master Odo," added Alyson, addressing the squire and grinning from ear to ear. Her cheeks were flushed, her eyes sparkling. The squire touched his cap and shyly returned her smile.

"You *know* this man?" I whispered incredulously as they dismounted and led the animals to the water trough.

"Oh, aye. That's Odo atte Elme; we're old friends."

"Not him," I snapped. "Him!" I pointed at The Poet.

"Master Geoffrey? Aye. Known him my whole life. He's a cousin of some sort. Papa says he's destined to come up in the world."

"Does he?"

"Aye. So mayhap you did better than you thought marrying Papa. If a relation rises, so does the whole family." There was no rancor in Alyson's tone. She bumped shoulders with me, smiling.

"Mayhap, I did," I said, suddenly thoughtful. The Poet . . . or, as I must now think of him, Master Geoffrey, had brokered this marriage, which now turned out to be to one of his relatives; someone I was beginning to realize had been unfairly maligned. I recalled the day I was locked in my bedroom. I'd seen Lady Clarice handing The Poet a purse before sending him on his way. Was it to present his relation with the dowry she offered?

As he approached, Master Geoffrey seemed uncertain about the welcome he'd receive. He took my hand cautiously and bowed, before releasing it and placing a kiss on Alyson's lips.

"You're looking very well, Mistress Alyson, and you too, Mistress Bigod."

"Call me Eleanor," I said. "After all, we are related."

Master Geoffrey laughed uncomfortably. "Ah, indeed. It's a very distant connection, through my grandfather."

We smiled like simpletons. Odo whistled as he removed the blankets and saddles from the mules.

It wasn't until Alyson gave me a shove and jerked her chin toward the house that I understood how remiss I was being. Of course, *I* was mistress. It was my duty to extend invitations to any guests. Bless her wrinkled apron; if I needed a sign things were going to be right between us, this was it. She was relinquishing her role as lady of the house to me. I reached for her hand and squeezed it.

"Please," I said to Master Geoffrey. "Come inside and let's have an ale. There's also some cold coney and ham hock as well. Then you can share your news, and what's brought you to Bigod Farm."

With an elegant bow, Master Geoffrey followed me and Alyson into the fortunately clean, mostly tidy, house. Apart from King

Claude, who, as was his wont, lolled on the chest under the window, contentedly licking his balls, his fur floating around like a snowstorm.

———•———

Over a few mazers of ale, Master Geoffrey regaled us not just with stories of Noke Manor and the people within its walls, but London, where he was studying under a fusty old lawyer named Master Derman. The man was so short-sighted, he would oft be caught addressing a sword and shield hanging in the Great Hall of Inner Temple as if it were one of his peers. Master Geoffrey also brought news of the court and the spendthrift ways of Queen Philippa and King Edward. It struck me as odd that those, like myself, who could least afford to spend, always enjoyed listening to stories of others who did.

After a few more ales, he even admitted to having been in trouble for beating a Franciscan friar. Odo coughed politely and turned his head away, but not before I'd seen the flash of pride upon his face.

I could scarce believe that Master Geoffrey, this slight man of even temperament, had been roused not only to strike a man of God, but fined for the privilege. When he told us it was because he came upon the friar beating a skinny young beggar black and bloody with a rod for no other sin than blocking a doorway in Fleet Street, I confess Master Geoffrey went up in my estimation. I began to imagine him beating Layamon. The picture conjured gave me a very warm and happy feeling (forgive me, O Lord).

As the afternoon wore on and the sun disappeared behind dark clouds, the wind growing stronger, there was a lull in the conversation. I could hear a rat scrabbling in the walls, the goats bleating. There was so much I wanted to ask Master Geoffrey—about Fulk, about the whys and wherefores of our marriage contract, about why he chose such a man for me—yet it didn't seem right with Alyson there.

Mayhap, she sensed this or, more likely, was driven by less noble intentions, for I'd noticed the looks she exchanged with Odo. Before long, she asked him to help her make the animals secure.

Finally, it was just me and Master Geoffrey. "Can I ask you something, sir?"

"You may ask whatever you wish," said Master Geoffrey affably. He relaxed on the bench, resting against the wall. We were seated opposite each other at the trestle table, the remnants of our meal in front of us.

I took a deep breath. "I wish to ask about Father Layamon."

Master Geoffrey wet the tip of a finger and carefully collected some crumbs from the table. He studied them before sucking and collecting more. "Two days ago, accompanied by Master Merriman, Father Layamon left Noke Manor bound for Bristol. From there, he will sail to France—where he'll remain." He chuckled. I didn't find it funny. I prayed the ship would capsize and drown Layamon. Everyone else was to be rescued, of course. I wasn't a complete barbarian.

When I didn't respond, but sat staring out the door, Master Geoffrey abandoned the crumbs and tapped the back of my hand. "A groat for your thoughts."

My eyes slid to his. Up close, he looked younger than from a distance. His cheeks were unlined, the curls of his scant beard soft and thin. To think I'd once thought him ancient. Being with Fulk put that in a different context.

"Why did you broker a marriage between me and Master Bigod? I thought at first you must either hate me or, following orders from Lady Clarice and Father Roman, seek to punish me. I couldn't understand why you'd plight me to such an old, dirty man. But now . . ." I glanced about. "Now I know you're related, that you know Master Bigod and the family, I just wonder . . . why?"

"*Hate* you?" Master Geoffrey's eyes widened. "Dear God, child, how could you think that? I scarce know you." Perturbed, he tugged his beard, his mind working. I had the strong impression that far from struggling to answer my question, Master Geoffrey was juggling with the idea I might dislike *him*.

"Please don't tell me you're unhappy, Mistress Eleanor," he said, sitting up straight. "For as God is my witness and Jesus my Savior, that was never my intention. Nor is it the impression I have. Not only do you and Alyson appear to have struck up a friendship, but I can see your influence everywhere." His arm drew a semicircle.

"I'm not unhappy—" I began.

"Thank God and all the saints." His head dropped into his hands.

"But I am curious . . . How did you know?"

"Know what?" He raised his face.

"That Master Bigod, my husband, was not like everyone said. I mean, it clearly wasn't just because you're related—"

"Distantly."

"Distantly." I smiled. "You knew, didn't you? You knew he wasn't what people said. You knew that once you look beneath the gruffness, the dirt, once he was in his own home, on his own land, he was a different man."

Master Geoffrey paused, then held up his mazer, nodding at the jug. I topped it up. "Aye, I knew."

Drinking deeply, he wiped his mouth on his sleeve and then tried, most unsuccessfully, to stifle a belch. Straddling the bench, he drummed his fingers on the table, thinking, thinking. Swiveling back to regard me, he appeared to come to a decision.

"I've known your husband for as long as I can remember and, during that time, I've seen him suffer and endure more than anyone has a right. Understand this, Eleanor." He waggled a long finger. "No matter what those shrews and prating old men say in the village, Fulk Bigod is not and never has been a bad man. He's simply a sad one. Just because some dunderheads can't tell the difference doesn't make them right."

My heart, which had been knocking against my ribs, began to settle. From the outset, I'd never sensed anything evil in my husband, but sadness? Aye, now I put it to mind, it oozed from him like the mist over the millpond at Noke Manor in autumn. It reminded me of Lady Clarice, how sometimes when she thought you weren't looking, she'd be staring out the window with her needlework untouched in her lap, sorrow rearranging her face into pools of shadow and deep lines. As soon as she sensed a presence, her expression would transform and you'd swear you imagined it. Papa had been the same.

Instead of going to the trouble of reorganizing his face for folk, my husband hid his sorrow beneath layers of dirt and gruff silence.

"How are you and Fulk related?" I asked quietly.

"My grandfather was a man named Robert Chaucer—"

"Is that your name, sir?"

"Aye. I'm Geoffrey Chaucer." He rose and gave a brief bow, staggering slightly. The ale was strong and, like me, he was becoming affected. Collapsing back onto the bench, he leaned over the table conspiratorially.

"Robert Chaucer hailed from a village on the outskirts of London, a village Fulk also hails from. Fulk's grandfather and mine were cousins. My grandfather was a mercer. My grandmother came from a reasonably well-to-do family, the de Comptons—"

"Wait," I said, sitting bolt upright. "Your grandmother was a de Compton? So was my mother."

"Aye, Eleanor, we're also very distantly related—by marriage. Cousins removed so many times—" He circled his hand in the air.

"But that means Fulk and I must be too."

"That was one concern regarding your marriage—consanguinity. But when I asked, the bishop said there were enough degrees of separation and approved it."

Here I was thinking I'd no family, not since Papa died, when the truth was, I'd an abundance of relations—by marriage. I stared at The Poet—Geoffrey—my cousin, with fresh eyes and a slightly dreamy half-smile.

"But I digress," continued Geoffrey, unaware of the strange mood that had descended on me. "From the moment my grandmother married Robert, who'd been apprenticed to her first husband, his fortunes changed. Not only did he become the owner of the business his wife had inherited when she was widowed, but he became deputy to the old King's butler. After a time, he was made Comptroller of Customs for wine levies. From mercer's apprentice to holding royal appointments, and all in one lifetime." He chuckled, and not without pride. "He used to say if he can do it, anyone can. Likewise, Fulk, a farmer by birth, married the daughter of a gentleman who held considerable land toward Bath.

Upon her father's death, his wife, an only child, inherited a good percentage, including what you see here. Suddenly Fulk went from being a landholder of minor means to one with a modest amount of property. But whereas my grandfather prospered, for Fulk it was a different story.

"Under normal circumstances, having land should have been a boon. But the weather was colder than usual, the rains heavier, and year after year crops failed. I'm too young to recall, but talk to anyone of a certain age and they'll tell you how hard it was to put food on the table; to feed the animals. How entire villages starved, babies died, their cattle and sheep, too. If they weren't slaughtered for food, they were left to perish in the fields. Floods and then famine ravaged the land, killing thousands." Geoffrey's face darkened.

I'd heard snippets from the old people in Bath-atte-Mere, and those at the manor, but never like this. It was as if people's memories could not go back further than the Botch, the deadly pestilence that struck over sixteen years ago, causing untold deaths and changing everything.

"But this is where your husband came into his own," continued Geoffrey. "Many people wanted to sell their land, move away. Fulk remained and took over their leases. Some said he was mad. That he was destined to fail. The land, they warned him, was dead and it would be the death of him. Nothing would grow. He would have been better off burying his coin and trying to grow his fortune that way.

"Only, instead of continuing to plant crops, Fulk dug them up and turned the land over to pasture. With the last of his wife's dowry, he bought sheep. Alas, she never survived to see how his decision succeeded—beyond anyone's expectations. She died in childbed—the babe too—and it broke Fulk's heart."

Master Geoffrey drank. "Anyhow," he said, putting the mazer down. "As you know from the villagers' tales, he went on to marry three more times. Despite what's said, he never killed his wives. Two he lost to pestilence, another to childbed. There were twins. They only lived a year before sickness took them as well. In the end, Fulk Bigod, the man with land and sheep aplenty, had no wife, no children from his loins, but he did have family." He tilted his head, waiting for me to respond.

"I know about Alyson, Theo, and Beton," I said. "I also know there are—were—others. I just don't know whose children they are."

Master Geoffrey nodded sagely. "Tell me, is that something a bad man does? A murderer? A miser and bully? Takes in the children of his fallen sister and raises them like his own."

"Sister?" This was the first I'd heard of a sister. "Where is she?"

Master Geoffrey considered his next words. "Swear on your everlasting soul that you'll never reveal what I'm about to tell you."

God's boils. A shiver ran from the back of my neck to the soles of my feet. "I swear."

Master Geoffrey lifted his rump off the bench and bent so far over the table, I thought he was intending to kiss me. "Fulk's sister," he whispered, though there was nobody but King Claude to overhear, "a woman named Loveday, was once happily married, boasted a fine house in Bath, a husband of means, and was herself a capable merchant, selling cloth and other fripperies to fine ladies. That was, until the Botch swept the town. Her husband died, and she found that not only did customers cease to call, but debtors came a-knocking. Once she'd paid them off, but was still owing lease-monies on the house, she'd no choice but to leave with her two boys. She was too proud to take Fulk's offer of a roof over her head, or his money. Instead, she went to London to try and make her fortune. She had some ells of cloth, a few coins, letters of recommendation from women too scared to darken her door but wanting to help in any way they could. Most of all, she had a great deal of pride."

He hesitated. I waited.

"It wasn't enough." He sighed. "It never is. Remember that, Eleanor. All too soon she was frequenting Gropecunt Lane, selling the only thing left to her once her cloth and coin were no more."

I frowned.

"Her queynte," explained Geoffrey.

"Oh."

"She became a meretrix, a whore. That's where my father found her and, when he saw the conditions she was living in, he brought her sons to Fulk.

"After that, there were other children. Theo and Beton and, finally, Alyson. Fulk refused to say whose they were. Likely in vengeance for his secrecy and success, folk spread rumors. How the children were here for other, less godly reasons—" He paused. "It didn't help that when he tried to hire servants, they took one look at the children, at the state of the farm, and ran away. I imagine for the city, as many young folk do."

Master Geoffrey's voice was slow and sad. "I only caught a glimpse of the old Fulk—the man before all the tragedy—when my family stayed here, on the farm, while the pestilence ravaged London."

"You were here?"

"Aye. I was but a lad. But I clearly remember the moment his beloved Evelot died. He changed, Eleanor, and with every loss he kept changing, until he rejected everyone, even those with his interests at heart."

"You?"

"Aye, even me." Geoffrey turned away, but not before I'd seen the tears swimming in his eyes. He passed his sleeve casually over his cheek, then continued in a low voice. "Father made me and my mother promise we would keep an eye out for Fulk. When I was made a page in Prince Lionel's house, I tried, not that it did much good. He refused my offers. When the chance came to study at Inner Temple, learn the legal process, I thought, why not? It would hold me and my family, including Fulk, in good stead. Why do you think I make a point of coming to Noke Manor, of asking to manage Lady Clarice's legal affairs? The manor is close, yet far enough not to arouse Fulk's suspicions that someone might be watching over him. He would loathe that, especially when he goes to so much trouble to keep everyone away." He gave a small smile to ensure I understood what he meant. I did.

"The grubby, gruff exterior," I sighed.

"It was his armor, his shield against the world. He used dirt and filth to ensure no one came near him ever again."

My soul swelled and ached. Heavy drops of rain began to fall. They struck the roof with a series of dull thuds that echoed on the ground, exploding the dirt. Aye, even the skies were weeping for Fulk Bigod. This was beyond terrible. It was tragic. How could I have thought so poorly of him? Listened to those ghastly people whose twisted minds turned a good man into a bad one, ensuring he'd no friends with whom he could unburden himself. The man was a veritable saint. People should be beating a pilgrimage to his door, buying cockle shells and ampullae filled with his essence.

"What happened to Loveday?" I asked, dabbing my cheeks with the ends of my apron.

Master Geoffrey shut his eyes and tilted his face toward the ceiling, before opening them again. "She worked for a few terrible years before she was beaten to death. Her body tossed into the Thames. Father had to go and identify her." He glanced out the door. The rain had become a thick watery curtain. Master Geoffrey was forced to raise his voice. "From the talk of Bath to a line in a coroner's record. She's buried here, you know—" He pointed out the door. "Under some tree by the brook. Alyson oft sits there—in the branches. All Loveday's children do . . ."

So that was where Alyson had run the night I arrived. Not to the coneys, as my husband had me believe, but to her mother. Fulk's sister. I couldn't hold back anymore, I buried my head in my hands and wept. Master Geoffrey rose from his side of the table and slid onto my bench, taking me in his arms. As I cried, he stroked my hair.

"You see, Eleanor. Rightly or wrongly, what happened between you and that sorry excuse for a priest was going to make *you* an outcast. Misunderstood, maligned. Any plans for a good marriage your father or Lady Clarice had made were ruined—hush, hush, not by you, child. Not by you. The moment I saw what was going on, caught wind of what the bishop and Layamon intended, which was to have you sent away, likely to serve someone cruel and unforgiving, I had to do something; find someone who wouldn't judge or punish you. It helped that you were of an age to be wed and I happened to know a man in need of a wife."

I sobbed harder.

"I also knew that Fulk could do with someone like you."

"L . . . L . . . Like me? But you said yourself, you don't know me," I wailed.

Master Geoffrey laughed; it wasn't unkind. "Ah, but from my visits to Noke Manor, I grew to know your father and those who worked with you. I know you're headstrong, clever, stubborn, and prefer to make up your own mind. Someone who, despite your tender years, wouldn't be swayed by hearsay and gossip."

I pulled away from him, aware that his chest was wet, that my nose was running, my hair had started to unravel and my scarf slip off.

"But . . . I listened. I even added to it . . ."

"Mayhap," said Master Geoffrey, smiling so gently it made me cry more. "But I doubt you'll make that mistake again. Will you?"

I shook my head fiercely, then buried it in his chest once more. He smelled of horses, musk, and smoke. His arms were comforting. I thought of Papa and all the times I wished he'd held me tight like this.

The longer I cried, the more I came to realize I was no longer howling for sorrow's sake, but with relief. I was glad to be on Bigod Farm. I was glad I was married to such a good man, such a kind man, even if he was old. And wrinkly. At least he didn't stink anymore. If I had my way, he never would again.

If I had my way. God, I sounded like a real wife.

Only, I thought, as my tears ceased to fall and I sniveled and tried to breathe, I wasn't a real wife, was I? Here I was, months later, still a child-woman and, until I bedded my husband, I would remain one. Sweet Jesu, that was something I had to ensure happened lest the marriage be annulled.

I freed myself from Master Geoffrey's embrace, wiped my face and downed some ale he'd poured. Then I took his hands and kissed first one and then the other.

"Thank you," I said. "Thank you." His skin was soft. A writer's hands, not a worker's.

"For what?" he said, though I could tell he damn well knew.

"For this—" I gestured about me. I meant more than just the house.

"You're very welcome, cousin." We both smiled.

After that, we sat quietly, asking each other questions that had nothing to do with the past, and everything to do with today and tomorrow.

When the rain began to ease, Master Geoffrey rose. "I hope that in future, you'll allow me to visit from time to time? See how you're faring?"

"If you don't, I'll find you and demand to know why."

He grinned. "If I can't visit, I'll write. I know you can't read, and nor can Fulk, but you can ask Father Elias at St. Michael's Without the Walls in Bath to read my missives. He's an old friend. You can trust him."

"You've a few of those, don't you?"

"Aye. Friends are what make life worth living." He took my hand in his. "I also hope that with you, I've not only a cousin, but a new friend as well."

"You do."

We grinned.

He let go of my fingers, stretched, and faced the door. The rain ceased, though dark clouds approaching from the west suggested another deluge. Alyson's and Odo's voices grew louder as they returned to the house.

Master Geoffrey pulled me to my feet beside him. "Let's have a toast," he said, putting a mazer into my hands and picking up his own. "To new friends. To family. May we always see the good beneath the surface and—" He moved his mazer out of the way as I went to clink it. He hadn't yet finished.

"May we always have the heart to give those requiring a second chance the opportunity to take it."

We struck cups and drank, not knowing then how much those words would come back to haunt us.

That night, as Geoffrey shared a bed with Theo below, I welcomed my husband to ours and became Mistress Fulk Bigod in every way.

And, in case you're wondering (and you are), my husband may have been old, but he was no monster . . . Nor was he the divine Cupid; not that I'm complaining—too much. Even so, as I shut my eyes and waited for it to be over, I comforted myself with the thought this was what women and wives had done since time began, young, old, and in-between—willing and unwilling. It was a duty, another expectation placed upon us by God and man. Gradually, I came to see my body, my queynte, as a tool, which, over time, I learned to wield to my advantage.

It was some years before I discovered I too could take pleasure from it. That, truth be told, was the beginning of my undoing.

EIGHT

Bigod Farm, London, and Bath
The Years of Our Lord 1364 to 1369
In the thirty-eighth to the forty-second years of the reign of Edward III

The seasons passed, summer relaxed into a cool autumn followed by a freezing winter and Yuletide. On Bigod Farm, more transformations were slowly wrought.

Alright, I wrought the changes and sometimes, I admit, not so slowly.

One of the first I insisted upon was maintaining the interior of the house and ourselves in a state of cleanliness. With Alyson's support, I refused to listen to objections and excuses as I first asked, and later demanded, that bathing was to happen at least once a month, more frequently if someone fell in shit or helped with birthing animals. Or if their lice or fleas were troublesome. If Theo, Beton, or even Fulk refused to adhere to this schedule, they were to sleep in the barn (Theo and Beton did a couple of times, until they decided it wasn't worth it). Likewise, the rushes were now changed fortnightly and were spread throughout the main room.

Though my husband was initially reluctant to abide by what he called my unnatural obsession with water, claiming his skin would slough off or he would catch any number of diseases, when I threatened to withhold sexual favors, he soon came around. I also knew part of my husband's reticence was fear that without the dirt to keep people away, he would be forced to endure society. What he gradually learned was that I would be by his side—at least until we'd turned those nasty rumors on their head.

For our first Christmas, I presented the family (how that word made me fizz with delight) with new clothes I'd woven and Alyson had sewn. Theo, Beton, and Fulk strutted about the house like peacocks and, when I suggested we hitch the cart to Pilgrim and attend mass in the chapel at the manor, were willing. The gratification I felt when the villagers didn't recognize Fulk is hard to describe. When Alyson, Theo, and Beton—the suspicious, grubby children the folk of Bath-atte-Mere had whispered about—entered the chapel beside their adopted father in fine woollen tunics and surcoats, clean, bright hose and boots, draped in cloaks lined with sheepskin, delicate embroidery tracing the edges, I couldn't have been prouder.

Lady Clarice was so taken aback, she made a point of not only welcoming us as she stood next to Father Roman when we left the chapel, but inviting us to the Great Hall for some wassailing and feasting. I sat with the other wives at a decorated table, served by young girls who, less than a year before, I'd worked beside. Whereas once I would have been most uncomfortable, expecting to be ignored, I was beset with questions and barely disguised comments—many flattering. I answered those I wished and pretended not to hear those I didn't. I also made sure I remembered my friends, wrapping May and Joan in my arms and disappearing briefly to visit Cook, as well as sitting with Mistress Bertha and Master Merriman. There were a few times I wanted to snap and scold a gossip, repeat back words she'd once used against my husband. But that was no way to secure a fresh place in this little community. Instead, I smiled a secret smile, shook or nodded my head, or bowed it in false modesty. For certes, I wasn't feeling the slightest bit humble.

I was bursting as I watched Alyson whirling about the floor with Odo, looking happier than I'd ever seen her in a lovely russet kirtle and golden surcoat. Theo and Beton were a fine sight, clean-shaven, their thick dark hair tamed. But most of all, I was proud of my husband. He stood to one side in the Great Hall, between Master Geoffrey and Lady Clarice, his mazer constantly filled, men in a tight circle about the three of them. He smiled on occasion, listened intently to what was being said, and kept me in his line of sight. Fulk, Geoffrey, and I shared many a look that night—the kind that comes from mutual understanding and more than a little bit of hard-earned triumph, tinged with rich irony.

In less than a year, circumstances had undergone an enormous change. Mine from serving girl to sinful wench to farmer's wife, and Fulk and his family from reclusive outsiders to folk in the thick of the village. Fulk raised his mazer in my direction. Aye, I deserved a toast. We all did.

That was just the beginning.

The following year, as our fleeces sold well and Fulk invested in more sheep, I persuaded my husband that if we wanted to make more money, we needed to diversify (a word Papa had been fond of using) and one way of doing that was by putting me and Alyson to work as well. We not only needed to invest in another loom for Alyson to work upon, but bigger ones. In order to make that kind of purchase worthwhile, we needed to be freed from daily household chores. That meant hiring servants.

Fulk had many positive attributes, and when it came to love and understanding, he was the most generous person on God's good earth. He was also a splendid listener and acknowledged the sense of my suggestions. But when it came to parting with coin, unless it was for the sole purpose of increasing the size of the flock, he became the worst of misers. That was, until I learned that once more, all I had to do was withhold my queynte—until he saw fit to give me what I wanted.

He held out for three days.

Two weeks later we welcomed first one maid, Milda, then another, Sophie, into the house. Milda was a poor widow of about thirty odd years of age from the other side of town. Her children had either died or left home to find their fortunes elsewhere. A stout woman with honey-colored hair, permanently rosy cheeks, and smiling hazelnut eyes, she had a quiet way about her that I liked immediately. Grateful for the work, she was respectful of my position, only offering advice when asked (which wasn't often, even though, mayhap, it should have been).

Sophie was a young girl of about ten from Bathampton, who came from a large villein family having trouble feeding everyone. She was delighted not to have to share a pallet.

Over summer we'd extended the house, building walls, and partitions, making private rooms for Alyson and the men. While Milda and Sophie first slept on pallet beds near the hearth, before long I used my usual methods of persuasion to get Fulk to build another room for them, at the opposite end of the house to ours and above Theo and Beton's.

If only I'd known it was so easy to have my wishes met! I could have deployed this strategy from the beginning. After we'd swived and Fulk was lying on his side snoring, I would lie awake and wonder. Was this the great secret all women knew? The power their queynte possessed to overcome even the strongest, stubbornest men and thus get their own way? Is this why God didn't want Adam to eat the apple? Because He knew the moment a man bit into its sweet flesh, instead of obeying God, he would obey woman, in thrall to her chamber of Venus?

Regardless, I began to use my power freely. I like to think wisely and well—mostly to benefit others. I became gatekeeper to my heavenly postern. My husband could only enter after paying a fee—submission to my will.

Nevertheless, there were times I felt Fulk was laughing at me and my demands. Not in a demeaning way, you understand, but as if I was a child he was indulging. I suppose, in retrospect, that's exactly what I was.

After two years, Bigod Farm was a growing concern when it came to sheep and pasture, our wool sought after by English merchants. Better still, alien merchants came from Flanders, Venice, and Brabant to purchase our fleeces. These men were not only prepared to pay good prices, but to hand over very large sums in advance for wool our flock had not yet grown. It took a bit of convincing to persuade Fulk to agree to terms, even though it advantaged us. This time, it wasn't my queynte that made him capitulate (I didn't even try), but Master Gerrish and a local brogger named Master Kenton, who explained these kinds of advance contracts were being offered and accepted by the biggest monasteries and sheep farmers throughout the south and west of England. Master Gerrish offered to lease a portion of our land and buy some of our flock, so keen was he to take the aliens' coin. I think that persuaded my husband more than the brogger's words. It wasn't the first time Master Gerrish, or Turbet, as I now called him, tried to buy our land and sheep. It wouldn't be the last.

As a consequence, the wool Alyson and I wove (Alyson long ago surpassed my skills on the loom, she was such a fast learner) was also much sought after. But this is where we struck a problem. The Guild of Weavers and Fullers in Bath caught wind of what we were about and objected. Oh, we could have our wool dyed by the local fullers and make cloth—providing we only clothed ourselves. As we weren't guild members and neither was Fulk, we were forbidden to sell it, even though the demand was there.

It wasn't fair.

When Fulk objected, the guild presented a compromise: we were allowed to sell our cloth to a merchant in Bath for a fair price (when you're dealing with merchants, you swiftly learn that "fair" is a synonym for "low," the lower the better). In turn, the merchant would sell the cloth himself for inflated prices and pocket the profits. The merchant suggested to us turned out to be the brother-in-law of the head of the guild.

Once again, it was Master Gerrish who persuaded us to ignore the rules. He convinced Fulk, who passed the task to Beton or Theo, to take our cloth to the bigger markets in Brighton, Divizes, Stow-on-Wold, and even, once, to London. There, though stillage was paid, we kept every coin earned. As a consequence, we had to produce greater quantities of cloth and more quickly (and secretly). We hired maids from the village to card and spin so Alyson and I might concentrate on weaving.

Our reputation not only as producers of fine wool, but as weavers, began to grow. It would have been easy to increase our output further, but something in me (and Fulk agreed) knew that if we kept our enterprise small, just me and Alyson, then not only were we less likely to be caught, but we maintained the quality and could thus ask better prices.

It was a risk that paid off.

At unexpected moments, Fulk would reach over and drop a kiss on my brow, or cup my face. Usually, when I was at the loom. "Little did I know when I married you, Eleanor, that the pretty head beneath that glorious hair contained such a clever mind."

Alyson would arch a brow then concentrate on weaving, but not before I saw the smile that crinkled her eyes.

A wall was built between the main room, now more like a hall, and the kitchen. A chimney breast was inserted and an oven installed in the kitchen, reducing the smoke that used to fill the entire house. Once that was no longer a problem, we hired men to plaster and whitewash the walls, which lightened the inside of the house considerably. I also persuaded Fulk to extend the house a room's width the entire length. This was then divided into three rooms: a new bedroom for us, so we no longer had to ascend the ladder to go to bed (our old room was turned over to much-needed storage); a solar, so the family and servants might sometimes retreat if there were guests (usually other merchants, Turbet, and twice in two years, Geoffrey); and a garderobe or *necessarium* as Fulk insisted on calling it. That was at the opposite end to our bedroom and the kitchen and, despite the deep pit dug, and the wide plank with the hole that sat over it, it was a small space that, no matter how hard the maids cleaned or how often the boys buried the waste, exuded a terrible stink. Still, it was better than throwing the contents of the jordan about the yard.

I should add we didn't spend all our time moving the shuttle back and forth and clacking on the looms. Nor did we remain on the farm day after day. As Fulk's confidence (and mine) grew around others, we would take occasional trips into Bath, about an hour's cart ride away. By now Pilgrim had companions in the form of three other beasts, including one old nag named Philippa, or Pippa for short, because she acted as though she was the Queen. We would joke that she and old Claude were a right royal pair. Unlike the real King and Queen, they could barely stand the sight of each other.

Each trip we made into Bath-atte-Mere seemed to last longer, as invitations for ale or food were proffered, everyone wanting to hear news from the farm or further afield.

On one occasion, I accompanied my husband to London.

I hadn't long turned sixteen. The city was everything I expected in many ways, but in others, it was better. My head just about swiveled off my neck, and, if I hadn't been warned about the crush, the noise, and how thieves were on the lookout for fresh faces, I doubt my purse would have survived. I know my pinched ass and ringing ears almost didn't. But I loved every second, and as we traveled home, weary yet bursting with excitement at what we'd seen, bought, and done, I couldn't wait to return.

It would be many, many years before I did, and then in very different circumstances. But I'm running ahead of myself.

———◆———

It was a much-altered Eleanor Bigod who met The Poet when he dismounted from his horse. For a start, I was seventeen, a matron by anyone's standard with five years of marriage under my belt. Still my womb hadn't quickened. It was a very sore point and, while Fulk never made an issue of it, he watched me like a limpid cow whenever my courses came and I pushed him away for the few days. He couldn't school his face, and not simply because he couldn't sard me. No one was more aware than me that he was growing older, slower, frailer, and time was running out.

What purpose did I serve if I didn't transition from wife to mother? I'd grown taller, was large-breasted with a slim waist and rounded hips. The epitome of womanhood, Fulk called me (I had to ask Father Elias what "epitome" meant and, when he asked how it had been said to me, blushed a shade of crimson I'd only ever seen on a wealthy Bath lady's kirtle). My skin was even more freckled from the work I did outside, and my hands, while callused from weaving, were also softened from the grease of the wool and the fact I rarely did the laundry or washed dishes. Nor did I sweep or shovel shit—those tasks were now assigned to one of the three girls and two extra boys we hired. Not all of them worked in the house. The boys helped with the sheep, or drew the plough and planted the fields, along with additional help from the village during harvest. They also maintained our two horses and four mules. Pilgrim died the same year as Lady Clarice. I know which I missed more.

When Master Geoffrey dismounted, brushing off his clothes and throwing the reins of his rather fine mount to his squire—no longer Odo, who had run off to war and broken Alyson's heart—the first thing I noticed was the insignia on his clothes. The insignia of the royal house.

Seems I wasn't the only one to ascend the Wheel of Fortune.

"May God give you good day, Geoffrey!" I exclaimed, walking into his open arms and kissing him roundly on the mouth.

"You too, Eleanor. Why, you're the picture of health."

I slapped his arm. "Look. Here comes Alyson."

Where the years had been kind to me, to Alyson they'd been less generous. After Odo ran away, she forswore men. I'd laughed, which just seemed to make her more determined. There were plenty of young men keen to attract her interest. Not only was she known as the daughter of a successful wool producer and farmer, but she was comely after a fashion. True, her skin was coarser than it had been, and she dedicated herself to the loom in what might have been considered an unhealthy way, except that what she produced was so intricate and fine, it put weavers in Ypres and Ghent to shame. I tried to encourage her outside, to enjoy the sun when it shone, even to stand in the rain or snow when it didn't, but she couldn't be persuaded. Wan of face, her hair lacked the luster it once had. I kept hoping time would lift her spirits, but nothing thus far had worked. Nevertheless, she was pleased to see Geoffrey.

We escorted him inside, showing him the additions that had been made since his last visit. The maids quickly took his cloak, brought over a jug of ale and some food to the table—a larger trestle. In what was rather a boastful gesture, I asked the girls to remove the food and drink to the solar.

"Solar?" exclaimed Geoffrey, his eyes widening. "Well, well, well, aren't you the fancy lady?"

"You don't know the half," I said, laughing. "And speaking of fancy," I said, flicking the insignia on his tunic. "What's this? Lancaster colors if I'm not mistaken."

"You're not," said Geoffrey, collapsing into one of the two fabric-covered chairs. I took the other as Alyson dragged over a stool and sat at my feet, her distaff and spindle already busy. "Since I was last here, much has happened. But tell me, cousin, when might I see your good husband?"

I explained Fulk was in the fields. October was when we planted our wheat and rye, and though Theo and Beton were perfectly capable of overseeing this, heavy frosts had made the ground so hard, and the process so time-consuming and difficult, Fulk had insisted on supervising. Theo and Beton were sent to check the flock. After I'd assured Geoffrey that Fulk would be back for nuncheon, I filled him in on what we'd been doing as we drank ale and picked at white bread and slices of goose left over from the Feast of St. Francis.

"Now, your turn, tell me what you've been up to."

Reluctant at first, Geoffrey revealed that not only was he in service to the King, but he was now married.

"Married!" I exclaimed. My face grew hot and it took all my composure not to wriggle in my seat. Alyson ceased to spin and shifted her gaze from Geoffrey to me and back again. I wasn't sure how I felt about him being wed. It wasn't jealousy exactly . . . But what was it?

Was it not our lot to marry, to go forth and multiply?

"Praise be," I said, with as much enthusiasm as I could muster. "What's she like, your wife?"

Geoffrey considered his answer. "Her name is Philippa de Roet. I'm told she's remarkably like her sister, Katherine Swynford, who's considered quite the beauty."

To his credit, he didn't preen. My hand crept to my cap, then to my cheek.

"She hails from Hainault, where the Queen is from," continued Geoffrey. "In fact, she arrived with the Queen's entourage."

I didn't know what to say. I didn't really care about that. I wanted to know if Philippa had nice eyes, teeth, a sparkling wit, breasts, hips. Was she bold, was she kind?

Geoffrey stared into his cup. Our drinking vessels were no longer made from wood, but silver. I wondered if he noticed. This was Geoffrey, of course he did.

"Come on," I said finally. "Out with it. It's clear you've something else to tell and don't know how. What is it you've done? From your letters, I know of the annuity the King has granted you. Congratulations. We heard Blanche, Duchess of Lancaster, died and that you wrote a tribute to her." He nodded. "I hope the Duke appreciated it."

Geoffrey shrugged. "I'm not persuaded John of Gaunt appreciates anything but himself."

Alyson stifled a giggle. I snorted. "And . . . what else?"

Geoffrey raised his head. "I wanted to let you know, I not only married, but I've a son."

My hand flew to my stomach; the pain that flared was so acute, it was as if all the children Fulk and I had been praying for had fallen over, unborn, in my womb.

Unable to hide my envy at this news, I was aware Geoffrey knew what a blow this was, that he who had never really sought to make a child should have one, and with such ease in so short a time. He had not only gained a bride but a family. Nevertheless, he should rejoice—and we should on his behalf. What would Fulk say? By telling me, Geoffrey had not only relieved himself of the duty, but was allowing me to break it to my husband when the time was right.

I pushed aside my grief for something I'd never had and smiled. It was genuine. I *was* happy for him. "God be praised. When did you welcome him? What is he named?"

"Thomas," said Geoffrey, relaxing a little. "His name is Thomas and he was born last year."

"Last year . . ." That hurt more. It had taken Geoffrey a long time to summon the courage to tell me. That wasn't fair. The man loathed to hurt me and I loved him for it. Or would again, once I'd thought upon this.

"I guess that means I've another cousin."

"Me too," added Alyson.

Geoffrey's face brightened then. "I guess it does. Lucky lad to have such a family." You'll recall I mentioned Geoffrey had a way with words.

We were interrupted by the arrival of Fulk and, soon after, Theo and Beton. Insisting Geoffrey stay and showing him to our guest room (the latest addition to our ever-expanding house), I occupied myself discussing with Milda what should be prepared for supper and making sure the ale was drinkable. We'd made a batch a few days earlier.

I filled the jugs and passed them to Sophie, listening to the voices of the men as Fulk showed Geoffrey about. He was so proud of what we'd accomplished. While I knew a great deal of it was due to my bribes and demands, my insistence things be done or bought or re-done a certain way, something Fulk boasted about, I also knew in my heart I'd denied my husband in the worst possible way.

I might have made him richer in coin, but I had failed to give him what his heart truly desired. Not just a child of his own, but a son to whom he could leave all that he'd labored so long to achieve.

I waited until Sophie left the kitchen and then, sitting on a stool, watched through tears as darkness crept in the open door, spread across the floor and, bit by bit, shrouded my barren body.

NINE

Bigod Farm
The Year of Our Lord 1369
In the forty-third year of the reign of Edward III

*I*t is said that those who enjoy the benefits of the Wheel of Fortune must also expect, at some time, to experience its woes.

They're right. In 1369, my time arrived.

Since the previous autumn, heavy rains had fallen, causing part of our land to flood. We lost a number of sheep, but weren't alone in that. Turbet had an entire field wash away, as did many of the farms around Bath. The Abbey lands became water-logged and half their flock caught the murrain and either died or had to be slaughtered. Those who survived were transferred to our higher pastures or Turbet's. What fleeces could be salvaged, when they weren't riddled with mold and infection, were impossible to wash and dry.

It wasn't only wool growers who suffered. For Bath and its surrounding villages, the never-ending rain meant thick, claggy mud. Ploughs became bogged, oxen, donkeys, horses—it mattered not what beasts were harnessed to the yoke, even men; the equipment couldn't move in the moribund earth. We only managed to sow wheat because the fields were on higher ground, but it was an anxious wait to see if anything sprouted. The rye we couldn't plant at all, and we were the lucky ones. That year, more fields were left fallow since the Botch almost twenty years earlier. This time, though, men and women were available to work the land, but it refused to yield what hungry mouths needed to survive. Famine came.

Because of Fulk's thrift, we were able to buy stores—sacks of grain to mill for bread, vegetables and fruit, some of it imported. We made ale, albeit not very pleasant-tasting, and either sold or traded it. We had a surfeit of meat, and took what we could spare to the manor and Abbey so it might be distributed among those less fortunate. Not even our brook could be relied upon for fish, or the River Avon, as it was too dangerous, the waters deep and swirling. Two lads fishing near Bathwick Mill fell in the river and drowned. Boats were washed ashore or sunk, bridges became impassable, which meant stores couldn't be delivered and markets were canceled.

Heavy rain also meant the men couldn't work the fields, so workers were sent home—extra maids as well. The rest were trapped indoors, underfoot. Fulk and I generally rubbed along quite well together, our arguments few and far between, but those months I'll remember not just for the worry over vittles and rain but the bitter words we exchanged. At the height of our quarrels, he would become so angry he would stride out the door, remaining in the barn tinkering until his temper cooled. Being inclined to choler, unlike my husband, who was far more phlegmatic, I would often throw things in my rage.

After one particularly nasty squabble on a dreary afternoon in April, I shattered a beautiful glass sphere my husband had bought me from the markets in Bedford. Alyson lifted her head from the loom by the window and said, "Oh, grow up, will you?"

Milda and Sophie pretended not to have heard, remaining focused on their carding and spinning.

I stared at Alyson, stricken. She usually took my side. With a cry of fury, I stomped off to the solar and would have slammed the door only the wood had swollen and it wouldn't shut.

So I kicked it, flopped into a chair, folded my arms, and brooded. The newly fitted shutters rattled as the rain lashed them. I could hear the braying of the beasts in the barn even above the noise. No doubt, Fulk was complaining to them about his shrewish wife. The brook had again burst its banks and the sound of water carving out new paths, taking with it the lodgings of all manner of creatures, as well as parts of our vegetable garden, just made me furious. Furious and despondent. Until, after an hour of self-indulgent pity, it didn't. After all, I thought, as my temper receded, how fortunate was I to have a roof over my head, food in my belly, when not only the little creatures were denied all these, but so many poorer folk. What about those who'd died?

I became stricken with guilt. Alyson was right. I was behaving like a child, throwing tantrums, complaining because my husband tracked mud into the house. Who did not? As he said, would I prefer it he never entered his own home? My hesitation had been enough to send him back outside, into the cold, the wet, the misery.

He hadn't deserved that. He was too old for such treatment.

Donning my cloak, flashing an apologetic smile in Alyson's direction, who gave me an undeservedly warm one in return, I ran out through the rain to the barn.

I couldn't see him at first; the interior was dark after the pale grayness of the day outside. I blinked the water out of my eyes and threw back my hood. The animals were unnaturally quiet, staring at me with somber faces. Only the chickens fussed and rooted in the hay, which was scattered in a most unseemly manner, not just in their roosts, but below their nesting boxes. Anger, always so close to the surface lately, flared again. Why, the hens might lay their eggs only to have them trampled. We needed eggs now more than ever. Dear God in Heaven, could no one be trusted to do a job correctly?

I scooped up a pile of hay and was about to share it among the nests, when I saw a body lying against the goats' stall.

"Fulk!" I screamed and, dropping the hay, fell to my knees.

He was lying on his back, eyes open, staring at the ceiling. His mouth was moving, but no sound came. I quickly checked him for any injuries, blood, but there was nothing. No broken limbs, no sign of an intruder, though there was a great lump on the back of his head. I shouted, screamed. The animals began to bray and bleat, distressed by my distress.

It was our combined noise that finally brought Alyson and Milda out of the house.

"Pa!" Alyson cried. Her hands fluttered uselessly, tears welled. I needed to take control, remain calm.

Milda began to secure the animals.

"Milda, tell Warren to fetch Doctor Jameson." Warren was one of our live-in workers from the village. A good rider.

Milda glanced at Fulk, her face pale, her mouth drawn. She wiped her eyes. "I'll be right back."

Between us, Alyson and I tried to make Fulk more comfortable. I kept whispering to him, saying how sorry I was as I fought back tears.

In no time at all, Warren was mounted and, with some coins in his purse and instructions ringing in his ears, riding toward town. Beton and Theo came in soon after and we managed to make a hurdle out of old sheets, roll Fulk onto it, and drag him to the house. Great slews of mud marked the floor. The irony wasn't lost on me.

Fulk appeared to have lost the ability to move his limbs and the power of speech. Only his eyes were working, darting here and there, looking so terribly afeared. It broke my heart.

We'd not long managed to get him into bed, cover him with many blankets in an effort to warm him, when the doctor arrived.

Young for a medical man, Doctor Jameson was no-nonsense and so knowledgeable. As Fulk oft noted when he'd cause to use him, he didn't waste time. He also charged reasonably.

I didn't want to leave Fulk's side, but Doctor Jameson insisted I drink some ale and get warm lest I too be struck down with illness. "Then who will look after your husband?"

"He's going to be alright then?" My voice was filled with hope.

"Alright? I'm not so certain. But he will live. For now."

Apoplexy was the doctor's diagnosis. A violent fit that rendered Fulk incapable of using his left arm, his legs, or able to go to the *necessarium*. He could barely swallow and couldn't speak, only grunt.

Each day the doctor came to check his progress. Fulk remained unchanged for over a month. Dependent, frustrated, sick, he refused to give up. His eyes would lock onto mine and somehow let me know that within the fleshy shell, he was still there.

If he was, so too would I be. I owed this man that and so much more.

God and the Fates must have decided our household had endured enough, for not long after Fulk was struck down, the rain ceased and, for a while, the sun shone. The fields were still muddy, but at least after a week or so, a plough only became stuck a few times. The brook and rivers receded to a manageable height, and the wheat we'd sown that hadn't washed away began to grow.

The animals were released from the barn and the sheep were left to roam the pastures, greedily cropping the lush green grass. I ordered the men, who'd returned with the sunshine, to ensure the sheepfolds were erected on high ground to minimize the risk of the flock getting stuck or breaking their legs in the muddy patches that persisted in lower areas. A couple had lambed and the poor little critters had become mired, their mothers' panicked bleating not heard until too late.

The cattle tended to linger where the foldcourses were placed, so moving the sheep kept them all reasonably safe.

Though I forwent weaving to tend my husband, Alyson kept working. For both her and Fulk's sake, I had to ensure the rest of the household performed their duties. There'd been many tears and wailing when Fulk first fell ill. I allowed Theo, Beton, Milda, Sophie, and Warren to express their sorrow then told them, if they had an excess of humors, they were best purged elsewhere. Mayhap, they thought me unfeeling, but they'd shed enough heavenly dew between them to float the ark. What I wanted my husband to hear and see—and Alyson agreed—was nothing but bright chatter, laughter, and, if not smiling faces, at least not faces swollen with weeping.

Fulk was much loved. A gentle master, a kind and generous one, his incapacity was a great blow to all. The girls struggled to hide their sadness, but once they understood it was affecting their master, they made a stellar effort. I was proud and told them so.

Each day, I'd prop the bedroom door open and ensure light and fresh air entered. I had Theo and Beton move Fulk's bed so that he could see and hear what was going on in the hall. Sitting beside him, my distaff and spindle twirling, I would greet the visitors—and there were many: Turbet, of course, but also Lord Hugh and his wife, and Master Merriman, who now walked with the aid of a stick, and folk from both Bath and the village. Some of the monks made a point of stopping by, as did two merchants from Venice who'd been buying our wool for years. I swear, it reminded me of London's Cheap Street some days. I hadn't realized how popular Fulk was. I would have basked in pleasure, only I couldn't, as I was afeared.

Still, the doctor refused to give up, and if Doctor Jameson wouldn't, then neither would I. Fulk's left arm slowly regained some movement. I fed him a few times a day, mostly ale and bread soaked in warm milk, waving away the swarms of flies that had arrived with the cessation of rain, but even so, he rarely finished what I gave him, often choking. Despite my care (and I prayed not because of it) his frame began to shrink, his cheeks hollowed, and his eyes, once so alert, began to lose their rain-washed clarity and sink into his skull.

What did I do? I laughed more loudly, spoke faster and more often, refusing to allow even a whisper of what I feared above all to be spoken. Except by Alyson. She shared my worries and would sometimes exchange a look that spoke of the helplessness we tried not to let overwhelm us.

Turbet Gerrish came most days and it was he who suggested we move Fulk's bed into the hall so it would be easier not only for him to be a part of the daily routines, but for folk to pay their respects. He also said I should resume weaving.

Propped near the hearth, the loom beckoned me. At first, I resisted its siren call. But once I moved it close to the bed, I found comfort in the familiar actions. Though I was the one to teach Alyson to weave, through her I came to appreciate how, when I was behind the loom, my fingers quick and busy, my body became still. The faint

trembling of the stationary warp against the over and under action of
the weft mimicked my form. I was all but unmoving on the outside,
but just like my busy hands, I was restless in my mind and heart as
my thoughts took flight. As the fabric slowly grew, row upon row of
color and sometimes patterns, I was reminded of the seasons and the
changes they wrought. We too were like cloth—even the animals
and the harvests: we grew in increments, woven by nature and God's
guiding hands, shaped by the care or abuse of those around us. We
stayed bright and well-kept, or faded and mended; or, if unfortunate,
torn, and ruined. Just as every bit of cloth held the story of its maker,
and the sheep, the wool, the carders, spinners, fullers, and weavers
who took part in its development, so did we. It was a wondrous thing
to consider and it helped, if not to accept Fulk's condition, to become
reconciled to it.

I stayed by my husband's side as much as possible, weaving cloth
and stories and sharing any gossip.

By early June, Fulk's grunts had turned into words of a sort. I
knew my name: "El." Alyson became "Al," which sounded much the
same. He could also make it known if he wanted Theo or Beton to
carry him to the *necessarium.*

As summer announced itself with hot and humid clarions, I had
to make decisions regarding the wool. What was to go for fulling,
what to remain undyed, where to sell it. I also had to decide whether
or not to buy more sheep to replace those we lost or let the flock re-
produce naturally. Turbet offered advice.

At these times, Fulk listened intently, becoming very still. Sometimes he'd reach for my hand and grip it as tightly as he was able.
"El, El, El," he would say, his eyes darting about. I knew he wished
to relay something important. I tried to guess, running a series of
words past him. It wasn't until I said "sheep?" that he raised his right
arm and let it fall against the bedclothes over and over. When I gave
an insistent Turbet permission to attend the markets in Bedford and
Brighton and purchase more sheep for *our* flock, not relinquish some
of our sheep to him, Fulk's arm ceased to flail.

At last, we'd worked out a way to communicate. Together, we
managed the sheep, wool, and our basic trade.

Not long after Turbet returned with the additional beasts, he drew me away from my husband's side.

We stood near the window, in Fulk's sight but not so close he could hear. "What is it you wish to say, Turbet, that cannot be said before Fulk?"

Turbet glanced across the room at my husband and sighed. "I don't know how to raise this with you, my dear—"

"Just speak what you must." I'd no patience with dissembling. I was no longer twelve. I'd also grown weary of Turbet's constant smile; as Alyson once observed, it promised more than it ever delivered— unless it was for his benefit.

"Very well," said Turbet, flashing me a glimpse of his great yellow teeth. "I feel it's incumbent upon me to tell you what others may not feel they have the right or are uncomfortable expressing."

I folded my arms.

"Ah . . . it's evident that Fulk, may God bless him, isn't going to recover anytime soon, or mayhap, and I say this with utmost respect and love for him, ever."

It was only gratitude for the help Turbet had rendered that prevented me from shoving him in the chest and ordering him from the house.

"In which case, you may need to reconsider not only your flock, but how you manage the lands."

"Is that so?" I used a tone that made Alyson and Milda pause in their work, and even Hereward and Wake raised their heads.

"I mean no offense, lady. On the contrary, what you have done holding together not only the household, but Fulk's affairs, defies belief. For one still so young, your business acumen is not what one would expect. It's unnatural."

Was it my youth or the fact I was a woman that gave him cause to marvel?

I remembered my manners. "Your praise means much." That was true. Gaining his approval was no mean feat. I think that's why what he said next caught me unawares.

"And so, I'm prepared to offer an excellent deal in exchange." Without hesitation, he did.

What?

"Correct me if I'm mistaken," I said when he'd finished. "But you were saying something about me releasing some of our land to you? A percentage of the flock?"

"Ah, aye, I was." He turned his back to Fulk. I made sure I faced my husband and repeated what Turbet said very carefully and loudly.

"You wish to purchase the lease on seventeen acres of pasture— the portion that adjoins your lands—and buy some thirty sheep being a mixture of wethers, hogs, and ewes. Is that correct?"

"And a ram," called out Alyson. Good. She'd been listening too.

Fulk became agitated, his arm thrashing the air. "El, El, El," he repeated.

"It's alright, husband. I understand." I tried to calm him, but it was difficult. Turbet Gerrish was obviously annoyed. He wouldn't go so far as to frown, but his smile was forced through thin lips.

"I think it's probably best I leave."

Fulk's cries grew guttural.

"Think on it, Eleanor," Gerrish said, his fingers curling around my forearm. "This—" he described the house and the lands beyond with a sweep of his arm, "is all your responsibility now. What I'm suggesting isn't much to lose in the scheme of things and would not only provide you with ready coin for doctors and medicines, but make management much easier. Something, as a woman, you need to consider."

Suddenly, I wanted him gone. To think of profiting from his friend's misfortune, my misery.

But of course, once an idea is planted, even one you know is somehow wrong, it takes root in the mind and grows like a weed, spreading to infect every sensible thought and some not so sensible ones. Though I managed to settle Fulk swiftly after Turbet left, his offer remained between us, and I turned it over and over like lumps of clod.

Was Turbet's proposal wrong? It made a great deal of sense in some respects to reduce the size of our holdings. We'd ample. And, with the coin we'd earn, I could not only pay for Fulk's treatment, but hire extra workers. And we could think about buying wool from other suppliers and concentrating on weaving. I could even seek advice on applying to the guild for membership. I knew it was unlikely they'd grant it to me, a woman, but if someone like Lord Hugh vouched . . . Or Master Geoffrey . . . Aye, I would go and see Father Elias and ask him to write a letter to his lordship on my behalf. Dear Lord, I owed Geoffrey a letter as well. I hadn't even told him about Fulk . . .

These thoughts occupied me over the next week or so. Every day, Turbet returned and repeated his offer. Oh, he used different words each time, and waited until we'd moved out of Fulk's earshot to deliver them, but he was beginning to wear me down.

As midsummer approached and preparations began for feasting, I had to organize crews of men to shear the sheep. This proved harder than usual as those we regularly hired had agreed to work elsewhere—where a man was in charge. That cut deep, I admit, and made my anger, which had lain dormant since Fulk's apoplexy, rise once more.

I sat by Fulk's bed a week before midsummer and bewailed our situation, then outlined as reasonably as I could why accepting Turbet's offer might be a good thing. I didn't mention the men being unable to shear. Anyway, Theo and Beton were more than capable of doing that and, bless, said they'd train Warren. Between them, they'd manage; it would just mean working harder.

"What do you think?" I asked Fulk. "Should we sell, husband?"

Fulk held my hand and stared at me with such earnestness, then said, as clear as the bell in the Noke Manor chapel, "Nay."

I stared, then leaped to my feet, shouting in joy.

"You spoke!"

"Nay. Nay. Nay," he repeated, smiling a lopsided grin.

Alyson threw aside the shuttle and darted to the bed.

"Pa!" she cried. Milda and Sophie slowly approached, hope writ on their faces.

We threw our arms around each other and danced about the bed, Fulk watching us, shouting out, "Nay, nay, nay!" as if he were a babe practicing his first word or mimicking a horse. Every time we passed the bed, we deposited a kiss on his sunken cheeks.

That night, I thanked the Lord, and the following day, delivered the verdict to Turbet, telling him that far from declining, as the doctor predicted, my husband was slowly recovering. Therefore, I rejected his most gracious offer.

A strained smile split Turbet's face. "God be praised," he said. "Though I'm disappointed you won't be selling, how can I not rejoice?"

If I doubted his sincerity, then the present he delivered a few days later in honor of Fulk's recovery, a recovery evidenced by the fact he also managed to say my name in full, made those doubts vanish. Turbet only stayed long enough to hand his gift to Sophie before he departed.

"Forgive me, Eleanor," he called from the doorway. "I've business in town."

Tomorrow, I'd be conducting the same business—with alien wool merchants keen to buy our fleece.

Turbet's gift was extraordinary and very thoughtful. It was a beautiful woven coverlet lined with rabbit fur to keep Fulk warm throughout winter. Since it was a colder-than-usual June day, I asked Sophie to spread it over Fulk. His eyes widened and his grin appeared. His good arm rubbed the soft fur, and he tried to press his cheek against where Sophie had tucked it around his neck. She lifted it to her face.

"This be lovely quality, madam. How generous of Master Gerrish."

"It is," I agreed, watching Turbet and his squire ride away. Had I misjudged him?

Master Turbet was in my thoughts as I accompanied Theo and Beton into the fields that afternoon, keen to learn what I could about shearing.

We returned when the sun was low on the horizon and, despite a few clouds, the sky was a wash of apricot and rose, throwing the silhouettes of the woods into stark relief. The evening was warm with the promise of summer. The soft bleating of shorn sheep, the smell of cattle and other animals as well as woodsmoke tinged the air. I recall breathing deeply and feeling not just weary, but a sense of accomplishment, of being at peace.

Remember what I said about the Fates and Fortune's bloody wheel? Aye, well, they were going to have the last laugh, weren't they, pack of wart-covered whores.

We walked into the house to be greeted by silence and a foul odor. The loom was still, neither Alyson nor Milda were to be seen. The fire had almost banked and Fulk was lying in shadows, no candles were lit. There was the sound of faint coughing, followed by whispering.

"Alyson?" I started to feel uneasy. I crossed to Fulk, snatching a candle and flint on the way. "Theo, stoke the fire, will you? Beton, find out where your sister is—and Milda and Sophie." I was cross poor Fulk had been left untended.

I lit the candle and, calling Fulk's name softly, held it above the bed.

"Dear God."

When I'd left that morning, Fulk had been comfortable, happy—with his gift and the warmth it gave. He appeared better than I'd seen him in a long, long time. What greeted me was a man bathed in sweat, his dry mouth gaping, his hands curled into claws. I threw back the blanket, his nightshirt lifting as I did so. His body was exposed and, to my horror, I saw black swellings bulging from his groin.

I tore his shift from his neck and shoulder. The buboes were forming in his armpits as well.

I began to back away, shaking my head. There was a cry from further in the house. Beton came running. "Eleanor, Eleanor—" he said. "Alyson, she . . . she's terribly ill . . ."

I glanced toward Fulk. "Your father, too," I whispered.

"What? What?" said Theo, panic making his eyes large as he looked from me to the figure on the bed.

"It's the Botch," I said.

"God help us," said Theo. The brothers crossed themselves.

I don't know what came over me. Call it strength—call it madness. First ordering the men to stay with their father, I swept through the other rooms and found Sophie moaning on her pallet, covered in black and purple swellings. Alyson was in a high fever but, as far as I could tell, bore no tokens. Milda was untouched, bravely bathing Alyson's clammy face, her own a picture of determination. When we found Warren, who'd remained in the fields awhile to stack the shorn fleeces, he was hiding in the barn. He also showed no sign of sickness.

Maintaining a distance, I ordered Warren to take a donkey, go to Father Elias and then Father Roman. I urged him to warn the village and then stay away. He hadn't come inside the house, hadn't been near Fulk, Sophie, Milda, or Alyson.

After Warren left, Theo, Beton, and I stood in the barn. Fear was a living breathing thing keeping us apart. I could feel its sharp teeth nibbling at my resolve to be strong.

All the stories Papa and the older folk from Noke Manor had spun about the Botch, the terrible deaths and their survival, stories I'd ghoulishly absorbed, were now lessons that might yet, God be praised, save us. I ordered water boiled, certain herbs to be crushed and steeped in bowls and mazers, the animals locked away, and the fire kept burning.

I returned to Fulk's side. Papa always said the pestilence was God's punishment for man's sin.

In other words, God wasn't going to help us, no matter what we asked of Him.

So I made sure we did everything we could to help ourselves.

TEN

Bigod Farm
The Year of Our Lord 1369
In the forty-third year of the reign of Edward III

Nothing helped. More buboes sprouted on Fulk and Sophie, swelling before our eyes, oozing pus and blood, filling the house with a rancid stench. When Theo sickened, I began to fear for all our lives. I banned Beton and Milda from touching Fulk or Sophie, or venturing close lest they inhale the same air. Milda, God bless her, ignored my orders, insisting on helping. Beton fetched water, threw wood on the fire, burning the herbs I'd gathered. He ensured the animals were fed, and sat in a corner staring into space when his chores were done.

When Alyson's fever worsened, I began to wonder, was the sickness in our clothing? In the wool? Or was it the animals who carried it? Hadn't it started after Turbet's blanket arrived? I wondered if, since it had come from London, it held the disease in its fur, like a secret courier biding its time to release the deadliest of messages. Did it even matter? With great care, I removed the cover from Fulk's body and threw it in the yard.

When Sophie died less than two days later, then Theo followed a few hours after, Beton was bereft. Alyson, though lost in the throes of febrile visions, understood and her cries of physical pain became ones of grief. I willed Fulk to wake, to get better, knowing if he did— *when* he did—it would be to news that would tear him asunder.

In the end, I never had to deliver the tragic blow. On the third day after he sickened, Fulk Bigod, a man with the mightiest of hearts, ceased to be.

Despite my care, all our care, the pestilence claimed my husband's gentle soul. I didn't weep. I consoled myself by believing it was a relief to see his pain end. The delirium that had him trying to call for his other wives, his lost children, me, was over. I was afraid if I let my sorrow show it would consume me.

We wrapped Fulk in his bedding, Milda, Beton, and I carried him outside and buried him alongside Sophie and Theo—down by the brook, beneath the tree where his sister was interred. The ground was soft on the sward, so digging wasn't a hard task. Unshriven, knowing neither Father Roman nor Father Elias could heed a summons even if we'd called them, we nevertheless prayed for Fulk's eternal soul, for the souls of all our dead, even though I was furious with God for taking them—not just from this life, but from me.

Pater Nosters and Aves were said, as I reassured Milda and Beton these would do in the absence of a priest. Afterward we constructed basic wooden crosses—just sticks tied with rope—and inserted them into the mud. I held my hand over my bare stomach and asked Fulk to forgive me for not giving him his heart's desire. Not for want of trying, you randy old goat. Over the years, our awkward early encounters, where he was careful not to hurt me and I was merely determined to do my duty, had transformed into something loving, tender and, dare I say, passionate. Venus had more than smiled upon our union.

Oh, how I would miss him.

It was then the hot tears flowed.

Before Beton or Milda could see, I turned back to the house, asking over my shoulder that they collect any eggs as we needed to eat, keep up our strength. I doubted I could hold down a mouthful.

Though the sun was gone and only a band of gold limned the horizon, the hills about dark and foreboding, I could see the sheep, glowing pearls stark against the gloaming. I stopped and stared. Much to my astonishment, not only had the foldcourses been moved, a man was herding the sheep into one and the entire flock had been shorn. There was only one person who could have organized that: Turbet. He must be well, then. A flash of guilt pierced my chest that I hadn't given the man a thought. It was followed by a rush of gratitude and relief, a bright, warm rush that made my heart swell. Turbet Gerrish. Dear God.

I crossed the pasture and, ensuring I kept a distance, shouted across to the shepherd. Wary, he remained where he was, and confirmed this was Turbet's doing. He'd also arranged for shearers and for the wool to be washed, dried, and packed.

I raised my face to the heavens, astonished to see God's lights twinkling in the firmament as if they were living creatures, chattering away about the disaster playing out below. Beautiful, they gave me something I hadn't felt for days, if not weeks: hope.

"Mayhap, Lord, you haven't deserted me." I took a few more steps then paused, peering into the silver-spangled night. "Shall we put it to the test?"

Once in bed, I prayed to God like never before. I swore that if He allowed Alyson to live, I would journey to a shrine, become a pilgrim, and give thanks to Him, His saints and all their glorious works.

Once the sickness had passed, I promised I would also give thanks to Turbet Gerrish. A man I hoped one day to be able to repay.

———— ◆ ————

It was a long time before we felt secure enough to venture beyond our land, and more weeks still before we were allowed to return to the village and town. While there'd been a huge number of deaths in London and the north, mostly children, other areas were more fortunate. Bath-atte-Mere only lost one family, and Thom Crease, the carter who'd been moving back and forth between the major ports and London.

Father Roman had been besieged by offerings and gifts—mainly food and ale. No wonder he looked plumper. I'd a suspicion his surplice was not only new, but had been decorated with jewels. According to Lord Hugh, the priest devoted all his sermons to reminding people about the might of God's judgment, ensuring that donations and offerings continued. Folk may not have understood Latin, but they did understand God's wrath.

Bath had more casualties. Within the walls, forty people died, the freshly turned earth of their graves a stark reminder of what we'd survived. Folk remained cautious, the older ones recalling what it had been like when the Great Mortality swept the land, asking God for clemency and offering prayers, coin, and gifts to the Abbey and the other chapels within and without the city walls. Funny how something like the Botch made those more oft inclined to ignore the harsher directives of the Lord disinclined to gamble with His mercy. I should know, I was one. God even answered my pleas: Alyson's recovery was slow, but her health, praise be, was restored.

Along with Beton, Alyson, Milda, and Warren (who'd returned), I made a great show of attending mass each Sunday—preferring to listen to Father Elias at St. Michael's Without the Walls than to pompous Father Roman in the village.

Once it was evident no one else was going to succumb to the pestilence, those who'd fled the town returned and trade resumed.

Our supplies had all but disappeared and though we picked fruit and vegetables, and harvested what we could of our grain, we'd been forced to leave a great deal to rot in the fields. What we'd managed to collect would mostly suffice as fodder for the animals. I just hoped once we sold the cloth I'd woven—I'd been busy and so had Alyson once her health was mended—we'd be able to purchase necessary stores and maybe even replenish the flock.

We were quiet in those early days. Looking inward, not just to each other, but to our thoughts. I don't know what I would have done without Milda. Throughout those long weeks, especially while Alyson was ill, I came to really know her. The way she'd wrap her slender fingers firmly around my shoulder, giving it a squeeze, when she'd pass by; her soft humming when the moans of the ill threatened to engulf me. The evening hours when she sat beside me, spinning, offering naught but her quiet companionship, a posset to soothe my fractured soul and, later, when Alyson joined us, hers too. I found myself studying her by the dying light of the candles. When had her golden hair ceded to so much gray? When had her stoutness transformed into a wiriness that reflected her inner strength? Were they recent things, attributable to the Botch? Or had I not noticed, just as I hadn't noticed the mole on her neck, the way one side of her mouth lifted when she was amused, or how she rapidly blinked when she disapproved of something? The Botch and our weeks of solitude brought me an appreciation of my maid who I would never again take for granted.

I knew Geoffrey had survived, a letter arriving not long after we were able to venture out again. Father Elias delivered it and read it to me. This missive prompted me to do something I hadn't done before: write to Geoffrey—well, not myself, but to have Father Elias scribe on my behalf. He'd volunteered many times, but I didn't like having to rely on someone to shape my words. How did I know they were writing what I said?

Now, I didn't care.

As soon as it was safe to do so, I made a special trip to St. Michael's Without the Walls and, sitting beside the Father, began to dictate. I'd thought long and hard about what to say. Father Elias sat at his desk, a piece of parchment stretched before him, an inkhorn and sharpened quill at the ready, together with some sand for blotting. I looked upon these tools with wonder. They allowed us not only to communicate with each other but, through them, with God—after all, what was the Bible but God's holy words? Never before had mine been recorded. It was hard to sit still as my insides lurched with excitement.

"How would you like to begin?" asked Father Elias, quill poised just so, a drop of ink swelling at the tip.

"Are there rules?" I asked.

"Well, it would be usual to commence it with 'Right Worshipful Mastership,' or something like that."

I pulled a face. "Really? So many honorifics? Mastership? Geoffrey's not the King. He's just a poet. He's my friend."

"And in showing him such respect you acknowledge that and more."

"Oh, very well, then." I waved my hand. "But maybe just Right Worshipful. Or sir. He's not my master, after all."

Father Elias tried not to smile. The scritch-scratch of the quill was a pleasant distraction. I was fascinated by the form my words took on the page. Whenever I paused, craning my neck to watch the letters he made, Father Elias urged me to continue.

After a while, he stopped. "You can't say that, Eleanor," he said.

"What? Goddamn?"

"Aye. You cannot take the Lord's name in vain."

"I can if I choose. And I'm goddamn madder with Him than I am with a baker who cheats the measures."

Father Elias's cheeks reddened and he coughed into his fist. "I understand, Eleanor, but I think another word might be better."

"Whose letter is this? If you choose my words, then it's hardly mine, is it?" I stabbed a finger at the page. "I'm paying you to write what I say. Right?"

Father Elias gave a deep sigh. "Right," he said. "May the Lord forgive me."

"If He doesn't," I added, "I will."

He chuckled. "That's a relief."

After that, I had him read back each completed part and, true to his word, he wrote everything I said, even when it caused him vexation.

The letter marked an alteration in my relations with the Father. From that day forward, I knew I could not only trust him but mayhap even call him friend. In fact, seeing Father Elias was one of the few bright spots in what were dark, sad times. Keeping busy also helped.

Attempts to ease my sorrow through work were often interrupted by Turbet. Every other morning, he'd arrive at the house. Early, he would shout through the door, then enter. Never empty-handed, he brought bread from his ovens, cheese, ale, jugs of wine. Then he'd ask if we needed anything, as if we weren't able to bake, churn, or brew (which we could, we just were too tired managing everything else and stores were scarce) before relaying any news.

Quarantine was only just over when Turbet saw to it our wool was packed and sold, going so far as to take a quantity to the markets in Burford himself. Upon his return, he deposited a purse of coins on the window ledge. It was this that enabled us to hire the help we needed to get back on our feet again. I employed two extra men and a young girl to help Milda. Turbet also brought me a contract to supply wool to the Datini Company in Prato, a city near Florence. Stunned he could be so generous as to share such a lucrative contact, let alone encourage these businessmen to look to us to part-supply their wool, I didn't know how to repay him.

As a consequence, though we'd lost animals, trade, and, most of all, people, we were not as poorly off as we might have been. Our losses were of the heart, the spiritual kind. These were much harder to recover from, and nothing that has happened since has persuaded me otherwise.

I half-expected to see Geoffrey before summer ended, especially when a lawyer from Bath sent a summons for me to appear in his offices. I had to ask Father Elias, who I'd asked to read it, what business a lawyer wanted. It was to make me cognizant (I asked the Father what that word meant) of my late husband's will.

"Would you like me to accompany you?" he asked.

"Aye, I would."

If Father Elias hadn't been with me I might have fallen off my stool when the lawyer, Sir Ormat le Lene (who, despite his name, was fatter than a butcher's dog), informed me that, even after Fulk's lands and all his possessions were divided three ways (it would have been four, but Theo's death reduced it to three) and taxes paid, I was a woman of means. I wasn't rich like Lord Hugh's wife, or Mistress Tiffany, whose husband was a goldsmith in Bath, but I'd more to my name than I'd ever believed possible for a—what was it Father Roman used to call me? Oh aye, "a peasant brogger's slutty get."

Mayhap, that was why, after I floated out of Master le Lene's office, leaving Father Elias a generous donation toward the church, and rode the cart back to the farm, listening to Milda, who chatted the entire way but about what, I couldn't have said, the last thing on my mind was Turbet Gerrish.

Celebrating our good fortune and thanking dear Fulk and the good Lord that we would be alright, Alyson, Beton, Milda, and I began to make plans.

These were all thrown awry when Turbet arrived unannounced. It was his second visit for the day. He had covered himself liberally in scent. I could detect sandalwood, musk, rosewater, and few other perfumes besides—ones that really shouldn't be mixed if you wish your companions to breathe.

I welcomed him and poured a goblet of wine from one of the jugs he'd brought. I hadn't considered why he might be here again, and so was unprepared when, sitting opposite, his eyes glinting in the candlelight, he asked me to marry him.

Turbet Gerrish, wealthy landowner, my husband's neighbor and business colleague, asked me, Eleanor Bigod, to be his wife before God and man. It was by anyone's measure, hasty—Fulk had only been in the ground six weeks or so—but this was motivated by material concerns, not amorous ones.

Alyson dropped the shuttle. Milda paused in her carding. Beton, who was playing a game of One and Thirty with two of our laborers, rose slowly, his eyes on me then Turbet.

I prudently drank the wine.

"Well, what say you, Eleanor? Will you make me a happy man?"

I stared into Turbet's eyes, or tried to. As usual, they were darting about, trying to fix on something behind me. I wasn't such a fool I didn't know marriage to me, just like his generous presents of food, his unsolicited help, was a way of getting what he wanted—the land and sheep, only in much greater quantity. But he wouldn't be the only one to profit from such an arrangement. As his wife, I'd be entitled to at least a third, if not more, of all our conjoined assets should anything happen to him. He wasn't a handsome man, but he wasn't an ugly one either. He was old and lined, but I was accustomed to a weathered face and knew it wasn't necessarily a sign of dotage or ill-health. When asking for my hand, he hadn't affected a smile, but been serious. He smelled good, had nice manners, and, for all his flaws, had been kind—even with intent.

All I could think about was God and His bloody lousy timing. For with Fulk's estate, He'd just given me the gift of liberty. Hours later, He throws Turbet in my path, and potentially takes it away. Upon marriage, my property would become my husband's.

Though, if I wed, there was a chance I could have what I'd always wanted—not just respectability and stability, but a child. I could be a mother.

Why do you do this to me, O Heavenly Father?

It was then I recalled the promise I made weeks ago. I'd sworn that if God allowed Alyson to live, I'd make a pilgrimage.

Sweet Jesu. The last thing I wanted to do was traipse about with a bunch of religious zealots determined to prove their godliness.

But it would give me time to consider Turbet's proposal.

Also, if word got out about the will and that Turbet, a man with decent holdings, had asked for my hand, well, who knows what other offers might come my way.

I lowered my eyes lest Turbet see the schemes forming behind them—though he'd have to look at me first. I pressed my hands together in an attitude of prayer and raised my eyes to the heavens.

After a while, Turbet cleared his throat. By now, Alyson had resumed working the loom, and Milda, one corner of her mouth twitching, started spinning. The men were focused on their card game again.

"Well?" he pressed, less confident. His squire coughed into his fist.

"I'm overwhelmed," I said. "While it would be an honor to be

Mistress Gerrish—" His face lit up, even his eyes ceased to rove. "There are those whose consideration must be sought before I give you my answer."

Anger flashed, though he quickly schooled it. "You mean, your family."

"Oh, aye, aye," I said quickly. "And the Holy Family, too."

His eyebrows rose.

"You see," I explained quickly. "I've long planned, well, since Fulk died, to go on a pilgrimage and thank God for our salvation from the Botch."

"And where do you intend to go?" His words were thin and sharp. "For how long?"

I racked my brains. Where did one go on pilgrimages? I knew the kings of old went to Jerusalem, but I'd no desire to venture all that way—the place was full of sand and bloody Saracens. Then there was that Compost place in Spain. What about somewhere closer? Ely? Was that far? What about Lincoln? Mayhap, that wasn't far enough. Then it occurred to me.

"Canterbury," I said. "I'm going to Canterbury."

Rising from the bench, Turbet drained his goblet and, pulling out a kerchief, dabbed his mouth. "Know this, Eleanor. If I do not have an answer by the end of the year, then I'm afraid my offer will be withdrawn."

Marriage was a business proposition, but most people weren't so obvious about it. My vanity took a blow. I thought Turbet might have desired *me*, even a little bit. It was Fulk's lands he wanted after all.

Not Fulk's lands. *Mine.* Mine and Alyson's and Beton's.

"You'll have my answer as soon as I've one to give you," I said, and walked him to the door.

He pressed a kiss to my hand, turning it over so it was my palm that received it. I resisted the urge to wipe it on my kirtle.

"I hope God gives you the guidance you seek and the response I desire. And don't forget, if you don't want to marry me, the offer for your lands and flock still stands."

I stared at him. "How can I resist."

Alyson coughed. Milda juggled the spindle.

I waited until Turbet and his squire were mounted before closing the door and joining the others.

What Turbet didn't know was, it wasn't God I needed to seek advice from. Since when had He been helpful? The person I wanted to ask was someone I'd written to only a few weeks earlier—the man who organized my first very happy marriage.

I would write to The Poet. To my friend and confidant, Geoffrey Chaucer. If he said to marry Turbet Gerrish, then by God, Eleanor Bigod would.

PILGRIMAGE TO CANTERBURY

—•—

A letter to
Master Geoffrey Chaucer
from
Mistress Eleanor Bigod, widow

*R*ight worshipful sir, I commend myself to you.

May it please you to know that once more I've sought the services of your dear friend and mine, Father Elias, in order to tell you of the latest events to have overtaken me. I'm most perplexed that you've not replied to my earlier letter seeking your urgent advice regarding a marriage proposal from Master Turbet Gerrish. I can only assume this missive went astray.

As noted previously, after the death of my husband, Fulk Bigod (I don't know why Father Elias insisted on writing his name in full, as if he were a stranger to you instead of a relation, for Godsakes—and aye, in case you're wondering, I made him write that too), I fulfilled my promise to my Lord Jesus Christ if He would spare the life of my Godsib, Alyson. That is, to undertake a pilgrimage.

My chosen destination was Canterbury and I was accompanied by Alyson and Milda. Truth is, I didn't really care where I went, I just knew I didn't want to leave England nor go very far. Turned out, the road to Canterbury is much traveled and easy to negotiate. Nevertheless, I was at first reluctant to set out. Not only was I anxious to know your thoughts on Turbet's offer, but I was worried about leaving the farm in the hands of Beton, who, though older, does not possess a wise head, especially when it comes to business. I also feared something may happen to him in my absence, even while I was on a holy mission, God being inclined to overlook me and those I love.

Father Elias and Master Gerrish promised to keep an eye on Beton and the farm. After Master Gerrish proved himself so helpful while sickness raged, I felt somewhat reassured, even as I understood he had other motives. He was looking to shore up potential assets, after all.

There were other reasons for me to go, so I did not tarry awaiting your reply. Fulk's death cut deep, Geoffrey. I found myself prone to bouts of sudden weeping. The death of a goat, a sheep mauled by wild dogs, Fulk's favorite goblet unused on the sideboard—these things could plunge me into deep sadness from which it was difficult to rise. Alyson coped slightly better. Milda, for whom grief is a familiar companion, felt leaving the farm awhile would remind us both how fortunate we still are, despite our grievous losses, and help us look to the future.

Master Gerrish believes that future lies with him.

Since I wrote to you, I've been besieged with offers, which I know will make you smile when you consider how hastily my first marriage was arranged. The same men who once decried me as whore and harlot now seek to make me wife (Father Roman, for obvious reasons, being an exception). I'm no longer so foolish as to think I'm the attraction rather than the lands and sheep, the house and all its comforts, to which I am one-third entitled. Alyson kindly suggests it's also my youth (I am but seventeen) and, possibly, my wide hips. For certes, no one except Fulk has ever mentioned my pretty face.

Truth is, Master Gerrish's offer is not unappealing, even though he too is long in the tooth (the lines and crevices on his face would match my Fulk's), inclined to snore (he's fallen asleep at our table on occasion), and has a rather melancholic temperament (for all he pretends otherwise). So, in the absence of a response from you, I used the trip to Canterbury to consider him and the other offers I have received. Once I reached the shrine of Thomas à Becket, I addressed my conundrum to God and to the good saint himself, but, as I fully expected, they both ignored my pleas as if I were the greatest of sinners, not a woman who had just dedicated weeks of her life to riding miles, prayer, ~~feasting~~, fasting, and making new friends among my fellow pilgrims. (I especially enjoyed the company of a monk named Oswald. It was a fine way to experience God's love here on earth. I wish you could see Father Elias's blushes.) Not to mention my bleeding feet, sore ass, and peeling nose. Anyhow, I'm now forced to ask for your wise counsel (again), my cousin and friend. Since you saw fit to organize my first marriage, I'm asking you a second time: should I wed Master Gerrish? Does not the Lord say to love thy neighbor?

Written on the Feast of St. Katherine, the Virgin and Martyr.

Yours, Eleanor.

Postscriptum: I thought Canterbury a crush and the ampullae filled with the saint's blood overpriced. I bought one each for me, Milda, and Alyson. I had to

queue to purchase them and couldn't help but wonder how one person, even a saint, could have so much
blood in them. I also bought a badge to pin upon the
gray cloak I purchased. And a staff to aid walking.
Brother Oswald said one is not a real pilgrim unless one
is in possession of a staff. Ever tried to hold one while
on a donkey? Almost impossible. The badges prove I've
visited the shrine (and you'll be pleased I also offered
prayers for Queen Philippa, may God assoil her). What's
the point of going if one cannot prove one has been?
At least it saves me prating endlessly about it as some
are wont to do; I just flash my badge and the story is
told. As for all the gold and silver plate surrounding
Becket's tomb, and the great garish ruby the French
king presented—why, it was almost the size of a goose
egg! It was tasteless, and that from a woman who years
ago almost lay with a priest. I'd sooner give my coin to
the beggars milling outside the cathedral. Which I did.

But, apart from Oswald—oh, and the manciple, a
Frenchman, oo la la!—it was an unremarkable journey
to a dirty, crowded, expensive town, keen on gulling
the unwary and charging for the privilege.

Needless to say, I plan to return soon. Or at least, to
make another pilgrimage, it was such an adventure. I'm
thinking mayhap Jerusalem.

The Tale of Husband the Second, Turbet Gerrish

1370 to 1377
It is an uncomely couple, by Christ, so me thinks
To give a young wench to an old feeble
Or wed any widow for the wealth of her goods,
That never shall a bairn bear but if it be in [her] arms.

—William Langland, *The Vision and Creed of Piers Plowman*, c.1370–1390

ELEVEN

Laverna Lodge
The Year of Our Lord 1370
In the forty-third year of the reign of Edward III

I've heard it said that a January bride will know only cold because the frost will get in her veins and cool her husband's ardor. If my marriage to Turbet Gerrish was anything to go by, this was no old wives' tale.

We were married by Father Elias on the threshold of St. Michael's Without the Walls on the Feast of St. Agnes the Virgin. Unlike my first wedding, there were invited guests, as well as many onlookers, who were there to admire Master Gerrish's new bride, the Widow Bigod, as I was called. Though I suspect most of the admiration was reserved for my new husband, who looked magnificent in a deep blue paltock with silver dragons embroidered around the collar, matching bonnet, cloak, elegant crimson hose, and fine black boots. Until I saw him I thought I looked resplendent. Alyson had organized for some of our wool to be dyed a deep shade of cramoisie, and though I knew the color would likely run when and if I ever washed it, despite the alum-water used to fix it, it occurred to me that once I became

Mistress Gerrish, I would never have to do laundry again. It was that thought and not, as Alyson later suggested, the snowflakes swirling around, that froze a big grin on my face as I rode atop our old palfrey, Pippa.

There I was, heading toward a house of God, committing the sin of pride in my brightly colored kirtle. My hair, apart from some curls escaping around my forehead and cheeks, was hidden by a fine veil into which we'd sewn some beads bought from a tinker (we couldn't afford jewels—not then). My surcoat, a gift from Turbet, was a deep golden hue, and lined with marten. Marten! I also wore a woollen cloak, but rather than fold it around me, in a fit of vanity, I threw it over my shoulders so all might see my new outfit. Was I cold? Satan's tits, I was colder than a duck's ass in December, but I basked in the warmth of folks' approval. I, Eleanor, who had first married in a hurried and shameful fashion. What a difference being a respectable widow made. Heads turned, women who'd scarce paid me attention pushed others out of the way and stood on tiptoes, craning their necks so they might catch a glimpse. I tilted my chin, smiled harder, and waved like I was royalty.

When the horse halted, Beton helped me dismount. Alyson, riding behind on one of our donkeys, brought me my old pattens so I wouldn't ruin my new slippers or muddy my garments.

Whispers rose to a crescendo. People pressed forward, but not so close they prevented me approaching Father Elias, who waited patiently by the church door. For the first time in weeks, the sun tore a hole in the canopy of gray clouds, clouds that, if we weren't fast, promised to mend the heavenly puncture and spit all over proceedings. The snow had been swept away so there was a half-decent path. I gripped Beton's arm on one side and Alyson's on the other. I'd insisted we were in this together, every step of the way (if I didn't slip over on my ass).

Vows were exchanged, rings too, and before God I married a second time. A great cheer erupted, then the bells rang to alert all and sundry that a troth had been plighted.

I was eighteen; my husband was two score years older. A spring chick compared to my last one.

Turbet paid Father Elias and we retired to The Corbie's Feet, an inn just inside the walls. Many joined us—the opportunity to wine and dine at someone else's expense too tempting to resist. Who could blame them, especially after the famine and the Botch last year? On the table were platters of mortews, froys, meat jellies, even a peacock and huge sturgeon drowning in a pale aspic. There were fruit sauces aplenty, green sauces, brown ones, and sweetmeats. And there was bread. When I wasn't drinking and smiling, I was eating.

I can't tell you how many times I was kissed and congratulated, tickled, pinched, had indecent suggestions put to me, nor how many ales I downed. Thrown from one pair of arms to another when the dancing started, it was all very jolly. When I stumbled back to my new husband, he was very solicitous, ordering more ale be fetched. Some of the women cast glances in my direction. Envy, no doubt. I wasn't above feeling a warm tingle at the notion.

Finally, as the church bells rang the hour, we left the celebrations amid blessings and more leers and drunken suggestions, mounting the horses and donkeys and riding to our new home. Snow fell steadily and evening was closing in. Assured it wasn't far, I hoped it wasn't, for now that the heat of the inn and the dancing was gone, I was chilled to the bone. Alyson's teeth chattered as she rode beside me.

When Turbet ordered our party to halt and found blankets for me and Alyson, I marveled at my good fortune. What a considerate husband. I caught Alyson's eye and raised a brow. Ever skeptical, continually expressing doubts as to the wisdom of the union, going out of her way to point out Turbet's faults and repeating rumors, she had to acknowledge this was an act of kindness. When I said as much, she leaned over and whispered, "He's just making sure the goods he's bought aren't frozen on arrival."

I burst out laughing.

Turbet's grooms rode ahead with lamps to ensure we didn't ride off the path. Turbet had seen to it our belongings were collected from Bigod Farm and delivered to his house, the prettily named Laverna Lodge. As yet, I'd not seen it. Turbet had insisted that I not cross the threshold until we were wed. I found his insistence odd, but also quite quaint.

What I didn't expect as we rode the mile or so from Bath's walls and turned off the main road, was the huge house rising above the trees. Why, there was a small tower and at least three chimneys. As we drew closer, the whole of Laverna Lodge was revealed. There were two stories and an outer courtyard crowded with servants—most shoveling and sweeping. They ceased work as we entered, laying down their implements and coming forward. Propped against the walls were empty carts, stacks of barrels, bundles of hay, buckets, chopped wood, a plough, and so much more. Don't think for a moment it was disorderly. It wasn't. Everything was neatly arranged, protected by the overhanging roof, so covered only by a light dusting of flakes.

Night had fallen. Light from behind the mullioned windows (windows!) cast little wells of brightness, making the banks of snow glisten invitingly. Two women ran out of the house with furs that had been warmed by a fire and threw them over my shoulders and Alyson's. Some men led the horses and donkeys off into a large barn to my right. There was a faint whiff of animal ordure and the sounds of low snuffles, bleats, and stamping hoofs. The barn was almost as big as Bigod House—after the extensions. I was agog. While I knew Turbet was a man of some means, I'd never considered his home before.

At the front door, I paused beneath the portico while Turbet issued orders. People had sprung into action, running here and there, crunching through the snow, murmuring, "Welcome, mistress," "May God bless you, mistress," "Congratulations, master, and may God bless you." A young man carrying a tray filled with steaming cups of mulled wine appeared at my elbow.

It was all too much. Alyson, Beton, and Milda were staring about with wide eyes. "Holy Jesus in a basket," said Beton, almost dropping the goblet placed in his stiff hand.

It wasn't until Hereward and Wake came bounding out of another doorway, a lad panting after them, that I began to relax. Something familiar and loved. The dogs threw themselves against us, making us spill our drinks and dissolve into laughter as we petted and fussed. Now, this was a welcome I was accustomed to receiving.

It was only later I recalled the boy who'd been tasked with managing the dogs running toward Turbet and throwing himself on the ground, uncaring of the cold and the snow.

"Forgive me, master. Forgive me, master," he said over and over.

The mayhem stopped, or maybe it was my imagination, as everyone focussed on the boy and Turbet.

Turbet bent down and pulled the lad to his feet, brushing his tunic and coat. "What are you worried about, boy? They are big hounds and you but a wisp. You'll not be looking after them again, will he, Jermyn?" The last comment was directed to a man of middling years supervising the activity, who I learned was Turbet's bailiff.

"Nay, my lord," said Jermyn, gesturing for the boy to get back inside.

Everyone returned to their tasks, the hounds settling beside me and Alyson. But there was an undercurrent. The joy manifested with our arrival was most definitely dimmed.

We were taken through the entrance into a small room that held a wooden table, some candles, and a mighty arras depicting an ancient battle. We shuffled down a short passage. To our right was another room, and beyond that, through a doorway, I caught a glimpse of a huge hall. We then passed through a room in which my loom and Alyson's had been placed, before we ascended some stairs and moved into a warmer one and were invited to sit. Extra drinks and more food were swiftly delivered. Turbet left us briefly to have a word with his housekeeper, Mistress Emmaline.

I removed my gloves, my cloak having already been taken by one of the maids. Unlike the other rooms, which were quite barren and cold, this one was small and cozy. Turbet had declared it the solar. It was certainly an improvement on my last one. A proper hearth held a blazing fire that gave out a great deal of warmth and light. Sconces with burning candles sat at intervals along the walls, lodged between tapestries, most depicting bloody battle scenes. Leather shields and swords also provided decoration. Turbet's family made their fortune fighting the King's campaigns—his father being rewarded with lands. Turbet himself had fought in the Battle of Sluys, but this room was almost like a shrine to war. Does not Venus fall where Mars is raised? I pressed my lips together and tried to dismiss the little voice tolling a warning in my head. There were two fabric-covered chairs, one of which I was enjoying, as well as three lovely carved ones with arms, and a stool. Of the two small tables, one held a silver jug and some goblets, and a bureau with enamel insets along the top sat against one wall. Upon it were some books. Alyson put down her drink and went to examine them.

"Jesus wept," said Beton, gazing around with wide eyes. "You've struck it lucky, Eleanor. Turbet must be richer than we thought."

"In debt more like," said Alyson dryly. "Did you notice who was at the wedding feast? Not one of the Bath gentry. Just a bunch of merchants and shopkeepers."

"Nothing wrong with that," sniffed Beton.

"I'm not saying there is, unless they came to do an accounting. From the look of this—" her arm swept the room, "the man lives like a lord—or pretends to. I'll guarantee any room that isn't public is wanting. Why, take this room. Never seen such threadbare cushions and wall hangings in my life."

"At least he has some," I said.

She sniffed. "The man is about making an impression. You wait, all those servants scurrying about—they'll be gone come morning. Hired to bedazzle is my guess."

"Nothing wrong with that," I said, echoing Beton. "We hire servants when there's extra work. What's a wedding if not that? What are we but additional mouths to feed?" I tried not to let my temper take hold. Didn't matter what Turbet did or said, Alyson would not budge in her low opinion. Yet, the only reason I was married to him was because Fulk, the only man she ever knew as a father and who she'd loved dearly, was dead. Uprooted from her old life and ways, I'd forced her into this. I just prayed she'd grow accustomed to Turbet. I prayed we all would. God knew, this bitter night, I thought I could.

"You need to give the man a chance, Alyson," I snapped. "You've taken a set against him."

"Have not," she replied with indignation. "Not without reason. My judgment is made from what I've observed and heard."

"Well, I've only observed *my* husband being generous and kind.

As for hearing anything, not one whiff of scandal have I been told aside from your whispers."

"Who'd dare tell *you*?" scoffed Alyson. "Once you agreed to marry him, no one was going to say anything, were they?"

"Why not?"

"Because you would have bitten their bloody heads off, as you do mine."

"You're one to talk—"

Milda began to blink; high color filled her cheeks.

"Ladies, ladies," said Beton, holding up his hands as if to fend off an attack. "Remember what day it is and where you are. For God's sake, cease your muck-spouting. Let's start as we mean to go on. Anyhow, it's too late to change anything. Eleanor is a Gerrish now. And, because we're family, we're all stuck with him, whoever and whatever he is."

It wasn't often Beton talked sense.

I brooded, even as I liked that Beton called us family. Alyson turned the pages of the book she couldn't read and shook her head, muttering, "I never wanted to come here. I'd have been content to stay at the farm." She snapped the book shut. A cloud of dust hit her in the face and she coughed. "But you two talked me out of it."

Beton and I had worked hard to persuade her that the rent monies she received as her share of the farm would go some way toward increasing her dowry and give her some independence. Not that a woman ever really had any.

If I'd been feeling more charitable, I would have reminded her that *I* wanted her here, with me. I wanted Beton and Milda, too. I hadn't been all that keen to leave the farm, but once I accepted Turbet's proposal, I'd little choice. It didn't help that Geoffrey never wrote back to me. Despite dictating two letters to Father Elias, one before my pilgrimage and one after, he never replied. It reached a point where I had to give Turbet an answer or lose him. Lose his lands, more like. Lose all this, I thought, looking around.

In the end, I'd capitulated. I was young, I needed a man's guidance. That's what Father Elias said. It's what Beton, Milda, and Mistress Bertha said as well. It's what they all said.

Except Alyson.

She pointed out I'd been the one to guide Fulk; I'd increased his prosperity. I could manage on my own. With her, Beton, and Milda beside me, I didn't need to rush into marriage. Not that I listened.

To make matters worse, Beton was remaining at Bigod Farm. Oh, he was with us for the wedding feast and the morrow, making sure we had everything we needed from our old life at the farm. Turbet convinced him (and me) it would be better if Beton stayed at Bigod Farm as a bailiff and, with a goodly wage, oversaw the serfs and the rents and generally looked after the place on our behalf.

"Our," of course, included Turbet. What was mine was now his and what was his remained so.

At first I'd objected to leaving Beton behind, even though I could see he was taken with the notion of having a title, some author-ity (and who could blame him for that), and money. When Alyson argued that whoever rented the farm would be the *only* tenant and would sublease the cottages so there was no need for a bailiff, Turbet smiled—the kind of smile someone gives you when you're being naive, if not downright stupid.

We talked and talked. Truth is, we argued and I threw things. I thought what Turbet said was practical. So did Beton. Milda didn't offer a view. Only Alyson wasn't happy.

Beton and I bullied her into accepting the idea. And it was then that she shared her wild belief.

Her eyes brimming with unshed tears, her hands balled into fists, she'd leaped to her feet and screamed. "I don't know how you, Beton, can work for that man, or you, *you*—" she pointed at me, her finger a dagger, "can consider marrying the person who killed Pa."

She shook like a wet cat. I was dumbstruck. Beton stared as if she'd grown horns and a tail.

Poor Alyson, Fulk's death had affected her worse than I thought.

"What do you mean?" I asked finally.

Alyson drew closer, resting an arm on the table. "Didn't you think it funny how Pa grew worse after Turbet gave him that gift?"

"The blanket?"

"Aye. Up until then, Pa was improving. The moment that fur was spread over him, he sickened—and not just him." She let her words hang.

My stomach roiled. Fulk had been showing signs of improvement before the Botch claimed him, Sophie, Theo, and the others. I had briefly wondered if the Botch had been carried in the fur . . .

"I was talking to some spinners in town," continued Alyson. "Some say the Botch came from London. That it was carried about the country in cloths. And what did Master Gerrish give Pa? Why, a lovely fur-lined cloth to keep him warm. That's what killed him. Could have killed us, too. It was God's good grace spared us or we'd be buried down by the brook and all."

I stared at her. "That's a terrible accusation. Anyway, not everyone who touched the fur died. And if what you say is true, what good would it have done Turbet for us all to die? He couldn't inherit Fulk's land."

"That's true. But he could lease it cheap after, couldn't he?"

Ready to challenge her, I stopped. She was right. Furthermore, only those who rubbed the fur against them died. Sophie had pulled it over Fulk and kept stroking it. Likewise, Theo had taken responsibility for bathing his father, lifted him to the jordan, pulling back the fur, wrapping it around him again and again . . .

What was I doing? I was allowing Alyson's grief, her desire to find someone to blame for Fulk's death, to influence me.

"Listen to yourself, Alyson. This is madness. Even if the disease did come here as you suggest, you can't think it was deliberate. Why, Turbet was as much at risk as Fulk and the carter. Did he not ride with the fur? With the other cloths too?"

"He survived the Great Pestilence before, why not again?" Alyson locked eyes with me. "Don't forget, Turbet had been at Pa to sell some land. Sheep too. Now he doesn't have to buy anything but your queynte and he has it and more besides."

I slapped Alyson across the face. Hard.

The tears came then, and not just hers. With one hand pressed to her flaming cheek and a look of utter betrayal, she ran into the night.

"Go after her, Beton," I whispered, sorrow and guilt thickening my words. "You know where to find her."

With a grim nod, he did. Before he went out the door, he turned. "She deserved that, Eleanor. She's wrong, you know. It's the grief talking, fear of change."

"I know," I said. "I know." My hand found the bench and I sank onto it. Milda came and sat beside me, holding my hand. "It's love makes her say that, mistress. It's love governs your choices, too." She added softly, "I don't mean for Master Gerrish."

I gave a bark of laughter and squeezed Milda's hand, ever-grateful for her solid presence. She knew Alyson wasn't the only one grieving. But I had to think of the future—not just mine, but Alyson's and Beton's, Milda's too. Turbet, for all his shortcomings, could at least give us one. It wasn't as if there was a queue of suitors lining up to offer for me, despite what I'd written to Geoffrey.

I buried my head in my hands, tears trickling down my cheeks and onto the table. Milda rubbed soothing patterns on my back. What if Alyson was right? What if Turbet had . . . Nay. Nay. No one could be that . . . that . . . wicked. Could they?

The doubts she planted tried to sprout, especially once we returned from Canterbury.

None of these thoughts made for good company on the very first evening in our new home.

Turbet found us a short time later, staring into our goblets, a dog lying upon my feet, another upon Alyson's, not speaking. In response to his unanswered question, Beton simply shrugged and said "women." Unperturbed, Turbet topped up our goblets, sat, and regaled us with what he'd seen and heard at our wedding feast.

As I listened and watched, I felt so conflicted. He was so . . . so . . . affable, so solicitous, if dull. As I reached down to stroke Hereward's ears, I thought, if only I could put Alyson's words aside, I could manage. This could be a good life. One where my husband was part of merchant circles, knew about sheep and wool, went out of his way to be generous to my family—including the dogs (King Claude and the weaned pups could not be shifted from the farm, but Beton would keep an eye on them). A life of comfort. How much more did I want?

An image of Fulk chuckling rose in my mind.

Alyson would come around, I thought as I gulped the heated

malmsey, burning my throat. Beton laughed at something Turbet said. I smiled, aware of my husband's eyes upon me. With remarkable restraint, Turbet had insisted we wait until our wedding night before consummating our union. I remembered how his lips felt upon mine at the church door, how his hand roamed along my back and cupped my buttocks before giving them a resounding slap, making me jump.

We could have a good life here. I repeated it like a mantra.

Couldn't we?

TWELVE

———◆———

Laverna Lodge
The Year of Our Lord 1370
In the forty-third year of the reign of Edward III

*F*or all Turbet acted as if he could barely contain his ardor prior to our vows, what with his hot kisses on my hands, as well as cheeky pinches and slaps, when it came to sarding on our wedding night, God's truth, he was unable.

Upon seeing me naked on the bed, an inviting smile upon my face, my warm and willing queynte on display, his spindle retreated into the gray thatch guarding his loins like a felled tree in a forest. Except a tree is at least firm. His prick was more like a hooked worm before the gaping mouth of a fish—cowering to the point it couldn't even be swallowed.

Frustrated beyond measure his rod wouldn't harden, despite his own efforts, he demanded I pleasure him. So, I rose to my knees, crawled across the bed and set to with gusto. After a time, I began to grow both weary and cold—I was unclothed, the covers had slipped from my shoulders. Still nothing happened.

I was like an old person given slops instead of a bone to chew.

Unsettled, he began to hiss—grabbing a fistful of my hair to keep me in place. I was ordered to suck harder, nay, softer, use my teeth, pull and pull with my fingers but gently, nay, more firmly. To spread my legs, close them, bend over, stand up straight. Keen to please, and aware his hand in my hair was beginning to hurt, I complied. He began to sweat, his face growing so very red. I could feel his rage boiling like a kettle. I half expected him to lash out and strike me, which made me both nervous and clumsy.

I accidentally bit him. He leaped back with a sharp cry and struck me hard across the face. I fell backward on the mattress in shock. The imprint of his hand burned my slick flesh. Tears gathered—not from sorrow, but from embarrassment.

"I'm sorry, I'm so sorry." I began to crawl toward him so I might inspect the damage.

He slapped my hands away and pushed me aside. "Get away, doxy," he shouted and turned his back so he might examine himself in private.

"I really am very sorry, sir." Repressed laughter made my voice high.

He spun around, eyes blazing. "You think this is funny?" His mouth twisted into a leer as his eyes roved over my body. "It's no wonder I couldn't . . . er . . . perform. Look at you! This is your fault." His hand swept toward me. "When all is said and done, you're an ugly little bitch."

He drew his shirt over his body, picked up his tunic, paltock, hose, and boots and, without another word, stormed out of the bedroom.

I fell back on the bed and stared at the ceiling. *My fault? Ugly little bitch?* How dare he, the maggot's cock. Fulk never had problems sarding me. On the contrary, as I'd grown older, we'd enjoyed many a romp between the sheets. How could it be *my* fault? I did everything and more, but still my husband's pole would not stand to attention. The fault lay with him, not me.

Ugly little bitch.

Was I? I know my hair was an uncommon color, being more red than brown, and my freckles were like speckles of dark paint splashed across my body, the gap in my teeth pronounced, but Fulk had thought me beautiful and said so often. Many of the merchants and carters in Bath and at the village market admired me as well. And what about Layamon all those years ago?

He'd been keen enough to swive me. Fulk, too . . . But he was no longer here.

My eyes began to burn.

Ugly little bitch . . .

Across the ceiling, shadows thrown by the candles looked like a phantom crowd cheering. I touched my cheek. It was on fire from the blow. Then, I ran my hands over my body. My skin was soft. I'd grown plump under Fulk's attentions, only to become thin immediately after he died. In the last month or so, Turbet, mayhap to woo me, ensured our table at Bigod Farm was always laden, and so my flesh had begun to fill out again. I touched my breasts. They were large, full, my nipples pink, and, as I pulled upon them, quick to harden. My stomach was nicely rounded and my thighs too. The hair that sat atop my quentye was soft as lambswool and, Fulk used to say, as inviting as a shepherd's sunset. I smiled, wishing he was here now. The man who found me beautiful. I rolled over onto my stomach, grabbed a pillow and lay upon it, making sure to drag the blankets over me.

After a while, I rubbed my eyes and moved my face only to place it straight on a damp patch.

Tears did no one any good, I thought, crying harder.

I didn't hear the door open, I only felt the covers rise, and a body slip in next to mine. A pair of arms drew me close.

"Don't you listen to him, you hear? It's him who's ugly."

I couldn't answer, words were banked up in my throat. I clung to Alyson and waited for her to say "I told you so." I cried and cried, and not just about what Turbet had (or hadn't) done and what he'd said, but because I'd wilfully ignored Alyson's warnings—not what she said about Fulk's death and Turbet being a potential murderer. I didn't believe that for a moment. It was her other concerns I'd dismissed, convincing myself they were simply uttered out of spite or envy.

I also hadn't listened to her because a part of me wanted to live a more comfortable life, to enjoy the privileges that came with having extra coin, being married to a man of standing in both the village and town. Prove Father Roman and his ilk wrong. Grasp opportunity, as Papa always said. When I began to sense that mayhap Alyson was right and Turbet was not all he appeared to be, I'd deliberately kept myself blind to the truth.

Now it was too late.

Ugly little bitch.

"No matter what happens," said Alyson softly, "no matter what I say to you or you throw back at me, I want you to know, hen, I'll always be here for you. We're in this together, you and me."

My throat clogged; my eyes swam and the room dissolved. She'd called me hen, our little joke that I, the younger one, was the hen and she the chick. It made my heart swell. I didn't deserve her.

She began to stroke my hair. "Turbet drank too much tonight, hen. He'll be sorry in the morning and make it up to you. Just you wait. We all say things we regret at times, as you and I have cause to know." She chuckled. I cried harder. "Hush, hush. It will be alright." She squeezed me tight. "If anyone can make it work—and I don't only mean his prick—"

That raised a short, sharp laugh from me.

"—then it's you. Look how happy you and Pa were. Who would ever have thought? A young thing like you and my grizzled old father? Mayhap, all Turbet needs is a chance." She paused. "Another one. And you, with your big heart, your big smile, and let's not forget your big nugs—" She gave them a squeeze. "You'll give him that and everything will be fine."

What was it Geoffrey said? Oh, aye. Everyone deserves a second chance.

Mayhap, even Turbet.

We lay there in silence, interrupted only by my snuffling. Moonbeams sliced through the thick glass, throwing puddles of argent light on the covers. Curled in each other's arms, we watched them creep across the bed. Outside, an owl hooted and one of the dogs barked, joined by the other soon enough. I wondered what had disturbed them. Had Turbet ventured outside to cool his temper? To think upon his words?

Somehow I doubted it. A man like that didn't dwell upon such things. To do so would be to admit fault and he was very clear the problem wasn't his.

I rammed my fists into my eyes. Alyson was right. I was married to Turbet and he to me. If I was to stay married, then I had to make it work—including swiving. We needed to make a child. Otherwise, what was a wife but a whore with a ring on her finger? God knows, I'd love to have a babe. My fingers ran lightly over my belly.

Born under the sign of Venus meant love was my speciality. But Mars was also my patron. For certes, Turbet didn't stand a chance if I decided to go to battle—and I would. For my marriage, my honor, the hope of a child, and for Alyson.

Did she sense I was thinking about her? Did she know how much it meant that she'd come to me and offered solace?

"Thank you, Alyson. Thank you." My voice was raspy.

"What for?" she asked sleepily, tightening her arms about me.

"For being here. Caring."

"Who says I care?" she chuckled. "Nay, this is what sisters do, isn't it? Look out for each other. Love one another—even when no one else does." There was a heaviness. "Especially then."

"Well, I love you, chick," I said. I meant it. I really did.

"I know." She kissed me and, moments later, was breathing steadily.

I shut my eyes and, moving so she was curled around my back, tried to sleep. Visions of Turbet's prick retreating into a forest of gray haunted my dreams as did his ice-cold rebuke followed by his insult, *"Ugly little bitch. This is all your fault."*

As it turned out, for once in my life, it really wasn't.

THIRTEEN

———— ❦ ————

Laverna Lodge
The Year of Our Lord 1370
In the forty-third and forty-fourth years of the reign of Edward III

*I*n those first few months, any attempts to consummate the marriage were unsuccessful. They more often resulted in Turbet striking me, hurling abuse, and thundering away. Or, worse, me laughing. I didn't mean to be cruel, I really didn't, but the sight of him with his breeches lowered, his wrinkly knees and his fleshy worm curled amidst that thatch of gray hair, became a source of hilarity. Looking back, I think mayhap I laughed because if I didn't, I would have wept. No woman wants to be blamed for murdering her husband's desire. Before long, Turbet made excuses not to come to my room, the solar, or even to be in the house. If I'd time to think about his increasing absences, I might have been more concerned. As it was, I'd other duties to occupy me.

When I was married to Fulk, it was understood I would learn how to manage the household and then help him in every way a woman possibly could with the farm. Due to Alyson's diligence and patience (our first few weeks together not withstanding)—Fulk's too—I'd not only come to master what was required of me, but made improvements.

But nothing and no one prepared me for life at Laverna Lodge. Whereas Fulk and I worked in tandem, like an oxen and the plough, with Alyson, Beton, Theo, Sophie, and Milda providing additional help when required, making a team, things worked very differently here.

First of all, the place was more than three times the size of Bigod Farm and, though not as big as Noke Manor, nor possessing that number of servants, it still had a few. They all needed supervision (even if most knew what to do without me looking over their shoulders). Then there was the lodge itself. There weren't only rooms for sleeping and eating, but a decent-sized kitchen and a room attached to that with an oven for baking. Every other day, the villeins and free-tenants on Turbet's lands (and some from nearby villages outside Bath) would queue to have their bread baked.

There were two tiny rooms for the live-in servants, who slept practically one on top of the other, and two huge barns, the animals being more spaciously housed than their masters. There was even an area for smoking meat and a buttery. Despite the convenience of such rooms, there was little food being stored. In the immediate grounds, there was a rather small vegetable garden that needed a good weeding, some straggly fruit trees, a pond—currently iced-over but apparently filled with fish—as well as chickens, ducks, geese, and three cows.

Fortunately, the housekeeper, Mistress Emmaline, a large woman with low-slung breasts (over which she'd fold her arms when displeased), who carried a great clank of keys about, was content to show me what was what—mainly because it gave her the opportunity both to complain about the extent of her duties, and to show off her accomplishments. I knew enough by now to pander to her and praise her handsomely, even if I didn't feel it was entirely deserved. I mean, how could one have so much help yet still have an untended garden? Being winter was no excuse. How could she allow her apron to be so grubby and her maids' shifts torn and poorly patched? The rooms were filled with furniture and objects but appeared neglected. I'd learned from my first weeks with Alyson not to make an enemy of someone who might turn out to be my only ally, so said nothing. Alyson and Milda kept their silence too, thank the Lord, though I could see Milda cataloguing what needed to be done. Emmeline was also a great source of stories about the former Mistress Gerrish and the few visitors who called here. I would get to meet them soon enough.

There were five live-in maids to care for the animals, the oven, the fireplaces, to draw water from the well, churn the butter, collect the cream, brew, make maslin and other types of bread, sweep the fireplaces, change the rushes and all manner of tasks, including laundry. To my astonishment, not one of them was encouraged to spin, though they all knew how. There were boys and men to tend the sheep, the horses (Turbet had no donkeys until we arrived), and to keep the store of weapons clean. Aye, Turbet had an armory of sorts where longbows were housed (there was even a butt for practicing), two heavy swords, and armor that had once been his father's. A blacksmith leased the smithy. Mornings rang with the sound of his hammer striking the anvil. It was quite musical. There was also Turbet's squire, Nicholas, who followed his master around like a browbeaten puppy. I was saddened to learn that the young boy who'd struggled to hold Hereward and Wake had been dismissed with a beating. From Bath, his name was Peter. I could tell Mistress Emmaline was surprised I'd asked after him. The extra servants who'd been buzzing about the lodge the night before were, as Alyson suspected, hired not only to help prepare the house for my arrival, but to give a grand impression.

By the time I'd finished the tour of the lodge, I was underwhelmed.

There'd once been a chapel, but that had fallen down and never been replaced. The household went to St. Michael's Without the Walls and sometimes Within for service, depending on the day. Turbet's lands, unlike Fulk's, were divided into strips for the villeins to live and work upon, and pasture. It was expected I would visit the villeins if they were sick or with child or dying. As steward, Jermyn was responsible for collecting rents, listening to complaints, and issuing fines or punishment at the regular manorial court. (As the months went by and the villeins became accustomed to me, I would hear what they thought of so-called manor justice, Jermyn, and even, on occasion, Turbet.) Jermyn basically looked after everything outside the walls of Laverna Lodge. With so much to learn, even if it wasn't something I could or would oversee, I was determined to be a good mistress. God knew, I couldn't be a good wife.

After a couple of weeks, I tried to quiz Turbet about his villeins. He dismissed my questions and, because the servants were present, I didn't press the issue. I tried again a few weeks later, as the snows began to melt and the scope of the pasture lands was revealed. I wanted to know what breed of sheep he preferred and what he felt about the quality of the wool. Hard not to think about these things when every single day, on top of my other tasks, I also spun and, now that Alyson and I had wool, weaved. Patient before others, Turbet evaded direct answers. But when the servants left the room, he came to where I was sitting with my distaff and spindle, the newly made thread fine and firm between my fingers.

"Don't you ever, ever question me about the sheep. Don't you ever question me about the villeins, or the land either. In fact," he said, leaning over so his face was only inches from mine and I could smell the malmsey on his breath, see the silver bristles limning his quivering jowls, "don't you dare ask me about *my* business, do you hear? Remember your place."

I stopped the spindle and gazed straight into his eyes as, true to form, they slid away and he pushed himself upright. "But, husband, how can I help if you don't tell me?"

"*Help* me? *You?*" He stared. "You're serious?" He began to laugh. A great affected belly-laugh. Alyson, her spindle turning, glanced in my direction. Milda paused in her actions. Waves of anger and humiliation washed over me.

"Dear God!" He made a great show of wiping his eyes. "Let me remind you that as a woman possessed of a simple, weak mind with no capacity for understanding, you don't need to know *anything*. You're not required to *help* me. You're required to do one thing and one thing only, and that is *obey* your husband." He poured himself a drink. "What I do with the land, the sheep, and villeins, doesn't concern you. Don't worry your—" he'd been about to say "pretty" but changed his mind, "head about such matters. All you'll achieve is a megrim." He glanced at me as he resumed his seat. "Help me," he chuckled. "You could no more help than a babe wield a sword."

"Then why are wives known as helpmeets?" I murmured. I didn't have the courage then to confront him. Not when I feared he might slap me or worse.

It was no surprise the story of my offer was repeated over dinner a few nights later when a group of merchants, including a man named Mervyn Slynge and his ward, Kit someone-or-other, came to dinner. Master Slynge was a respected Bath wool grower and his ward a handsome young fop with chestnut curls and a faint mustache. What I said became a source of great hilarity; the redder I blushed, the harder the men laughed.

The only person failing to find amusement was Master Slynge. He eyed me over his goblet and, as I fought not to cry and wished the floor would swallow me, I could have sworn, gave a great big wink.

Milda, who'd been such a boon at Bigod Farm, proved herself again at Laverna Lodge. Though she disapproved of Mistress Emmaline's housekeeping, she determined to make a friend of her. They could oft be heard gossiping in the kitchen or, as the weather grew warmer and the snows began to melt, the birds to nest and sing, in the garden. When she wasn't spinning, she was also popular with the other maids, helping them with their chores. Milda was able to gauge moods and the temperature of the household, report back if I was doing something deemed foolish, dangerous, or even, on occasion (rare, I admit) wise. She'd already proven her worth at Bigod Farm and as a traveling companion when we went to Canterbury. Now I couldn't imagine life without her.

I quickly picked up what was required of me as Mistress Gerrish. I'd always known there'd been another wife, many years ago. What I didn't know was she died from a strange wasting illness, languishing in her bed for over six months before she passed away. The household didn't talk about what happened, it was forbidden. Nor did they mention Turbet's two children: a son and daughter. I discovered their existence quite by accident when I was exploring the attic and found some worn-out children's toys. Milda learned the daughter was married to a merchant in York and the son was based in Calais and had something to do with the Staple there. When I tried to ask about his children, Turbet responded sharply.

"They're none of your business."

I remember the incident clearly. We were in the Great Hall. It was Candlemas, a day when all women who had borne children brought a candle to church and celebrated the Holy Mother Mary. We'd not long returned from St. Michael's. I'd invited Father Elias to join us. Master Mervyn Slynge and Kit were present, along with some other merchants and their wives. Master Mervyn was seated across from me. At the tone in Turbet's voice, everyone had fallen silent, casting looks in our direction.

Hurt by his answer, embarrassed he could speak to me so before guests, I bit back. "Since I don't have my own to be concerned about," I said quietly, "it's natural I'd be curious about yours."

He'd slammed his fist on the table. "Natural? There's nothing natural about you, woman! You've too much to say for yourself. Curiosity is the devil's itch and curse you for always wishing to scratch it!" Leaving his food uneaten, he marched from the hall. Nicholas waited a moment, then dashed after him. Alyson reached for my hand under the table. Father Elias shot me a sympathetic look and began to fill the uncomfortable silence with observations of the recent plantings in the lodge's gardens (I had managed some improvements there, at least). Mervyn Slynge signaled for the musicians to keep playing.

I did learn his children's names: Tamsyn was the daughter, Perkyn, the son. But after a few months, I gave up trying to find out more; I even ceased to ask my husband about his business, much as I wanted to question him about the debts we seemed to be accruing faster than you can say "usurer's ledger." Confronted with reminders of monies owed whenever I ventured into Bath, it wasn't as if I could pretend there wasn't a problem. Not to mention the many folk who braved the winter snows after we were first married to try and collect what was owed to them. Only later did I find out these various shopkeepers and merchants were relying on what I had brought to the union to pay them.

Months later, they were still waiting.

I pushed this to the back of my mind as I did so many other things in those early days, especially as weaving came to dominate my life. Turbet had been insistent that both Alyson and I not only work the looms, but train other women, men as well, to weave to our standard.

The head of Bath Abbey, John Harewell, also known as the Bishop of Bath and Wells, came to dine one evening, accompanied by his cellarer, a number of higher-ranked monks and the precentor, who took notes. They sat at the table in the Great Hall like a row of crows in their dark Benedictine robes, their hoods flung back, tonsures shining in the flickering light of the sconces and candelabra. The only exception was the bishop, who wore a white alb and cincture. The fine wool was a sight to behold. I longed to rub the cloth between my fingers, but durst not. Sitting opposite them were some of Bath's leading wool producers and merchants—my husband, sitting at one end of the table, among them. I sat quietly at the other, terrified lest I be sent away. I needn't have worried; the only person to notice me was Master Slynge, who offered a reassuring smile.

Between them, the men discussed the prices of wool, everyone deferring to the monks, who had the largest flock and therefore the most wool. Keen to recoup any losses caused by the Botch, they were prepared to bend regulations. Turbet argued that prices should be raised. The bishop and one of the Bath merchants countered that if the price per bale was increased, then buyers would go elsewhere. Turbet said there were plenty who could afford to pay more, especially the alien merchants—he indicated the two he'd invited. From Flanders, they were a father and son. But if that happened, the monks argued, it meant regardless of what was paid to them, all the real profit would still go to the aliens (beg pardon, good sirs), when they sold the wool in their markets at higher rates, English wool being in such demand. And so it went, back and forth.

Finally, it was agreed to raise the price per bale by half the amount Turbet initially proposed. The men shook hands and, after toasting a successful outcome, dispersed. Much to my surprise, Turbet told me to see our guests to the door.

It took some time for everyone to get sorted and leave. I was bidding farewell to Mervyn Slynge, who was without the company of Kit this night, when I heard voices coming from the Great Hall. Not everyone had left after all. I waited until Master Slynge was mounted, then returned, stifling a yawn, eager to escort the stragglers out. I was keen for bed.

Far from departing, the remaining men were thick in discussion. I recognized the two alien merchants and Master Kenton, the brogger. Instincts told me to stay in the shadows of the doorway.

"You're right," Turbet was saying. "I've no intention of selling our wool to any local markets. Instead, what I want is to negotiate private contracts with you, good sirs—" He was addressing the aliens, Georg and Ludolf van Haarlem. Pale of skin and with long noses, they'd barely partaken of either the food or wine and hardly spoken until now.

"This is what we're here to do," said Ludolf. "Lock in a contract for the next few years."

"Few years?" said Turbet, flashing that smile of his. "That's a long time. The price would have to be right."

"We heard what price you're preparing to sell your wool for," said the father, Georg. "We can offer more—providing you deal exclusively with us."

Sweet Jesu. Turbet had deliberately invited these men to the table so they'd hear the price the Bath growers were setting for their wool and then encourage them to raise it—for himself. Part of me loathed his cunning, the other part admired it.

"That's what I was hoping you'd say," said Turbet and, with a wave of his hand, signaled for more wine to be brought to the table.

I took that as my cue to leave. As I mounted the stairs, my mind buzzed like bees around gillyflowers. Here was my husband, a Bath wool grower and merchant, openly cutting out those he'd just agreed to work with cooperatively, so all our wool might sell and we'd profit handsomely. Could his agreement with the alien merchants harm the others? I hoped not. As the monks said, the extra coin made on their wool would aid St. John's Hospital. Help feed so many poor. For all my doubts about priests and monks, the ones at Bath Abbey and St. Peter's poured what they earned from wool and cloth-making into maintaining the infirmary, which looked after the elderly, the sick, and poor as well as any pilgrims who passed through town, and those who came to enjoy the healing waters of the hot baths—something I was yet to experience. The hospital relied on tithes and donations to operate. Ever since the Botch decimated their ranks decades ago, there hadn't been as many benefactors and so they were forced to find other means to survive. Hence the wool and cloth-making. If my husband were to disrupt their efforts, I wasn't sure my soul could bear it. I knew Fulk would be rolling over in his grave. But who could I tell? Did I even want to, when, as Turbet's wife, I would be perceived as complicit in his plans, even if I had no say?

It was an interrupted sleep that night, filled with dark dreams.

———·———

As winter melted into spring and March arrived in a flurry of wind and rain, Lent preoccupied us. I refused to dwell on my growing concerns about Turbet and his plans, except to keep an ear to the ground. Anyway, by the time the bells sounded for none each day and I sat down to weave, I was so tired, I doubt I could have given them sensible consideration. As Turbet continually reminded me, was I not the "weaker vessel"? A mere woman? When it eventually dawned on me that I should have been insistent, specifically about how Turbet's decisions would affect the sheep and property I'd brought to the marriage, it was too late.

While I was fraught and distracted about the kind of man my husband was and the situation I found myself in (and had brought Alyson and Milda into), Turbet was frantically enjoying *my* assets, and not the physical kind. Turns out his worldly goods didn't amount to nearly as much as he liked everyone to think. He lived well beyond his means on the strength of his first wife's dowry, and he, a knight's youngest and disappointing son, had grown accustomed to doing so. Everything I owned became his not only to manage, but to divest himself of as he felt necessary.

Turbet not only thought it necessary to break up my pastures and turn the land into small strips, placing tenants in poorly built cottages to work it, but to sell off parts of it as well. It was quick coin—used not to reduce debt, but to enable him to spend more. Foolishly, he then brought my sheep into his own flock, uncaring that the land he possessed could only hold so many and the sheepfolds were too small.

Too late, I learned that while Turbet could sound as if he knew what he was doing when he talked business, like his sometimes charming demeanor, his lavish clothes and dinners, the large house and stables, it was all for bloody show.

A show that needed a young wife with land, sheep, and funds, and the attentions of false friends and cunning bargains to keep it all running.

FOURTEEN

Laverna Lodge
The Year of Our Lord 1371
In the forty-fifth year of the reign of Edward III

I was married to Turbet for over a year before I finally heard from Geoffrey. It wasn't that he'd ignored me, as I'd begun to believe, but rather that my letters had chased him across various countries, always arriving just after he'd departed.

The King had sent his newly minted diplomat to France, and from there to accompany Prince John of Gaunt, the King's third son, to Aquitaine. My letter found him on the day Gregory XI became Pope. Geoffrey had sat down in his lodgings at Avignon immediately to respond.

He wrote two letters that day—one to the King informing him of the outcome of the Papal elections, and another to me, which arrived via Father Elias.

By the time Father Elias came to the lodge to read it to me, winter was once more on the wane. Yuletide and the Feast of the Epiphany had been the most miserable I remembered. Not only had my husband arrived home drunk on Christmas Eve with a bunch of merchants he'd invited from London, but that duplicitous brogger, bloody Master Kenton, tagged along. The only welcome person as far as I was concerned was Mervyn Slynge. I tried not to let the fact Kit accompanied him affect me. That laughing popinjay could go to hell and stay there as far as I was concerned.

Immediately after Christmas, my husband left on a long trip, which was just as well, for I was heartily sick of his constant barbs.

But back to Geoffrey's letter.

Apart from his travails and service to the King, Geoffrey thought to answer my question of whether or not I should marry Turbet Gerrish. Though he knew his response would arrive much too late to be of use, in typical fashion, he still saw fit to proffer advice, such is the way of men that they must be heard even when what they have to say is beyond useless.

Naturally, he warned me against wedding Turbet.

When Father Elias relayed that bit, Alyson arched a brow and gave me a pointed look. I ignored her. May Geoffrey's balls rot in his breeches. What was the point of saying anything if not to arouse my ire? My regret? To prove himself right and me wrong?

I stormed about the solar, and if there'd been something to throw, apart from a decorative crucifix upon the wall or one of Turbet's cherished armaments, I would have hurled them out the window.

When I'd finally calmed enough to hear the rest of Geoffrey's missive, he also said if I did marry Gerrish, then I would make the best of it and seek to learn what I could from a man who knew how to extract the most from those around him. Did he know the man extracted coin the way a pardoner did confessions?

I glanced at Father Elias.

"Is Geoffrey saying what I think he is?"

"What's that, dear Eleanor?" The good Father was relieved my pacing had ceased and my choler cooled.

"That my husband is a thief?"

Father Elias did his usual blushing and dissembling whenever I asked something he found difficult. The day I told him my husband's prick was so small and inclined to withdraw in the face of womanly desire, and confessed that attempting sex was about as successful as trying to light a fire with a wet ribbon, he'd spluttered and turned such a shade of puce, I thought he was choking on the Host. I was quite ready to shout for the doctor. Instead, I threw holy water over him and he recovered faster than a drowned fish. He then had the gall to chastise me for wasting blessed liquid.

I retorted God wouldn't mind; it wasn't like He drank it, was it?

By the time Father Elias finished the letter, my temper had completely dissipated and aye, regret had taken over. I sank into a chair, not daring to look at Alyson as she clicked and clacked at the loom in the corner.

God's truth, the more I unearthed about Turbet, the more I wished I'd waited for Geoffrey's reply, no matter how long it took. Guilt was not a cloth I wore lightly or well, yet it was one I donned daily. If my decision to wed Turbet had only impacted upon me, I might have been able to tolerate it—nay, that's not the right word—to become reconciled to my choice. But with every passing day, each time I learned something about my husband, his dealings with others, the servants, the tenants, the reckless decisions he made, his overbearing manner toward those less powerful or fortunate, never mind his treatment of me, I felt a pressing weight upon my soul. I wanted to blame Geoffrey, lash out and scold him, hold him accountable for *my* lack of insight. But it wasn't his fault. I'd closed my ears to Alyson's warnings; worse, I'd made a mockery of her doubts and twisted them into something nasty that lived within her, when the opposite was true.

Truth, ha. Geoffrey's words, the kindness in the way he framed them, knowing I would have capitulated to the demands of those around me, been tempted by what Turbet appeared to offer, juddered the truth free so I was forced to face it once and for all.

I'd married a sweet-smelling wastrel.

Not even learning about Turbet's past helped. Through Mistress Emmeline and others, I discovered that, as a child and young man, Turbet had been a disappointment to his domineering bully of a father and later, to his shrew of a wife. Married young and under the illusion that once he took possession of his wife's fortune he'd be free to carve his own path, on the contrary, she managed both it and him. The children grew to despise their weak father as much, if not more, than their mother did. After their mother died, the children had nothing to do with him, which explained why he preferred not to discuss them.

Still, I couldn't understand what I'd done to deserve his public derision and private disregard. For months, I tried to pretend his actions didn't hurt, to excuse them as the result of his upbringing and previous marriage. In the end, I could not. Instead of having sympathy for those who were weaker, Turbet took the opportunity to intimidate and browbeat. His targets were servants, workers, the young, the frail, and, of course, women.

My forbearance came to an end the day he sat to nuncheon, having invited Master Kenton, and proceeded to boast about what he planned to do once the bill of sale on some land was finalized.

"Excuse me, husband, but did you say the northern pastures were to be sold?"

He paused, the knife halfway to his mouth, a piece of bloodied lamb skewered on the end. "Listen to her, Kenton. She talks as if she understands men's business." He snorted and pushed the meat between his lips, casting an amused look in Master Kenton's direction.

Master Kenton sniggered.

A rush of anger made me rash.

"But, sir, the northern land is mine. There's a flock dedicated to those pastures and they produce very good wool." Turbet continued to chew, ignoring me. Master Kenton slurped from his mazer. I was less than a gadfly for all the attention they paid me. "Surely, husband, this is something you should discuss . . . with me."

Turbet paused. He carefully put down his knife and then slammed his fist on the table. Such was the force, his mazer toppled, spilling wine. "Who do you think you are? Eh?" One of the servants rushed to mop up the spill. Turbet half rose from his seat and, as the young lad attempted to wipe the table, shoved him aside. The boy staggered and fell on his ass.

I went to help, horrified Turbet would behave in such a manner.

"Sit down!" he bellowed.

The boy leaped to his feet and scurried away. With great reluctance, I resumed my seat.

Turbet stood over the table. His face was slick and red, his eyes bloodshot. "You will remember your place, woman. Just as you will remember that the lands are no longer yours, they're *mine*. It's not for you, a mere servant's get, to question your husband's decisions—not now, not ever, am I clear?"

Dear God, I wanted to rise up and slap his face. I wanted to shout him into submission. But, what he said was true. The lands were no longer mine.

Satisfied with my silence, Turbet sat back down, signaling for a servant to refill his goblet. As the wine was poured, I noted how shabby the boy's shirt was, how frayed the collar. Yet there sat my husband in his fine wool, with his bejewelled hands and velvet coat. The other servants' attire was also worn and tired.

"Forgive that display, Kenton, would you?" said Turbet, picking up his knife. "My wife is but young, unschooled in the ways of her betters."

"Then, it's just as well she has you to teach her, sir."

The lack of sincerity in Master Kenton's words was breathtaking as was the sycophantic look he gave Turbet. My husband preened.

Sweet Jesu, my husband was not only mean in every way, he was a bona fide fool.

"If you cannot keep the peace, Eleanor, you can leave," said Turbet smugly.

I should have left. Should have picked up what remained of my dignity and departed. But I knew if I did, either I, Alyson, or one of the other servants would pay for my boldness. I remained. But I also made up my mind that I would discover the fate of my lands and sheep.

As I listened to the banter between Turbet and Master Kenton, it was clear the only reason Turbet wooed and wed me was because he thought I'd be malleable.

Thus far, keen to be a good wife, to make something of our marriage, keep accord, I'd been that. Look what it had cost me. Me, Alyson, and Beton.

Shame on me.

Over the next few weeks, I found that not only had my husband

sold much of the land I'd inherited from Fulk, but he'd persuaded
Beton to entrust him with his portion as well. Then he'd sold it to
buy more sheep. This might have worked but he'd gone to markets
in York and purchased unwisely, spreading disease among the flock.

It was only because I went behind my husband's back and ordered
the shepherd remove any healthy sheep to a separate foldcourse, pretending to speak with Turbet's authority, that the entire flock wasn't
affected.

After we'd culled the sick sheep, the remainder were moved to
another pasture and enclosed. I told Beton to ensure any sheep the
tenants ran or that strayed from the monks' lands were kept clear of
Turbet's. In this way, the rest were saved.

When he found out what I'd done, Turbet didn't thank me, of
course not. He leveled blame for the losses at Beton.

In the end, all that was left of our inheritance was a mere few
acres. The new resident at Bigod Farm, a freeman from the Cots-
wolds (to whom, it became apparent, Turbet owed money), ploughed
some of Alyson's lands, planting them with his crops. Surreptitiously,
he shifted the boundaries, taking more than was his right. When
Beton tried to argue on his sister's behalf and even took the matter
to manor court, he was fined for affray and told to back off or else.

Sickened by the gross injustice, I couldn't ignore what was happening any longer. Alyson and Beton didn't deserve to lose the little
that their father had worked so hard to provide.

Bursting into Turbet's office, I found him deep in discussion with
Jermyn.

When he saw who'd entered, and without knocking, his face
darkened.

"What do you want?" he growled.

"And a God's good day to you too, husband," I said with false
cheer.

"God's good—et cetera." He flapped a wrist. "I ask again, what
do you want? Can't you see we're busy?" He gestured to the pile of
scrolls on his desk.

"I want to talk to you about Bigod Farm, about Beton," I said
swiftly.

"Beton? That lazy, good-for-nothing drunk," said Turbet.

I was taken aback. Surely he was talking about a different person.

"Aye, your stepson, nephew, whatever he is, has proved to be a right burden." Jermyn passed his master a piece of paper. "One has only to look at this to see his record-keeping is atrocious. How can anyone judge what crops belong to whom let alone animals and equipment when nothing is written down? When there's no proof? How's a court or bailiff to pass judgment? It's one man's word against another's." He shoved the paper in my direction.

There was no point debating the issue. We both knew I couldn't read or write and Beton was illiterate. As Turbet had known when he'd appointed him to oversee the farm. He'd assured me and Beton that either Jermyn or his squire, Nicholas, would aid him in that regard. The help had never been forthcoming, both men always being too busy. Unable to manage, it's no wonder Beton started to drink.

Before the year was out, Beton disappeared. He told Father Elias he was heading to London to seek his fortune. He didn't even say goodbye. Was it shame that prevented him farewelling us? Or worse, did he believe Alyson and I endorsed his shabby treatment?

Did not a husband speak for his wife? The very thought Turbet was regarded as my mouthpiece mortified me. But, by not speaking up, hadn't I been complicit?

Debt mounted and it became impossible to venture to Bath without being followed by the cries of those to whom Turbet owed money. How could I pay? Turbet controlled the purse strings.

If it hadn't been for our weaving venture, I don't know what we would have done. Alyson and I worked hard to train the servants—two girls, Aggy and Rag (Ragnilda, but she only answered to Rag), and, much to my surprise, a big, gangly youth with a mop of thick hair, wide-spaced blue eyes, and lovely long fingers, named Hob. Even with the extra coin the weaving brought, it didn't bode well for the future; not the way my husband spent.

I worried that in order to meet our obligations, obligations my husband had incurred by his poor business sense and lavish lifestyle, and the contracts he'd signed with Meneer van Haarlem, which meant most of our wool was sold before it was even grown, weighed, or the quality assayed, I might have to put off some of the servants. Since Turbet refused to discuss the manor records and ensured that when he was away, Jermyn didn't either, I was never sure. To those who came to the house seeking to have bills settled, I played ignorant, as much as it pained me. Fulk could never abide debt, and I know Papa didn't approve of people living beyond their means, not when it was at the expense of those who scraped to survive.

I was nobody's fool (except when it came to my choice of second husband) and knew if something didn't change and soon, then the life I'd foisted upon Alyson and Beton and Milda would turn out to be like one of those mirages in an exotic tale, and would disappear in a shimmer of remorse.

FIFTEEN

Laverna Lodge and Bath
The Year of Our Lord 1371
In the forty-fifth year of the reign of Edward III

*S*o, hen, what're you thinking?" Alyson didn't even look up from the spindle. A few of us were in the solar spinning. It was a freezing-cold day. The windows were sealed with frost, and a bitter draught managed to ease its way through the cracks and crevices, diluting the warmth of the fire that we practically sat upon. Hereward and Wake were curled at my feet. Part of me wished I could lie beside them or borrow their thick coats a while.

Trust Alyson to notice I was preoccupied. I watched the thread growing between her experienced fingers. She was waiting patiently for an answer.

I glanced at the servants. Hob and Aggy had just come in from finishing their chores and were preparing to work the loom. They were pretending not to listen while soaking up every tidbit to share it in the kitchen later. Milda and Rag were in the barn fetching more wool to spin. Though I trusted Hob, Rag and Aggy, and Milda of course, I couldn't risk what I had to say being heard, let alone repeated. For Alyson was right. I'd spent weeks wool-gathering until, this very day, I believed I'd finally found a way to deal with my spendthrift husband.

"Why don't we walk in the garden?" I abandoned the spinning and stood.

"What?" exclaimed Alyson, recoiling in horror. "Outside? In all the snow and wind and freeze our bloody tits off?"

I jerked my head toward Aggy and Hob.

It was easy to forget the servants. I know that sounds callous and cruel, but when I was a servant at Noke Manor it was our God-given duty to blend in, to become all but invisible. We used to pride ourselves on not being noticed. If we were, then we'd failed in our duties. Worse, we'd have nothing to gossip about.

"Now you mention it," said Alyson, rising, "a walk in the fresh air is just what I need."

"The hounds too," I added. "We'll take them."

Just the word "hounds" was enough to propel the dogs to their feet.

Before long, with cloaks, gloves, and clogs over our soft boots, we were trudging about the grounds. Hereward, Wake, and two puppies we'd kept, part of a fourth litter who'd grown fast, came with us, fanning out, snuffling and exploring, glad to be outdoors. The hoofprints of the horse of yet another creditor were stark in the snow.

We walked in silence, watching the dogs, waving to Milda and Rag as they returned to the house, their breath escaping in torrents of white mist. The blacksmith's shed gave us a welcome blast of warmth and we slowed our pace to enjoy it. Inside, we could see Master Ironside's huge silhouette against the flames as he plunged a piece of molten metal into water, his leather-aproned apprentice beside him. Almost immediately, they were hidden by steam.

We continued, coming upon another of the servants, a tall man with thin brown hair and stooped shoulders, chopping wood in a corner of the courtyard and moaning as pain shot up his cold arms. Drew and Arnold, a pair of young men who had six teeth between them, most lost in brawls, were raking up horseshit in the barn, whistling and shouting insults to each other in jest. Drew was as short and burly as Arnold was tall and lanky. Upon spying us, they stopped, doffed their caps—Drew exposing his already balding head and Arnold his mop of pale curls—and leaned on their rakes, curious to see us outside. Neither had family to speak of, just each other. We'd barely passed from sight when we heard them discussing the state of our minds. As far as they were concerned, we must be loonmad to be out in the weather when we could be in the warm solar.

Once beyond the courtyard, we set out toward the nearest of the drystone fences that marked the boundary between the grounds of the lodge and the pastures. Before us the land rose to the west, a cluster of charcoal trunks at the crest of the hill the only color against the snow. Even the sheep were hard to see, but they were there, huddled beneath the trees, released from the barn for a brief time to forage and move about. A servant named Wy, who was training one of the other pups that had come to us, a big young hound named Titan, was responsible for herding them. Wy was a slight, shy man with a terrible stutter, a pronounced limp, and scars on his hands from where the knife had cut him when he was first learning to shear. He was good with all the animals. Patient. Gentle. Mistress Emmaline said he preferred the company of beasts to folk. They never mocked his speech or asked why he limped. Milda heard that when he was younger, a group of boys beat him badly, jumping on his leg and breaking it. If it hadn't been for Drew and Arnold pulling him out of the ditch into which he'd been thrown and taking him to the barber in Bath to have the bone set, he might have died. The three had been close ever since. Drew and Arnold would not hear a word said against Wy, and were always watching out for him. I liked them a great deal for that.

To the east, the land was flat, a huge expanse of snow broken only by drystone walls. Underneath the thick blanket lay a mix of pasture and the fields of the villeins. Men and women were abroad even today, shoveling the snow, trying to expose the topsoil. A few children tagged along, one throwing a stick for a rangy dog that bounded through the drifts, shaking its coat every time it returned to the child's feet. Laughter and voices carried. The cottages were dark blots on the landscape, their coated roofs the only exception, gray smoke spiraling skyward. There were more houses without smoke to identify them. In the past months, once the harvest had been brought in, and excess stock slaughtered at Martinmas, the occupants had abandoned them. One day they were there, the next they were gone. Rents were owed, tithes too. My heart sank upon seeing them empty. At least four families had gone, two with small children. Not that I blamed them, not when the land they'd been given was so meager and the expectations of their landlord so great. Mayhap, just mayhap, if I trod carefully, I could change that. Papa's words from so long ago echoed. *"Of men, the best and wisest don't care who has control over what or who in the world."*

What I could do with all this if I had control. If I had a say.

To the southeast, the hills dipped into a shallow valley, the church spires of Bath spindly fingertips pointing heavenward. A mixture of thick smoke and mist hovered over the town, marking its location the way a shingle does a shop. It was reassuring to know that a short ride away, there were people, trade, markets, Father Elias. Over the last few months, my reception in the town had been a great deal more welcoming as people understood I was working hard to pay off Turbet's debts. If only I could prevent him from incurring more, we might actually inch into profit one day.

I looked out over the landscape, inhaling the clean, almost metallic smell of the snow, and listened to the snuffles and happy barks of the hounds. Mayhap, there was a way. It was cruel, it was dangerous too, but if something bad achieved something good, was it a sin? Was it evil?

Alyson leaned against the stone wall and released a long sigh.

I rested next to her. "You were right. I've been thinking—"

"God help us," she said, crossing herself.

I elbowed her in the ribs. "I've been thinking," I repeated. "I might have found a way to stop Turbet running up more debt and being so free with our inheritance. What's left of it. Mismanaging the tenants and so on." I nodded in the direction of the empty cottages and thought of the wool contracts. "Racking up more and more debt."

"Isn't it too late for that?" she asked, shielding her eyes with her hands as she surveyed the area. Even though there was no sun, the snow gave off a powerful glare.

"Mayhap. But for all that Turbet's a profligate of the highest order, he's not making the sort of money he needs to maintain his lifestyle. At least, he isn't if this—" my arm encompassed the land, "and his debtors are anything to go by."

"You know they are," said Alyson. "And to be blunt, Eleanor, I'm looking forward to just once going into town and not having some poor sod run up to us with a weepy story about how your husband owes them money."

"Me too," I sighed.

"Milda told me the cordwainer *and* the grocer are refusing to serve us until the last bill's paid," said Alyson dourly, examining the thin leather of her boots.

I looked down at my worn clogs. "Aye. They're not the only ones. The miller and fishmonger said the same. In starting to pay off Turbet's debts with the little coin I keep aside from weaving, I've made matters worse. There's now an expectation they'll all be paid before we can purchase anything else or ask for credit again."

"Have you told Turbet?"

I gave a dry bark of laughter. It echoed. "I've tried. But you know how he is. Things are so bad, even Jermyn's tried to make him see sense. Mistress Emmaline. Father Elias. Turbet refuses to listen. Says it will all be fine once summer comes and the harvest is done and the wool sold. What he actually means is when the rest of the contract money is paid."

Alyson made a harrumphing sound. "That's months away."

"Exactly. And there's no guarantees even then. Not after what he did last year, buying those bloody northern sheep. The flock's reduced, the condition of their coats is not known. He sold those alien merchants an unknown quantity and quality. Worse, a false promise. And look at the tenants' lands. Turbet made them plant all their strips instead of leaving every third one fallow. What if the wheat's diseased? What if the rains are like they were a few years ago? The villeins have nothing to fall back on."

"He's a fool." Alyson screwed up her eyes. "He's unable to plan for more than his next fine paltock, fur, barrel of wine, or ham hock."

I clasped my hands together. "I tried to tell him that." I touched my breast. "But what would I know? You've heard him; doesn't even matter the evidence is before his eyes, if I say it, then it's foolish. I don't know what I'm talking about."

"Pa didn't feel that way," said Alyson quietly.

A wave of longing washed over me. "He did not." I kicked the snow about with my clog. One of the pups paused in her digging and cocked her head to watch me.

I continued wistfully. "As long as my husband listens to the likes of alien merchants, never mind bloody Kenton Haveton and that fop, Master Kit, who all agree women are wicked, stupid, and prone to playing men false with all our wiles, he'll not give consideration to anything I say." My hand described a broad arc. "Certainly not about this."

"Then how can you ever hope to make a difference?" asked Alyson, watching the hounds galivant about.

I gave a grim smile. "By giving him no choice but to listen—to listen and do exactly as I say. After all, it really doesn't matter who's in control, does it? So long as the result benefits everyone."

Alyson slowly turned to face me, her expression doubtful. "Really? That's what you've been thinking about? That's your words of wisdom?"

I laughed. It was genuine. "Nay, not mine, but Papa's or, rather, someone called Toll-a-me. He believed it didn't matter which sex is in charge, as long as good is done in the world."

"Was he a eunuch?"

I laughed harder. "Mayhap." My laughter died. "But if I can gain control over everything, including paying off debts properly, then we might be able to make something of this. I mean, look at what's here, Alyson. There's so much land, fine land, and that's before you include ours. Yet it's being mismanaged. The house too." I turned and leaned back against the wall, facing it. Alyson did likewise. The lodge looked rather imposing with its two stories and chimneys. "We could do so much. We just need to be considered, thrifty. All I need is for Turbet to give me authority to make changes, even for a while . . ."

Alyson frowned. I could tell she wasn't convinced. "And young Gaunt there," she said, pointing to the larger of the pups, who was busy chasing his tail, "might transform into a dragon." She spun back around and rested her elbows on the wall. "How, in God's name, do you propose to make this miracle occur? How are you ever going to make Turbet Gerrish listen to you, a hapless, hopeless woman?"

"Like this," I said, and there by the drystone wall that separated the pasture and villeins' lands from the lodge grounds, with no one but the hounds, the sheep, the wind, and dazzling light to hear us, I outlined my plan.

SIXTEEN

———◆———

Laverna Lodge
The Year of Our Lord 1371
In the forty-fifth year of the reign of Edward III

Three nights later, I put my plan into action. I knocked on my husband's bedroom door, took a deep breath, and entered.

Turbet didn't acknowledge me. Seated on a chair near the window, a blanket over his lap and another around his shoulders, he was reading. A candle flickered on the table before him and a few melted in sconces on the walls. Every time I came to his room (which wasn't often), I was overwhelmed by the tapestries. Every single one depicted knights bearing down on distressed naked maidens, swords drawn. They froze my blood. Sweet Jesu. Imagine going to sleep with those images in your head. Mayhap, that's the kind of sport my husband enjoyed; I wouldn't know as he never drew his sword from its sheath in my presence. I shuddered, closed the door, and joined him.

A goblet in one hand, Turbet's other sat atop a document unfurled in his lap. His gaze was fixed outside. Snow brushed against the mullioned window, its gentle touch a beckoning whisper. Behind him was the huge bed, the curtains drawn to keep in any warmth. An empty pallet was made up beside it. Good, Nicholas wasn't there.

I'd almost reached his side when he spoke. "I don't recall summoning you." Wine stained his lips, made his words thick. He'd consumed a few. Whether this would work in my favor, I'd soon learn.

"You did not, sir. But I need to speak with you."

"Well," he said, putting his goblet down, winding up the document and flinging it on the table. It struck the top, rolled a few times then came to a halt against the jug. "I don't *need* to speak to you. And I certainly don't want to hear you prate. Begone." Without even looking in my direction, he flicked his fingers.

Heat rose up my neck, ignited in my chest.

I raised my voice. "I'm not certain, sir, who it is you think you're addressing, but I'm your wife and you *will* hear what I have to say." I stood behind the chair opposite, gripping the top.

"I don't care for your tone," he said loudly. "Out, I say. You're not wanted."

"Oh, you've made that more than evident from the moment we married. To be exact—" I paused, "since our wedding night."

His top lip curled in a snarl. "And whose fault was that, eh?"

"As I recall, you were the one who had difficulty ah . . . how shall I put it, standing to attention." His eyelids fluttered. "Fulk Bigod never had such problems and he was older than you by at least ten years." My heart was slamming against my ribs, I was standing on my tiptoes, ready to flee.

"*You* dare to say such things to *me*?" He began to rise from his seat then changed his mind. I wasn't worth it. "The reason I couldn't . . . I didn't . . ." he searched for words, spit gathered in the corner of his mouth, "was because I find you physically repulsive—" His hard eyes met my steady gaze. "And your freckles abhorrent."

If he thought his words would hurt, then he was mistaken. Not only had I heard them before, I knew they weren't true. I'd caught the looks he gave me when he thought I wasn't watching. I knew he'd told Fulk on many occasions he was fortunate to have such a pretty and willing wife. The men he invited to the house made it clear they found me desirable. The only exception was Mervyn Slynge, but his ward, the obnoxious Kit, made up for that. Why, every time I saw him he undressed me with his eyes. Lest you think me vain, I knew I wasn't everyone's mazer of ale, but I also suspected my husband was insulting me to mask his own failings. Part of me felt pity, part of me felt fury I was cheated of my wifely rights, the comfort and pleasure of sex. But this wasn't the moment to be thinking about that. It was the last thing I wanted from this man.

With a sneer, his eyes raked me from top to toe. "Why, you're covered in the huckery things." His wrist flipped in the direction of my breasts. "They're all over your chest, your great heavy nugs—why, a babe would crawl over iron nails to escape from those things. They're like overstuffed cushions and just as likely to suffocate any soul who comes near them."

I curled my hands into fists at my side. I wouldn't bury them beneath my arms, hide the bosoms he dreaded, as much as I wanted to. Instead, I thrust them forward.

"They're even on your quoniam, I'm sure. Marks of the devil, placed there to sap a man's seed, his desire." He began to make dark, hollow sounds that might have been laughs. They ceased as quickly as they began. "If I couldn't perform, the fault's not mine, but yours, you Satan-sent daughter of a whore-son."

His lungs were spent bellows as he wheezed and puffed, staring at me, waiting for me to collapse under the weight of his contempt. When had he become so very old? So very cruel?

I let the torrent wash over me and, instead, leaned over the chair so my heavy nugs swung, and exposed my gapped teeth by giving him a huge smile. Even if Turbet Gerrish hated my body, it had afforded my first husband and me much joy.

I willed my heart to cease its wild percussions, my breathing to slow.

Turbet grabbed his goblet and sank further into his seat.

Below, the sounds of the house continued. Low voices, footsteps, a shout. A door closed, another opened. Wind whistled through the window, making the candle gutter before it took hold again. A strong flame, firm. A trickle of sweat made its way from the corner of my brow, down my neck, and disappeared beneath my shift. I held my ground; watched my husband. His brows knitted, his hooded eyes roved back and forth, back and forth from window to table, to his lap, with a mere flash in my direction. Without a nightcap I could see how thin the hair on his head had become, his scalp gleaming. It made him look frail. Aye, weak. Easy to control . . . I knew this was what his first wife had done—dominated him and the household, forcing him to cede to her will through the withholding of not just sexual favors, but money, his children's affections, hers. It had been a savage thing to do, whatever her reasoning, but that didn't give him the right to inflict the same punishment upon me. Nor was it an excuse for me to deploy her tactics to have my way. But since my queynte didn't work as it had with Fulk, I wasn't left with much choice. I inhaled and prepared to go into battle.

Before I could, he spoke. "You forced me to say that. You wouldn't leave when I insisted. But there it is, you have the truth. I find you—"

"I know," I said, walking around the chair and sitting down. "I know." I clasped my hands in my lap. I was afraid if I didn't, I'd lean over and punch him in the face. "I'm not deaf. I heard you clearly along with the rest of the household. You've said it before. Many times. Lest you're forgetting, I'm also an ugly little bitch. It's not slipped my memory."

Did he flinch?

"I'll have you know," I said softly, "I've been called worse."

(Just for the record, I hadn't—not then.)

He glanced at me.

"They're just words." (I was yet to learn the power they had to inflict injury—The Poet taught me that.) "But none of that matters," I continued. "And nothing you say, no crude insults or *unkind* words, will prevent me from speaking tonight. All I ask is that you listen very carefully."

He released a long, weary sigh, drained his goblet, then quickly refilled it. He didn't offer me any.

"You're a stubborn bitch, aren't you? I knew that already, of course. Fulk used to say much the same, only he found it endearing."

My heart swelled.

"Funny, I thought I might too," said Turbet wearily. "Very well. If it's the only way I can get you to quit my sight, have your bloody say and leave."

Somewhere in the house, something was dropped, the sound reverberated. A hound barked and the others joined. There was a scurry of feet, low voices, something being dragged, then silence. I said two Ave Marias in my head and, just when I thought my husband's patience would expire, began.

"I know you killed Fulk Bigod."

There was a beat. Turbet blinked, then sat bolt upright. "I *what*? Wait. What did you say?"

"I said," speaking coldly, "I know you murdered Fulk."

Honestly, the look on his face was beyond priceless.

"*Murdered* him? Are you mad, woman?"

"Aye, mad, bad, *and* ugly, ask my husband. God's truth, I know you're responsible for Fulk's death and nothing you or anyone else says will persuade me otherwise."

It was the longest he'd ever held my gaze. Then he drank. When he'd wiped his mouth, he began to shake his head. "I'd nothing to do with your late husband's death and you know it. You're *non compos mentis*. Evil spirits have deprived you of your senses. Thank God and all the saints I never sarded you lest a child result."

"I'm in perfect health, thank you, husband, and my mind is sound. I think when I agreed to marry you, it was a little unhinged. That's why it's taken until now to know that what I suspected all along is true: you killed Fulk."

"Repeating it over and over doesn't make it so, woman. But, alright, I'll play your little game. Tell me how I killed him."

"By gifting him with a fur that was infected with pestilence."

"*What?*"

"Aye. The moment my husband was covered with the fur you brought to the house, he sickened. He died swiftly and painfully, thus leaving his widow and her inheritance at your disposal. Those lands you'd been trying to acquire, which he refused to sell, were in your grasp. It was a cunning, wicked plan but it worked."

His jaw dropped, he started forward in the chair, his goblet forgotten. He closed his eyes and massaged his temples. He opened one eye, then the other. "You're really quite mad, aren't you?"

He pulled the blankets around his shoulders and tucked another around his legs. "In the morning, I'll have Jermyn make arrangements for you to be sent to St. Bethlehem's in London. You'll be better off there. We all will."

Ignoring his threat, I continued. "You went out of your way to purchase a fur that arrived on a vessel from Kaffa, where the pestilence was raging. You placed it among the other cloths you'd imported and delivered it straight to our door. Straight to my husband. You never touched the fur—or the other cloth for that matter, not even when they were unloaded in Bath. I know, I asked."

"Why would I touch it? Touch them? There's no reason. I've servants to do that for me. The carter—" He pressed his lips together as he remembered. The carter had died. "It was God's will, a great misfortune." His voice quivered, his fingers curled around the edges of the blanket.

"Not only did you kill my husband, but you infected at least four other families in Bath, causing the deaths of thirteen people. Not that you cared; you got what you wanted. Fulk's land and sheep to sell and thus maintain your extravagance—as anyone in town will admit, you didn't use it to pay your debts."

Turbet stared at me for a long, long time. "What utter rubbish." He began to chuckle. "Oh. My. They're going to love you in Bedlam. You do know that people pay to stare at the loons through the gates each day? What entertainment you'll provide. Why, I'd pay a groat to listen to your fabulations. Your friend Geoffrey must be proud." His laughter died suddenly. He poured more wine, regarding me with amusement over the rim of his goblet. "You stupid little fool. I've never heard anything so ridiculous in all my life!"

I stood, smoothing my shift, pressing it into the contours of my body. I fetched another goblet and helped myself to the jug. I took a long draught. It was good.

"Neither have I," I said and sat back down.

Ready to contest, to argue further, Turbet was momentarily lost for words. "Did I hear alright? You *admit* this is nonsense."

"Aye, I do. It's a complete and utter fabrication. To you. But, imag-

ine this, dear husband. Tonight, the moment I leave this room, I start
to tell the servants this version. I whisper in Jermyn's ear, Milda's, the
blacksmith's, all of the household, including your unhappy tenants."

Turbet sat up straight. "I won't allow it. I'll call for Jermyn this
moment and have you gagged."

I shrugged. "Matters not what you do. Word will still escape. Do
you think I've kept this to myself?"

His eyes bulged, his cheeks paled.

"All too soon," I went on, lowering my voice, making it sinister,
"all of Bath will know what I'm accusing you of. How long before your fine friends, Master Mervyn, the bishop, and your fellow
merchants, learn what you've done? Master Kenton? Then where
will your reputation be, husband? You'll be known as a levereter—
corrupt to the core. Do you think people will keep giving you
credit, buying your wool, your cloth, if there's even a whisper of
doubt attached to it? If someone is just a tiny bit anxious that what
they're buying might, just might, be infected not only with pestilence but with the sins of the man who used such a method to
dispatch his enemies?"

"Enemies? But Fulk wasn't my enemy, nor those poor souls who
died from the sickness. I don't have any enemies."

"Everyone has enemies, husband," I said carefully. "Especially
those who work hard to cultivate the esteem of others but never repay them—in coin or kind. Fancy dinners and promises only go so
far—ask the King, ask the princes. And what about your arrangement with the monks and other merchants? What if a whisper of
your business with Master Kenton or the Hollander merchants was
to escape? What would the guild do to you, your business? Other
merchants? What damage would such knowledge do to your standing then?"

Turbet shook his head in horror. "Dear God. I've married a hedge-
born Jezebel." He stared about in dismay, his cheeks ashen, his eyes
sunken in the half-light. "No one's going to believe you," he said
hoarsely.

I leaned back in my chair and put on my best smirk. "Oh, husband, I thought you understood. I don't need anyone to *believe* me.

I just need them to *listen*, something you've failed to do for a long time."

Turbet was listening now. I could almost hear the whirring of his mind as he calculated the damage such a rumor would do. Whether it was true or not, made not a whit of difference. To a man who prided himself on his reputation, who did everything in his power to maintain a facade of wealth, business acumen, congeniality, popularity, this would be a death knell.

His hands began to shake. "This . . . this . . . it would ruin you as well."

"What do I care about my position? What is it, anyhow? I'm hardly a wife. You keep reminding me I'm nothing."

"I . . . I can change that."

"Even though you find me physically repulsive?"

"I didn't mean it that way, I—"

"I don't care whether you did or not."

"Wife, *Eleanor*, I want—"

I held up my hand to prevent him saying more. "I don't care what *you* want, Turbet Gerrish. It's my turn to tell you what *I* want, what you must do if you don't want this nasty rumor to spread . . . like a personal pestilence." I lowered my hand.

"Go on."

Better than "begone."

"You're to give me control of not only the household, but all your business interests that involve the sheep, pastures, villeins, and their lands."

His eyes became so round, I thought they would roll out his head. "Surely, you jest? *You*? The household is already yours, the villeins, I can concede, but the sheep? By them you mean wool production."

"I do."

"Never!" he exclaimed, flinging himself backward in his chair, fist thumping the arm. "Why, it's men's business, *my* business. It's what *I* do. I can't have a woman running my affairs. I'd be a laughing stock. I'd be seen as a loiter-sack, a weak man who allows his woman unnatural authority." He heaved himself out of the chair, the blankets pooling in a heap on the floor.

He began to pace, words tripping out of his mouth.

I had to put a stop to this. I leaped up and grabbed a hold of his arm, wrenching him around to face me. "I haven't finished."

"Oh, I think you have."

"No one can call you a cumberworld or whatever else you're imagining if they remain ignorant of our arrangement."

He halted.

"If they don't know I'm managing your affairs, how can they say anything? Cease your pacing. Sit. Listen to me, Turbet Gerrish." I led him back to the chair, poured him another drink, pushed it into his hand. I piled the blankets over him once more, fussing like a real wife, as if there was affection when facts were, I didn't want him so cold he couldn't focus. I knelt before him, my hands gripping either side of the chair. He was a captive audience. "How do you think Fulk's fortunes improved once he married me?"

Turbet gave a half-shrug. "I never asked . . ."

"It was *me*. I was the one who advised him about increasing the flock, hiring extra servants so I might weave. It was me who trained the others, just as I am now. And I was doing it well before Fulk's illness. But I can do so much more. Nay. Your task is to listen," I said sternly, when he tried to interrupt. "I know you've sold my land to the Abbey, well, most of it, that you lease other parts and demand the villeins do boon-work. But, just as you have with your lands, you haven't given them enough to be self-sufficient, you've given too much over to pasture. Aye, I know you intended the villeins would card and spin and maintain our wool supplies, but that idea went to hell in a handbasket when they up and left, didn't it?"

He had the grace to look uncomfortable.

"Increasing the size of the flock the way you did, without selecting which sheep to mix with those we already had, brought disease. We've lost almost half. Thus the villeins were not only deprived of land they needed to grow food, they lost the extra income from spinning fleeces as well.

"What did you do about that? Instead of making concessions so they remained, cultivating and strengthening the sheep we kept healthy—and that was only because I insisted they be kept apart—

you sold more land to buy more sheep, sheep that have a poor-quality coat which no one wants to buy."

"Aye, but in time, with inter-breeding, the quality will improve. The flock will be fine."

"The flock might be, eventually, but what about your tenants? *My* tenants? Those who haven't left to seek better conditions? They're hungry and sick. Do you know they've been out working the fields in the snow? Aye, shoveling it away so they might till the soil, tend whatever they've planted. Do you think they'll remain once the snows melt and they find the crop has failed? Nay. They'll be off to find a better master. Somewhere they can at least earn a living. It isn't hard these days. Masters are prepared to pay well for good laborers. How will you maintain your lands when there's no one left to work them? How will you make money when you've been forced to sell all you own?"

I didn't add, all I own as well.

Turbet considered my words, then pouted. "And what would you have me do, eh?"

I sighed. How could he not see what to me was so obvious?

"What you should have been doing in the first place: buying wool from the markets, from the goddamn monks if you have to, and giving it to the villeins to spin on our behalf. Alyson and the others can weave it. As can I. In the short term, we can raise the prices of our cloth to cover the cost of buying in and still make profit. As it is, we're adding to our debts, watching any earnings being pissed against the wall." I hefted the jug. "After it has been drunk."

I sat back on my haunches.

"Unless you let me make some much-needed changes, Turbet Gerrish, cede control to me, I swear on God's bones I will take us all down. At least if I do it, it will happen quickly instead of the long drawn-out way you're going about it. At least my way will only impact those it deserves to."

"I don't deserve it," he whimpered.

I could barely stand the sight of him. How could I have once thought this man husband material? He wasn't worthy to lick Fulk's boots, covered in cow shit and all.

I rose. "Think on what I've said, Turbet. I'll give you until the morrow. Remember, no one need ever know it's me behind the decisions. It will appear as if it's all you. Your reputation won't be harmed, I assure you."

"Won't it?" he asked. "Seems to me whichever way I decide, it is. If not my reputation, then my life. What man gives his wife authority?"

I was heading to the door when he spoke. I turned. "A man who has no choice."

SEVENTEEN

Laverna Lodge and Bath
The Years of Our Lord 1371 to 1375
In the forty-fifth to the forty-ninth years of the reign of Edward III

*O*ver the following years, much to the amazement of everyone in Bath and the surrounding villages, but mostly Turbet Gerrish, my husband's fortunes underwent a dramatic reversal. The only ones not surprised were myself, Alyson, Milda, and Master Geoffrey.

The morning after I gave Turbet my ultimatum, he summoned me to his office and ceded control to me. The proviso that no one knew was emphasized, with the intention we revisit the arrangement within the year. I agreed.

And so with my husband's blessing—oh alright, that's an exaggeration—reluctant cooperation, I began to make changes. The only thing I hadn't considered was that in order to make it work, Jermyn had to be informed.

The first time I went to see the steward and told him to move the foldcourses and check the boundaries marking the villeins' properties, he had conniptions.

"I'm sorry, mistress, but until the master tells me, I'm not doing nothing. I don't take orders from a woman, I don't care who she's married to."

I almost stamped my feet in frustration. "I'm speaking with your master's voice," I insisted.

"Well, I'm not hearing it," the stubborn goat replied. He even had the gall to put his fingers in his ears.

There was no help for it, I dragged Turbet from where he was still sulking, and demanded he tell Jermyn that he was not only to obey my orders, but keep me abreast of the lodge's affairs—the tenants' rents, tithes, sheep losses, wool prices, markets, broggers' offers, merchants as well.

Jermyn fell into his chair when the words were dragged from Turbet. I swear his face went a sickly shade of yellow. I poured him wine and waited until he'd drunk it all.

After that rocky start, over the years Jermyn and I developed a workable relationship. Though he doubted my judgment to begin with, insisting upon checking everything I said with Turbet. (I even caught my husband undermining me a couple of times. When he did, I simply uttered the word "fur"—I even sang it loudly on one occasion—regardless of who was within earshot and that quickly put a stop to his efforts.) Over time, once Jermyn saw the results, his initial reserve turned into a grudging respect.

One of the first things I embarked upon was suspension of the villeins' tithes. If they didn't have enough to feed themselves, how could anyone expect them to give up a tenth of their grain, vegetables, livestock, and anything else they'd grown to the church? Or to us? That caused a stand-up row with Jermyn, but I had my way and in doing so gained the eternal gratitude and loyalty of our tenants. When summer arrived, only one family left to live elsewhere, but three more came to replace those who'd gone (including a very handsome young man named Jon). By the following year, when word about the better conditions, extra land, and coin spread, we had full occupancy.

I ordered the boundaries between the villeins' plots be remeasured and marked, their ploughs repaired, and oxen bought and shared. We could also lease the beasts to the Abbey's tenants and even those at Noke Manor. The same with ploughs and other farming equipment. I asked Master Ironside to make tools that could be shared among the tenants—scythes, hammers, shovels, spare parts for the plough and such. With good equipment, it meant it was easier and quicker to work the land. I also insisted the foldcourses be moved across the tenants' fields, including those left fallow, so they might benefit from the sheep's droppings. The yield that summer was the best it had been in ages, and so a system began to develop.

Likewise, the flock, which had been badly reduced from the murrain, in addition to the effect on their coats when Turbet foolishly introduced a different breed, were separated. After a season, the thinner, coarser-coated sheep were sold, taken back north, where that breed of sheep thrived. With the money made, we were able to buy more of the curly-haired type preferred by the alien merchants. The first year, though we were obliged to meet the contract my husband made with the Hollanders, we kept aside a small portion to sell ourselves. Through Father Elias, I wrote to Geoffrey to see if he could use his connections and recommend any alien merchants who weren't swindlers to purchase some. We received a good price when one buyer from Flanders, and another from Genoa, began to haggle.

With the money received, we bought more sheep, allowing some to remain on the tenants' land and for them to benefit from their milk. The wool we'd kept aside was spun into thread, employing the female villeins to spin as well. While Alyson, Hob, Rag, and Aggy weaved our thread, I trained some of the cottagers and even a couple of the young novices from the Abbey. It was a good skill to have and the pay would tide the villeins over in winter. There were some days when the Great Hall was more like a weavers' workshop, it was so full of carders, spinners, and clicking and clacking looms, women and men chatting and even, at times, singing.

Fortunately, the monks and the guild never found out about either the contract my husband made or the fact we were selling our cloth or, if they did, they were too worried about making enemies of the alien merchants who we were all beginning to rely upon to raise the matter. What's that saying Papa was fond of? The enemy of my enemy is my friend.

In just over two years, we'd paid almost all of Turbet's debts, and without sacrificing too much of our quality of life. Some of the servants left. Two of the men joined the army to fight in France. After they left, I went into Bath specially to hunt down young Peter, the lad who'd been unable to control Hereward and Wake the night I arrived at the lodge. A small lad of nine, he was miserable working at a local tannery. Once he overcame his disbelief I was actually offering him a place in the household, one that meant he never had to dip his hands in piss again, he was grateful. I put him to work in the house. He even managed to make friends with Hereward, Wake, and the constant brood of pups.

A couple of the female servants married. Rather than hire live-in servants to replace them, I asked the mother of one of the cottagers, Goody Babelot, a grandmother nine times over with a wealth of stories and experience, to come in daily and help in the kitchen and assist Mistress Emmeline about the house. She also happened to be an experienced spinner.

Don't think for a moment every year was good. There were frosts that killed the crops; wild dogs tore into the sheep, and that was the same year the murrain returned and decimated one-third of them. We'd only just shorn them, so while we gained from their wool, we lost the beasts. It was a horrible way for them to die, and I confess, I wept as the men dug a huge pit for the carcasses. The new tenant, Master Jon, threw an arm over my shoulders, an action that caused a few brows to raise and, God forgive me, my heart to quicken.

"Be alright, mistress. They be with God now."

If heaven was one big pasture where sheep frolicked for eternity, what would they do with all that wool?

"Make gowns for the angels, of course," said Alyson, when I posed the question. We laughed at the notion. From then on, every time we went to church, we'd find an image of an angel on the walls or in the brilliant windows and try to guess which breed of sheep was responsible for their gown.

Then there was the year summer was never-ending and so very dry and hot. I was twenty-two. Crops withered in the ground, animals perished and their corpses rotted where they fell. The harvest was scant and folk went hungry. They became sick as well. Alyson fell ill for a time, coughing and spewing, her flesh aflame and sweaty. I nursed her carefully and, after a week or so, she came good. I went to church to thank the Lord.

That was also the year Mistress Emmeline died. It was midsummer. She started vomiting, shitting herself, and was unable to drink even a small ale. Goody Babelot and Milda made special potions for her, but to no avail.

Hereward and Wake, after giving us many years of joy, also died. One day apart. I swear they couldn't live without each other. I cried more over their deaths than I did Fulk's. After that, I imagined them in heaven rounding up the sheep, sitting at Jesus's feet the way they used to mine, scratching their fleas so hard they made heaven's foundations shake. I liked that idea. They left behind their grandchildren for us to remember them by. I visited their graves by the drystone wall on occasion, just to say hello.

Mayhap, God smiled upon what we were doing, mayhap, Fortuna decided it was time my fortunes rose, but slowly, the wheel turned and we gained more than we lost.

The following spring, just as rumors of plague in the north reached us, the sheep were shorn and the wool washed and dried. That summer, we spun the wool into thread, and welcomed women from nearby villages, those too old or young to work the fields and whoever else could turn a distaff and work a spindle, to join us. It was a merry sight that would attract the attention of the workers when they had cause to visit the barn or lodge. When Master Jon arrived, I'd oft spy him leaning against a doorway, his big arms folded across his brawny chest, chewing a piece of straw, his eyes drifting toward me. I grew a little clumsy under his gaze, a bit warm. Alyson would nudge me and nod in his direction.

"Someone'd like you to thread his needle, hen," she'd chuckle.

When Turbet happened to be home, I'd sometimes see him standing in the main doorway of the Great Hall. If he noticed Master Jon, he didn't say, mayhap because Jon would make himself scarce. The women would curtsey and call out blessings to Turbet. After all, here was their generous master who gave them work and allowed them to contribute to their families. Gracious, he would wave and sometimes even smile and doff his hat.

"You be a lucky one, my lady," the women would say, bestowing knowing looks. I accepted them with a smile. Alyson would snigger. "If only they knew," she'd murmur.

By midsummer, the servants and tenants gathered fruit, began hay-mowing, weeding (we had terrible problems with dock, chicory, and marigolds), then started their threshing, reaping, and gleaning. We provided ale and food for the workers doing the boon-work on our behalf and for those we'd hired to get the crops harvested. Watching how much harder those who were being paid worked compared to those who were obliged, I decided to offer pay to our villeins as well. Only a small amount, mind, but the difference it made to their willingness was remarkable. Jermyn objected strongly and took my decision to Turbet. Much to my complete astonishment, Turbet told Jermyn to do what I said.

I made sure to thank Turbet—not that he had a choice, but I liked to let him think he did.

Never again did I expect the villeins to work for nothing, not when they attended to their tasks so well. But it was more than that. Conversations over dinner with the likes of Master Slynge, who kept his ear to the ground, and other landowners in the area, indicated things had changed. With each passing year, fewer tenants were doing boon-work for their lords, preferring to be paid cash. Papa always said if lords weren't careful to look after their own tenants, then there would be others who would. Labor was scarce, and far better to pay those already leasing the land to work the fields than hire outsiders who weren't invested—especially those who had fled the plague-ravaged northern counties. It made sense and, in the end, paid off in ways that cannot be quantified.

On the last day of the harvest that summer, Lammas to be exact, after the final cart laden with corn was driven into the barn, a sheaf laid ceremonially atop, the sun was low in the golden sky, the birds were chirruping and floating in the warm breeze, the festivities began.

A huge bonfire blazed in the courtyard. Some of the tenants

brought their instruments and began to play. In the Great Hall, tables were laid with a veritable feast. Milda, Goody Babelot, and the new cook, a man named Henry Bacon, had been busy. There were roast chickens, capons, mutton dressed with vinegar, apples aplenty, pottages of barley and herbs, steaming loaves straight from the oven. Ale flowed and Turbet even brought out jugs of wine. Suspicious of fancy French drink, most of the villeins avoided it, preferring ale. Not so the servants, who knew Turbet kept a fine cellar.

That year, the mood was joyful, children, dogs, and even some startled chickens and pigs running underfoot as evening embraced us and the stars shone. The dancing grew wilder, the laughter louder, and singing began. Garlands of greenery and flowers were hastily made and flung around people's necks, placed on heads. Someone, I think Alyson, put one on mine and, as I danced, my veil slipped off and my hair came unbound. It tumbled well past my waist, whirling around, sticking to my hot face as I twirled and passed from one set of brawny arms to another.

Through the smoke and curtain of hair, Master Jon reached for me and drew me into his arms. My heart began to beat its own rhythm and my knees went weak. Sweet Mother Mary and all the saints, he was a lusty young man, with his golden hair falling over his face, those dark flashing eyes and teeth so white in his sun-brown face. I knew it was wrong to press myself into him, to squeeze the hand that held mine so tightly, enjoy how he pressed my bottom to his groin, but I couldn't help it. Venus rose and my quentye and every other part of me burned more than the bonfire around which we spun. When he danced me into the shadows and bent and kissed me, I responded. It had been so long . . .

The courtyard swam, the folk gallivanting about became devilish shapes, black and twisted against the flames. He released my lips and buried his face in my neck. "By God, you're a sweet piece. Such a temptation."

By God. Bigod.

As I shoved Jon away, laughing at his temerity, he threw back his head and chuckled deeply, winking.

I thought of Fulk, about the way he would hold me, love me. I ached. I wanted to pull Jon back, lift my skirts, and husbands be damned.

I took a step forward, when another pair of arms found me, and pulled me back into the light. A great cheer rose as Turbet Gerrish, my husband, drew me into the dance.

Startled, my first instinct was to pull away, but he held me firm—as firm as Jon had. In the firelight, his thin, gray hair glinted, his eyes were unreadable, but when they met mine, they didn't slide away.

With one arm around my waist, the other entwined about my fingers, we danced through and around the others, my skirts flying, my hair too. I was panting hard, wondering why Turbet had not only seen fit to join us, but taken hold of me. Had he seen me with Jon? Had he witnessed our wild kisses? He'd shown no interest in me, never done anything so bold.

I liked it.

When he kept hold of my hand after the dance ended, and pulled me away from the others, there were a few knowing shouts of encouragement and much laughter. When the music started again, he led me toward the side door and I didn't object. After all, was he not my husband? From there, we went up a narrow, winding staircase to his bedroom. Without a word, he shut the door and brought me to the bed, pushing me onto it.

Taken aback, before I knew it he flung himself down. Not on top, but lying next to me. Then, gently and with great clumsiness, he began to undo my tunic. I pushed away his fingers and did it myself, ordering him to do the same with his own clothes.

Half-expecting a protest, he grinned. Dear God, he shed ten years when he smiled, really smiled like that. I said as much.

His surprisingly gentle mouth met mine. "Don't talk," he said. "Just let me do this."

"Do what?"

"What I should have done long ago."

And he did.

It wasn't as good as being with Fulk, but it wasn't all bad either. At least his prick stayed hard, till it didn't.

When he'd finished and rolled away, keeping a hand on my thigh, I twisted so I could see his face.

"Well, my lord, you're full of surprises, aren't you?"

"Not half as much as you've turned out to be, wife."

I found a perverse pleasure in him calling me that. At least I truly was now his wife.

"Not so bad for an ugly little bitch, am I?"

He winced, his body stiffening. I leaned over and kissed his cheek to take the sting out of my rebuke.

"Aye, you're not, my hedge-born Jezebel, my Hadean Lilith," he sighed. "Is it some cruel cosmic joke, that all I had to do to truly be the master of my domain was surrender the role to you? Little did I suspect that a brogger's child, a former servant and goodwife, would possess such know-how."

For once in my life, I remained silent. God be praised.

He let out a contented sigh, folded his arms behind his head, and stared at the ceiling. Outside, the celebrations continued, raucous and merry. Part of me wanted to rejoin them, but another part knew I had to remain. I tried to read Turbet's face in the moonlight, but it was inscrutable. All I could see was his straight nose, the rise and fall of his chest, the cobwebs of silver hair that veiled it.

"I can imagine God is having a good laugh," said Turbet finally. "Not just at me, but at all men."

Well, if not Him, I certainly was.

EIGHTEEN

Laverna Lodge and Bath
The Year of Our Lord 1377
In the fifty-first and final year of the reign of Edward III

It didn't take long for me to work out why my lord had been so eager to swive me that Lammas. It wasn't that he'd suddenly had his eyes opened to my beauty, as I hoped, or found me desirable. It was the attention of other men. Turbet had a jealous streak as wide as the London Road. Upon seeing lusty Master Jon fancied me, he thought to stake his claim—or claim his stake as may be. In other words, it wasn't until other men wanted what was rightfully his, handled his property, that he did too. Not that I'm complaining. Once I worked this out, I used it to my advantage as often as I could, and not just when my passions needed dousing.

Over the following years, I found that when I responded to the ogling, suggestive murmurs, caresses, and offers of other men, or spoke of how these overtures made me feel, my husband would bestow upon me a variety of gifts—from a lovely bolt of silk, to colorful ribbons, a sparkling bracelet, or a fine pair of slippers. For allowing Mervyn Slynge's ward, Kit, to kiss me upon the lips three times in succession and squeeze my buttocks after dinner one evening, I was given a headdress that was the envy of the parish.

Why had it taken so long to discover this? First it was the power of my queynte, and now it was men's need to triumph over their own sex when it came to women. It was so damn simple. When I said as much to Alyson, she frowned.

"Alright for some. You attract men the way a flower does bees or the pieman dogs. No one wants my honey."

"That's not true," I objected. A number of men had tried to court Alyson, but she simply wasn't interested. Said she was happy where she was and who she was with—meaning me. I couldn't help but be flattered (and grateful), and while I wished her to know the love of a good man, they were in short supply. Truth be told, I was also afraid that should one come along, they might snatch her away, and then where would I be? I didn't encourage her to pursue her swains as much as I probably should have. Worse, I made a point of always trying to find fault with any who did step forward.

Was I selfish? Aye, I was. And one day, I would beg God's forgiveness.

Our fortunes continued to rise and our wool and cloth were in great demand. I was developing quite the reputation as a weaver, not that I deserved it. Those I'd trained outdid me. The best by far was Alyson. Not only was her weave tight and smooth, but she had a great eye for color. Alyson deserved all the kudos, but she was most content when I shone and she basked in my shade. Conceited wretch, I was content with that too.

Part of the reason I was happy to be lauded for weaving was because it meant no one paid too much attention to the other business I conducted—what by rights was Turbet's to manage. People still noticed, said it was only since I married Turbet that his wool sales had increased and his cloth was sought after. Likewise, the tenants sang his praises and, of course, what he owed was paid almost as fast as it accrued. I continued to be harried each time I ventured to Bath, but whereas once it had been to settle my husband's debts, now it was to make purchases.

Though I enjoyed the largesse of my husband—both in the gifts he gave and the various feasts he hosted, inviting his merchant colleagues and other acquaintances—I was quite thrifty and always made sure I kept coins aside—I never really trusted Turbet not to fall back into his old ways. I'd never forgotten how almost everything had been frittered away, and right beneath our noses. I didn't want to risk that ever happening again.

But of all the folk who marveled at Turbet's success and congratulated him upon it, there was one (apart from Jermyn) who knew the real reason. Master Mervyn Slynge revealed this one evening after we'd enjoyed a long and delicious repast in the Great Hall. I'd received a letter from Geoffrey that very morning. In it, he announced that his second child, Elizabeth, had become a novice at the Priory of St. Helen's. The rest was filled with excuses as to why he had to deny my request for aid in selling wool. You see, when he'd returned from Genoa a few years earlier, Geoffrey had been given a new post—that of Comptroller of the Wool Customs. Comptrollers were generally loathed, as they made sure the correct taxes were paid on whatever goods were exported. That Geoffrey should be responsible for this was both amusing and offended my sensibilities as a producer. Everyone knew the King and his lackeys (of which Geoffrey was now most assuredly one) granted the alien merchants licenses willy-nilly and gave them such extraordinary concessions when it came to excise that they paid a fraction of the rate home-grown English wool merchants were levied. No wonder Papa had encouraged Lady Clarice to entrust her wool to smugglers and thus evade taxes and port duties. Turbet had tried to get Fulk to rely on the same avenues. I'd considered doing this with ours as well but thought, mayhap, with Geoffrey in the role, I wouldn't have to . . . Would he turn a blind eye? Dismiss or lower our taxes? Record a lesser weight for our sacks so the duty wasn't so high?

Nay. He would not. Geoffrey was as honest as the day was long. No wonder the court appointed him. He was likely to make sure the Wool Collector—the man who operated in partnership with the Comptroller and was despised even more—didn't swindle the royal coffers any more than they already did.

Unsurprised that he had declined (and secretly filled with admiration), I was sitting in the solar, thinking over what Geoffrey had written and wondering what to write in reply (knowing Father Elias kept my friend abreast of what went on in Bath and at the lodge), when who should enter but Master Mervyn.

"Good sir." I went to rise, slightly annoyed my peace was disturbed. I'd drunk quite a bit at dinner and felt a megrim starting. "If it's my husband you seek, you'll find him in the office. I believe he's taken Masters Godfrey and Bevan there to show them his new seal."

Master Slynge waved for me to sit and, accepting a goblet of wine from one of the servants, dragged a chair closer. "It's not him I wish to speak to."

"Oh?" I looked about for his ever-present ward to find he was nowhere to be seen. Though a spoiled young man when I first met him, Kit had matured over the years into a fine-looking fellow, even if he still adopted airs and graces to which he had no right. "And why would that be?"

Mervyn sank into the seat, his eyes never leaving mine. Being accustomed to a husband who still had difficulty returning my gaze, I found it both refreshing and unnerving.

"How old are you now, Eleanor? Twenty-two? Twenty-three? Younger? I know you married Bigod while still a maid."

In every sense, I thought.

"I'm twenty-five . . ." I answered cautiously. What did my age have to do with anything?

"Excellent, excellent." He studied the room, his eyes alighting on the new arras I'd had made depicting a sylvan scene. There was also a lovely silver box and a burnished bowl atop the cabinet. He took in the new ornaments and I was pleased to see an expression of approval. Why I cared, I'm uncertain. Mayhap, an awareness of my humble beginnings, beginnings that I liked to think were no longer so apparent.

Finally, he faced me. "I've been meaning to speak to you for a while. Actually, what I wish to do is tender an apology."

"Apology? What for, sir?"

"You see, my dear—and this isn't easy for me to admit—I'm a

man who likes to think he's a good judge not only of character, but prospects. But, when it came to you, my judgment failed."

"You were blinded by natural male prejudice, sir," I said, smiling prettily.

Mervyn Slynge's eyes narrowed and I worried I'd gone too far. Then, he laughed. "You're right. I was too much of a bigot to believe a woman could possess a mind let alone a good head for business. But you, my dear, contradict everything I thought to be true."

I didn't want to say that if I contradicted it, then how many other women might? Either way, it made his premise false. "How have I accomplished such a remarkable concession, sir?"

He put his elbows on his knees. "I've known Turbet since he was in breeches and if there's one thing I can confidently say, it's that he lacks any sense for commerce. In fact, if he hadn't married well the first time, he'd be in hock right up to his neck. Instead of investing and trying to increase his wealth, the fool spent his wife's inheritance faster than the King does ransom money. It was good luck, not good sense, that anything was left. Even then, when he met you, he'd been living off goodwill and the largesse of acquaintances—" He tapped his chest to indicate he was one. He sighed. "But goodwill only goes so far, and when his offers of marriage to other well-endowed women came to naught, he set his sights closer to home. Frankly, I thought he'd lost his mind when he wed you. Why, your beginnings were very humble, regardless of the fact you inherited lands that abutted Turbet's and came with a decent flock. He was risking his reputation, his social standing, wedding so far beneath his station. But he was wiser than anyone knew. He saw in you what Fulk must have."

"Oh? And what might that be, sir?" My mind was racing. Do I deny everything and attribute all the decisions being made to Turbet as I'd promised?

"A cash cow. Or should it be, sheep?"

My eyes widened. The rude bastard. "I beg your pardon?" I said, my voice slightly shrill.

Master Mervyn chortled and held up his hand in a sign of peace. "Stay. Stay, good lady. I don't mean to offend, though I know the words do. But this is me you're talking with—"

Was I? Seemed to me he was the one doing all the prating.

"And I refuse to pretend. I'm too old for that. Have seen too much." He paused and took a long drink. "Turbet was in dire straits and doing everything he could to pretend otherwise. Then you, Mistress Business-Head, come into his life and turn his fortunes around. Why, the man who could scarce tell the difference between a wether and a weaner now has one of the finest flocks, is producing wool of such quality it's fought over by alien merchants, is weaving marvelous patterns, and, furthermore, has happy villeins who, unlike those on neighboring lands, remain put. This is not the work of Turbet Gerrish, nor his man, Jermyn, who I know does what his master tells him. Nay, my lady, this is down to the one thing that has changed in Turbet's life. This is down to *you*."

I should have objected.

"Nay. Do not insult me by pretending this isn't the case."

I wasn't.

"I'm no fool either. And that's why, I wish to offer *you* something—"

I held my breath.

"If ever you find yourself in need of an ally, someone whom you can rely upon to give you an honest opinion about a venture, a business decision, then I'm at your disposal."

I released my breath in a rush of disappointment. "I find this odd considering you've spent the last few years listening to others insult me." Never mind the last few minutes . . .

"Oh, my dear, it was nothing personal. Ask the others. They say the same about all women." He laughed at the expression on my face. "But whereas there are some who deserve their . . . opprobrium, you, my dear, don't. You're something entirely different. Just what, I don't know . . . Yet."

"I'm merely a wife." I lowered my eyes and tried to appear demure.

Master Mervyn stood. "Ha!" he said and drained his drink. "You may be a wife, but there's nothing *mere* about you." He went to leave, then changed his mind. "In fact, someone like you would be enough to convince me to venture into wedlock. At my age too. Mayhap. One day." He shuffled out of the room, pausing at the doorway. "Let me know if you ever become available."

Aye, I thought, and lambs might fly south.

I thought I was the only one privy to the conversation, one which I repeated to Alyson that very night, but I sometimes forget the Almighty is also listening, as is Fortuna. Though I dismissed Master Mervyn's offer as cup-shotten nonsense, knowing by then his predilection for young men, I should have understood that God the all Great and Powerful also has a mighty sense of humor.

Too soon, I was to feel its full force.

———◆———

Geoffrey didn't only write letters. He even came to visit on two occasions. The first was back in September 1374. The weather was still very warm, the ground dry. Alyson was abed with sickness, though improving. Some of the villeins were ill and two had even died. I hoped it was because they were elderly, though, when I went to their funerals, I was shocked to learn they were younger than Turbet.

But I was telling you about Geoffrey.

We spent the morning together, walking about the grounds, and I showed him the weavers busy in the Great Hall, the pastures, yellow stubble rather than green, but dotted with healthy looking sheep. As we wandered, we talked. Conversation was never a problem and I so enjoyed his company and hearing his news. He was comfortably ensconced in his London house, an apartment above Aldgate, one of the busier entrances to the city. From its windows, he could see people making their daily pilgrimage to and from the city, carting and carrying their wares, herding animals. Soldiers were oft escorting prisoners, while noblemen and women would ride out en route to their great estates. He could also see the river, and his office, which was at Wool Quay, was only a short stroll away. He invited me to come and visit one day. I said I would. I said a lot of things I meant back then.

I asked about his wife and children. When the old Queen died, Philippa had gone to serve John of Gaunt's new wife, Constance of Castile.

He shrugged. "I'm afraid I barely see them."

I stopped in my tracks. "What do you mean? Now that you're back in England, in London no less, I thought you and your family would be under the same roof. Philippa must have missed you greatly . . ."

The expression on his face told me all I needed to know. My heart tripped. "Philippa is accustomed to being her own woman," he said stiffly. "I'm sure you of all people understand."

Did I? I was hardly my own woman, I belonged to Turbet, and before him, Fulk, and before him, Papa. What woman could really be called "her own"? What did that even mean?

Unaware of my ruminations, Geoffrey continued. "The apartment is not really suitable for young children, what with the noise of the street and such. It's also quite dark and damp. Anyhow, Philippa has a lovely suite of rooms at the Savoy and, when the family aren't there, they're at Kenilworth or one of Gaunt's other palaces."

"That sounds like excuses, Geoffrey." In the harsh light of the sun, I could see his skin was lightly pocked, the lines around his eyes and mouth had deepened. Tiny veins scattered his cheeks. Only his eyes retained their familiar brightness, their shining hope. But, the more I looked, I saw what I'd failed to notice before. A blight that could only be sorrow. "Oh, Geoffrey, what is it?" I clasped one of his hands in both of mine and drew them to my breast.

He sighed and looked at his shoes. "I don't know, Eleanor." He shook his head, as if to clear it. "For all that I read and write about love, devotion, hope, I seem to be unable to salvage any for myself."

I squeezed his hand.

He returned the gesture. "Did I tell you I'm writing again? I've ideas for a poem about what goes on in parliament, about the crowing and chest-beating and ridiculousness of our representatives."

"Father Elias did mention it," I said. "You're embracing your other self. Remember, we used to call you The Poet."

He chuckled. "As I recall, it was said to mock me."

I couldn't argue.

"I'm also in the middle of writing about good women. It's something you inspired—not because you are one, mind," he added with a grin when he noticed my chest puffing up.

"Ah. So I'm a muse now, am I?"

"You certainly amuse me," he said.

I punched him gently on the shoulder.

"I find that even my best intentions are thwarted. I want to write about good women, but all I can think about is how, like a unicorn or a dragon, a good woman is a mythical creature that we men search and search for and fail to find."

"Oy," I said. "Speak for yourself."

"I am, my dear. I am."

As usual, Geoffrey had taken a roundabout route to get to the point.

"You're not happy with Philippa?" I prompted.

He shrugged. "How do I even know when we've barely lived under the same roof? Barely shared a bed?"

"You must have shared one at some stage. You've two children after all," I exclaimed.

Geoffrey gazed skyward, squinting. "*Philippa* has two children."

After that, we meandered back to the house where ale and rabbit awaited. I never did ask Geoffrey what he meant and swiftly dismissed his words.

The next time he visited was three years later. It was the day after my conversation with Mervyn Slynge.

A great deal had happened since. Not so much at Laverna Lodge or in Bath, where time seemed to march on the spot. Apart from another outbreak of the Great Sickness a year after Geoffrey last graced our door, people came and went, died, were born, fell ill, recovered or didn't. But in Geoffrey's world, the world of merchants, politicians, court, and words, everything changed all the time. I wondered how he could bear it, spinning around and around like a dizzy girl on a maypole.

Sitting in the solar, I listened as he shared his news. Much I knew already, but it was so different hearing it from someone who lived and breathed it, felt its impact, saw its consequences. Though he'd been to Calais and back since we'd last been together, the biggest news by far was the death of Edward of Woodstock, the King's eldest son and heir to the throne, the hero of Poitiers and other battles besides. It had been a long, lingering death that Geoffrey said no one would wish on their worst enemy. Services had been held, the country plunged into mourning—even here in Bath we'd grieved. Geoffrey said it was a tragedy that the King, already frail, would never recover from.

The parliament had created its first Speaker of the House of Commons, which Geoffrey said meant ordinary folk like him and me, like my villeins, now had a greater say in how we were governed. Alyson snorted loudly.

"That'll never happen until we rid ourselves of the monarchy and elect a leader," she said.

I stared at her in horror. "Have you been listening to those preachers at the cross in Bath again?"

She pursed her lips.

Geoffrey arched a brow. "I didn't know the ideas of John Wycliffe had spread beyond Oxford."

"Spread might be an exaggeration, but they're discussing them hereabouts," admitted Alyson when she understood she wasn't going to be shouted at. Turbet wouldn't tolerate any mention of the scholar Wycliffe and his followers. Called Lollards, they decried the authority of the Pope and priests and the rituals of the church and believed that anyone could have a relationship with the Lord without a priest to be their intermediary. Alyson had told me about them, but I didn't much care. Not then.

With Geoffrey a willing audience, she continued, "They say the bread they give in church isn't really Christ. That we don't need to have that to know Him."

"I hope you don't repeat such things around Father Elias," I said.

"Or anyone else," warned Geoffrey. "They're dangerous words, Alyson. Dangerous ideas."

"I'm not stupid," she said.

Nay, she wasn't. Just inclined to listen to those she shouldn't. I half-suspected she'd taken a shine to one of the young preachers.

We moved on to discuss the King's failing health and how his mistress, a woman named Alice Perrers, was making enemies faster than a London merchant chips his silver coins. I wanted to know more about this woman. We'd heard of her, of course, how she'd turned the good King's aging head, was lavish with his money, buying clothes and jewels and properties for herself in his name, ruining the exchequer in the process. Part of me admired her gall, most of me envied her. She'd risen from low beginnings, been a servant too—admittedly, in the dead Queen's chambers, but still a servant. Made my accomplishments pale in comparison. I said as much.

"Eleanor, Eleanor, Eleanor," said Geoffrey. "All I have to do is look around to see what miracles you've wrought, what your common sense has done. Turbet couldn't be happier. Just ask him."

I beamed and fluttered my beringed fingers. "Mistress Perrers isn't the only one who knows how to extract largesse from a man."

"I can see that as well," laughed Geoffrey.

"Even so," I said, suddenly wistful, "I'd give it all away if I could have a child."

Alyson slowed her spindle, looking anxiously at me. She knew how much the lack of a baby pained me. For Turbet, who already had two children (whom I'd still never met), it wasn't such an issue. But for me, it was a constant feeling of failure.

"Oh, Eleanor," said Geoffrey and took my hand. "You're young. There's still time."

I snatched my hand back. "Young? I'm twenty-five. I know next to Turbet I'm a babe in swaddling, but truth is, I'm an old matron, sir. No pretty words or sympathy will change that, certainly not while I'm married to Turbet."

Geoffrey dropped his voice to a whisper. "Mayhap, with your next husband?"

Cheeky bastard. Discussing such things while my husband was somewhere about the house, living and breathing (and wheezing and struggling to mount his horse, let alone me). It was then I told Geoffrey about Mervyn's strange proposal.

"If it's a child you're a wanting, you'll not be getting one with him," said Geoffrey, smirking and accepting the drink Alyson poured him.

"That's what I said." She clinked his goblet with her own. They drank.

"Still, if it's riches and a fancy house in town, then mayhap

Mervyn is your man. You've a fine head for business, Eleanor, and what's marriage if not legitimate women's business—one where, if she's canny, she can profit."

"Aye, that, or whoring," I added quietly, before quickly changing the mood and begging a story.

—————— •—•—— ——————

Was it a cruel irony that, two days later, the same day beloved King Edward passed from this earthly realm to sit at God's side in heaven up above, my husband also died? King Edward perished in bed, they say, his wily mistress by his side, pulling a large sparkling ring off his finger as he drew his final breath and claiming it as her own.

That very morning, a gray day in June, my husband managed to mount his horse without aid. Intending to ride down to the Abbey, he told his squire, Nicholas, to remain and attend to other duties. Less than a mile from the house, he fell. He was found late that evening, his neck broken.

Was I sorrowful? Only at the manner of his death, and that a way of life I'd grown accustomed to would be altered. I didn't shed tears, though my heart was heavy.

Geoffrey was still with us when they brought the body back. I can't remember whether what I decided over the following weeks was at his suggestion or my own idea. But, in the wake of Turbet's death and the inevitable sorrow and fears for the future that followed, and with Mervyn Slynge immediately reminding me of his offer, I did the only thing I could.

Not content to seek God's wisdom alone over such an important question (though I did ask Father Elias and pray), and after first seeing Turbet buried and making sure everything was in order at home—my will written, debts paid, tenants looked after—I applied for a passport and papers to allow me and Alyson to leave England for a time.

Geoffrey and Father Elias helped, both putting in a word with the bishop and relevant people in officialdom.

After permissions were granted and I had the relevant documents, I packed enough clothes to last a long journey, told Alyson to do the same and, digging out my pilgrim's cloak, hat, scrip, and staff, set off.

I told you I'd rather fancied another pilgrimage.

I took one and dragged Alyson along. Milda begged to remain behind.

It occurred to me that in order to ask the Almighty about any new marriage I might make, I needed to be as close to Him as I could without leaving earth.

So, I went to the next best place: I went to Rome.

PILGRIMAGE TO ROME

—————◆—————

A letter to
Master Geoffrey Chaucer
from
Mistress Eleanor Gerrish, widow

I send my greetings from Rome, Geoffrey, and God's and all the saints' blessings, and mine.

When I first trudged down the Godforsaken hill and into this damned city, I was cursing you from here to Bath and back again. Forget my aches and endless pains, forget my swollen feet. I thought at least when we got to Rome, we could repair our physical selves as well as our souls. That's what I kept telling Alyson and our fellow travellers, who, let me tell you, make my whining sound like a chorus of angels.

How can one repair oneself when all about, everything is broken? There's not a building standing that doesn't have blocks of stone or rubble strewn about like some giant's game of dice, nor a street where the cobbles haven't lifted. Street is a generous word. Not only are they narrow and higgledy-piggledy (with few exceptions, the ancient Romans knew what they were doing, but they're long gone), but when you eventually get to the church, monument, shrine, or whatever other marvel we're being asked to ogle (and leave coin at), stumbling into these large open spaces they call piazzas, it's as if we've come upon a farmyard, what with all the goats, chickens, and pigs roaming about.

Ancient wonder? The place is in bloody ruins. Wolves come out at night and vermin rummage everywhere. Speaking of vermin, on almost every corner there's a Roman shouting at us to buy their wares. Or they're trying to drag you into this shop, to that stall, or some place that passes for an inn. I thought Alyson and I were going to be kidnapped and sold in some exotic flesh market (not that I'd mind too much if some of the gentlemen I've seen around here bought me—they might be loud, these Romans, and not very tall, but my God, Geoffrey, they're big where it counts, if you know what I mean).

Every time I turn around it's to find some Roman pissing in a corner or in the middle of the street, up against one of the bleeding arches or columns that pop up out of nowhere. Or it's a wretched beggar having a shit just where you're about to step. Horse's droppings, goats, pigs, sheep, turkeys, geese, human—you name it—it's everywhere.

Then there's the robbers—worse than those we encountered getting here, I tell you! They'll cut your scrip clean off your body if you're not vigilant, steal your purse, never mind the bread from your mouth. Worse, they'll sell you what they swear on Mother Mary's tits is a genuine relic for a vast sum only for you to discover that what you thought was a bit of Jesus's five loaves is really dried horse dung. That's what happened to the silly manciple who's part of our group. Mayhap, you know him? Says he knows you. Bit into the stuff, didn't he, hoping for a miracle. He got one alright—a mouth full of shit. Alyson couldn't stop laughing, since she knows what that's like (I'll tell you that story another time).

Just when you think you can bear it no longer, your guide leads you up another bloody hill, along a never-ending path, and orders you to look. And what happens? The heavens part, sunlight beams down, and glorious soft light, like God's breath, illuminates everything. All those bits of rock and broken stone suddenly take on the wisdom of the ages, the stories of all those who have lived, breathed, loved, wept, fought, and walked these winding, squeezy streets and straight wide roads, pour into your head. The river, usually a thick green sludge, is transformed into a vein of beauty that carves a path through the city and gives it succor. The trees, which are the most peculiar shapes, become majestic sentinels on the crests of the hills. The church spires rise to the heavens, God's spears in salute. From this magisterial vantage point, our guide points out all the places he's taken us. Finally, he turns to us with shining eyes and a wide, cavernous smile, moves his arm in a great arc and says, "St. Peter's."

We all gasp as our eyes alight on the glory of Rome, sacred home of the Veronica. Aye, we went there too. Peter's tomb lies there also. They even let you poke your head through a small opening and speak to the saint himself, which I did. How he heard me above the wailing, hair-tearing, and weeping of the other pilgrims, I'm uncertain, though I did give my lungs a good working. Some of the pilgrims put on a show with their hysterics and devotions. I was forced to slap one woman who wouldn't stop howling and tossing her head around. She ceased immediately and, as I was receiving the gratitude of others who were equally annoyed by her performance, she punched me in the head. God's truth, Geoffrey.

I had to pull Alyson off her, as my Godsib pummeled her furiously. Made me laugh to see Alyson so outraged—and in one of the holiest of places. We were forced to leave after that, but not before Alyson pulled a great hank of the woman's hair from her head. "Cheaper than buying one of them bloody relics," she said, twining it into a switch. We're telling folk it's Mary Magdalene's tresses—for certes, the woman fought like a whore.

If there's one thing I've learned (apart from not to share a bed with a nun—my God, her farts would put a soldier's to shame), it's that traveling afar brings you closer to home—not in the physical sense, which would make it both an irony and a terrible waste, but in the spiritual one. God may not have spoken to me quite as oft as I wished, but home has called to me almost every night of late and I miss it. I miss England. What I won't miss is the English folk I've traveled with. That's another thing I've learned—some of those who travel do so because they're not tolerated at home. Dear God, it would be easy for others to believe we're nothing more than a nation of moaners and tight-fisted ass-wisps.

Was it worth spending months on Via Francigena to get here? You might recall, we came via Boulogne, and saw Notre-Dame de la Mer, which was where King Edward II married Isabella of France, but I suppose you know that. Was it worth the badge, an image of the Virgin Mother and Child in a sickle of a boat? Worth the blisters, the swollen feet, the bedbugs, the snoring of the old women (and men) Alyson and I had to share beds with, their constant praying, tears, their judgey faces and words, the endless complaining of the two friars and their great clanking beads? Was it worth the dreadful food, the sickness in my belly, and the subsequent squits? Was it worth the terrible drenching we received outside Langres? The freezing cold of Gran san Bernardo—even if the monks were good hosts? Was it worth the flies, the hot sun burning the back of our hands as we rode from Lucca to Siena (now that's a city), the holes in my soles, thirst, the gnawing hunger when we couldn't find a hostel to take us? Was it worth traveling with thirteen strangers (Alyson not included) to reach the Eternal City?

You'll be pleased to know, Geoffrey, I have to say, once I stood on that hill on that cold day in November, and was able to drink in all that I'd seen and done in one fell swoop, I decided it was.

From where I stood, I could see not just the city, but beyond it to the glory of Christ and all His saints and apostles and all the blessed martyrs, and sing His praises and theirs. Mind you, all I really have to do to remember them is touch the souvenirs I bought—my cloak and hat (and Alyson's too), now carry not just ampulla from Canterbury, but my badge with a key and sword and my small patch of cloth, my vernicle, which I've pinned to my cloak. And let's not forget the whore's hair. I tell you, Geoffrey, I spent a great deal on these holy trinkets, which prove where I've been. I'd rather part with pennies for these than the plenaries every dirty monk and his one-eared dog try to sell.

The scribe is growing weary and tells me he has run out of quills. I will draw to a close, my friend. Know that I've prayed for you at every blessed shrine and church. At St. Peter's and St. Mary's, I left a tiny wax image of a child in the hope that if not the Holy Mother or St. Peter, then the Almighty might see fit to grant me my greatest wish. Though, if I grant Mervyn Slynge his and marry him, then my own may have to wait.

That's the one question for which I still have no answer, my friend. Am I foremost a wife and business-woman? Or do I wish to be, as God and almost everyone else commands, a wife and mother? Be damned if I'll be a crone.

I hope God in His wisdom helps me find the answer before I reach home.

Written on the Feast of the Conception of Our Lady.

Yours, Eleanor.

The Tale of Husband the Third, Mervyn Slynge

1378 to 1380
Some say the tags we desire most are these:
Freedom to do exactly as we please,
With no one to reprove our faults and lies,
Rather to have one call us good and wise.

—The Wife of Bath's Tale, *The Canterbury Tales* by Geoffrey Chaucer, translated by Neville Coghill

NINETEEN

Bath
The Year of Our Lord 1378
In the first year of the reign of Richard II

$\mathcal{M}$y third wedding was a quiet affair—just me, Mervyn, Alyson, Milda, and Geoffrey, all huddled around Father Elias at the church door. Instead of a feast, we had supper at Mervyn's town house on the corner of Locks Lane and Cheap Street in Bath. Missing from the list of witnesses was Kit, who, not long after I left for Rome, ran away with a Scottish laird's daughter, breaking Mervyn's heart. He was now living somewhere north of Aberdeen, knee-deep in heath and haggis. Though I'd miss his kisses and caresses, I was glad I never had to listen to his gripes about women again. God help his poor wife.

Whereas a first wedding is generally a cause for celebration, and a second grudgingly accepted as necessary to maintain the social order and preserve or create a family, for a woman to be married thrice due to widowhood, and without a babe to call her own, attracts gossip the way rancid milk does flies. It hovers about, buzzing and wheezing before sticking and stinking. And not only because the new wife's three-score-and-twelve latest husband is thought to be a sodomite.

In the minds of many, Fulk's and Turbet's deaths were my fault—I'd killed them with my queynte.

Some might say, what a way to go.

Regardless, many prayed for Mervyn, while at the same time there was a great deal of envy directed toward me. In marrying a Slynge, I not only moved upward in terms of wealth and status, but geographically. I went from lodge and land to a three-story house inside the walls of the town.

I was now a wife of Bath.

And let me tell you, the other wives, prepared to tolerate me when I lived two or more miles away, out of sight, didn't much like it.

Not that I cared. Not after what I'd been through to get to the altar again, to once more shore up a position and rebuild my life and wealth—the latter having been ripped away through the wiles of men and their progeny in my absence.

When Alyson and I returned from Rome that cold, snow-bound day in late January, the Feast of St. Wolstan the Bishop, it was to find Laverna Lodge occupied.

While the servants, especially Milda, were happy to see me, they also conveyed, through awkward silences and long, knowing looks as they escorted us to the solar, a level of growing distress that made me deeply uneasy. Milda was fretful and shaking, but unable to say why in front of the other servants.

Seated in my chair by the hearth, one of the blankets Alyson had woven wrapped about her legs, getting familiar with my favorite goblet and wine, was a woman I didn't know. Standing next to her, a possessive hand on her thin shoulder, looking every part the lord of the lodge, was a man of medium height with dark hair combed back from a pinched, pale face. Though I'd never seen him before either, he was not unfamiliar. Those shifting eyes, wide teeth, and the heavy chin that jutted worse than the top story of a goldsmith's house, declared who he was. It was Turbet's son, the never-to-be-talked-about Perkyn. The woman was his wife, Gennet. Their children, Nonce and Dunce (I don't remember their names and neither do I care to), were in the nursery—my old bedroom it turns out—with their nursemaid.

While I was away seeking God's guidance and paying my spiritual debt or accruing credit (depending which way you see it), Perkyn, learning of his father's demise and my convenient absence, descended upon Laverna Lodge and staked his claim. Though my late husband had made many promises at the church door, he failed to enshrine his promises according to law. In other words, he never altered his goddamn will. A widow is generally entitled to at least a third (and often more) of her husband's estate. My husband's written wishes failed to acknowledge the wife he was married to for eight bloody years, and this combined with the power of Perkyn and his fancy London lawyers, saw to it that my portion was nothing more than my clothes, a horse, a bed, a loom, and a few other possessions.

Upon learning who I was, Perkyn ordered Jermyn to produce the documents that outlined my rights. A load of scribbles and flourishes with wax seals hanging off the end was flaunted. Fat lot of good. I couldn't read and from the smirk on Perkyn's immensely slappable face, he knew it. As if to compensate for the shock, I was invited to stay the night, along with Alyson—whom they barely deigned to look at—in the servants' quarters.

I fought the will, of course I did, writing to Geoffrey. He sent the name of a lawyer, Master Abel le Dun, a squat little man who rode down from London. He would have been better named Un-Abel. In the end, it didn't matter one iota that it had been *my* endeavors, *my* decisions, *my* negotiations, that carried Turbet out of debt and made Laverna Lodge and its wool a solvent, growing enterprise. It was as if I was invisible or, worse, had never been there. Everything belonged to Perkyn and his willowy, beak-nosed sister, Tamsyn, she of the protuberant brown eyes who also descended on the solar that evening. With their ability to cast my future, the pair put the Fates to shame.

To make matters worse and rub salt into a festering, pus-filled wound, part of the reason I'd no grounds for contesting the will was entirely my fault. When I'd made Turbet the promise that everyone would believe he was in charge of business, I shot myself with a quiver full of arrows—and not just once. No one would consider it was me, a woman, an ignorant illiterate servant and farmer's wife, who'd turned the Gerrish fortunes around. Jermyn wouldn't speak on my behalf because to do so would not only reflect badly on him, working for a woman, but as steward, he was seen as Turbet's right-hand man and therefore partly to credit for his master's success. For the first time in his life, Jermyn was held in some esteem.

"Good luck maintaining all you've done," I hissed at him as I left the courtroom after the pompous judge upheld the will.

The only person to offer testimony for me was Mervyn. But even with his connections, it wasn't enough.

Knowing it didn't matter what I said or what the truth was, knowing that everything I'd endured, including bloody Turbet, had been for naught, sent me spiraling into darkness. The last fifteen years meant nothing. Nay, it was worse than that, because somehow, I'd also managed to lose everything Fulk had worked for, which meant Alyson had nothing to show for her loyalty and labor either. She'd hitched her cart to mine and I'd broken both. I was sickened, enraged, and heartsore. Beton had made the right decision when he fled to London. If he'd been a night carter, he couldn't have fared worse than we did.

And what of poor Milda? When I'd traveled to Rome, she'd a home and position. Now, she was the unpaid servant of a destitute woman.

After the judgment was given, I retreated to The Corbie's Feet in Bath, where we'd taken rooms. I lay in bed for a week, unable to move or eat, staring at the walls, going over everything and plotting ways to kill spineless Perkyn and his greedy sister.

The only good thing to come of the entire mess was that when they learned I wasn't returning to Laverna Lodge, Rag, Aggy, Drew, Arnold, Wy, Hob, and Peter left. They said they'd rather labor at anything else than remain with *that* man and woman.

Young Peter came to where we were staying and, with his cap screwed up tightly in his hands, announced, "I'd prefer to put me hands in piss for the rest of me life than stay out there with 'im, mistress." I learned later that Perkyn was fond of whipping the servants—the men with his crop, the women with his bare hands.

The entire time I wallowed in self-pity, Alyson remained by my side. Just as she shared the room, she shared my self-recrimination.

She didn't cast blame—not a word of anger or judgment passed her lips as I whined, raged, planned, and surrendered. How she tolerated this, I cannot fathom. She sat in a corner, her distaff and spindle twirling, her hands busy as she hummed. She would organize medicants, for any messages to be sent. She'd insist I dress and meet with Father Elias in the taproom when he came, Master Un-Abel as well. A spring of goodwill and determination—I don't think I ever thanked Alyson enough. I doubt I'd have survived if she hadn't been there to pick me up and dust me off each day, let alone encourage me to grasp opportunity when it finally presented itself again.

As for Milda, she took responsibility for our meals and laundry, ensuring we were mostly undisturbed, and kept her ear to the ground. Out of the room most days, she'd return and fill us in on general gossip. We'd been the talk of the town for a few weeks, but eventually another event pushed us to the periphery of the public mind.

I never thought I'd have cause to be grateful to the Pope. But when Pope Gregory died a huge row erupted over his replacement, an Italian named Urban VI. There were some unhappy with Urban, so they elected another Pope—this time, a Frenchman named Clement VII who hotfooted it to Avignon. Now there was one Pope in Rome and another in Avignon. Imagine it. Two bloody Popes. How the Almighty was meant to know which one to listen to—after all, wasn't the Pope God's messenger on earth?—let alone us poor souls, was anyone's guess. It was all folk were speaking about, according to Milda. While it was good to know we weren't the subject of tittle-tattle anymore, I couldn't help but be offended that our Pope (England was for Urban—we'd never back a Frenchie) was in the city I'd just spent months traveling to! Think how many dispensations walking in the same footsteps as His Holiness would have earned, how much spiritual surplus that would have given me. God knew I needed it, what with all the twisted, murderous thoughts filling my head.

Just when I thought I'd have no recourse but to go to London and sell the only thing I had of any worth, even if it was slightly used, who should come to me with an offer I was in no position to refuse but Mervyn Slynge.

On returning from my pilgrimage and learning of my penury, I'd refused to marry him. Rather than have him suffer the embarrassment of withdrawing his offer (a woman with property and prospects is a very different proposition to one with nothing—not even my private places were an asset with Master Slynge), I told him I couldn't, wouldn't be his bride.

When I didn't hear from him—apart from when he spoke before the judge—we'd no more contact. I pushed him to the back of my mind. It was hard, because his house, a tall, pretty place with real windows, was across the way from the inn.

So, imagine my surprise when Milda announced Master Slynge was downstairs asking to see us.

I washed and dressed hastily and, clutching Alyson's hand, went downstairs to a small room to the side of the noisy taproom. Mervyn knew everyone there was to know in Bath and had secured privacy. Over cups of wine, he laid out a plan for me, for us, with Alyson as witness.

What he proposed was that we marry but, to all intents and purposes, it would be in name only. He'd no desire to bed me, no desire to share a bedroom. He simply wanted to use my business head, my instincts for increasing profit when it came to wool and weaving and apply them to his commercial interests.

"You will work for me by recreating what you did out at Laverna Lodge, only on a larger scale."

"You mean, weaving?"

"Aye. I want you to set up a similar enterprise. As you know, I'm considered reasonably successful when it comes to producing fine wool and selling it. But the excise, duties, and regulations the King has imposed make it nigh on impossible to enjoy much profit. Therefore, using a percentage of my wool, I wish to branch out into producing cloth. It worked for Turbet, and it will work for me. Rather, you will."

Alyson and I exchanged a look. Milda beamed. A growing sense of anticipation, of lightness, bloomed in my chest.

"We will start on a small scale. I'll have looms made, you will hire and train the weavers—oversee the production of the cloth."

"But the guild—"

"Leave them to me." He made a steeple of his fingers, assessing me over the top of them. "Unlike Turbet, I wish to work with their blessing. With your talent for weaving and training, I've no doubt we'll achieve that and the business will grow. I want our cloth to be the reason the alien merchants come to Bath."

I was about to admit Alyson was a much better weaver and teacher than I ever could be, but she placed a warning hand on my arm and shook her head slightly. Inwardly, I sighed.

I missed what Mervyn said next, catching only the end. "Make no bones about it, Eleanor. I will work you hard. You too, Alyson."

"I'm not afraid of hard work, sir."

"Me neither," said Alyson. There was a sparkle in her eyes. Her dimples appeared.

"I know," he said.

He then explained that by marrying him, not only would I gain the name, money, and status that came with being a Slynge of Bath, but if I was discreet, he added, he would give me freedoms most women would envy.

I was puzzled. Surely, there had to be something I was missing. This was too good to be true. What, apart from setting up a weaving business, did this man want from me? What did I have that he was prepared to give me so much?

I asked.

Mervyn looked from me to Alyson, to Milda, and back again, choosing his words. The fire spat. Voices carried from outside. A pot was being struck with a spoon, a child was wailing for his mother. Someone emptied a jordan from a window above, their warning cry too late for some poor sod passing by who began abusing the thrower loudly. Because a shutter was half open, some of the stinking contents splashed over the window sill. Milda closed the shutters, plunging the room into semidarkness but also reducing the noise. She kicked the rushes around until the herbs strewn within them released their scent, managing to mostly mask the stench. Satisfied, she returned to her place near the door. Not a word had been exchanged the entire time. The muffled cries of the child continued.

With a long sigh, Mervyn finally spoke. "I don't think I'm mistaken in believing you're all, as women of the world, aware that . . . how do I put it?" He glanced at the ceiling, searched the room. "That my tastes don't run to . . . that I'm not inclined to . . ." His hands waggled in our direction.

"Dresses?" I supplied. Alyson coughed to cover a laugh. Milda's expression revealed nothing. I knew damn well what he meant, but I wanted him to say it.

"That's one way of putting it," he said, shifting uncomfortably. "What's underneath them would be more to the point."

"Ah."

"Ah, indeed. As you know, the church, the law, does not look . . . kindly upon men with my tastes. In fact, I believe there's a special place in hell reserved for us." He released a weary sigh. "The thing is, ever since that scoundrel Kit . . . abandoned me, forgoing his rights as my ward, there have been those inclined to use his sudden departure to ponder why I've never wed. Kit's leaving has unleashed an unwholesome curiosity among the townsfolk, my friends, and business acquaintances. Normally, I could take this in my stride, but it's beginning to have an impact on my dealings. Those able to turn a blind eye to what they don't see, cannot unhear what's being whispered or claim ignorance. I don't like it. I'm quite prepared to do whatever it takes to put a stop to it."

He rose from his chair and crossed to the hearth, his back to us as he stared into the flames. The walls of the room were thin and the noise from the taproom was growing as men entered The Corbie's Feet and sought to down a midday ale and purchase some vittles.

"I've thought about this for a while. Marriage is my only solution. For my business and legacy, whatever that may be." He turned around. I'd never really looked properly at Mervyn Slynge before. Age had begun to wither his legs, his shoulders were slightly slumped, his hair had slunk away from his scalp until only a few strands straggled across his pate. His brows were dark and thick, a pair of wings about to take flight. But his teeth were good, and within the folds of his face, his eyes were sharp. I knew he could be vicious, cruel even, but also loyal. He'd stood by me when few others would. There was an honesty about him I liked. Geoffrey had said he wasn't what he seemed and while it would be easy to interpret that in terms of his . . . tastes, I liked to think of it in another way.

"I find you're someone I could tolerate sharing my life with, what remains of it anyhow, Mistress Eleanor. You too, Mistress Alyson, Mistress Milda, for if there's one thing I've observed it's that where one of you goes, the others follow. With you beneath my roof, I believe we will put paid to one type of gossip and replace it with another. What I gain by marrying you, Eleanor, will far outweigh whatever I have left to lose."

He sat back down.

Turns out, my cunt was an asset after all.

"And the truth is, I'm tired. Tired of resisting the pressures of this town to be what it insists I should be. What God insists. I am who I am, and I think, I pray, what I am won't be objectionable to you." He stared at me. "Am I right in thinking this?"

"You are," I said.

"And you, Mistress Alyson? Do you object?"

"It's not for me to object, sir."

"Milda?"

"Nor me, sir," said Milda.

"Excellent," said Mervyn, slapping his hands against his thighs. "So, what's your answer to be, Eleanor? Will you do me the honor of becoming my wife—to share the profits of our partnership and any losses that may incur? Shall we put paid to the prating of my neighbors and associates? To yours as well?" He reached out his hand.

I took it. The skin was papery, dry. His fingers were long.

"Before I answer, sir, there's things I need to know."

"Ask away."

"Do you have any children or relations hidden away? About whom you do not speak?"

He chuckled. "Who might swoop upon you after my death and take what's rightfully yours?"

No use pretending. I nodded.

"Nay, my dear, and unlike Turbet, may God assoil him, I'll make certain my will is most clear about what you'll be entitled to. In fact, I give you my word, it will be written and witnessed before we even plight our troth."

I studied his hand holding mine as I stood, one arm wrapped across my middle. I extricated my fingers from his. If I agreed to Mervyn's offer, my desire to have a child would be put on hold, if not thwarted altogether.

Yet . . . this was no longer about my own desires. There were others who needed me, had once relied upon me and, due to forces beyond my control, I'd let them down. Mayhap, I could make amends.

"If I agree, sir, would it be possible for me to include not just Milda, but some of my former servants in your household?"

Mervyn's eyes crinkled beneath the folds. "Of course. For, once you become Mistress Slynge, it's your household too."

"Oh, and three dogs, two are pups. Hera and Siren." I pointed toward the yard outside. In my absence, Titan's bitch, Rhea, had given birth. I found them all shivering in the barn the night I returned to Laverna Lodge. I'd felt no guilt about taking them.

"They will be companions to my dog, Bountiful."

But there was still one last matter. Never again did I want to be in a position where I didn't possess full knowledge of what my husband or anyone else I had to deal with was planning. I would remain in ignorance no longer.

"I wish to hire a tutor who will teach me to both read and write. Alyson too, if she desires. I'll need your approval to proceed."

Alyson pulled an extraordinary face—whether in pleasure or pain, I couldn't tell.

"And you have it," said Master Mervyn. "Furthermore, I know just the man."

"Then," I said, rising to my feet, "I accept your proposal."

I held out my hand. He placed his in it.

"You will be my wife?" He stood and looked me in the eyes. His were a dark blue. A large mole sat under the right one.

"I will."

Alyson fell back in her chair with such relieved force, I swear it would have been felt in the catacombs of Rome. Milda released a long, happy sigh.

———•———

Mervyn was as good as his word. A will was drawn up and witnessed. Geoffrey even made himself available to read it on my behalf and both he and Father Elias authenticated the contents.

My husband-to-be gave me coin to refresh a tired wardrobe and outfit myself in a manner becoming to Mistress Slynge and her beloved companion, nay, her sister, Alyson. Milda too. We moved into the best room at The Corbie's Feet and enjoyed good food, ale, and wine. Rhea, Hera, and Siren also joined us.

A few weeks later, after the banns were read, we were wed.

And so began my brief, happy life as Mistress Eleanor Slynge.

TWENTY

—◆—

*U*nlike my previous two marriages where I had met some resistance and even resentment, I was welcomed into Slynge House. The main reason, I was to discover from the very chatty housekeeper, the widow Oriel, was because the servants were so relieved their master had finally married.

They too knew the rumors that abounded but, unlike Mervyn, who had wealth and the power that came with it, they were sorely affected. Excluded, judged, life hadn't been easy for them, especially when, as they described it, the "young master"—Kit—lived there. "I prayed every Sunday the master would find someone with whom to share his life," admitted Mistress Oriel, crossing herself, her eyes welling as she welcomed us. "God took His time, but you came, mistress."

She couldn't have been more grateful if I'd arrived on the doorstep with pots of gold. Alyson screwed up her face in an effort not to say anything. I merely nodded and smiled.

The servants weren't the only ones to pass comment. For all it was a town, Bath was a small place.

"Funny, I'd always thought he wasn't one for the ladies," was a constant refrain around Market Cross.

"Always preferred male company," said some gentleman outside the Mercers' Guild one day.

"Who doesn't?" mumbled his whiskered companion.

"Never thought old Slynge would plight his troth. Used to call women the Blight of Wrath, remember?" said a tall thin man with a blue birthmark upon one cheek.

"Was young Kit said that, if I recall," said the merchant beside him. "Not that Slynge corrected him."

"That's because the lad was right," grumbled blue-face.

Folk spent hours trying to work out what I had that other women didn't. I could have told them—a mind that was regarded as an asset. Not that anyone would have given this credence for a moment.

These snippets were only what I overheard. In the first few weeks after we wed, people would generally stop talking when I approached, either turning away or obsequiously congratulating me. Mervyn was right about marrying a Slynge, it gave you status. The power of money to make people ignore what would otherwise make you a pariah—your birth, your past, your tastes in the bedroom. It never ceased to amaze me, or Alyson.

We'd oft sit up late at night talking about men and marriage. How, through my three very different husbands, I'd found myself living such a varied life. For certes, it was not one I ever imagined.

"Can I ask you something, Eleanor?"

We were in our bedroom. Though we both had our own rooms, we preferred to share a bed. It wasn't as if Mervyn would complain. We gave Milda Alyson's room. Though it was considerably smaller, she'd never had a real bed or her own space before and was forever thanking us. It was the least she deserved.

Alyson was in a chair near the hearth, a candle burning by her elbow as she worked her distaff and spindle. She'd spent most of the day on the loom, weaving. She only left it to eat, and to demonstrate how to work the shuttle and tighten the weave for some of the new people we'd hired. Including Aggy and Rag, we had seven weavers set up in the hall downstairs. From Bath mainly, they were mostly women, though Hob was there, and an older man as well. Those who didn't show quite the skill needed, Alyson and I put to carding and spinning. We'd need to find extra weavers, as more looms were being built and there was room to fit at least a dozen in the space comfortably.

I watched Alyson for a moment, the way she didn't even have to look at what she was doing. It was like second nature to her. "You, chick, may ask me anything," I said. It still amused me, our private joke, that I called her chick and she referred to me as hen. "You rule the roost," she'd say.

"Do you miss sarding?"

Her question so caught me by surprise, I choked on my wine. Without missing a turn, she leaned over and slapped me on the back.

"It's not like I don't know you enjoy being swived, hen. By St. John's ears, I used to hear you and Pa at it all the time, worse than when we hired a ram to service the sheep. I've never been so bloody grateful when we extended the house and me, Beton, and Theo had our own rooms—at the opposite end." A flash of sorrow crossed her face. "I used to give them wool to stuff in their ears."

Caught between hot embarrassment and laughter, I wasn't sure how to respond.

"If I'd known . . ." I began.

"Wouldn't have changed a bloody thing." Alyson dared me to contradict her.

We both burst out laughing. I took another drink and considered her question.

"Your pa was the kind of lover every young wife needs. Considerate, undemanding . . ." I began to lose myself in memories of his soft kisses, the way Fulk would worship my body. How, as I grew older, I learned to take pleasure from what he did . . .

A different kind of heat began to distract me.

"I didn't bloody miss it until you made me think about it, wench!" I gave her a shove.

"So, was Turbet a decent lover?"

Grateful we had moved on from discussing her pa, I gave her question serious thought. "He wasn't anything like your father. Decent? That might be a stretch. He swived me to prove to himself and others he was a man. There was no thought for my satisfaction."

"But you sarded him anyway."

"A wife has no choice, Alyson. It's part of our vows. It's why God put us on this earth, to marry and do our duty, which includes allowing husbands to bed us. Doesn't matter whether we wish it or not, if he's got a distaff—" I nodded toward hers, "a flagpole, or a baby turnip. We can't choose the size of his prick or how he wields it."

"What size was he?" I knew she wasn't asking about her father.

"One day you'll learn, chick, it's not the size that matters, but how it's deployed." I waited. "But since you ask, beanpole size." I waggled a finger to indicate. "And he was clumsier than a novice in a whore house."

We fell about.

"Even so," I continued, "I took gratification from him. He wasn't allowed to cease until I said."

After we'd wiped our eyes and Alyson found her rhythm again, she asked one final question.

"For all that this . . . arrangement with Mervyn is working, how are you, Eleanor, a woman of passions—born under the sign of Venus no less—going to cope without someone to love you?"

"But, I do have someone."

Alyson raised a brow.

"I've you."

She gave me one of her beautiful smiles, the kind that make you feel like melted butter. "Aye, you do, hen." A wistful look crossed her face. "But you be a woman who needs a man."

I let out a long, heavy sigh. Truth be told, the thought had crossed my mind more than once. "Mayhap, I don't need them in my bed."

Alyson guffawed. "Aye, right. And I be a Moor's spawn."

I glanced toward the window. The candle flame was reflected in the thick glass, turning it molten gold. I feared Alyson was correct and that my desires would lead me into dangerous temptation.

"Nay, you wait," said Alyson. "One day, you'll be swept off your feet, a prisoner in love's shackles. Then you'll do what all those in thrall to Venus and who have a fine instrument needing to be plucked do."

"Oh? What's that?"

"Take a lover."

I stared at her for a while before finishing my drink and climbing into bed. If people knew the truth of my marriage, they could hardly blame me, could they?

But if I was led into temptation, who'd deliver me from evil?

———◆———

Living in Bath was very different from visiting it on market days. Gradually, I became accustomed to its quirks, finding beauty in the strangest places. The hardest thing to get used to was the smell. It grew worse as the afternoon wore on unless a wind blew from the south and carried it away. Some days, if we were lucky, you barely noticed it, except in summer, when the heat was at its worst. Then it trapped the town in its pungent embrace. In terms of physical space, Bath wasn't very big, but in other ways—the river, the gardens, the bridge, abbey, churches, towers, and gates—it contained a world of different folk. There were black-garbed monks and veiled nuns. There were elegantly dressed gentry and local and foreign merchants. Servants, paupers, knights, fisherfolk, even people who lived on the barges that drifted by, all made up the population. Then there were the farmers and those outside the walls, the merchants, tinkers, and vendors who, as I once had, came for business, increasing the town's size each day. It was like a tiny country.

Filled with a mixture of wood and stone houses, many of which tilted to one side or the other like a group of exhausted shearers, it also had large gardens in which anyone could walk—if they were prepared to dodge sheep, geese, chicken, and pigs, who also shared the grounds. Birds would swoop and glide, singing prettily on fine days, chirping their misery on the many wet ones. Spring flowers provided a cavalcade of color and their heady scent battled with the usual miasma.

Mostly comprised of a few wide streets, Bath also had lots of little compacted earthen lanes piled with refuse and the usual assortment of dogs, cats, chickens, and hogs rummaging about, if not orphans and beggars as well. Two- and three-story houses shared plots of land in which grew a variety of vegetables and herbs; meaner houses had no garden but would open onto courtyards. By the river were ramshackle dwellings with rickety wharves that jutted over the water, many with small craft moored alongside. Shops and inns lined almost every street, crowded with customers who would lean on the hinged counters, wander inside the open doors, or prowl the carts and barrows of the street vendors. Calls of "hot pies," "fresh eels," "fine shiny apples," "silk ribbons," and "lovely lace for the ladies" echoed most days.

By far the biggest attraction in Bath, apart from the thermal waters that bubbled up from under the ground and were enclosed in pools called variously Kings, Hot, and the *Balneum Leproforum* (for lepers), was St. Peter's. A huge church near the east wall, it had soaring towers and what Geoffrey called flying buttresses (why, I don't know, as they always stayed put). Much like the cathedrals we saw in France and Italy, it was magnificent, but didn't quite match their grandeur. Still, I didn't correct the other wives when they'd boast about it. Wasn't their fault they hadn't set foot outside the borough, nor that their husbands hadn't died (yet) leaving them free to explore this marvelous world if they were so inclined. Made me realize how fortunate I was.

I also became a regular at St. John's Hospital. Call it penance for Turbet's past activities, or salving my own conscience. I would bring the monks any leftover pieces of cloth, clothes that were no longer being worn but could be reused with some patching, as well as small donations of coins. I never went to the Abbey. I left that to Mervyn, who knew the bishop. I walked past it many a time, admiring its grace and sturdiness, catching glimpses of the monks and novices within its walls, the general air of busyness, but it was not a place where women were welcome.

Mervyn managed to broker an excellent deal with the monks whereby they not only bought some of our wool, but wove the cloth according to patterns Alyson designed. One day a week, a group of monks came to Slynge House and sat with our ever-growing workforce, helping us train them in return for introductions to the alien merchants Mervyn and I dealt with.

It hadn't been hard to recruit more weavers, for the new lord of Laverna Lodge, Perkyn Gerrish, proved to be as astute at business as his father. Forced to use broggers to sell his wool, he lost a small percentage. This was made worse when he recruited spinners to turn the wool he kept into thread. Because they were his villeins, he refused to pay them, considering it boon-work. Naturally, the villeins left—first the lodge, then the lands. Now he had no tenants and no spinners and, because Rag, Aggy, and Hob had left to work for me, no weavers either. Served the rapacious fool right.

In summer, Mervyn struck a deal that increased his fortunes considerably. He managed to bypass English customs altogether and sell his wool directly to both Ypres and Ghent merchants. Earlier in the year, he'd invited a number to stay. Their second day under our roof—after a dinner that was a feast by anyone's standards, filled as it was with many courses of meat, fish, and wonderful subtleties that the cook, Master Quintrill, created, all of which looked like sheep, looms, or something else to do with the trade—he took them to visit his lands. Mervyn owned huge tracts outside the western walls. There he had two enormous flocks, which were well managed by a number of shepherds who had dedicated cottages. He'd also constructed three barns for housing the sheep in winter and for shearing them come spring. As a consequence, their fleeces were soft and white and, before they were even washed, cleaner than most. A further barn with a thatched roof and huge double doors so carts could be rolled in and out with ease was where sacks were stored until they could be sold, reducing cartage and potential weathering and damage. I'd never seen land and buildings designed just for the maintenance of sheep and wool production before. Neither had the merchants—not in this part of the world. That night, they agreed to work exclusively with him, enabling him to bypass many of the duties and excise imposed on English wool producers. It was these men who introduced us to a Venetian merchant who ended up buying a great deal of our cloth as well as that of the monks—under the same conditions. You might recall I said the King imposed better conditions and generous subsidies on alien dealers. It's no wonder we took advantage. I couldn't help but wonder what Geoffrey would think, being Comptroller and all. Needless to say, there was no mention of any of this in my letters.

Ah, my letters . . .

My husband was as good as his word when it came to finding me a tutor. We weren't even married a week when he introduced me to an old friend of his, a scholar from Oxford who was a widower raising a young son and keen for work. Master Binder was a Hollander by birth who spoke Dutch, Latin, French, and English. Long-limbed and thin, with a sunken belly and cheeks, he had pale blue eyes and a thick-lipped mouth that never smiled. But he was patient. Once a week, he would come to the house and teach me. First, it was to read (and what a trial that was), encouraging me to identify and pronounce letters he drew on his wax tablet. Eventually, I was allowed to write myself. He would even set me tasks to complete between our appointments. I wish I could tell you these skills came easily to me, but they didn't. It was more difficult to unravel than a skein of northern wool, and I was besieged by knots and breaks. But, like a newly minted soldier, I was determined to emerge victorious from this battle.

When Master Binder brought his son with him, a fresh-faced boy who could nonetheless read and write fluently, my initial lack of progress shamed me. Here was a lad of twelve or so able to read and write in more than one language with ease. In all fairness, the boy never made me feel a fool. On the contrary, he tried to help.

The good news is, after a year of lessons I was able to read the documents Master Binder brought fluently. Ever since the old King made parliament and the law courts use English, there was a variety of poems, romances, and other works for me to listen to and read for myself. There was a poem called "Piers Plowman," about a man named Will who has dreams involving kings and paupers and wit and conscience. It wasn't complete, but because Master Binder knew the poet, he'd been given a copy to comment upon. There were other works as well—romances with knights and fair maidens, sinners, and the sinned against. I'd heard many of the tales from the bards in the markets or the mouths of jongleurs who visited Noke Manor. And, of course, from Geoffrey.

It was being able to read Geoffrey's letters that gave me the greatest pleasure. The day I wrote my first letter to Geoffrey, I didn't think I could be any prouder. When he sent it back correcting my mistakes, I wasn't offended, not when I was able to read for myself how the new King had graciously added to the annuity granted by the old one and Geoffrey was now twenty pounds a year richer.

Mayhap, the Wheel of Fortune was turning in both our favors, God be praised.

Becoming educated and weaving was not all I did. As Mistress Slynge, it was expected that I would, time permitting, stroll about town like some of the other wealthier merchants' wives. Keen to emulate the gentry living in Bath, these women would dress in their finest and, accompanied by a maidservant or two and sometimes a groom or small boy, strut about, throwing back their heads, laughing, chattering, and above all, being seen. To me, it was a complete and utter waste of time, but as Mervyn said, I'd a role to play and I couldn't disappoint.

I didn't care much about these women or what they thought, but I didn't want to upset Mervyn. For all I believed him a nice if somewhat strange man when I first met him, after we married and he grew older and more frail, happy to oblige me in almost every regard, I knew him to be, as Geoffrey had anticipated, much more than that. He was thoroughly enjoying the talk our marriage and now the weaving business generated; talk I precipitated. I'd no idea my every move and action were being so carefully scrutinized and debated— in dining halls, solars, farmhouses, and inns. The day I crossed the street when I spied Tamsyn Gerrish in town, determined to ignore her, became the subject of gossip for days after. Geoffrey even heard about it in London.

And so, I learned to read, write, perambulate without purpose, weave, teach, run the household, and look after my increasingly poorly husband. Indulgent, Mervyn would insist I wore the best tunics and hose, all made from scarlet and dyed my favorite crimson. My handkerchiefs and veils were made of gossamer-thin materials, and I began to wear rings on my fingers and little gold spurs on my kid-boots—the latter a gift from Mervyn and a complete affectation.

Did I begin to take my new position as a wife of the town too seriously? Mayhap, a tad. But when you come from nothing, to be given something can make one vain and more than a little greedy.

Something else that came with marrying Mervyn was a better position in church. When I'd been a servant at Noke Manor, it was all I could do to squeeze into the back of the chapel. If I hadn't been held upright between the other maids and servants, I would have keeled over with boredom. Once I became Mistress Bigod, I was at least able to stand without being pushed and buffeted. Still relegated to the back when communion was given, it wasn't until I married Turbet that I earned a place halfway down the nave. As Mistress Slynge, I was reserved a spot toward the front, only slightly further back than Lord and Lady Frondwyn and their brood. Most importantly, I was above the Gerrishes, and thus if I didn't want to pay them attention, I bloody well wouldn't.

When Father Elias came to see me later that first week and I told him this, he was most displeased by my lack of Christian charity.

"I'm only showing the Gerrishes exactly the kind of Christian charity they showed me," I said.

He made the sign of the cross.

When, the following Sunday, Master Perkyn and his wife dared to approach the altar right behind Lady Frondwyn and before me, that flat-chested nonce of a sister in their wake, I rose to my feet and shoved them aside so hard, they fell against each other like skittles. A cry went up in the church as folk sought to prevent them falling (and, to my great delight, failed), while others simply tut-tutted. Not so much at me, but at these upstarts who ignored the hierarchy. Be damned if I'd allow them to remind me of my origins; they were no better than thieves.

Thrusting out my bosoms, I took my time approaching the altar, Father Elias too busy conferring with God to notice the commotion behind me. After that, no one dared to precede me. Did I enjoy my rapid ascent to the almost top? By God, I did (and he would've too—Fulk that is, not the Almighty).

After that Sunday, when I put Perkyn and his petty family back in their place, I knew that nothing and no one would ever wrest me from mine.

Was I tempting Fate with such thoughts? Of course.

But temptation, and answering its siren call, were swiftly becoming my hallmark.

TWENTY-ONE

Bath
The Year of Our Lord 1379
In the first and second years of the reign of Richard II

Summer bid adieu and autumn took the stage before winter announced itself with icy flurries that blew the ever-present smell of the tannery away and scattered the morning mists. By now, Alyson, Milda, the dogs, and I were a regular sight around Bath. In a dress made especially for me by Goody Brown, the best seamstress in town, I would oft be seen on market day, trying to strike a bargain with the vendors. My kirtle would attract admiring glances and even comments. Alyson said they weren't looks of appreciation but consternation at my ridiculous hat. I'd had a few made, modeled on the ones I wore to Canterbury and Rome. Broad-brimmed, they protected my face from the sun, thus preventing more freckles forming. Until I married Mervyn, I'd only ever owned a small number of dresses and almost all of those were made by me, Alyson, and Milda. All that changed when my new husband insisted I avail myself of some new kirtles, tunics, shifts, gloves, cloaks, hats, and hose, and that Alyson should do so as well. He also gave me enough coin to

ensure all the servants were well-clothed and that the Slynge coat
of arms (earned on the battlefields of France) was embroidered over
their breasts.

When summer came around again, not only was I part of the
town and parish, but I declared proudly to Alyson and Milda that it
would take a catastrophe to pry me from it.

Milda crossed herself, Alyson stared at me in dismay. "What possessed you to say that? Now you've done it."

"Done what?" I asked carelessly, biting into a delicious pastry
Master Quintrell had made. Crumbs flecked my décolletage and I
picked them up carefully, slipping them into my mouth. Waste not.
I pulled at the laces, trying to create more room. Seemed Goody
Brown had made this tunic a bit small. Of late, a few had been cut
to a different measure.

"Tempted Fate," sighed Alyson.

"If Fate finds me tempting, who am I to quarrel?" I declared and,
before Alyson or Milda could decry my rash words, flounced out of
the room.

I'd taken to visiting Mervyn each morning. More and more of
late, he preferred to remain abed until the sun was high in the sky
and he'd had a few mazers of small ale and some coddled eggs and
bread. Ably assisted by Drew, who along with Arnold had joined
the household, both now manservants, Sweteman, Mervyn's squire,
would see to it that he was comfortable against his pillows, dressed
in a shift and the fire blazing—even on warm days. Mervyn was so
thin, despite what he ate. He was forever complaining of the cold.

Perched on the edge of the bed, I would break off bits of bread
and dip them in the eggs, feeding him and discussing how many ells
of cloth were ready to sell and where they were going, how the flock
was faring, the price of wool and anything else of interest. I would
keep him abreast of gossip (something both Sweteman and the lads
also did) and even read to him. I was very proud of my prowess. He
particularly enjoyed Geoffrey's letters.

I'd received one a few months back written from Milan, where
Geoffrey had gone to conduct business for the King. In it, he said
he'd finished a work on Saint Cecilia and was writing a poem en-

titled "The House of Fame." Similar to that Plowman one I liked, it was about a vision. What was it with poets and dreams and visions? Couldn't one write about real people and events? He should consider writing about people who weren't inclined to fantasies but were just like me, Alyson, Father Elias, Drew, Arnold, Wy, Rag, Oriel, and Milda. He was also writing about a couple of love-struck knights. Well, maybe that was more in line with what I meant. Any knight I'd met only ever thought about two things—war and sarding—and not necessarily in that order.

Sadly, Geoffrey rarely wrote about his wife or children. I didn't suppose there was much to say what with Philippa being in Lincoln-shire ensconced in one of Prince John's many houses. His daughter, Elizabeth, was shut away in that nunnery. No wonder the man wrote about dreams and love so much. Mayhap, I wasn't the only one missing out on a good swiving. As I heard one traveling merchant whisper drunkenly to another one night, "Absence doesn't make the heart ache as much as it does your balls."

Aye, and my queynte and all.

Geoffrey prayed we'd escaped the latest outbreak of the pestilence in England that had spread from Bristol and ravaged the countryside. Towns in the north had suffered terribly, many lives being lost, but thus far, praise God, Bath had been spared. Only those carrying certificates of good health were admitted through the gates. No doubt there were unscrupulous doctors growing rich issuing those.

I'd folded this particular letter and placed it my placket, then taken Mervyn's hand. While this latest outbreak of the Botch hadn't struck down my husband, he was nonetheless suffering. Didn't matter which physician or doctor came, or prescribed bloodletting, read his charts, or gave him fancy stones to put under his pillow, or ghastly concoctions to drink that combined everything from flowers and herbs to fish heads, kitten's tails, and horseshit (alright, maybe it wasn't that bad, but it wasn't far off), he never improved. Fortunately, though his body was failing and his lungs wheezed like over-worked bellows, his mind was sharp and he'd send the quacks away with fleas in their ears and refuse to pay them.

It was probably around this time I first began to notice the husband of one of the weavers we'd hired. I'd like to think it was because, unlike my husband, he was so healthy. But it was a great deal more than that. A maker of looms, his name was Durand Slaywright, and his wife, a skinny wench with lank mousy hair and a chin that collapsed into her neck, was Basilia. She wasn't particularly good at weaving, but she tried so very hard and at first I didn't have the heart to set her to spinning (which any nonce can do). But the day Durand arrived at the house with a freshly carved loom ready to have the warp strings tied, I suddenly found myself very interested in everything Basilia was doing.

A large man, and by that I don't mean fat, Durand was tall, broad-shouldered, possessed of arms that looked fit to burst from his shirt like an overripe fruit its skin. His vest barely laced across his chest and his thighs, well, they looked like nuts in casings, they were so defined. He'd a thick head of barley-colored hair and the darkest eyes. But it was his smile that captured me. God's truth.

Basilia rose when he entered and shyly introduced us. I barely remember what I did or said, all I know is that when those lips pulled back to reveal white, even teeth and I looked into those onyx eyes, my center turned to liquid and I became very chatty and conscious of the state of my veil, my face, the stains on my old tunic. Dear Lord in Heaven, my fingers fluttered like butterflies cavorting over blooms. When I tripped over the edge of another worker's loom trying to get to the other side of the one Durand was moving into place, he caught me around my waist to prevent me toppling. He pulled me close and I breathed in the very maleness of him. My head spun, my breathing became difficult. I giggled, thanked him prettily, and slowly untangled myself from his firm grasp.

"Madam, madam!" Basilia had fussed, pulling over a stool for me to sit upon. Milda fetched me an ale. "Are you alright?"

"Aye, I am," I managed to say, not looking at Basilia, but at her husband.

Was he aware of the effect he was having? I'm sure he was, for when he took his leave, he stood in the doorway, out of sight of his wife, and waited until our eyes met. In that silent conversation much was promised.

It wasn't until I was returning to my loom that I was doused with the equivalent of a bucket of river water. "That's a mighty handsome man," said Alyson, moving her shuttle across the strings.

"Was he?" I said, flicking a strand of hair and taking my seat. "I barely noticed."

"Aye. I saw how little you noticed him."

I pulled a face.

"Lest you forget, hen. He's Basilia's man."

Bloody Alyson. She was right. I had to put him out of mind. But like a devilish sprite, he'd dance through my dreams.

When I encountered Durand unexpectedly a few days later, it was on the road to do my weekly visit to the flock and report back to Mervyn. I'd been doing this since early spring when he became too ill to make the journey himself. At first, I'd protested. Not that I couldn't do it, as I was very familiar with what was required—had I not taken over from Turbet? But that was the precise reason I didn't want to usurp Mervyn's position. I'd plenty of authority and didn't need to wrest it from him. What would people say?

It was a conversation I'll never forget.

"Since when do you worry about what people say?" Mervyn smiled, head tilting to one side like a bird.

I blinked. "I've always had a mind to what others say. Being a man, you wouldn't understand, but us women are at the mercy of others' tongues—most often, those of our own sex."

Mervyn nodded sagely. "Mayhap, you're right." Then he beckoned me closer and took my hand. "Listen, Eleanor. You're not to worry about what others say about you or me—not anymore. Wait," he said, "let me finish. You're no longer a Noke Manor lackey, a farmer's wife, or the hidden talent behind Laverna Lodge's short-lived success. You're someone. You train and employ people, you deal with servants, merchants, wives, gentry, priests, and bishops. You're my wife and I won't have you tolerating anything you don't have to, which includes twisted tongues and rumor-mongering. You stood up to Fulk, you stood up to Turbet. It's time you trusted who you are and stand up to anyone else who would try to belittle you. And that includes me. Do you hear me? Use your voice, woman, use it for yourself and for those who don't have one. And use it well."

If I was a lantern, I would have glowed. I never thought I could love Mervyn Slynge, but in that moment, I did.

Alas, it wasn't my voice I was thinking about when I spied Durand driving a cart on his way back to town; he'd been collecting wood to carve another loom. Milda was upon a mule beside me, Peter on a pony the other side, while Drew and Arnold rode ahead, axes slung across one shoulder, bows on the other. Brigands were known to sometimes rob travelers, so I always brought protection.

Durand and I drew alongside and exchanged polite greetings. The dogs gamboled about the horses' hooves. I barely recall what was said with our mouths, it was the secret conversation we had with our eyes, hands, the unspoken, that held me in thrall.

Two days later, he came upon me in our small garden where I'd gone to collect some herbs to put in a drink for Mervyn. Without a word, we scuttered behind a hedge and fell upon each other, tugging and pulling at our clothes, mouths hot, fingers burning. We didn't just sard once, but twice, collapsing on each other, sated. His kisses were the stuff of legend, his pole—a barge pole—was like his body, hard and thick in all the right places.

Being used to old men's bodies, which had their own particular beauty—or at least, Fulk's had, I barely saw Turbet's, and Mervyn's was mostly a mystery to me—I'd never enjoyed a younger man's before. Oh, I'd seen Layamon's, years ago, but he was a mere boy compared to Durand. Thirty-two years old and a worker, Durand was built for pleasing. And I, a woman of twenty-seven, was built to be pleased. His hands could span my waist when he lifted me onto his prick. I would wrap my legs around him and ride till he bucked and shouted and I joined his cries with blissful ones of my own.

Durand became my lover and for a few weeks, I was deaf to anything but our whispered words, the looks we exchanged; I was blind to anyone but him. No space was safe from our swiving—the back of his cart, the small yard, the secret space beneath the stairs. Often, we would race to the solar when no one was there. One time, when I was certain everyone was either in the hall weaving, kitchen cooking, or tending Mervyn, I took him in my bedroom.

That was the beginning of my undoing, that and the air of distraction I carried. A glazed look that showed all too clearly what was going on in my head. I started to forget to visit my husband, or when I did, I was vague about the flock, the fabric we wove, sales. I was keen to get away lest Durand be waiting. I drifted off in the middle of conversations, my dreams were filled with heaving bodies, hot lips, and a prick that, like a magic wand, cast a spell over me. Thinking back on it, I'm appalled. My selfishness, my unkindness in sarding another woman's man. For allowing him to take up space in my head and heart that others deserved more. I didn't love him. I didn't know him. I just knew his body and the way it made mine feel.

For certes, we barely spoke. There wasn't anything for us to say—we'd nothing in common, not really. It was his pole and my queynte did the talking. Whatever lay between us was purely carnal, a desperate sating of mutual appetites. I never doubted he loved his wife, but it was me he wanted.

The madness came to an end when, firstly, Alyson confronted me after Durand and I had spent the afternoon in my bedroom, naked and bold as you like. She found a lace from his shirt, torn when I ripped it from his body. She could also smell him, smell us. I didn't deny it, how could I? And what would be the point?

"You must cease this folly now, sister," she said sternly.

Like a child, I became angry, defensive. "Why? Do I not deserve love? Do I not, a young woman who's been married to old men, deserve to enjoy what other wives know?"

I should have stopped. The hurt on Alyson's face was raw. Fulk was so much more to her, to me, than an "old man." But I didn't. The devil stole my tongue. "Be with someone who can transport me to bowers of bliss?"

"Oh, aye," Alyson hissed, throwing the lace at my face. "And what of Basilia? Isn't that what he's supposed to do to her?"

"She doesn't satisfy him."

"How do you know? Has he told you that?"

I was about to bark a retort when I realized he'd never said anything of the kind. All he'd ever done was pant and express joy at feeling and seeing my various body parts—especially my quoniam. "Not in so many words."

"I'm surprised he'd know any. The man's thicker than a tile. Nay, that's not fair on tiles."

I threw myself on the bed, pretending an indifference I didn't feel. "It's none of your business who I swive."

"Oh, but that's where you're wrong, Eleanor." She stood before me, hands on hips, little bolts of lightning flashing from her eyes. "When your actions affect the business, and, worse, the workers you profess to care about, then it *is* my bloody business. It's yours too."

I rolled over and raised myself on my elbows. "What are you talking about?"

"Have you even taken one look at Basilia? Nay, of course not, you're too busy gazing at her man to notice the impact your bloody assignations are having on the poor woman."

"What do you mean?"

"Her eyes are permanently swollen, she's thinner than a river reed, and so pale she puts the moon to shame. When she thinks no one can see, she weeps and weeps and refuses to eat or drink."

I went to reply, but what could I say? I hadn't noticed. I hadn't really given Basilia a thought. My stomach became heavy. I sat up.

Alyson plonked beside me on the bed. "And then there's Mervyn. You haven't been to see him for days. When you did, you were so keen to get away, you neglected to feed him."

"There are others to do that."

"But he wants you."

I leaped to my feet. "I don't know why. He's made it perfectly clear he's not interested in women."

"Not in that way. You're more than a woman to him, Eleanor. You're his wife; you're his friend."

That stopped me in my tracks. I ran my fingers through my hair. It was true. "Do you think he knows?" I asked Alyson.

"About Durand?"

I nodded, biting my lip.

"The entire household does."

I felt a strange urge to cry.

"Mervyn would hardly care if I swive another man. Why would anyone else?"

"He might not care about the swiving, but he does when you make yourself the subject of gossip. And when you hurt one of your workers, *you* should." She joined me at the window, lifting my hand from where it hung limp by my side and placed it between her two cool ones. "I never took you to be a bitch, Eleanor. Well, that's not entirely true. I did when I first met you." She half-smiled. "You were a right little one then."

I began to feel heat travel up my neck. My eyes began to swim.

"But, as I came to know you—to love you—I knew you to be kind, loyal, someone who gave people a chance. I never thought you'd turn into the kind of woman who coveted another's husband. Nor did I ever think you'd be the kind of woman who was indifferent to the hurt and pain she caused others. And, you know what makes it so much worse? You're not even doing it deliberately. You're doing it uncaringly, because you're thinking only of yourself."

She was right. I hadn't given a tinker's cuss about anyone but me and my needs. I hadn't even noticed Basilia or her suffering. As for Mervyn—dear God. The man had given me, us, so much and how did I repay him? By doing everything I could to either avoid being with him or, when I'd no choice, getting away as swiftly as possible.

"And what if you were to make a child with this man, eh?" added Alyson quietly. "Then what would you do? What would *we* do?"

My insides flickered, I felt lit from within. My hand pressed protectively across my stomach before the truth struck me with all the weight of a church bell, tolling a warning against my worst instincts.

Alyson's words echoed. *What would we do?*

I tried to extract my hand from hers, but she held me tighter.

"I don't know how you can bear me," I said hoarsely. "You're right. I've been so goddamn selfish. Oh, dear God." I sank to the floor. The tears came thick and fast. Aye, I was sorry for myself, sorry to hear the truth and see what I'd become through others' eyes. Know that the goodwill I'd worked so hard to earn, the good name I'd struggled to achieve, was on the cusp of being ruined by my own thoughtless, wicked actions. I was nothing but a worthless whore.

"I don't deserve you," I breathed, and fell into her arms.

I wept for what seemed a long time. Gathered in Alyson's lap, she held me tight, stroked my hair, murmuring words not so much of comfort, but acknowledgment of what I blathered and sobbed. I determined then and there to end it with Durand, to try and make it up to Basilia, to all the servants. But mostly, to Mervyn.

And to Alyson.

"They must ha . . . ha . . . hate me . . ." I choked and sniffled.

"The workers? Our servants? Nay, hen, they don't hate you. How could they? You've done so much for them, given them lives, wages, hope, and a future. They're just confused that the woman they trust to be better has proven, in essence, to be just the same as them."

"The same?"

"A sinner."

I cried for a little longer, then ceased abruptly. I heaved myself upright and took the kerchief Alyson passed me, wiped my eyes and cheeks, and blew my nose.

She kissed me on the forehead. "I'll get you some wine to drink and water to wash your face. We'll fix your hair up and make you presentable."

"What for?" I'd no intention of leaving my room ever again. Well, not for a few days at least. Until I had Durand out of my blood, and this could all blow over.

Alyson dragged me to my unwilling feet. "So you can do what all sinners must."

I shook my head, confused.

"Ask forgiveness."

"Oh." I took a deep breath. "Alright. I'll go and see Father Elias."

"You'll see him alright and make a confession. But I don't mean him."

I stared at her in horror. "If you think I'm going to go and ask forgiveness of everyone, then you're very much mistaken."

"Am I? If you don't, then you're not who I think you are, Mistress Eleanor Slynge."

I searched for excuses. Rubbed my nose, hiccoughed, and straightened my damn tight kirtle. Bloody Alyson was right. I had to apologize and ask forgiveness from all those I'd wronged. If I didn't, then I was no better than the likes of Layamon, or Turbet and his pox-ridden family. And be damned if I'd be compared to them. I was Fulk Bigod's widow, Alyson Bigod's Godsib, Eleanor, Mistress of Slynge House, and a wife of Bath.

I would make my penance and pay, in whatever way I must, for my lusty, selfish ways.

TWENTY-TWO

—◆—

Bath
The Years of Our Lord 1379 to 1380
In the second and third years of the reign of Richard II

*I*n a matter of months, I learned some hard lessons. Among them was to think twice before putting your desires so far above others you fail to see their needs, and, when a male is offered queynte, it will be taken, even if the man already is.

The main lesson was also the most painful: in order to truly pay for your sins, you must allow others to set the price.

Whereas Father Elias demanded a succession of Hail Marys and dispensed a mountain of advice on how to avoid repeating my trespasses in the future, Mervyn merely smiled ruefully and more than a little mournfully at my confession. His hollow cheeks quivered, his shadowed eyes were pools of sorrow as he held my hand and drew me closer so Sweteman, Arnold, and Drew couldn't overhear and said he wished he was both younger and inclined toward my sex. In which case he would have absolved me by reasserting his conjugal rights. He even attempted to thrust his brittle hips. I laughed as I was supposed to and all was forgiven. "I married a full-blooded woman, Eleanor. I'm surprised it took you this long to take another to your bed."

I swore to my husband then and there I would never do it again, not as long as he lived. It was his turn to chuckle. "Glad you have the sense not to make promises that can't be kept, lady wife, since I'm not long for this world."

I'd hugged him then, shocked at how prominent his rib cage felt beneath his shift, his lungs battling to seize each breath. The thought he might die soon shook me to the core. Mervyn may not have met all my needs, but he damn well satisfied ones I never even knew I had: to be respected, listened to, spoken to as if I had a mind of my own, and supported. There's a great deal to be said for that. Alyson had the right of it—Mervyn and I would never be lovers, but we were friends. And what saddened me the most that day was the realization my friend was dying.

When I told Durand we couldn't see each other again, he merely shrugged. "I think you mean 'swive,' because unless you tend to blind me, you be hard to miss, madam." Then, doffing his cap, he wandered away down the street. But it was Basilia whom I found hardest to approach. I was ashamed to admit what I'd been doing, I felt sullied and humiliated—I was her employer, supposed to be her better. But that was the point, wasn't it? If it was easy to ask forgiveness, then everyone would. Most of all, I felt I was unworthy.

As it was, she had already worked out a way to forgive me. No doubt in cahoots with her philandering husband.

Displaying few of the signs of distress Alyson had described, a rosy-cheeked Basilia listened to my confession then calmly said if I paid her the sum of five pounds, all would be forgiven and forgotten. I was speechless at first then, as you'd expect, paid the money, even though it was a huge amount. She never came back to work and last I heard, she and Durand were living somewhere outside the walls of London. Afterward, I was able to see the funny side. That's why, when I next wrote to Geoffrey, I included the tale of my lust and the various ways I had paid my penance, giving the greatest space to Basilia's sudden transformation from hollow-cheeked cuckold to negotiator extraordinaire.

Call it serendipity, Fortuna, or the Hand of God, but just as Geoffrey would have been reading my letter and composing a very priggish one in return, full of reproaches for allowing the sin of lust to overcome my good sense et cetera et cetera (this from a man who wrote of love-sick knights slaying one another over a woman—the cheek of it), a new customer swam into our ken.

A young friend of Lady Frondwyn's, her name was Cecilia Champain. Her stepmother was none other than the former King's infamous mistress, Alice Perrers. Cecilia had come to Bath at Lady Frondwyn's invitation. As I showed her the weavers at work in the Great Hall and she gushed her admiration for our cloth, she revealed we had a mutual friend—Geoffrey. From the way she said his name, all a-blushing and coy, I began to wonder what kind of "friend" Geoffrey was. The more she prattled, the less I listened as it dawned on me that I wasn't the only one allowing a married man to dip his wick in my wax.

I took a good hard look at Cecilia. Slender, short, she had fine blonde hair and almost nonexistent eyebrows that had been plucked into such thin arches she looked constantly surprised. Mayhap, she was. The thought of Geoffrey, with his forked beard and little paunch, panting and pushing over this one, almost undid me. She would have been no more than twenty. Yet there was a sly look about her, the way she pursed her little rosebud mouth. That night, I admitted to Alyson I didn't like her.

"You're just jealous Geoffrey has another friend," said Alyson, punching the pillow as she prepared to settle.

I stared at the ceiling. "Nay. I'm not. Truly. I'm more annoyed that if he's sarding her, he had the gall to accuse me of peddling Eve's wares and risking the salvation of heaven. What's good for gander is not for goose to ponder. There's something about the woman I find . . . false. False and more than a little avaricious. Did you note the expression on her face when she told us that Geoffrey's been forced to hire a lawyer to defend an accusation of trespass and contempt?"

"Aye. I did. She was delighted. She went on and on about how he might have to pay a fine but how it was well within his means."

"Exactly. Ten pounds, wasn't it? What sort of person finds glee in another's misfortune?"

"Not a friend."

"Nay. Either an enemy, or someone who enjoys revenge."

Alyson ceased to strike her pillow and, turning on her side, considered me. "What has Geoffrey Chaucer done that a young woman like that would seek revenge?"

I shrugged. "I don't know, Alyson. But I like it not."

As it turned out, my feelings were right. But, before I could write to Geoffrey and warn him (as well as point out that sanctimony only works if you're a saint), events overtook me.

———◆———

After the Great Apology (as I came to think of it), life in Slynge House and Bath continued as normal. I resumed my daily visits to Mervyn, weekly ones to our pastures and flock, as well as to mass. Father Elias was a regular at dinner or supper, as were some of the older merchants, Mervyn's long-time friends and colleagues. We oft took the meal in Mervyn's bedroom for, as autumn segued into winter, he became completely bedbound.

I also continued my lessons with Master Binder, who, when he developed a terrible cough, asked his son to take his place. Jankin, by now fourteen or thereabouts, was tall, learned and becoming very, very handsome. I'd grown quite fond of him. He took almost as much pride in my accomplishments as I did. After our lesson was complete and he'd set me tasks for the following week, we'd sit in the solar, drink wine, and either read to each other or simply talk. Jankin was going up to Oxford, following in his father's footsteps, becoming a scholar and, likely, a monk. He quite fancied the Benedictine Order, and though he should have joined them by now, his father's declining health kept him close.

"But between Pa, Father Elias, the monks at the Abbey, and you, Mistress Eleanor, my education is not lacking. I've other pupils too."

Whereas I didn't feel jealous at the idea of Geoffrey having an attractive younger friend, the notion that I shared Jankin with others caused a sharp pain in my ribs that I was quite unprepared for. It wasn't that I was attracted to Jankin, though apart from his youth, there was no reason why not, it was just that I so enjoyed our discussions, our exchange of ideas and stories. It reminded me of my correspondence with Geoffrey, only better, for here my confidant was in the flesh.

The fact he was younger and prettier didn't matter. Much.

"Be careful, Eleanor," Alyson would warn. Again.

"Of what? He's but a child," I scoffed.

"A child doesn't look at you the way he does."

"Oh? How's that?"

"As if he might devour you."

I'd seen what she meant in his eyes, heard it in his tone. It was somewhere between loathing and desire. It was heady. I loved that I'd the ability to discommode this young man who would be a monk and a man of learning.

Fool that I was, I thought I'd the upper hand. Once again, I was but a tool of Venus and Mars.

It wasn't until after the Feast of the Epiphany, in the third year of King Richard's reign, that Mervyn's health declined sharply. Each day Father Elias came to the house, half-expecting to be administering last rites. Along with Sweteman, Arnold, and Drew, I'd taken to sleeping in Mervyn's room, on a pallet at the foot of his bed so that, like the men, I could be there to meet his needs. I owed my husband, this clever, generous sodomite, so much.

After making his final will and offering a last confession, three days after the Ides of January, on the Feast of St. Marcel, Pope, and Martyr, Mervyn Slynge received extreme unction and passed from the world quietly, surrounded by his priest, loyal servants, and mostly loyal wife. It was a dismal day, the sky heavy and gray, the wind fierce, matching my sorrow.

The world and my life would be diminished now Mervyn was no longer in it.

In response to a note, Geoffrey arrived the following day, even though the London Road was snowbound and difficult to traverse.

We'd already washed and clothed Mervyn. It was the first time

I'd seen him naked. Wrinkled and much reduced, he was like a child and man all rolled into one. I could see the span of his life in his ancient body. It was humbling and there was a strange beauty in the sagging, spotted, and moled flesh of his face, arms, and knees compared to the nearly flawless allure of his stomach and upper thighs. I wondered, as we ran the scented cloth gently over his limbs, his groin, how many lovers he'd had, and if he'd found forgiveness for his sins in the Lord's arms. Or did the Lord refuse admittance to men who loved other men, even if every other action in their lives warranted a place in the Kingdom of Heaven?

Alyson and I spoke on this during the night and though I couldn't see her face in the dark, I heard the tremble in her voice as she tried to quell her sorrow. It was a question we'd oft pondered of late.

We buried Mervyn beneath the chapel floor in St. Michael's Without the Walls. Though Mervyn could have afforded to be buried in St. Peter's, and indeed, the bishop had tried to persuade him, claiming that God would look kindlier if he chose that church, it had long been arranged with Father Elias where he would lie. Mervyn knew the bishop's insistence had little to do with God's attention and everything to do with what he bequeathed St. Michael's Without upon his death: enough to have masses said for many years and alms for the poor. Mervyn always said there were far more commons inclined to attend mass outside Bath's walls and be welcomed than there were within.

On returning to the house, we adjourned to the hall. The looms had been moved to the sides of the room and trestle tables erected. We had a splendid feast. Cook outdid himself. Ale and wine flowed and, as the night wore on, pipes, gitterns, and drums played while folk danced. There were many merchants present, as well as Master Binder—who'd dragged himself from his sickbed—and Jankin. I also invited the servants to join us and remember their master.

I concealed my sorrow beneath a facade of hospitality, but each reminder of Mervyn, of his kindness, his intelligence, quite undid me. I moved about the room, noting the grief on the faces of those present, listening to their memories of my husband, how his ability to see the best in folk allowed them to rise to be that—myself included. By St. Sebastian's ribs, what would become of me now he was no longer here? Instead of allowing my sadness to escape, the tears that had pooled in my chest to flow, I diluted them with wine.

By the time the bells rang for compline, I was stumbling about the place, throwing my arms around whoever stood nearby, alternately wailing and laughing. I remember sharing a dance with Jankin, who kept pressing his body into mine, not that I objected. Likewise, I was flung from one set of arms to another until the room whirled. I was breathless and more than a little bit ill. A group of merchants' wives stood near one of the tables watching me, their faces carved into expressions of disapproval. Their censure aroused me to new heights and I found Jankin again and, in front to everyone, pressed a kiss upon him, a farewell as the lad was off to Oxford in a week. I also kissed the grocer, his daughter, five merchants, and their sons. I would have kissed Father Elias as well had he not held up his cross to warn me away. It wasn't until Geoffrey and another man, Simon de la Pole, a brogger who Mervyn had dealt with on occasion, sat me down and forced me to remain still that I began to take stock.

The room was crowded and, despite the cold outside, the raging wind and sleet, I was sweating. A sea of slick, smiling faces swam before me; the odor of the rushes, dogs' leavings, and urine as well as greasy food made my stomach churn. I could smell sweat, ale, wine, and smoke and not just from the man who remained by my side, Simon, while Geoffrey fetched Alyson and Milda.

I tilted my chin, trying to see who it was that had been such a gentleman as to remove me from the floor before I fell and disgraced myself and Mervyn's memory. Though I could imagine him laughing if I'd toppled face first into the rushes.

"We've met before, haven't we?" I said slowly, trying not to slur my words.

"Indeed, we have, mistress," said Master Simon, touching his fine cap. In fact, all his clothes were rather fancy for a brogger. But then, I guess he'd know quality wool and the best spinners and weavers.

I pinched his coat, my fingers rubbing the fabric. It was a deep blue with cream stitching along the cuff and neck. "This is mighty fine," I said, narrowing my eyes so I might see it better.

"From your own workshop."

"Ah, that explains it," I said, a smirk appearing. "You've a good eye."

"I know," he said, with such a roguish smile and pointed look that even in my drunken state, I knew wasn't just about the fabric. His eyes dropped to my breasts. As the night had worn on, my neckline had slipped, and my heavy breasts were bursting from their confines. Be damned if I didn't experience a sudden rush of liquid heat between my legs. I returned his bold gaze. He'd a mop of dark brown hair upon which his hat sat jauntily. His eyes were the color of burned chestnuts and his skin was weathered, but in that attractive way young men possess—before age destroys their complexions. How old was he? Thirty? Mayhap, a bit older. He was tall, but not too tall. And strong. Geoffrey was but a wisp compared to him.

His eyes had dropped to my lips. I licked them. He began to lean into me but, before anything untoward should happen, Alyson and Geoffrey appeared.

"Come, sister," said Alyson, glaring at Master Simon and slipping her hand beneath my arm and heaving me upright. "Time for bed."

"Allow me to help—" began Master Simon.

Alyson shoved him so hard in the chest, he fell onto a stool. I began to giggle.

"You've helped more than enough. If you could but take her other side, Geoffrey," she said, draping my arm over her shoulders. "God, you're a weight."

I mumbled something, trying to smile reassuringly at Master Simon. Already he was distracted by a merchant's sister, a pretty dark-haired child of about fifteen. Evidently, his eyes strayed only slightly faster than his mind.

My head was sluggish and slow and, as we wended our way

through the hall, Alyson and Geoffrey explained to our guests that I was overcome with grief and going to retire. I recall thinking what they were saying wasn't exactly untrue. The loss of Mervyn, while leaving me very well off, as I was destined to receive more than half his worldly goods, also left me feeling empty. Once more, I was a widow. A woman whose husbands died on her faster than flies in a castle kitchen.

Mervyn was gone.

All the life drained from me. Without further complaint, I went to bed. I said goodnight to Geoffrey, who promised to look after those still downstairs, and as Alyson and Milda helped me undress, I barely said a word.

Milda left and Alyson tucked me under the covers, stoked the fire and, eventually, clambered in beside me, releasing a big sigh.

"Sometimes, Eleanor, you're such a trial. Of all the places to display desire, you choose your husband's funeral."

I winced. I'd sobered enough to understand my behavior was wanting. "I know. I'm sorry."

"You don't have to be sorry, hen. People will understand and if they don't, then they're not worth a pinch of . . ." She searched for the appropriate word. "Spice."

"I think you'll find it's salt."

"That's what I said."

I smiled. "I hope you're right." We lay there in silence, the muffled noises of dancing and music reaching us through the floor. The window rattled as the wind shook the house.

"We might have trouble convincing people to leave until the storm passes. I doubt we'll get much sleep before then," said Alyson wistfully.

"I don't think I can sleep. Not yet. Despite all I've drunk. Too much to think about."

"Aye," sighed Alyson. "What are we going to do now you're a widow again?"

I found Alyson's hand under the covers. "I imagine go on as we have. You know, weaving, selling our wool and cloth."

"There are those will make it difficult for you, despite your experience, your name and standing. You're a woman alone—a feme sole."

"Aye. Even though I'm a widow and not really alone." I squeezed her fingers and rolled onto my side. "I'll be pressed to marry again. Even tonight, there were men seeking my company, paying more attention than they ever have, though I've known them for years."

"Like Simon de la Pole."

"Exactly like him. How did I never notice how . . . how handsome he is?"

"Never had cause."

"Nay. Don't suppose I did." I traced patterns on the sheet.

The fire crackled and the wood split, a shower of sparks brightening the room momentarily. I could see the outline of Alyson's face, the lucent glow of her eyes, boring into mine.

"I can't stop thinking about what Father Elias said at the funeral today."

"What's that?" asked Alyson wearily.

"He said that we all, no matter whether popes, emperors, kings, queens, paupers, or beggars, whether high born, low born, rich, or poor, the one thing we all have in common is death."

"He's right."

"Then he read that passage from his psalter: *We have all come here to this world like pilgrims so that we are to leave it.*"

"And . . .?" Alyson waited for me to say more. "Oh, nay. Eleanor . . ." She half sat up. "Don't tell me you have a mind to wander again. Look what happened last time we went away." She fell back on the pillow.

"Last time," I said, "I went too far. This time, I don't intend to travel quite that distance."

"I suppose that means Walsingham or Canterbury?" Alyson sounded so despondent.

"I was thinking maybe Cologne."

"*Cologne?*" She turned to look at me in shock before burying her face in her hands and kicking her heels. "God, Eleanor." She removed her hands. "That's miles away and over the sea! Have you gone entirely mad?"

"Aye, Godsib. I have." I waited for her to calm down. "What say you? Fancy a trip through France?"

"While we're at war?" Alyson threw her arms out and began to chuckle. "If it's with you, Eleanor, then why the hell not? What could go wrong?"

PILGRIMAGE TO COLOGNE

A letter to
Master Geoffrey Chaucer
from
Mistress Eleanor Slynge, widow

My most meaningful blessings, et cetera, et cetera, upon you, Geoffrey.

I know I should have listened when you warned that visiting the shrine of the Three Magi in Cologne meant not only returning to places I swore I'd never go again, as well as a journey by sea, but I didn't. When you cautioned I was unlikely to encounter fellow Englishmen traveling to this part of the world and would struggle talking to anyone, I didn't listen either. When you said I should take at least three of my own men to serve as guards, I ignored you. Why? Now I've had time to consider my stubbornness, my insistence on doing almost the complete opposite of what you recommended (I did take two men), I've fathomed the reasons. I was cross with you, Geoffrey Chaucer. Cross at your stubbornness, your refusal to acknowledge I was right regarding that doxy Cecilia Champain.

But whereas I closed my ears to your prognostica-
tions of disaster—and rightly, as Cologne and the
entire journey has been both entertaining and worthwhile—you, my friend, should have heeded me. Am I
not a woman? Do I not possess a queynte? Do I not recognize in my kind the sort of habits, temperament, and
inclinations the good Lord and Father Elias say need to
be mastered? The moment I set eyes on her, I knew
what Cecilia Champain was, and I knew you were a
fool to trust her.

You may thank me and apologize when we see each
other again—in any order.

I won't dwell on the painful matter anymore, except
to say I was shocked when Alyson, Milda, Drew, Arnold,
and I arrived in London to join the pilgrims and called
upon your residence in Aldgate to learn, firstly, you
weren't there and secondly, that the little bitch had
accused you of *raptus*. You! A rapist! I can only assume
it's either a case of mistaken identity or you're not the
honest man you appear to be. Then again, one cannot
write the things you do, Geoffrey, and deny the lustful inclinations that come naturally to your sex. I quite
understand that on occasion your desires must overcome you—especially in the absence of your wife—
but with Cecilia Champain? That loathsome serpent? I
shudder at the thought. I've always said, never trust a
person without brows, a maxim that has proven true on
more than one occasion. (Remember Father Roman?)

I can only urge you, if you haven't already, to use the
advantage of your friendship with Alice Perrers to seek
redress. Is she not Cecilia's stepmother? I'm aware Mistress Perrers has fallen out of favor since King Edward's
death, but surely the woman still has enough influence
to mitigate what promises to be a disastrous outcome
for you. Not to mention the influence of your other
important connections in London.

If I thought it would have done any good, Geoffrey, I'd have remained in the city and shouted from the rooftops about your gentilesse, talents, and kindness, and how unlikely it was that you would force a woman into your bed. As it was, we'd booked passage on a ship from Southampton, and these captains wait for no man, or woman, once the tide has turned. I did leave a note with your fellow, and pray he passed it on. Forgive my lack of correspondence in between, there's been little time to write, and less confidence any letter will reach its destination before I do.

As my eyes once more turn toward home, I pray it's to find the matter resolved. If not, then I offer my services and voice once more. My late husband once told me to use it to help others, and it would give me no greater pleasure than to use it on your behalf.

If you were right about one thing, Geoffrey, it's the kind of pilgrims we'd encounter on this journey. From the moment we disembarked at Boulogne and met our guide, a portly man with a mustache that looked like he'd detached it from a besom, Herr Wolfram von Kühn, we were thrust together with a group of rough-looking men who, if they didn't have yellow crosses dangling down their fronts and backs, were wearing knives, axes, staves, and other sharp-looking instruments around their necks. When I asked Herr von Kühn, who could communicate in what he thought was English but was a mixture of Latin and some sort of London parlance (I did come to understand him—eventually), why these men were so adorned, he explained the crosses were worn by accused heretics while the other men were murderers. *Murderers*, I tell you! Their punishment was to walk to whatever number of shrines the judge sentencing them saw fit. Whether they were put to death after begging forgiveness and seeking indulgences, I didn't dare ask. I was apoplectic when I understood who and what were to accompany us on our journey. Until Alyson pointed out that at least while we traveled with criminals we were unlikely to be set upon by the same. It was solid reasoning, and that was before I learned that armed guards were also traveling with us. (As it was, we had only one brief incident, which saw the brigands turn tail the moment our worthy murderers wielded their various weapons and shouted like berserkers. It was thrilling!)

After a blessing from a ridiculously indifferent bishop, we set off from Boulogne, twenty or so of us, Alyson, Milda, and I the only women flung together with cutthroats, thieves, heretics, two monks, a franklin, a widower-shipman from St. Omer, a knight, Sir Jacques, who'd been to Jerusalem, and, of course, our guide, the portly Herr Wolfram von Kühn. I couldn't have asked for more interesting companions if I'd ordered them straight from the Almighty Himself.

For all your blathering about my being unable to speak the tongue of the natives, what you, Poet, a man of words no less, appear to have conveniently forgotten is the common language men and women all speak, particularly when flung together, night and day. What language is that? Why love, of course. And, trust me when I tell you, Geoffrey, not only did Herr von Kühn, *mein liebe*, speak the same tongue, but so did one of the monks—Italian, and we know they're experts in *amore*. Between them and one of the thieves who stole my heart and whose name eludes me, the journey afforded many pleasures. And then there was the rugged farmer near Bruges who killed his wife's lover with his staff. He almost killed me with it too, if you know what I mean.

Before you rush to judge, Master Raptus, explain this: if we're meant to turn our minds toward the spiritual, why are there constant reminders of the pleasures of the flesh? Even the monks have damned badges shaped like women's quoniam pinned to their cloaks, while all along the way, the churches are decorated with statues shaped like men's pricks, and any number of reliquaries and souvenirs shaped like cocks and cunts are everywhere to purchase. After a few days, I stopped pondering the whys, and determined to enjoy my widowhood and the freedoms that come with being my own woman. I've encouraged Milda to do the same, Alyson too—though, in her usual fashion, she keeps to herself and shuns the offers made, preferring instead to ensure I'm only bothered to the degree I want to be. On this pilgrimage, it's been more than I ever knew I would.

I can feel your blushes, Geoffrey. The way you pretend not to be amused, turning your chuckles into hollow coughs. Dear God, man, if I cannot share my intimate thoughts with you, The Poet who captures the very heart of lust and love, of a woman's part, then with whom?

Rest assured, being away has done me the world of good. Cologne is a sacred town—it has to be with so many bloody churches (twelve at last count)—the cathedral notwithstanding. The Hanseatic League are here, a canny mob of merchants and traders if ever there was one and, if I had mastery of German and French and all the other languages from which these men seem to borrow, I would strike up negotiations with them here and now.

As I walk, admiring the stone houses, cobbled streets, and enter the grand cathedral, or the Dom, as it's called, I find myself strangely disappointed. It's not properly built. It's crawling with scaffolding, builders, stonemasons, workers of all stripes, and you should see the state of other parts—the twin spires everyone's boasting about look more like the nubs of goat horns. It will be centuries before the damn thing is finished.

This hasn't prevented us admiring the beautiful golden reliquary containing the remains of the Three Wise Men, which glows like honey beneath an enormous arched window and is what everyone really comes to see. It was worth the entire trip just to lay eyes upon it.

Alyson and I had many nights in hotels and mon-asteries when we could discuss what I should do with all the offers for my hand that flooded in before I left Bath. Whether it was old Sir Percy, that down-on-his-luck merchant Richard de Angle, or the mercer Henry Makeward, I've decided that three husbands is more than enough. I'm happier being free of men and marriage. As a widow, I've the liberty to love where I choose and without judgment—even yours—well, not as much. I've control over my own destiny, and Fortuna can decide how far to turn her wheel on my behalf without the burden of a husband beside me.

That is what I wanted to tell you, Geoffrey. I'm fore-swearing marriage. From hereon, I wish to be known as the Widow of Bath. I will enjoy the fruits of my labors. As will Alyson, Milda, and my workers.

Alyson asks that I send you her blessings and we both ask you to do the same on our behalf to Father Elias, Oriel, Sweteman, Wy, and young Jankin should you be in Bath any time soon. I was so sorry to learn of Master Binder's passing. I'm relieved Jankin is doing well in his studies and that these will go some way to being a much-needed distraction in his time of sorrow.

I hope to be home before winter, Geoffrey, by which time I pray this matter with Cecilia will be put to bed (a poor choice of words). Just importune the Almighty there's no child that will bind you forever to that termagant.

Written on the Feast of St. Swithun.

I remain your constant friend—whatever the verdict, Eleanor.

The Tale of Husband the Fourth, Simon de la Pole

1380 to 1384
That's very near the truth it seems to me;
A man can win us best with flattery.
To dance attendance on us, make a fuss,
Ensnare us all, the best and worst of us.

—The Wife of Bath's Tale, *The Canterbury Tales* by
Geoffrey Chaucer, translated by Neville Coghill

TWENTY-THREE

Bath
The Year of Our Lord 1380
In the third year of the reign of Richard II

I married the brogger, Simon de la Pole, on the steps of St. Michael's Without the Walls on a cool morning in late June with Geoffrey's and Alyson's disapproval ringing louder in my ears than the bloody church bells.

Despite all the promises I'd made, the exciting plans shored up, the intentions I'd held close, once I returned to Bath from Cologne, they fell by the wayside the moment Simon de la Pole appeared on my doorstep.

He'd made quite the impression at Mervyn's funeral. Partly because something about him reminded me of Durand and the passions he'd aroused, and partly because he appeared to so swiftly forget me when I wasn't looking at him. I was curious, inflamed, and determined to win his attention—a deadly combination.

For all that I'd been married three times, and enjoyed many trysts on my last pilgrimage, I wasn't nearly as experienced with men as I liked to believe. I was, however, excellent at business and, I hoped, at managing my by now quite large household. I also thought I was a good friend, but short-sightedness, and refusing to hear what you don't wish to hear, can make a poor one of the best of us.

This isn't something I'd have recognized back then. It's only now, as an old woman reflecting on my younger years, I understand how ignorant I was, how foolish, and also, how desperate to be loved.

That was my undoing—and not just with Simon.

When Geoffrey learned I was intending to marry Simon, he made it his mission to come to Bath and dissuade me. Luckily for him, the case Cecilia Champain brought against him hadn't proceeded, in no small part due to the powerful men he had to testify on his behalf.

Geoffrey descended upon Slynge House in an uproar. I was hardly inclined to listen. As I said in the long letter from Cologne, and then shouted to his face, who was he to preach to me about poor choices when he carelessly shoved his prod in an unwed heifer? A heifer inclined to accuse him of a grievous crime? Simon, by contrast, wasn't prepared to sard me until we were wed, and I was used goods and all.

When Alyson added her concerns to Geoffrey's, I was about ready to box their ears and order the two of them from the house. Instead, as we raged at each other one night, I balled my fists and stood my ground. They could do their worst.

"Ask Mistress Ketch," cried Alyson, half out of her chair, pointing toward the window. "She'll tell you what he did to her daughter. What he did to their neighbors' girls as well."

"Who on God's good earth is Mistress Ketch and why should I care about her, her daughter, or their bloody neighbors?"

"They're farmers, that's who, and those girls, who were virgins until your debaucher came a-knocking, are about to drop de la Pole lambs, aren't they?"

"Who says they're Simon's?" I screeched.

"The girls!" yelled Alyson.

I'd no doubt the entire household could hear us. We stood feet apart in the solar, Geoffrey between us, Milda pretending to fold linens as we hollered and roared. I'd never seen Alyson so angry. Nay, angry is not the right word. Determined. Determined to have her say and make me listen. Alas, I was deaf to her entreaties. The fact Simon had fathered babes was confirmation his prick worked and I felt thrilled at the prospect he might fill me with child as well.

I was love-sick. Afflicted with a disease of the heart. Geoffrey called me cunt-dazed.

When rumors about Simon's first wife dying from neglect reached us, I put it down to jealousy. Likewise when we heard a maid in Lady Frondwyn's house had died giving birth to a child claimed to be his. A laundress at the Abbey said he'd forced himself upon her and was so shamed she threw herself in the river. She survived, but left Bath forthwith.

Next there'd be folk claiming he fathered the entire choir of St. Michael's, or the tinker's children who performed on market days. Stories about his womanizing reached such a point of absurdity, I closed my ears and instead chose to judge the man who paid court to me by his actions—toward me. The man who arrived dressed in his best clothes to escort me to church, the market, the pasture to see the flock, freely giving his advice about their fleeces, which he judged to be among the finest he'd seen (he was a brogger, after all). The man who never once tried to kiss my lips, or take advantage (God knows, I wanted him to), but treated me as if I were a princess, a virgin, and a martyr all rolled into one. He would admire my eyes, teeth, mouth, and body—not with his hands, lips, or tongue (though he told me oft how much he desired me—one look at his breeches and I knew this to be true), but with words.

I told Geoffrey he would do well to ape my lover's words in his writing. I'd never seen Geoffrey look so hurt. "And you would expect me to ask a queen how to thread a loom just because she wears your cloth?"

That silenced me.

"Why rush, Eleanor?" he said eventually, his face red, his eyes pained. "Not so long ago you claimed you'd never marry again."

"That was before Simon."

"Seems that no sooner is one husband dead and gone, you find some other Christian man to take you on," he whispered.

Picking up her sewing once more, Alyson raised her head. "Haven't you heard, Master Geoffrey? Simon de la Pole is no Christian, he's a Lollard."

"Don't you dare use that against him, Alyson," I said. "Yesterday you were saying it was the only thing about him you approved of."

"It is," she said. "Doesn't mean I approve of *him*, though."

I clucked in annoyance. "Nowhere does God say there's a limit to the number of husbands a woman can have." I dared Geoffrey to challenge me.

He didn't. I took it as a cue to continue.

"Where did the Lord command virginity? Tell me that, eh. On the contrary, He tells us to go forth and multiply. There's no finite number of husbands for women, nor wives for men, so why not multiply them? It's not as if I'm committing bigamy or adultery. My husbands are dead—may God assoil them. I love the Lord and my husbands equally. One in bed, the other in my heart and head."

Geoffrey gave a weak smile. "That as may be, Eleanor, but St. Paul believes that one can only truly come to God if one remains chaste."

"Of course, that's something a priest would say. But how many priests do you know who are virgins? Ha!" I threw up my hands. "Answer me this, Poet. If seed is never sown, then how can fresh virgins be grown? Look," I went and sat beside him, "I've nothing against virgins, as you and Alyson well know. You can quote all you like from St. Paul—who I reckon must have been a virgin to bleat about the state so—or Ptolemy or whoever, but it's not like I can turn into one now, can I? That horse has bolted, the sheep's been shorn, the gate's been breached. I may as well tune my desires using the instrument of wedlock."

I never admitted to them how much Simon's courting filled an emptiness I hadn't known existed until he reappeared with his pretty manners and even prettier words. Aye, it was flattery, good and true, and I needed to hear it. Like one of Geoffrey's love-sick fools, I believed his every utterance, about his desire, my beauty, even while my little ivory mirror, which I'd bought at the Haymarket in Cologne, told me otherwise. Even as Simon declared his love, a tiny voice whispered warnings, told me to proceed cautiously. Between them, my inner demons, Geoffrey and Alyson and even

Father Elias, my stubbornness was inflamed to greater acts of resistance. The more they objected, the closer I came to saying "aye" to Simon's proposal. I was afraid that changing my mind now would be an act of weakness.

Too late, I learned it would have signified strength.

In the end it made no difference what anyone said or what stories I heard—or even what I saw with my own eyes. I made excuses for everything. I married Simon amid a crowd of the curious, the doubtful, and the concerned, and as soon as I could, I tore him away from our marriage feast and the attractive servant he was talking to, and brought him to my—nay, *our*—bedroom.

There, Simon de la Pole took me as his wife. For all I'd longed for this moment, it was but brief. Oh, his pole was de-la-lightful. Hard, his thrusts keen, but he barely kissed my mouth, he didn't try to disrobe me, nor enjoy the flesh about which he'd rhapsodized so much over the months. He threw my skirts over my head, and pushed his way into my bower. Ready for him—as I had been for weeks—it was an easy entry and he was soon spent. I was just beginning, and wanting to be held and caressed until he was ready for round two. Instead, he leaped from the bed, pulled up his breeches, laced them, tidied his shirt and then, with a quick farewell, returned to the festivities downstairs.

I lay there staring at the ceiling wondering what in heaven's name had just happened. Here I was, on my wedding night, alone, while my husband celebrated his marriage the way, so it turned out, he preferred to live: *sans* wife.

Sans me.

TWENTY-FOUR

❖

Bath, Kent, and London
The Year of Our Lord 1381
In the fourth and fifth years of the reign of Richard II

There's not much to tell about my marriage to Simon de la Pole, not for the first years. It was exactly as Geoffrey and Alyson, and anyone else who possessed the courage to try and warn me had predicted: I worked and increased our wealth, while my husband not only strayed continuously, but kept a paramour.

What everyone implied, but I'd been too caught up in the fairy-tale of romance to see, was that he'd had a woman for years, long before he met me. A whore in a brothel in the center of town. She had a hold over him that nothing, not two marriages and numerous other affairs, could break. She went by the name Viola, though I was told her real name was Agatha Brown. Dressed like a lady (a wardrobe my coin contributed to after my marriage to Simon), she was a harlot, albeit a clever one. A lord's by-blow was the story, who, years earlier, had come to Bath after following the King's army and even, it was whispered, abandoning a baby.

Winsome, with long, dark curls, she was a beauty. Creamy flesh, long, delicate fingers, and a mouth even I wanted to kiss. I was eaten up with jealousy. I would sometimes hover outside the whorehouse just to catch a glimpse of her. Many times, I spotted her with my husband. It was a dirk driven into my heart, painful and enraging. This didn't stop me seeking them out. I was a glutton; I couldn't get enough. Each time, Alyson would grip me by the elbow and steer me back home, into the workshop, and sit me at a loom with a goblet of wine. Only weaving calmed me. Weaving and the solace of stories.

The one thing wealth, even modest wealth, allows you is books. With the help of Father Elias and Geoffrey, as well as the books Mervyn had left, I now had a small library of fifteen tomes. If it hadn't been for the tales of Ovid (which Father Elias read to me), the epics of Homer, Virgil, and the ancients, I don't know how I would have got through those early months as I reeled in shock from having my eyes opened to my husband's ways.

Of course I confronted him. He simply laughed.

"I never tried to hide Viola, you fool," he said, and wrapped his arms around me. "Whatever made you think I'd be satisfied with just one woman?"

"You married me."

Simon kissed the top of my head, then placed a long finger against my lips. "Aye. And that should be more than enough . . . for you."

That night, he made love to me the way I'd prayed he would on my wedding night. Instead of relishing it, all I could do as he kissed my breasts, ran his hands up and down my body, parted my legs, was wonder if he was thinking of her. When that wasn't distracting me, I was wishing I *was* her and that my russet-colored hair was dark, my teeth not quite so large and gapped, and that my freckles would vanish.

Never one to doubt myself (too much), as the months went past and spring arrived sending forth tiny, perfumed blooms and sweet gambolling lambs, I began to drink to forget. Night after night, I downed ales and wine, settling in the solar, trying not to think about who my wayward husband was swiving or where he went until well past curfew. The servants learned not to bother me; Oriel and Milda too. Only Alyson stayed by my side, dismissing the others and keeping me and my misery company. Everyone knew what my husband was and where he went on those long nights. The pitying looks at church were more than I could bear, so for a while I stopped attending, preferring to pay a fine.

Worried for my welfare, likely encouraged by Alyson, Father Elias visited, popping over most evenings and even some mornings, forcing me to rise from my stupor and my megrims to entertain him. Soon the loom ceased to provide any sort of comfort, and even reading or being read to held no joy. I began to replace the people in the tales with Simon and the sluts he bedded.

At the beginning of June, Geoffrey arrived. The news he brought was enough to rouse me from self-pity for a time. While I wallowed and my husband jabbed his fleshy spear in countless women, not only had Geoffrey been blessed with another son, Lewis, but around the country, rebellion was fomenting.

We sat in the solar, the full light from an overcast day streaming in the window. Milda and Oriel had brought ale and vittles. I merely picked. For certes, my kirtle and tunics were starting to hang. We ate and exchanged pleasantries—well, Alyson and Geoffrey did—as I wondered whether, if I continued to starve myself, I would resemble the slender Viola more . . .

"I'm surprised you haven't heard—" Geoffrey was saying.

"Heard what?" I asked, absently.

"That men from Bath Abbey lands have joined the rebels."

"Joined *who*?" I couldn't imagine Simon wanting any male company in the boudoir.

"I told you about this," said Alyson. "See, Geoffrey, you can't get through to her anymore. She's dwelling on another plane. That man will be the death of her."

Moving his seat closer, Geoffrey gathered my hands in his. "Listen carefully, Eleanor, lest what is happening beyond your walls starts to impact upon you."

I made the effort to sit up and focus. "I'm listening."

"The commons are rising against parliament. Against the poll tax and other duties. It's more than they can tolerate. In Fobbing, there was an attempt to kill a steward when he tried to collect his lord's dues. He escaped, but three of his clerks were beheaded. The men rioted, carting the heads about to impede anyone who tried to stop them."

I stared at him in disbelief. "The commons are rebelling? But . . . they'll be arrested and put to death."

"It's no deterrent," said Geoffrey. "The numbers joining the cause are growing. There've been riots in Kent, Gravesend, Maidstone, and around London. In the north of the country too. Men have picked up their tools and joined the rebellion—including men from here: the Abbey, lands owned by the Gerrish family—"

I gasped.

"And many more besides. They're refusing to pay any more taxes."

"You can't blame them for that," I said. The heavy taxes had long been an unfair burden, and not only on the poor. "The demands made by our lords, the King, have always been too much."

"And with the wars in France and Scotland, they're set to increase as his Grace looks to fund more battles." Geoffrey dragged his fingers through his hair.

I shook my head. "King Richard is only a boy—it's not him seeking war, but his advisors."

"That's true—especially Simon Sudbury, who is now both Archbishop of Canterbury and Chancellor. He sees this as his opportunity to make his mark."

I looked through the open window and, for the first time in weeks, actually saw what was out there. The streets were bustling with activity. There were carts laden with fruit, vegetables, and fish; men and women shouted to draw customers; mules and horses meandered in an orderly fashion down the middle of the street, and close behind them strolled elegantly dressed women, who paused to examine the vendors' produce. Shop fronts were open and inviting, their smiling owners beckoning people inside. Two milkmaids balanced yokes on their slender necks, stopping to fill a jug here, a beaker there. Urchins dashed between hooves and skirts, whether to pick pockets or beg coin, or even chase a stray dog for sport, I could not tell. A group of nuns scurried through the crowd, heads bowed, hands hidden in voluminous sleeves. A lone monk, his hood flung back to enjoy the weak sun, laughed uproariously with the owner of The Corbie's Feet, who was standing on his stoop. Funny that all this went on outside while I not only sat indoors, but inside my own head, brooding. Papa would be ashamed. But no more than I was myself. I'd let life go on while I stopped.

No man was worth this . . . Not even a husband.

I sat up properly.

"What do you think will happen, Geoffrey? With the rebels. Are we in danger?"

Geoffrey sighed. "Have you lost any workers yet?"

Much to my embarrassment, I didn't know. Me, who'd always prided myself on caring about my workers' well-being.

Alyson leveled a look of such compassion, it made me feel worse. "Young Damyan didn't show for work yesterday or today. I heard his father didn't go to the mill either. Other than that," she shrugged, "everyone else is accounted for."

Geoffrey grunted. "Confirms what I suspected. You've not only been generous to your servants, workers, and tenants, Eleanor, but in their minds, you're one of them."

I raised a brow.

"Common."

Aye, well, I was.

"Common-born doesn't mean common of mind or heart." I thought of Jankin and Alyson. Milda, Arnold, Drew, Wy, Oriel, and Sweteman too.

Geoffrey nodded. "John Ball, a priest from Essex, would agree. He's part of the rebellion and has everyone chanting lines from that song you hear in every inn and alehouse, *When Adam delved and Eve span, who was then the gentleman?*"

"There's great truth in that," said Alyson. "God didn't differenti-ate when he made us. Adam was born of the earth, and Eve of his body. He didn't bestow titles or riches upon them and deny those who followed. That's something we did. Something the church en-forces as well."

"Hush, Alyson," I said. "Enough of your Lollardy, even if I hap-pen to agree." I turned back to Geoffrey. "What do you think is the purpose of this uprising? Apart from abolishing taxes? It's unprec-edented."

"In England, aye. But it's no accident it's started when the King's armies are fighting on different fronts, when London and his Grace are without defenses."

"You think the commons will overthrow the King?" My heart began to pound.

"The rebels keep saying they're for King Richard."

"But don't they understand that the King represents the nobles and his court too?"

Geoffrey didn't answer at first. "The rebel leader, an archer who fought in the French War, I believe, has the commons persuaded that if they can just parley with the King, he'll come around to their way of thinking."

"Which is?"

"To abolish villeins, reduce taxes; allow men to rent land, to work it of their own free will, not in boon to a lord. To treat all men as equal."

"But," I stared at Geoffrey in disbelief, "that's impossible. We're not all equal. As Alyson said, we haven't been since we were expelled from Paradise."

"That doesn't mean we can't be again," said Alyson hotly. "At least by giving men free will—to work, to pray—they have a kind of equality; the equality of choice."

"You're sounding like one of these rebels yourself, Alyson," said Geoffrey, not unkindly.

The fight left her. "Nay, I'm no rebel, but as a woman, I can sym-pathize with them."

So could I. "We've no choice except those men give us." Choice should be a right, not a privilege one was born to or granted be-cause one was in possession of a prick. "What do you suggest we do, Geoffrey? What are you going to do? Are we safe here in town?"

"I think you should continue as you have, just be aware, be cautious. As for me, I'm going to return to London and pray that through some miracle this ends well. Only, I fear . . ." He stopped.

"What do you fear?"

"I fear it's only just begun and won't finish until blood is shed."

———◆———

Over the next few weeks, as more and more workers and servants left the outlying farms and Abbey lands, slipping away in the early morning, London-bound, news of the rebellion and the numbers involved grew. It was all anyone was talking about—some nervously, some with an unbecoming boldness that saw them being rude to the monks, to Lord and Lady Frondwyn, the wealthier merchants and shopkeepers, Father Elias and the other priests; all those they saw as their oppressors.

Even Simon ceased his nocturnal roaming, returning home still reeking of perfume and other scents, but keen to discover what we'd heard. He knew Geoffrey wrote and that Father Elias had connections that meant the news wasn't very old by the time it reached us. I confess I enjoyed those evenings sitting in the solar, deep in discussion with my husband, Alyson, Milda, Oriel, Master Sweteman, Drew, Arnold, and Jankin, too, when he came up from Oxford.

On the ides of June, the young King sought to parley with the rebels, traveling by barge to Greenwich. Instead of landing and talking, he remained on board and returned to the Tower. From all over the countryside, men marched toward London, the greatest number pouring in from Kent. Upon reaching Southwark, they attacked a bathhouse run by Flemish women. When the mayor of London tried to prevent the now bloodthirsty crowd crossing the bridge, the mob, joined by men from all over Southwark, defied him and ordered the bridgekeepers to let them cross or be killed. They were admitted.

In fear of his life as Comptroller of Customs, Geoffrey locked himself in his Aldgate apartment, bearing witness to the hordes marching beneath him. When it was all over and he came to see us, he described the moment these angry, tired, and desperate men— among them farmers, lesser merchants, priests, soldiers, and land-owners—swarmed through the gate.

"The building shook as they marched. The noise of their fury, their shouts and chants, the smell, was like the bowels of hell had opened. They swarmed through, uncaring of any in their path, and if they met someone of Flemish or alien origins, they slaughtered them then and there."

Once news of the attacks on aliens reached Bath, the few Flemings and Italians in town—mostly merchants there for wool and cloth—hid indoors lest they too be punished for something our King and parliament had instigated.

Then, unexpectedly, news reached us the rebellion was over. Just as swiftly as it erupted, it was finished. Wat Tyler, the leader, was dead. Only later did we learn there'd been two meetings between the King and the rebels. At the first, the King ceded to Tyler's demands. He promised to end serfdom and for justice to prevail. While this was happening, a group of rebels broke into the Tower and murdered Archbishop Sudbury and another monk. Whether that was the reason the King revoked his word, I don't know. Upon the second meeting, the King was accompanied by the Lord Mayor of London, William Walworth. The mayor smote Wat Tyler with a dagger, grievously wounding him, and later cut off his head and mounted it on a pole. The King, sensing the rebels were about to retaliate, rode out to meet them at Smithfield and ordered his soldiers to do them no harm. He promised them everything again; even had it written down and sealed in a document.

The rebels, believing their sovereign, went home. We heard the story from those who returned to Bath, how the fourteen-year-old King was so brave, so bold. How bloody war nearly broke out between the commons and the King's men on English soil. The returned rebels were full of praise for our ruler, excited by what he had promised and, most of all, about the future.

For a few weeks, so was I. What did this portend for our country? For relations between the nobility, gentry, and commons? Dear God, were we about to witness the impossible?

As with anything impossible, it didn't happen. The King's charter of equality and the general amnesty for the rebels were revoked and, come winter, parliament announced that the rebels were to be fined.

Those who weren't granted a royal pardon, among them the leaders, were put to death.

In the quiet of our home, we'd oft discuss what happened that day at Smithfield, when a rebel leader was killed and the King prevented a war by appeasing an angry mob. Was he lying when he agreed to their terms? Was he merely biding his time before he wrought vengeance? Or was he the puppet of his advisors? Not even Geoffrey had the answers.

In the meantime, as the rebellion reached its ugly conclusion, and Geoffrey continued to be estranged from his wife and children, my marriage was making me increasingly unhappy. Taking a leaf out of King Richard's book, I made plans of my own.

Vengeance is mine, sayeth the Lord.

So does Eleanor de la Pole.

TWENTY-FIVE

❖

Bath
The Years of Our Lord 1382 to 1384
In the fifth to seventh years of the reign of Richard II

I wish I could blame someone else for what unfolded, for the person I became. Above all, I wish I could blame Simon bloody de la bloody Pole. But if I did, that would be taking the easy path and, as Alyson oft noted, that wasn't in my bloody nature.

You'd think the rebellion led by Jack Straw, Wat Tyler, whatever his real name was (may God assoil him) would have knocked some sense into me, led me to conclude that no matter what happens, your birth dictates whether you're a commoner or not. But the way I saw it, I was a commoner who'd had good fortune thrust upon me. Unlike so many in servitude to cruel lords, the men I'd married had allowed me mastery, which meant I'd a better chance at succeeding than most. If I now had a husband with a roving prick, then at least I had one and that, for better and worse, gave me a kind of respectability.

But I was also a woman and that put me at the greatest of disadvantages. Did folk look askance at Simon and think less of him because he continued to explore other female flesh? Nay. It was my fault he made the beast with two backs with whomever he fancied. I'd become a laughing stock, fodder for the gossips, and while I was furious with Simon and desperately hurt, I was angrier with myself that I'd allowed someone who could have stepped out of one of Geoffrey's tales to turn my head.

Judas's balls. I wasn't twelve anymore.

In order to quench the rage burning inside me, I sought ways to make my philandering groom's life as miserable as mine had become. What I failed to understand was that misery begets misery. In acting like a shrew, I became one.

I would point out faults in Simon's dress, business dealings, manner, and announce them, regardless of who was present. I'd fire shot after shot, convinced I was weakening the Simon stronghold. My husband, curse his white teeth, would laugh as if it were all in jest, lifting my hand and dropping a kiss upon it. He would call for more wine, encourage me to think of more insults. The worse I behaved, the more charming he became. I could see guests casting horrified looks in my direction and pitying ones at him. More than once I heard people whispering that Mistress de la Pole was a right witch and the only reason poor Simon remained was because I'd cast a terrible spell. No wonder he strayed when being with me was so unpleasant.

Not so unpleasant he didn't continue to enjoy my wealth.

Sometimes, when the mood took me, I would put aside my scolding and be coy and loving, coaxing him to the bedroom. I would wait until I'd secured him behind a closed door and let fly. I would throw things, shout, pummel his chest, accuse him of all manner of crimes, and not just because he sarded anything with a queynte.

He would clutch my wrists, cock his head and say, "I was warned women are duplicitous by nature and that they hide their faults until such time as the ring is upon the finger. I'd believed you different, my love. How you dismay me."

Lost for words, driving my nails into my palms so I didn't reach for the poker and strike him, I would stammer and stutter. He would take my confusion, my fury, as an opportunity to disappear, blowing me a kiss from the doorway.

"Go to your Viola, then," I'd scream. "And may her queynte be filled with disease and shrivel your prick!"

One night, I told him that though I couldn't stop him being free with my goods, he could no longer have my body. He laughed uproariously and left. Afterward, through a veil of tears, I flung open the chest in which his clothes were kept and cut up every single piece.

He bought more. With my coin.

I sold his favorite horse: for a groat.

He bought another: for a pound.

I sent a parcel of cow shit to his whore.

She sent it back—flung against my door.

When I saw Oriel supervising two of the maids as they cleaned it, I felt ashamed. I sent them away and did it myself, earning strange looks and some laughs from passersby.

Oh, my arguments with Simon provided the best sport for the good folk of Bath.

All the while, Simon continued to flatter, cajole, and charm every single person he encountered. I began to repel them. Rumors started that my previous husbands had been fortunate to die and escape being hitched to a scold. Invitations dwindled. Visitors, apart from those Simon encouraged, all but ceased.

The only person I was hurting was myself.

In the meantime, life continued. I vaguely remember hearing that the King married a girl named Anne of Bohemia. (Did that place have any worthwhile shrines to visit?) Geoffrey and I corresponded regularly, his letters filled with news about the fine new customs house built at Woolwharf, replete with a weighing machine and an accounting room. What most excited him was the fact there was also a privy installed, so he didn't have to piss in a corner or shit in a jordan. Bemused he would think I cared about such trivialities, I was nonetheless grateful he shared them. I needed distractions.

When Geoffrey's mother died, I sent my sympathies. Alyson grew all excited when, the next time Geoffrey visited, he told us that John Wycliffe, the Lollard priest, had translated the Bible into English (I confess, I was quite thrilled to learn that too, but expressing it didn't suit the version of myself I had become at that time). At some stage,

Geoffrey's daughter became a fully-fledged nun at Barking Abbey in London. He didn't tell me, a merchant did. Wasn't Geoffrey proud of his children's accomplishments? (If you could call becoming a nun an accomplishment.) Or was it something else? The Abbey had a reputation for late-night parties and many, many visitors of the male variety. Mayhap, taking the veil wasn't such a bad option?

To make matters worse, whenever Geoffrey stayed with us, Simon made sure to ply him with the finest wines and ordered delicacies from the kitchen. He would take Geoffrey on a tour of our pastures, bring him into the hall where the weavers and spinners sat working, as if he was responsible for the fine fleeces and the quality of the cloth. I watched as Geoffrey laughed and chatted and retired with my husband to his office in the evening. Over nuncheon one day, I even had to endure Simon being critical of women who had multiple husbands. Whereas once I would have sat quietly and fumed, I drew upon the reading I'd done to at least offer up some examples of much-wed men.

"What of Lamech, who took two wives?" I said smugly.

Geoffrey buried his chin in his cup, hiding a smile. My husband gave one of his infuriating nods.

"Ah, I see you've been heeding the words of Father Elias, Eleanor. My wife, you'll note, Master Geoffrey, is excellent at parroting the words of her betters, even if it's to defend the indefensible."

I ground my teeth. "I'm no exotic bird to echo men's utterances, husband, not even good Father Elias's. I did read of Lamach, sir, as well as of Abraham who took several brides, in the Wycliffe Bible."

Raising his goblet, my husband chuckled. "You certainly aren't exotic, my dear. But a solid—very solid—common woman. An attribute some appreciate, isn't that so, Geoffrey?"

See what I had to contend with?

But when Geoffrey defended Simon, I knew I was losing the battle.

Come autumn, I changed tactics. Showing Simon how much his behavior upset me hadn't worked, so I strove to make him jealous.

I sent invitations to the men who'd once been eager for my hand. Whereas it took some persuasion to convince them to come—my new reputation making them cautious—they did. Simon had no choice but to be present, as discussion of business was often the pretext for their visits. Over a fine meal, I made sure to flirt outrageously, my breasts positively bursting from low-cut kirtles, letting my fingers linger on the arms and even the thighs of those next to me. When Master James Roberts followed me into the passage after a long meal, staggering from the number of drinks he'd downed, I allowed him to free my breasts and squeeze my buttocks, praying the whole time Simon would find us. He did, just in time to see James extract his hand from beneath my dress. What did he do? Clap the man around the shoulders, tell him he'd do better digging in a ditch than in those regions, and escorted him back to the table.

Later, when we were alone, he said he'd observed how I lost all sense when I was in my cups, and, if I wanted a grubby merchant to fondle me, I'd be better off with Harold Foysdyck, who at least had clean fingers.

Unlike Turbet, the attention of other men wasn't going to work with Simon. What if he couldn't see what I was up to? His imagination would fire and he'd think the worst and seek to at least parley. For certes, my imaginings went awry when I didn't know what he was doing.

I reduced the amount I drank, took more care with my appearance. The moment my husband returned home, I would leave, neither informing him of where I was going nor when I'd be back. I would make the rounds of various houses, watch processions, applaud the loudest at a play, weep the most at weddings, purchase all sorts at shops. Did I have dalliances on those days? Those evenings? Sometimes. Never with a married man. But those I had only served one purpose—a purpose that ultimately, like all my efforts, failed.

My sadness knew no bounds. I forgot to smile. To laugh. My dignity was in tatters and I didn't know how to repair it.

One year passed into another and time dragged.

On the upside, the weaving business was doing well—in no small part due to Alyson. Between them, Milda, Sweteman, Drew, Hob, Arnold, and Oriel saw that the flocks and the house ran smoothly. Wy cared for the hounds, hens, and other domestic animals. I continued to write to Geoffrey, albeit a bit more frequently. I was in need of a friend, someone outside the household, and as much as Father Elias was a marvelous confidant, outside the town. Bath could feel very, very small.

Recognizing my despair, Geoffrey organized for Jankin, who'd finished his studies and was biding his time before taking the cloth, to return to Bath and live in Slynge House so I could continue my lessons. Since I'd gone to Cologne, I'd neglected them. At first, I was resistant. But as Geoffrey reminded me, in the past I'd found much solace in learning, and there was no reason to believe I would not do so again.

Jankin arrived in the spring and at first I didn't recognize him. The lad who'd first accompanied his father to the house all those years ago, and later taken over my lessons, had matured into a very fine young man. Possessed of broad shoulders and legs that could have been the work of an Italian sculptor, he was an unexpected pleasure. For my senses, you understand. He was still a child in so many ways, please don't think me one to prey on the vulnerable. But his smile lit a room, his melodious voice plucked at my soul, his patience and praise were a welcome balm for my ills. Not at first, mind. At first, I used him as a pawn in my never-ending battle with Simon, whining and moaning about my wayward husband, pleased to have such a handsome advocate under my roof. To my satisfaction, Jankin would rouse to anger at my stories, his usually sweet face twisting into an alarming rage. On those occasions, I would swiftly counter Simon's dark deeds with other tales. Jankin's choler would cool and I was content.

Along with Alyson, Jankin and I would sometimes wander about town, making purchases. Then we'd take a picnic into the surrounding hills and lie beneath the trees, talking about all manner of things from God, a passage in the Wycliffe Bible, and even ourselves. Sometimes our hands would meet, our fingers stroke, our laughter meld. More oft, we enjoyed blessed silence. Birds would sing, butterflies dance, and lambs gambol. When I was with Jankin and Alyson, away from the house and the town and the curious and judgmental stares, I could forget my husband's antics and the turmoil they caused.

Simon and I continued to argue and play games with each other. I'm not sure why I was so desperate to gain his attention. I didn't love him. Oh, I wanted his admiration, for him to admit desire, but it became like a competition I had to win. Problem was, Simon wasn't even aware there was one.

What finally began to shake me out of my reckless behavior was Alyson. She came to my room one morning when I was struggling to rise. Simon hadn't come home again and I'd fallen into bed in a drunken stupor, anything to blot out images of what he might be doing.

She sank onto the side of the bed and waited.

I opened first one eye, then the other, and pressed my fingers into my forehead. Another day, another megrim. My tongue was furry and sour. "How can you look so good so early?" I moaned. She smelled good too. Roses and violets.

"Eleanor, I need to speak with you."

"If it's about Simon, I don't want to hear it."

Alyson released a long, long sigh. So long, it was enough for me to haul myself up the pillows. "What is it, chick?"

She stared at me, chewing her lip, her hands in a ball. A great tear rolled down her cheek. That undid me. Alyson never cried.

I reached over and collected it on the tip of my finger, a veritable jewel. "Out with it. If someone or something has upset you, I want to know. I will run them through with a sword, shout at them until their ears bleed. I will throw them from the house." Tears continued to fall. "Come on, chick. You can tell me anything."

"I used to think that was true. What's not so certain is whether you will listen."

I threw myself back on the pillows with a groan. "Please, Alyson, it's too early for another scolding."

"It's not a scolding I'm here to give." She wiped her eyes. "I'm here to tell you I'm leaving."

I sat bolt upright. "Leaving?" The room spun.

"I've taken a lease on the house next door, the small cottage next to the apothecary's. You need time to sort things out with that husband of yours."

I rubbed my face. I stared at Alyson. Surely, I'd misheard. "But, whatever's going on between me and Simon, there's no reason for *you* to leave."

"My dearest Godsib . . . you haven't a clue, do you?"

"About what?" I'd endured enough insults from my husband, I didn't need Alyson to start.

"From where I stand, sit, sleep, work, there's every reason." She wriggled closer, waiting for me to meet her eyes. A great weight began to crush my chest. The megrim that greeted me transformed into something larger, something that encompassed my entire being. My limbs refused to cooperate.

"I can no longer bear to see you contorting yourself into so many shapes. I've forgotten, nay *you've* forgotten, what the original was." She paused and stared at her hands. "This marriage, this set you have against your husband, your desire to quash him and emerge the victor, it's changed you, Eleanor. I don't deny for a minute the man's a scoundrel, a scoundrel who can charm the birds from the trees, but you're destroying yourself, your beautiful, worthy self and for someone who, frankly, doesn't deserve you. I can't stand it. And, Eleanor—" she raised her eyes to meet mine. I'd never noticed before how many other colors were in the blue—there was emerald, a touch of honey. Most of all, there was the color of sorrow—deep, striking, and unbearable to see.

"I cannot stand what you've become. I fear if I don't go, then the love I bear you will also change into something horrid . . ."

"Hate?" I whispered, doing my utmost not to cry.

"Oh no," she said, shaking her head, her eyes welling again. "Something much, much worse, hen." She leaned toward me until our foreheads were touching. "Indifference."

Then, she pressed her lips to mine, rose, and without another word left the room.

With my blessing, Milda went with her until Alyson could hire someone. Arnold as well. Aggy also moved in, coming to work at Slynge House each day. Drew, Peter, and a few of the others would wander between the houses, the hounds likewise. And, while I still saw Alyson, it wasn't the same. There was a hollow in my heart that only having her beside me could fill.

I didn't need Simon, it turned out. I needed her.

More than ever, I had to loosen the unnatural hold he had over me.

This time, it was Geoffrey who showed me the way.

It was late autumn, 1384. Geoffrey came to visit when Simon was away in Bristol or Dover, wherever it was business took him. I pretended not to care. When Geoffrey settled down in the solar, asking after Alyson and Simon, Jankin, who was with us, coughed and asked politely if he should leave the room. I said it wasn't necessary. I'd nothing to hide. Not anymore.

I told Geoffrey where Alyson was and even the why of it. After all, I'd shared my triumphs with Geoffrey, why not my failures as well?

He sat still, neither drinking nor talking, for some time. When he spoke, it was quietly. "If what you say about your husband is true, Eleanor—"

My face grew red. I opened my mouth to let forth a stream of invective. How dare Geoffrey doubt me. But then he said something that vanquished the insults.

"Then I think the time has come for you to leave as well."

"Leave?" I sputtered. "As if I'm not shamed enough. If I leave, not only will it be admitting defeat, confirm what he says about me is true—" I gave Geoffrey a pointed look, "but what will people say?"

"Wait. Let me finish. If you go on a pilgrimage, then they will say nothing but words filled with esteem for your ability to admit your mistakes, to seek penance, and they will praise your piety. If ever you wanted a way to avenge yourself on your husband, to reclaim the person you were, then you need to put space between you, between your carnal desires and mishaps in that direction—" his cheeks filled with color, "and seek out more spiritual ones. What better way to do that than on a pilgrimage?"

Stunned, I fell back in my chair. Holy Moses in a hay cart. A pilgrimage. A romp in God's name. It *was* a solution of sorts. A trip would give me time to think. Wherever I chose to go, over land or sea, not only would I discover unfamiliar people and places and have adventures, more importantly, I might find someone who was once familiar to me and who I'd lost.

I might find me.

Warmth burst in my chest and my eyes gleamed. "Why, Geoffrey, that's a grand idea. But, where would I go? I would have to seek my husband's permission and . . ." I frowned. It was not done for wives to go traipsing about without it. But who was I kidding? Simon would sign anything to have me gone a while, to be free to pursue his . . . interests. I would also have to ask for Father Elias's blessing, mayhap the bishop's as well. I couldn't see that being a barrier.

"I think, my dear," said Geoffrey, smiling at the evident delight on my face, "that you should consider going to the one place you've always expressed a longing to see."

My eyes widened. "But . . . that would take months and months! I'll be gone forever."

"Not forever, but a goodly time. Time enough to mend what is broken both within this house—" he nodded in the direction of first, my bedroom, and then the house next door, "and much more importantly, within you."

I glanced at Jankin. "Would you accompany me?"

Jankin sucked in his breath, his chest puffing out. "I would accompany you anywhere, mistress," he said gallantly. Then, he paused. "May I enquire where it is we're going?"

I grinned, my face shining. "Where else, but the holiest of holy cities?"

"You don't mean—" Jankin began.

"Aye, I do. We're going to Jerusalem."

PILGRIMAGE TO JERUSALEM

———◆———

A letter to
Master Geoffrey Chaucer
from
Mistress Eleanor de la Pole, wife

After dutiful commendation, I beg for your blessing as humbly as I can, dear Geoffrey.

I pray you received the missives I sent from Venice, and know we reached that marvel upon the water in relatively good health, despite the journey being rudely interrupted. Unlike my earlier letters, when I was still raw and angry from the manner in which I left Bath, in a fury with my husband and telling him, and anyone else outside the church that last Sunday, I wished him dead, I've had time to reflect upon my actions (and his) and reach an inner accord . . . of sorts.

When I boarded ship in Southampton with Alyson, Jankin, Drew, and Arnold, Fortuna smiled upon me by including among our merry group a very affable priest with a wonderful sense of humor prepared to listen to a recounting of my many sins. Of course, he cannot speak a word of English, nor me of Spanish, but that hardly matters because God knows all—no matter what language it's spoken in—and it is He who listens and intercedes. The priest is merely His earthly medium and mouthpiece. I do recall both you and Father Elias saying this often. Do not accuse *me* of failing to listen.

Your advice to leave Bath and, indeed, English shores was both wise and well-timed, Geoffrey, because I fear if I hadn't, I may well have acted upon my threat and struck my husband dead where he stood—with his prick inside the little milkmaid. God forgive me.

While my newly found peace is good news, the bad news is, we were forced to leave Arnold in Venice. He failed to recover from the fever he caught just before our arrival. The captain of our vessel wouldn't allow him to board for fear of contagion, memories of the Botch large in his mind. I left enough coin that he might be accommodated in a modest palazzo, and acquired the services of a kind *dottore* to care for him. He's under instructions that once he's well enough, he can either wait for our return or head home on his own.

As a consequence, only Alyson, Jankin, and Drew made the journey with me to the Holy Land. Milda, as you know, deemed herself too old to set out with us, and I've promised to offer many prayers to the good Lord on her behalf. I will for you also, my friend.

Though you expressed concern about Jankin accompanying us, for reasons you failed to disclose, he's proven his worth over and over. His ability to speak foreign tongues has proved a boon and prevented many a misunderstanding. Not being able to correspond so frequently, I've found him to be a keen and discreet confidant. Of course, Alyson is her usual reliable self, but I also value gaining a male perspective, particularly from someone not inclined to hold me to account all the time. I've said to him on a few occasions, if ever I were a widow again, I would wed him.

And so, back to our journey. We boarded ship again in Venice, a cramped vessel filled to the brim with other pilgrims and so many animals it was impossible not to step in shit either above or below deck.

As part of our fee for sailing, the Venetian captain, a strapping fellow named Alessandro de Mare, has included ale, wine, brackish water, and any port taxes. It's all very convenient. Our papers, which we acquired before leaving (and once again, I thank you for your assistance) were in order, unlike a gentleman from Assisi who was left at our first stop, Rovigno.

After Rovigno, we sailed to Methoni (dull) then on to Crete (a small mountain arising out of the sea with a bottomless lake). I should add, the moment the ship raised anchor, Alyson became ill and was forced to lie in our cabin for days, unable to keep down anything but the tiniest bit of wine. I was most concerned, but the smell of vomit and shit in the cramped quarters made it hard to remain any length of time. I ended up sleeping on deck, among a number of my fellow travelers, which wasn't a bad way to while away time. For certes, it meant I was among the first to catch sight of each new town or city and marvel. It's so beautiful here, Geoffrey, a tad hot—I find myself tempted to remove my shift and wear just a kirtle, but know that wouldn't be wise, especially not as the further south we go, we come closer to Mosselmen country, where such liberties are frowned upon. And that's before I discuss the liberties some of my fellow passengers might take come nightfall if they knew my flesh was but a layer of linen away.

In Crete, our only choice of accommodation was a brothel. There were very few objections from the priests—only the nun and abbess (the only other women on board—and they don't really count) were vocal, but the proprietor, a Belgian woman named

Gerta, cleared the house. Alyson was so relieved to be in an unmoving bed, she even tolerated the fleas.

Next was Rhodes, a floating fortress by any other name, filled with magnificent-looking knights, raucous markets crammed with teetering baskets of fruit, fish, lumps of meat, bolts of glimmering fabric, and so much more besides. Beggars missing limbs sat with bowls and the piteous expressions they all wear, regardless of where they hail from, and I did divest my purse of much coin as I cannot bear the sight of such suffering.

Then we sailed to the isle of Cyprus (lots of white sand), the birthplace of Aphrodite, under whose sign, as I believe I've mentioned, I was born. I did honor the goddess by leaving an offering. What do you think the chances are that she might heed my prayers, since God Almighty has failed to thus far?

Once we left that island, the mood on board underwent a transformation. Those who'd made this journey before were filled with eagerness, a kind of desperation. They would spend each day leaning over one side of the ship, eyes fixed on the horizon. I wondered if they too had been overcome by fever, and they had, in a way.

I'd just brought Alyson up from below deck. The wind was sweet, the air clean. The sun shone and large fish were breaching the waters, almost dancing before us as we sped across the shimmering surface. I began to think of those stories of Odysseus and his crew carving through wine-dark oceans as they head home—before the gods intervene, that is. As we came on deck, my fellow pilgrims burst into a chorus of song, some fell to their knees, laughing with joy, throwing their arms about each other and pointing toward the distant shore and the low hills of Palestine—the Holy Land. Kisses and warm smiles were exchanged, and that night there was a feast and much drinking. The magnificent ululations of the crew echoed long into the night.

We'd arrived. Almost.

We docked in the port of Jaffa and were greeted (if you can call it that) by officialdom. Our papers were checked and rechecked and then, after a rather firm lecture, we were spirited away to some dark and gloomy accommodation where we waited for days to be given permission to travel to the Holy City. I thought England held the crown when it came to administration—nay, 'tis the Saracens. Finally, when I thought we may as well just board our vessel and sail back home, the guide, along with armed guards, arrived to lead us through Palestine.

Twenty men accompanied us, all heavily armed with swords that curved like a goat's horn, which was just as well, because one night a group of Bedouins attacked. One of our guards was killed, along with three of the tribesmen. Put rather a damper on proceedings, let me tell you.

We were all eager to get to the Holy City and a degree of safety. When we first sighted those sacred walls, what can I say? Safety was not foremost in my mind. Geoffrey, you know I'm not one for displays—oh, alright, displays of religious devotion—but when I laid eyes upon the walls of Jerusalem, like the other pilgrims I slid off the donkey and fell to my knees. Jankin, Drew, and Alyson also. My eyes swam with unshed tears, my heart sang. O Jerusalem!

We entered through Fish Gate and made our way to the church of the Holy Sepulchre. Much to my disappointment, we were forbidden to enter and had to simply look upon its facade. How one can truly appreciate great lumps of rock, even if they house a miracle, defeats me. Yet, when the English friar pompously declared this very place was worshipped by the entire world, you'd swear he'd said, "Oh look, there's the Almighty!" as the other pilgrims fell to the ground, began to weep and make the most terrible fuss. The abbess and nun bellowed like cattle in labor, our Spanish pilgrims lay unmoving with their faces in the dirt, arms and legs splayed. The rest knelt and began to pray. Loudly. What did I do, I hear you ask? Nothing, but watched in bemusement, as did Alyson, Drew, and Jankin.

After a time (too long), we were taken to our lodgings. The friar and other priests were led up to a convent on Mount Sion while the rest of us ungodly ones had to make do with the hospital of St. John, a place in dire need of improvements. There were great holes in the walls, doors missing and windows without shutters or hide to keep the swarms of flies and biting insects out, never mind prying eyes. A small group of Franciscans welcomed us and, the following day, along with our guide, a portly man of middling years who I think was called Shalom (at least, that's what he and the Franciscans kept saying), we were taken to all the holy sites.

Now, Geoffrey, I'm all for visiting a shrine, as you're well aware, but never in my thirty-odd years have I encountered so many as I did here. Not one to be skeptical, it nevertheless seemed that every ancient bough—especially if it was an olive tree—cairn of rubble, stone, pebble, doorway, broken step, chapel, church, or narrow passage wending between rows of stalls selling devotions and badges, had some holy significance.

If it wasn't Mother Mary's tears or Christ Our Savior's blood, it was the stone upon which Peter stood denying his Lord (how they knew it was that particular one and not the hundreds of others, I couldn't fathom), or where the Virgin waited while her Son was being tried.

Or it was pus from Jesus's wound or a piece of some saint's foreskin. On it went, for days—places where someone was beheaded, whipped, prayed, had a shit, lost a tooth (I made those up), said "Hello, did you miss me? I'm back." We saw them all.

Finally, we were admitted inside that most sacred of places, the Church of the Holy Sepulchre. The first thing I noticed was how dark and cool it was, and I offered an immediate prayer of thanks for being able to escape the glare and scorching heat. We processed around what was more or less a giant cave with rooms, stairs to different levels, and shrines in many corners. Groups of other pilgrims offered devotions to the Lord in a cacophony of tongues. Candles glowed, giving the hollows and shadows of the interior an almost festive feel. Kisses were given to the many, many relics and indulgences collected (I've more than my fair share).

Finally, we came to Jesus's tomb. Much to my disappointment, it was empty. Jankin said what did I expect, considering our Lord had long ago ascended into heaven above. I can honestly say I'm not sure, but more than a scraped-out rocky hollow reeking of incense, even if it did have a godly aura about it. This was swiftly ruined by us all being led to different corners and given a meal.

Before we left, I found a sharp rock and, like others before me, inscribed my name on the outside of Jesus's tomb. For posterity, you understand.

We returned to the church of the Holy Sepulchre on two more occasions and, along with Shalom, went to Bethlehem and saw the site of the Nativity. The manger was made of pale marble, which, as I noted to Jankin, was unlikely considering Jesus was born to poor Mary and Joseph in a stable. What bloody stable has a manger made of white marble? We also went to the Jordan River, where I dipped myself in the sacred waters. Alyson, Drew, and Jankin preferred to fill our bottles with the stuff instead.

All up, I entered Jerusalem three times, Geoffrey. Three times. The same number as the Holy Trinity. The same as the number of days Jesus waited before arising. If that's not a sign, I don't know what is.

So now, as I write to you, I'm spending my final evening in this loud, reeking, holy city—a city that, when you consider all the wars and the blood shed in order to claim it, simmers with rage.

However, Geoffrey, I no longer do. This pilgrimage has allowed me (as you thought it might) time to reflect upon my actions. Not only my haste in marrying after claiming I wouldn't, but my terrible dark drive to force my husband to capitulate and be true to me. Above all, I've learned that only once one is true to God can one be true to oneself. It's in Simon's nature to roam, to seek out other women. So be it. What's become apparent is that it's in my nature to care about what he does. When I return, I'll lead my life in a godly way, taking care of those who rely upon me, working to better myself with Jankin by my side, reading and writing and expanding my knowledge. I will work to build the business. I will also work to build my relationship with my husband on terms that make us both content. Not that this will stop me praying to God for his death, because, for certes, that would gratify me. Jankin and Alyson both tell me asking such a thing of our Lord isn't appropriate. There was a time I might have agreed, but frankly, after Jankin translated what some of these aliens were praying for, and in the holiest of churches, I think requesting your swiving pig of a husband be sent to hell to make the earth a better place is more than suitable. Praise be to God.

Thank you for your advice, Geoffrey. I'm forever grateful I heeded it and that the distance I needed to put between me and my husband will be my salvation.

I hope that God has blessed you and kept you in my absence. We've heard rumors that John Wycliffe is very ill, news that made Alyson quite distressed. I offered a prayer for his soul. I figure with so many different faiths here in the one city, God has room for Lollards too.

May peace find you, Geoffrey.

Written on the Feast of the Eleven Thousand Virgins (the irony is not lost on me).

Yours, Eleanor.

The Tale of Husband the Fifth, Jankin Binder

1385 to 1386
And Venus falls where Mercury is raised
And women therefore never can be praised
By learned men, old scribes who cannot do
The works of Venus more than my old shoe.

—The Wife of Bath's Prologue, *The Canterbury Tales* by
Geoffrey Chaucer, translated by Neville Coghill

TWENTY-SIX

Bath
The Year of Our Lord 1385
In the eighth year of the reign of Richard II

God, it seems, had a change of heart. He finally answered my prayers. Less than a month after returning from Jerusalem, in the middle of a bitter winter, my fourth husband, Simon de la Pole, was found dead, facedown in a puddle near his whore Viola's residence.

I didn't learn about this until the following morning, when a chalk-faced sergeant knocked on the door and Oriel brought him to the solar.

At first, I thought it a jest. How was it the man who'd caused me so much angst, whose death I'd prayed for the entire time I was heading to Jerusalem (I didn't quite so much when homeward bound, being filled with the Holy Spirit), should have ceased to exist? If I could have fallen to my knees and offered thanks to the Almighty, I would have. I tried hard to school my face. Alyson, who'd been brought upstairs from the workroom, ran to my side and squeezed my hand so tightly, it was all I could do not to call out.

"Try not to look quite so pleased," she hissed.

And here I was, thinking I was doing a fine job.

The sergeant explained that the coroner was with my husband's body (strange, isn't it, how a person in possession of a name, a life, family, history, enemies, a wife, and friends, is suddenly reduced to a mere corpse) and seeking any witnesses. At that moment Jankin staggered into the room.

His hair was unruly, his shirt tied incorrectly, and the marks of sleep were upon his face. There was a rather nasty cut on his lip and a reddened mark on one cheek. Had he been in another alehouse brawl? For a scholar, he was mighty ready with his fists, a notion that gave me an undue sense of pride and something else I wasn't yet ready to acknowledge.

"I heard about Master Simon," panted Jankin. "Peter told us." Of course, the servants would know. Soon, all of Bath would. "I came over straightaway."

In an effort to curtail the rumors my husband and his friends had started about my young tutor and the relationship we'd developed, upon our return from Jerusalem, Jankin boarded with Alyson next door. He crouched by my side and took my hand. "Are you alright, Mistress Eleanor?"

Have you ever tried to summon tears when the well is dry? I bowed my head and said something unintelligible, praying I looked the part of the grieving widow. I sniffed, screwed up my eyes. The sergeant blathered on about too much drink, Simon slipping and likely being knocked insensible and having the bad fortune to drown in less than a few inches of water. All the time my mind was screaming, how was this possible? Not the manner of death. The fact that Simon de la Pole, the man who had made my life a misery, was dead. Hallelujah!

The sergeant added the coroner would be in touch when his report was complete, which may take some weeks, and left as soon as was decent. Like most men, he couldn't cope with tears—even fake ones. As soon as we were certain he was out of earshot and no other servants were about, Alyson, Jankin, and I huddled together, staring in disbelief.

"Simon is dead. Praise be to God," I said, raising my eyes to the heavens and crossing myself.

"Praise the Lord," said Jankin, grinning from ear to ear.

Alyson withdrew her arm from my shoulders. "You should both be ashamed of yourselves. It's not right to be praising the Almighty for someone's death."

"Even though he was a lying, cheating scoundrel whose demise I'd longed for?" I dared her to defy me.

"Precisely because of that."

Determined not to let her spoil my sense of the world being set to rights, I continued. "Regardless," I said breezily, "I know the Lord will understand. That's why—" I moved from the comfort of Jankin's sympathetic presence and went to the sideboard to pour some wine, "I'm going to celebrate. Who will join me?" I held the jug aloft.

Alyson shook her head. "I've work to do—as do you, Eleanor. The servants need to be told. Formally. Irrespective of what you thought of your husband, the house has to be seen to mourn."

"Oh, we will. I will. I'll mourn that I was ever married to the swine." I passed a goblet to Jankin. "Don't look at me like that, Alyson." I blew a kiss. "Rest assured, I'll behave and perform my wifely duties one last time. It's the least I can offer the roving prick."

Alyson tut-tutted. "Be careful, Eleanor. It's ungodly to talk in such a manner and He will punish you for it."

"Not today He won't."

With another noise of disapproval, Alyson left. I turned to Jankin and raised my goblet. "Here's to my newfound and blessed liberty. Praise be to God. Or should that be the devil? I'm sure he's got Simon's soul now."

"Praise be to God, to Satan," said Jankin, his goblet kissing mine, "and to His agents here on earth."

I arched a brow. "What do you mean?"

"Don't you think it odd a strong man like Simon died in a puddle?"

"Depends how much he drank, I guess. Or how deep the puddle."

"Puddle implies it was shallow or—"

This is what happens when you keep company with a scholar; they dissect everything.

"That someone made sure he couldn't rise."

We clicked goblets again. "Then bless God's agents too," I said and laughed.

A few days later, Simon was buried inside the church of St. Michael's Without the Walls, Father Elias presiding. I'd written to Geoffrey immediately and he'd come straight to Bath. It was good to see him, to know he cared enough to be there in my hour of triumph . . . I mean, need.

There was a respectable turnout. Merchants, neighbors, monks from the Abbey, our weavers, guild members, a few broggers, some traveling quite the distance to be there. I stood across from my husband's shroud, hidden inside the coffin I'd bought. Geoffrey and Alyson stood beside me, the servants forming a protective arc. On the other side of the church stood a suspicious number of red-eyed women, including Viola, who even in her grief managed to look striking. There was a great deal of weeping, including from some merchants' wives. Not even the stern looks of their husbands or the shocked faces of their children stemmed the flow.

My handkerchief was barely damp as I tried to squeeze out tears. Fortunately, the veil I wore hid my face, so I made sure my shoulders slumped and my feet dragged. I leaned against Alyson or Geoffrey, both of whom made a show of holding me upright. Geoffrey didn't approve of my light-hearted attitude either, but being a friend, withheld judgment—this time.

"Just make sure if you marry again, Eleanor, you don't rush."

His words echoed in my mind as Simon's coffin was lowered into the church floor. Instead of bowing my head while prayers were said, I took the opportunity to assess those attending—well, alright, the men. I started to imagine which among them I'd consider a fit husband. There was Master Attenoke, the mercer, who had bow legs but hands so delicate, they looked like a woman's. Rumor had it he strangled his last wife and lusted after her daughters. I shuddered at the thought of those hands touching me. Then there was Master Monemaker, the silversmith. He was a secret Jew and evidently not very good at it. Master le Ould had outlived three wives and was so ancient, he made Mervyn seem a spring lamb. I glanced at Master Saper, a powerful merchant who was prone to threatening anyone who disagreed with him and was said to have killed three fellows last year alone. Master Clavynger was a decent, wealthy man as well as presentable but lived with his sister in a spacious house where only one bedroom was used. Enough said. My mind ticked over as Father Elias droned and the incense permeated my nostrils, kirtle, and cloak.

Geoffrey hissed at me to be still.

Right there and then, before God the Creator, and beneath the cross that bore His emaciated Son, who gave His life so we might have one everlasting, I made a solemn vow. If ever I married again, it would be for love—not lust, nor money or security—God knew, thanks to my first three husbands, well numbers one and three, I had those. I would allow my heart to dictate my future this time, not my queynte.

In answer to my silent communion, a beam of light struck Jankin. Curls of golden hair shone against the black of his paltock and cap and made his youthful face luminous. My eyes traveled, noticing anew how broad his chest, how chiseled his legs. How he bulged in his hose in a way that made my insides molten. Though I'd appreciated so many of his qualities before, only now, before my dead husband, did I appreciate the bits that made him so very, very manly. I swallowed.

Dear Lord, but it was hot in church. My heart began to beat erratically, my ribs expanded until my dress felt so tight, I found it difficult to breathe. I was like a virgin widow and me, all of thirty-three years. An aged woman by any standard, except in my head. Except in my heart. And, goddamn it, except in my queynte.

After the requiem, I invited everyone back to Slynge House. It was an opportunity to show those who'd believed Simon's version of me they'd been gulled. I was not a termagant, or a common slut who shared my favors with any man.

Not too many took advantage of my hospitality, but enough to make a slow difference. Their condolences were mixed with compliments on the fine repast and promises to extend invitations in due course, once my mourning was over. I didn't admit it already was.

Along with the servants, Alyson, and Jankin, I donned black, and out of respect for Simon's memory, we ceased to work for two days.

Geoffrey remained for that period. Together with Jankin and Alyson, we threw on our warmest cloaks and walked in the fields outside town, away from others. There was something about the cold, the snow, the defiant buds pushing through the layers as spring tried to make its presence felt, that gave me hope; the notion I could and would start again. We spoke of the future, of maintaining the business, mayhap even expanding it a little. We talked about the trip to Jerusalem, all the places we visited, sights we saw, and people we met. The only subject we didn't discuss was Simon's death, yet its specter haunted our every step. Still, I managed to laugh, link arms with my friends, one-up a story and joke.

Throughout these jaunts, our daily interactions, Geoffrey watched me as a hawk does a fieldmouse. I knew he was biding his time to say something, no doubt something I'd not want to hear.

He waited until our last evening together. We'd had a lovely long supper in the solar. When the bells tolled for vespers, Alyson and Jankin (who were still living next door, as the lease hadn't yet expired) made to leave. They were giving me and Geoffrey some time together. As a widow, I'd no need for a chaperone.

"Eleanor," Geoffrey began once we were alone. I knew that tone and resisted the urge to sigh. "I pray I'm wrong here, but I get a strong sense you have designs on young Jankin."

"Jankin?" I gave a forced laugh. "Why would you think that? The lad is young enough to be my son."

"Grandson. Why, you're two score years to his one."

"I am not!" I was most indignant. "Alyson is coming up to two score years, I'm nowhere near her age." I was six years younger—that was eons. "Anyway, so what if I have? I'm free to desire whom I want."

"Desire, aye . . . but what I'm sensing from you goes beyond that."

Damn if Geoffrey wasn't right. I'd been having dreams about being with Jankin. "What if I am? He'd make a fine husband. And being so much younger, he's not likely to die on me, is he?"

"Eleanor," he said softly. "You know I care about you deeply, that as your friend, your family, I've only your interests at heart. And it's the heart I want to talk about. I understand you must be flattered by the attention the boy gives you. Why, he worships you like a son. Did you not say he has no mother?"

My mind was reeling. Surely no son kissed their mother the way Jankin had kissed me over the last two days. Geoffrey couldn't know about those stolen kisses, could he? The fumbles we'd enjoyed. Why, Jankin might be young, but those hands, those lips, and that tongue knew what they were doing. The boy aroused such a heat in me, it turned my body into a furnace.

"His mother died when he was a babe."

"Well, that explains it," said Geoffrey, sinking back into his seat, a satisfied look on his face.

"Explains what?"

"The lad's unnatural attraction to you."

"Unnatural?" I virtually shrieked. "What's wrong with me, eh?" I dared him to speak. Alas, Geoffrey, for all his writing about women with such insight and knowledge, was utterly clueless.

"Look at you, Eleanor. To him, you're an old woman. Your hair has threads of silver, and while you have a slim waist, not having been blessed with a child, you're wide in the hips and large in the breasts."

"I've had no complaints," I muttered, wishing for the umpteenth time my waist had thickened.

Unabashed, Geoffrey continued. "You're not exactly a beauty—though I find you beautiful," he added hurriedly. "But I know you, Eleanor." He studied me, steepling his fingers and resting his chin on the fingertips. "Mayhap, Alyson is right and the lad feels a sense of pride because he taught you to read and write."

"You've discussed me with Alyson?"

"Of course."

I tried to appear indignant and failed. "'Twas his father taught me."

"The lad's continued the lessons." He frowned. "Was I mistaken to advise you to resume? It might have been better if Jankin had remained in Oxford."

"Why on earth would you say that?" I leaped to my feet. "You of all people know what a comfort he's been to me. When you, Geoffrey, refused to believe the kind of man Simon was, took his side, Jankin at

least supported me." I prodded my breast. "Jankin listened and protected me—here and when we went to Jerusalem." I downed the rest
of my drink. "Which is more than I can say for some."

"You're wrong, Eleanor. I knew exactly what kind of man your
husband was. And I warned you. The point was, you chose to marry
him and, as a wife, as a woman, it's not your place to object to what
your husband does."

"Not my place? As a wife? As a woman?" My voice was getting
louder. "Nay," I said, suddenly flopping back into the seat. "You're
right. We women have no rights, no place but beneath a man in every
regard—bed, home, business. We must obey all his commands, as if
he were a god and it's him we worship."

"That's blasphemy."

"But it's men who've made it that way. What is a husband to a
wife but a false idol? Tell me that, Geoffrey Chaucer. Why did God
give women queyntes, desires, if not to have us fulfill them? Why are
your needs, *your* wants, more important than mine just because you
have a prick?"

"Eleanor, calm down."

"Nay, I won't. Nor will I listen anymore, Geoffrey." I put my
goblet down hard on the table. With a straight back, I faced him.
"All my life, you've given me advice. Sweet Jesu, you arranged my
first marriage to a man old enough to be my grandfather and now
you're telling me I cannot marry a man young enough to be my son.
What's that if not hypocrisy of the highest order? Let me finish." I
took a deep breath. "I've heeded your words, Geoffrey—mostly—
and sometimes they've brought me great happiness and other times
they have not. Sometimes, your advice has been tardy and I've had
to abide by my own choices, but at least they were *mine*. So, thank
you for giving me counsel I never asked for. But I'm no longer twelve
nor twenty. I'm no longer a maiden, nor a mother, but a widow. Four.
Times. Over. Be damned if I'll be a lonely old one. I no longer need
your guidance, especially when I don't ask for it. I don't even need
your approval. What I do need is your friendship. A friendship that's
given unreservedly. Can you give me that?"

Geoffrey put down his drink, his eyes never leaving mine. "Depends."

"On what?"

"What you do next."

I sighed. "Once again, you seek to control me. To reward me for doing what you say or punish me for disobeying you. You're not my husband, Geoffrey."

He shrugged. "That's not what I meant. Rather, like Alyson, I cannot stand by and see you make a ruin of your life, a life you've a chance to make something of—with the right choices."

"Jankin won't ruin it!" I said. "He'll complete it."

"If you think that, then you're a bigger fool than I ever took you for."

I narrowed my eyes. "At least I'm my own fool."

This was a threshold moment. I could either stay one side of the line I'd drawn, or cross it and be damned.

You know what I chose.

Geoffrey didn't try and talk me out of my decision. He simply stood, smoothed out his paltock, tugged his sleeves, then embraced me long and hard. In that moment, I was taken back to the first time I smelled him—damp wool, old books, ink, and musty but not unpleasant sweat. Without another word, just a wistful smile, he left the room.

He was gone from the house when I woke next morning.

Despite my sending him an invitation, he never did come to my wedding to Jankin. Few did, but then, unlike my previous marriages, I kept this one very quiet.

Four weeks to the day after Simon was buried, I became Eleanor Binder. For a few weeks, I was blissfully happy, blissfully unaware of what I'd done.

The day after the wedding, I received a visit from the coroner. Out of courtesy, he came to the house. Jankin happened to be next door, packing up the last of his belongings to shift into Slynge House.

Master Reyngud, the coroner, was an officious, cold man. He sat in the solar and delivered his verdict, uncaring of the effect it would have on me.

Simon didn't drown as we'd first been told. According to the coroner, he was already dead when he fell in the puddle. A blow to the head and a broken neck caused by the vicious stomp of a large boot extinguished his life. I decided not to share this news—not with Alyson nor with Jankin. I didn't want to spoil what should have been a joyous occasion. I would have told Geoffrey, only I'd made a point of steering my own course.

Instead, I pushed what the coroner said to the back of my mind: the fact that my bastard husband, Simon de la Pole, was murdered and the killer, whoever he was, remained at large.

TWENTY-SEVEN

The first few weeks of my marriage to Jankin were everything that, as a young girl, I'd dreamed. He was attentive, kind, and courteous to me and the servants. Better still, he appreciated my humor, laughing with rather than at me. It was so refreshing, so different from life under Simon's baleful eye. At first, I was on tenterhooks, waiting for the barb to strike, the cutting remark to score, the bitter whisper in the ear. There were none.

In the bedroom, he was a fine lover, an ardent one, and I was sated in a way I'd never been. On our wedding night, I was initially coy, so aware of the differences in our ages, of his physical beauty and the shortcomings of my well-worn body, which Geoffrey had cruelly pointed out. Shocked I was so modest when he thought me the contrary, Jankin insisted on learning the origins of this newfound shyness. Reluctant to admit the cause lest in pointing out my flaws I drew attention to them, when I finally whispered what Geoffrey said, Jankin solemnly sat astride my naked body and slowly, with sensuous deliberation, lathed every single part of me with his tongue.

Never before have I been transported to such heights—except when I did the same for him, taking intense pleasure from his deep moans and groans and the shudders that racked his body.

We made excuses to meet in the bedroom, our sanctuary, stealing what hours we could from the day for lovemaking. He called me his beauty, his joy, and dear God, I wanted to believe that's what I was to him because, for certes, he was that to me and more.

Even Alyson started to relax, unable to ignore the happiness I exuded, and spoke of moving back as soon as the lease on her cottage expired come Hocktide. Likewise, the servants and workers basked in the glow of our serenity. Oriel hummed, Milda sang. The only blight on my otherwise perfect days, filled as they were with weaving, managing the house, being welcomed back into Bath merchant society, and my beautiful husband's youthful arms, was Geoffrey. We hadn't communicated since he failed to attend the wedding. I wanted to believe it was the demands of his role that kept him away. Then I heard from one of the many London wool merchants he'd been given a deputy to help with his onerous workload.

As the days went past, I thought of Geoffrey less and less, and instead enjoyed my husband.

It was the best of times.

I should have known they wouldn't last.

At the end of March, the coroner's report arrived. Until that moment, Jankin could do no wrong. But, instead of passing the letter to me, the addressee, he broke the seal and read it. I was about to give him a drubbing, when I saw his face pale.

"My colt, my darling, what is it?"

"It says here Simon's death was unnatural."

He thrust the letter toward me as if it were a burning coal. I scanned the contents. "Aye, I know. Terrible business. I've found myself dwelling on it occasionally. Wondering if Simon was afeared in his last moments, if he knew his killer . . ."

"You knew about this?" he said.

"The day after we wed, the coroner informed me."

"Why didn't you tell me?" His eyes glinted darkly.

"Tell you?" I raised my voice. "Why should I? Anyway, I didn't want to spoil our happiness."

"I've a right to know what's being claimed."

My brows became perfect arches. "Pray, why is that?"

"Because . . . I'm your husband."

"Aye, *now*. But this—" I shook the report, "is about *my* former husband. This happened prior to *our* marriage. Ergo, it has nothing to do with you."

"It has everything to do with me," said Jankin. His voice was strained, his cheeks red.

"Why is that?"

"You always said what would make you happiest was Simon's death. Now I find out you think upon the scoundrel in a sympathetic way, the man who caused you so much pain."

"I'm not a complete scold." I forced a laugh. "He was *murdered*, Jankin. I'd be heartless if I didn't spare him a thought."

"But you wanted him dead!"

"I wanted him out of my life—aye, dead, if that's what the good Lord decided. But not even I wished him *murdered*. That would be a terrible sin."

"But you toasted God's agents on earth—you drank to them, with me."

"I wasn't serious. Sweet Jesu, you cannot for a moment have thought I was."

Jankin stared at me. Sweat beaded his forehead and he was gulping in a most peculiar fashion.

"Frankly, I hope whoever is responsible hangs." I flicked the letter. "No doubt, they'll uncover the culprit. There's to be an investigation."

Jankin rubbed the back of his neck. "I don't understand how you can be so . . . so . . . changeable, Eleanor."

"Changeable? How? This doesn't change what's really important." I smiled and held out my hands to show him what I meant.

He locked eyes with me. "But it does."

What a child he was being. No wonder I sought to protect him. I took a step, intending to cup his face, kiss those beautiful lips. "Come now, my colt. Any good Christian soul should care about murder, it doesn't mean anything—"

He slapped my hands away. Hard. My flesh burned.

"How *dare* you!" I shoved my hands under my arms.

"How dare you patronize me." He stamped his boot. "I'm not a child!"

"Then stop acting like one!" I cried.

He raised his arm. I held my breath, waiting for the blow to fall, wondering what I would do, how I would react, when he spun on his heel and marched from the room. Stunned, I sank into a chair.

I ran my fingers through my hair, which was not yet dressed. Jankin's voice carried up the stairs as he ordered a horse saddled. I could hear the faint whir and clack of the looms and the low chatter of the workers below. Outside, mules and carts trundled past, vendors calling out their wares. It was still early, the morning was gray, dull. A brisk wind blew leaves and other debris down the street. What a start to the day. My mood, which had been light and filled with enthusiasm, was now wretched and heavy. Like the sky. Aye, it was terrible to learn that Simon had likely been murdered, but not a shock; not before, not then. The man dipped his wick wherever he pleased. I'd no doubt there'd be many a jealous husband keen to trim it and put a stop to his womanising. Then there was the drinking, gambling and God knew what else. What did it matter? Simon's death was what brought us together. Why did Jankin react so?

Our first argument. Was that why I felt peculiar? Almost drunk, I felt so off-kilter. God knew, there'd be more. I tried to shuck off my sadness, my sense of terrible foreboding. I picked up the report, trying to bring the words into focus. Simon was punched a few times before being struck from behind and, while on the ground, jumped on. His neck was broken before, it's believed, he was dragged and placed facedown in the puddle.

Even for Simon de la Pole, it was cruel way to die. A useless way. According to the report, Simon had grazes on his knuckles and a swollen eye. He'd been in an altercation. Not the first time. Jankin was right. I'd often wished him dead. Why, on the trip to Jerusalem, I'd even told Jankin about a dream I had where Simon lay broken and bloody and how pleased that had made me. Remorse flickered in my chest. Truth was, I hadn't dreamed it at all; well, I'd daydreamed it, Simon's death. Many times. But never, in all my wildest imaginings had I meant for it to become a reality, please God . . .

Why did Jankin care so much? Was it the report or the fact I hadn't shared the outcome that made him so angry?

Jankin would oft say he'd teach my husband a lesson and make sure he could never hurt me again. I'd laugh and chuck his chin, kiss his sweet lips. I'd never taken his earnest vows seriously. And yet, even back then, Jankin was no child to be pacified with a mere peck, a motherly stroke of the face. I'd hold him, sometimes for ages, crooning, soothing, enjoying the feel of his body curled into mine, his fine beard nuzzling against my breasts. When we'd returned from the Holy City, I'd kept him at arm's length to staunch the rumors. Since then, he'd been in more brawls than I could count. The morning we were told of Simon's death he'd evidently been in another. He had a cut lip, a bruised face. He'd been drinking and slept late as well . . .

My stomach lurched.

Was he God's agent? Satan's agent? Could Jankin have killed Simon?

I began to pace the room, my thoughts unraveling faster than a poor weave. The room grew smaller. Heat traveled through my body to be replaced by a river of ice. A thousand pairs of black wings took flight, battering the edges of my mind. What was it Geoffrey said?

Why, he worships you, but more like a son does a mother.

Alyson had made the same claim, many times. Only since we'd wed had she ceased her jibes.

A man would protect his love. But a son, a son would do anything to protect his mother. I was both to Jankin.

I rose unsteadily, one hand against my mouth, the other pressed to my stomach. I had to find Alyson, the only person I could confide in.

I had to ask her if she thought what I feared more than anything might be true.

That I'd not only married my husband's killer—worse, I'd created him.

TWENTY-EIGHT

<hr />

Bath
The Year of Our Lord 1385
In the eighth year of the reign of Richard II

*T*o think a few words on a page could turn one's life upside down, inside out and scatter it into eternity. From the day the coroner's report was delivered, everything changed.

Jankin changed.

From a loving, caring husband he became a caustic-tongued, violent man who would first slay me with his clever words and arguments and then, when I argued back, became a pugilist who used both me and Alyson to vent his rage.

And Simon had been the one to tell me it was women who altered the moment the ring was placed on their finger.

Let me tell you what happened when I confided my worst fears about Jankin to Alyson. She ceased what she was doing and stared at me as if my head had begun to rotate on my neck.

"I thought him too young for you, Eleanor, too impressionable, I admit that. I never thought for a moment he was capable of murder . . . I still don't." She pressed her lips together and folded her arms. "Why, the man's a scholar, not a brute."

"But what about all the scraps he's in?"

"What young man trying to prove his worth isn't?" she countered. "It's more important for Jankin to fight precisely because he's a man of words. He needs to show he's also one of action."

I dissolved into tears as all my pent-up emotions released in a torrent. "I want to believe you, on both counts," I wept. "Only, I'm afeared I've made a bad impression on Jankin by constantly harping about Simon and all his faults, building him up to be the greatest of sinners and myself a saint. Not once did I present a fair portrait of the man. If Jankin did kill Simon, then there's no one to blame but me. It's my fault. *My* fault. He was a puppet and I his puppet master."

"Nay, nay," said ever-loyal Alyson, gathering me in her arms, rocking me back and forth. "You're not to blame. For all I called Jankin a child, he's still a man who has his own conscience. He's answerable for *his* actions, to God and the law. If you're right, and he did murder Simon, it was *his* choice, not your doing."

We argued as I tried to take the burden of blame and Alyson refused to let me. Finally, we sat holding hands.

"Eleanor, even if you're right and Jankin killed Simon," said Alyson softly, "what then? Simon can't be brought back from the dead."

I made a noise of protest.

"Exactly." She tucked a tendril of hair behind my ear. "I may not have approved of your latest marriage, but I know you love him."

I sniffed loudly. "I did." I stared over Alyson's shoulder, out the window, watching the way the endless mizzle fell from the sky, tiny droplets of moisture. Tears from heaven; tears from my soul. "Nay, I do. God help me, even if he's guilty of murder, I still do. What does that make me, eh?"

I turned to her, fearing what I'd see. There was nothing but understanding and love on her face.

"I'll tell you what," I said, before she could answer. "It makes me a fool, enslaved to my heart—and my c—"

"It makes you a good wife," she interjected. "Prepared to give your husband the benefit of the doubt."

"Good wife?" A dry, bitter laugh escaped. "I should be by now. I've had plenty of practice."

Alyson released my hands. She rose, dropped a kiss on my head, and went to fetch ale from the jug on the sideboard.

"Will you confront him with your suspicions?" she asked.

My stomach lurched. Would I? I should. A part of me was afraid; afraid that if he confessed to killing Simon then I would be obliged to do something. I was a coward. I preferred wilful ignorance to dire knowledge.

"Nay. I will not. I cannot."

Alyson passed over a brimming mazer. "It's not our place to prosecute and judge, hen. If Jankin is guilty, he will answer to God. Some day."

If Jankin was guilty, then I'd have to own my part in his crime. I took the drink from Alyson and sipped it gratefully.

"When you're ready, dry your eyes. Wash your face," she said. "We've work to do and you can't appear before Milda, or Oriel and the weavers, like that."

"Like what?" I asked, using my apron to wipe my eyes.

"Like a child who's lost her favorite toy."

I choked back a sob. Not lost it—broken it.

———————

That very night, Alyson and I waited in the solar for Jankin to come home, trying to act as if all was well. He'd been gone all day, God knows where. We'd spent the day weaving, Alyson doing her utmost to ensure I wasn't disturbed. What a pity she couldn't protect me from my thoughts as well.

It was well after vespers before Jankin swaggered into the room. I'd dismissed the servants, given Oriel and Sweteman the night off. Peter and Drew we'd sent to Alyson's house with a few jugs of ale as a reward for their work. They didn't question us, but took the offering gratefully, as we'd hoped. Milda, sensing something was afoot, went next door to make sure Aggy and Rag were occupied as well. Wy, as was his preference, shared the stables with the hounds and horses. We were alone in the house.

Jankin had been drinking, the smell of ale and wine was strong on him, as was woodsmoke. His cheeks were flushed, his eyes bright. His face was unreadable as he glanced first at Alyson before settling his gaze upon me.

"Where have you been, my colt? We've been concerned," I said softly. "You dashed away as if the hounds of hell were snapping at your heels."

He grimaced. "Mayhap, they were." Casual as you like, he went to the sideboard and poured himself some wine. Shadows from the candles and the hearth danced across his back. He took a long draught and then turned.

"If you must know, wife—" Where was the endearment? The love that so often enveloped my title? "I went away to think. God knows, it's impossible in this house with the constant stream of people, the clatter of looms, the ceaseless chatter. A man cannot focus his mind."

"And pray, husband—" I made sure to imbue the word with affection, "where did you go?"

"Goody Parson's alehouse."

"All that way?" Goody Parson had an establishment on the road to London, about three miles outside the walls of Bath. It was popular with couriers and merchants. "And did you manage to do your thinking there?"

"Some. After that, I went to the Abbey."

"And what did you think about there?"

"For Godsakes, wife," shouted Jankin. Alyson and I leaped in fright. "If you can keep your thoughts private, then the least you can allow is your husband to do the same." He lobbed his goblet down on the sideboard. A chip of wood flew across the room.

My heart slammed against my ribs. Never before had he raised his voice, let alone damaged a piece of furniture. Alyson ceased spinning, her brow furrowed with concern.

Before I could say anything, Jankin continued. "You who sees fit to keep a coroner's findings from your husband, express sympathy for your dead spouse, dares to ask me what I think?" He laughed. It was dark, forced. He ran a finger over the gouge he'd made. "I thought about many things. And then, as I'm wont to do when disturbed, read." He moved to the chair opposite mine and waited.

"What did you read?" My throat was so very dry.

"I read about the nature of marriage. About husbands and wives. But most of all, wife, as I read I thought about you." His tone told me the color of those thoughts.

"I should have known," he continued, stretching out his legs before him. "You women are all the same, whether your husband is duplicitous and a philanderer, or whether he is honorable and true. You are secretive, disloyal." He waved his goblet. "It's all written down for any man of learning to find—the warnings, the examples. The Romans, priests, the ancient wordsmiths had the right of it. Women play men false, you lure us into believing you're one thing when really you're another."

I tried not to sigh. It wasn't as if I hadn't heard these things before. I just never expected to hear them tumble out of my sweet Jankin's mouth.

"Oh?" I said, gently, but defiantly. "And how do we do this, sir?"

"As easily as breathing." He held up a finger. "Look at Eve. Did she not tempt Adam to eat the apple, exiling mankind from Paradise, from God's Grace? And what of Delilah? She seduced the mighty warrior Samson into her bed before shearing off his locks, taking all his strength, rendering him weak and pitiful. She turned him into a slave to her sick desires."

Dear Lord, but these men sang from the same hymn sheet, regardless of their age.

"Treacherous, lustful, greedy—there's a veritable roll call of wicked women, wicked wives. And today, after the many revelations, I took myself away to contemplate their meaning. Afterward I spoke to the librarian at the Abbey. Now I understand something I'd been blind to."

"What's that?"

Jankin curled his lip. "I've a woman, God help me, a wife, who, with her wily whispers, evil intent, lusty mouth and body, tempted me to commit the most heinous of crimes."

Alyson and I exchanged a swift look. My chest grew tight. "What crime might that be, Jankin?"

There was a beat. "I coveted another man's wife."

The breath I was holding released. I searched for Alyson's hand. I needed to touch her.

But Jankin wasn't finished. "I coveted you, you devil-sent temptress, Satan's whore, and you forced me into sin."

I ask you, how is a woman supposed to respond to that? Before tonight, Jankin had never referred to me except by delicious, loving titles. I thought he must be jesting. I began to laugh.

I didn't see the blow coming. My head slammed into the back of the chair. Sparks of light danced before my eyes. There was a cry. As my vision cleared, Jankin had Alyson's hands imprisoned in one of his. Her face was a rictus of fury, she was shouting, but I couldn't hear what she was saying for the ringing in my ears.

Then he smashed his forehead into her face. Blood exploded as he connected with her nose. She fell to the floor. He began to kick.

I roared and threw myself at him, knocking him sideways. He might be a large young man, but I was a good size and I'd righteous anger propelling me. How dare he strike us. What on God's good earth possessed him? I rained punches on his back, into his ribs. He tried to dodge the blows, then with a bellow of rage, swung his arm and his elbow hit my temple.

Pain was an explosion of white, before everything went black.

———— ◆ ————

Warm, comforting arms enveloped me. My head throbbed. I could smell fusty fabric, sweat, a tinge of orris root and leather. My eyes fluttered open. Across from where I lay, Alyson sat on the floor, a vermillion kerchief pressed to the middle of her face. Her eyes, shot with red, were swollen and discolored. When she saw me staring, her mouth opened and she crawled toward me. What happened?

Then I remembered. I tipped my chin, wincing that such a slight movement caused spears to lance my head. I was in Jankin's arms, hauled into his lap, and he was showering me with tender kisses.

I tried to twist and push him away, but he wouldn't let me. He was telling me something, but it was difficult to hear.

It was only because he kept repeating the same thing over and over that I finally understood. "Sorry, sorry, sorry. My beloved, my heart's core, my angel on earth. I'm sorry. Forgive me, Eleanor. God, forgive me. The devil was in me and enslaved my tongue, my fists, my boots." He buried his head in my chest and wept like the child he was.

What did I do? The only thing I could. I stroked his hair, his shoulders, pressed kisses upon his head, and stared blindly at Alyson, who regarded me with confused, bright, and purpling eyes.

Dear God. Of all my husbands, I thought Jankin the least likely to turn upon me. I recoiled at the blood on Alyson's face and hands, the blood that stained my tunic. He was like tinder to dry leaves, he just burned with anger. An anger that was now, please God, spent. If he was capable of such wrath, of striking us poor women, what else could he do?

What else had he done?

More importantly, what did I do now? What if he'd kept beating Alyson? Beating me? But he'd ceased, and admitted the error of his ways. Listening to him as he cried into my bosom, as I felt the trembling in his limbs, heard the words he kept murmuring, I knew his regret was real. His fury had frightened him as well.

I rested my hand on his hard shoulder. The hand that had so recently struck me gently found mine. He was both child and husband. I was doubly responsible. If he'd coveted another man's wife, it was because I made him do it.

But I was also responsible for Alyson. My sister, cousin, Godsib, and my stepdaughter all rolled into one. He would not hurt her again.

As I bled over my weeping husband, Alyson and I spoke over his head. We decided that no one must ever know what had occurred this night. It wouldn't change anything and it certainly wouldn't bring Simon back—thank the Lord. Nor would we confess to Father Elias lest he make our sins—real or imagined—known by a change of manner toward us. Should anyone ask, we would find excuses for our injuries. We must take the events of this night, this horrible, horrible night, to our graves.

"And from there, to hell," said Jankin finally. He'd been listening after all. He twisted so he could look at me. He ran his fingers through my hair then along my cheek, tracking more blood onto my face.

How long we remained on the floor in that terrible tableau of tears and blood, I cannot recall. It seemed an eternity.

Eventually, Jankin ceased to weep. Alyson's nose stopped bleeding, leaving it strangely misshapen. My ears no longer rang, but my head ached. We all ached.

When we retired to our beds that night, Alyson creeping into her house long after the servants had gone home, Jankin and I made tender love. With each thrust, he whispered, "I'm sorry, I love you. I'm sorry, I love you." When we'd finished, he simply held me again, sated, remorseful.

"I swear, Eleanor, I will never lay a hand upon you again."

Fool that I was, I believed him.

TWENTY-NINE

Bath
The Year of Our Lord 1385
In the eighth and ninth years of the reign of Richard II

*E*ngland was at war. Again. Tired of all the skirmishes and border raids of the Scots, the King and John of Gaunt put together a rag-tag force and marched north. Men were called upon to serve his Grace. This time, Drew, Hob, and a few others begged leave to go, taking the bows and quivers they practiced with each week, keen to test their skills in battle. Though my heart was heavy, I gave permission—what choice did I have? I prayed to God they would return unharmed. Arnold remained with Wy—we were afraid Wy would follow the army if he didn't. War was no place for someone like him.

A part of me wished my husband would join up as well. Alas, Jankin didn't. Instead, while Alyson and I worked the looms, super-vised the making of cloth, its sale and distribution, and I negotiated with the guild and various merchants and broggers over sacks of wool, he locked himself in his study and buried his head in books.

My humble library now numbered over forty volumes. Jankin had brought papers with him from Oxford as well as a number of treatises in Greek and Latin. Inspired by Geoffrey's poetry and translations from the continent, which were garnering praise in certain circles, Jankin had made the decision to devote himself to translating the work of the Roman poet Ovid into English. He began to go regularly to the Abbey, befriending one of the librarians there, Father Alistair Durling.

Grateful my husband was distracted and unlikely to be moping around or staring balefully in my direction as if I'd suddenly sprouted horns and cloven feet, I was also curious about what he was doing.

Curiosity had always been my undoing.

After that dreadful night when he'd lost control and beaten me and Alyson, there'd been an uneasy truce. For days after, Jankin treated us both with such consideration, it was easy to believe he was genuinely remorseful and that the vicious side of him was an aberration brought on by the shock of the coroner's report.

Yet in the back of my mind, I kept wondering why he had disappeared for an entire day only to come home and lash out? When he said I'd caused him to sin, did he mean sin by desiring a married woman or by killing her husband? I was too afraid to ask for clarification; afraid what the answer would do to me, to all of us.

People would stop me in the street to comment on my fine husband, his manners, and the respect with which he spoke of me. I would bow and smile, and thank them prettily. Wives whom I'd once have been delighted to make envious, I avoided, lest I inadvertently revealed my sadness and confusion.

I invited the bishop, his senior monks, and just about any merchant in town to dine. Jankin would emerge from his study and become, for a few hours, the most perfect of hosts. I would watch with a mixture of pride and trepidation, but at least I wasn't alone with him. That would be much later, when he'd come to our bedroom and slip beneath the covers. Sometimes he would seek me out, and I came to him willingly, even if my mind was filled with broken shards. Most oft, however, he would curl up with his back to me and fall into a fitful sleep, sometimes crying out. On more than one occasion, I could have sworn he yelled Simon's name. My heart would pound and I'd lie unmoving in case he mistook me for the demons he was wrestling.

I felt it was just a matter of time before the fury erupted again. I prayed that when it did, neither Alyson nor I, nor any of the servants, were victims of it.

When Hocktide came, I encouraged Alyson to renew the lease on the house next door, this time paying for it out of my own purse. It was telling that she didn't argue.

Jankin and I danced around each other, full of courtesies (especially when there were others present). I made every effort to please him. Once more, I grew pale, and my clothes began to hang.

My appearance must have undergone a considerable alteration because one day when I was at the market with Milda, trying to choose some leather for new shoes for Aggy and Rag, a nearby grocer mistook me for Alyson. Taken aback, I'd forgotten that once upon a time Fulk had thought we looked alike.

As I wandered home, stopping to buy some eggs from a farm maid, I asked Milda if she thought there was a resemblance.

"Oh my word, aye. I've always thought you two could be sisters, what with your hair being so similar, the freckles and your eyes. And, forgive me, mistress, but lately your gowns are as loose as Mistress Alyson's have always been. Aye, it's easy to mistake you, one for the other."

I studied Alyson more closely than usual as she worked the loom that afternoon, taking note of the way her shoulders stooped, how the lines around her eyes creased when she smiled. Was I so old-looking? If she kept her mouth shut, concealing her missing teeth, and one ignored the slightly misshapen nose, then I suppose we did appear similar. We both had dimples, and my cheeks and eyes bore faint furrows. Her neck was ringed with lines, the flesh growing loose. I noted how her breasts sagged. Vain, I raised a hand to my head. My hair had darkened over the years, but was it threaded with as much white as my dear sister? Did my bosoms sit so low, did my neck have a wattle?

Yet, the more I gazed at her, taking into account the signs of age, the tiny mole on her jawline, the more I saw her beauty, her strength. Each and every line told a story. They were maps that charted a life. Those fingers that deftly moved the shuttle and twisted the threads were clever, experienced, and gentle when they needed to be. They could weave, dress hair, slap an errant servant, pet hounds, wring chickens' necks, and so much more. They'd held my hand in excitement when we first saw Thomas à Becket's shrine, and clutched me as she vomited over the deck of Captain de Mare's ship on the way to Jerusalem. That mouth had laughed when she learned I'd bedded the lusty friar in Rome, and tightened in disapproval when I agreed to marry Simon de la Pole. It had kissed and offered words of comfort when Fulk died, and shouted abuse at me when I first arrived at Bigod Farm. Dear God, how she'd hated me. And I'd been so afeared of that fine chin and those flashing eyes that lit from within. I watched her now as she nodded at something Aggy said. When she smiled, which was less often these days, it was as if the sun had burst forth. If I was a man, I'd find her desirable (and I knew this thought was as much as a salve to my own vanity as it was an assessment of Alyson), yet she'd never, to my knowledge, lain with one. Any suitors who had come forward, and there'd been a few over the years, she'd gently rejected, preferring, as she always insisted, to share her bed with no one, and her life with me and those we'd gathered about us.

I studied them, my workers, my servants . . . nay, they were so much more. They were family. What would I do without Milda's quiet, calming presence? The woman who would appear by my side ready to offer an ale, a cloth, soothing words, or arms to fall into. She was like the aunt I never had, organizing, caring, unfussy. Then there was craggy Aggy, with her crippled husband and two little boys. I'd known her since she was a young girl, uncertain and nervous in Gerrish's big house, but keen to learn to weave. Dear God, what a burden she had, but she never complained, just worked hard, took her coin, remained loyal and constant. Or funny Ragnilda, Rag, slender as a reed, her fair hair and fierce intelligence hidden beneath a silence that only a fool tried to disturb. She'd been stepping out with that lovely young ostler, Hugh Strongbow. Aware of my scrutiny, she flashed a shy smile that warmed me to my very toes.

As for Oriel, she was a serious woman, but a loyal one. A good worker, able to preempt your wishes and fulfil them. Above all, she was tolerant and kind. They were the reasons Mervyn had adored her. Me as well.

The other women chatted or hummed, keeping the rhythm of their looms, their shuttles like stiff little birds flying between and beneath the threads, building our beautiful cloth strand by strand as Arnold counted the ells, and Wy and the ever-present hounds flitted between them.

How did this happen? This marvelous workshop of color and quality—of bonds tighter than the weave itself? I couldn't take all the credit. It had been a combined effort. It had started with me, Alyson, and Fulk, but every husband, every household, had added its own ingredients—coin, wool, skills, but above all, people. Contributions that ceased with the arrival of Jankin. Unlike my other husbands, he never showed an interest in the workers, the business, or came to the workroom. His life was with books and words, not wool, weft, and weave.

It was better that way.

That night, as Jankin lay next to me quietly snoring, I wondered, as I did every other night, why he married me. A woman almost twice his age. Why did I marry him? Was it because, just as I could see the beauty and strength in Alyson's aging body, he enjoyed mine? Was that why I kept him? Because a younger husband maintained my own sense of youth? Draining him of vitality to ensure my own?

June came and the town emptied as the shearing proceeded at a furious pace. Those who didn't work with wool were called upon to weed the fields in preparation for the harvest next month. I'd spent the last few days out on the pastures, along with Sweteman, Arnold, and Wy, supervising the shearers and ensuring the wool sacks were tied and stored properly. We'd filled more than ever before and, despite news that the campaign in Scotland was proving to be a disaster—I prayed that Drew, Hob, and the others would return to us—I was feeling very satisfied.

Over the last few weeks I had gradually relaxed my vigilance around Jankin. I began to believe his attack those months ago was just the consequence of shock. And while I had my own views on how and why Simon died, and even notions about who killed him, I refused to admit them even to myself. After all, what did it say about me, unnatural woman that I was, that I could sleep with the man I thought might be Simon's killer?

Come summer, I'd buried those thoughts beneath more pleasant memories. Once more, I enjoyed my young husband and the admiration being wed to him brought. If Jankin said that he would never hit me again, then I had to believe him. He'd been confused, upset. Hadn't we all? As God is my witness, there'd been truth in his cruel words. He *had* coveted another man's wife. Why? Because she'd made certain that he did. Just as the Lord had created Adam, I'd taken the clay that was Jankin and fashioned him to suit my purpose. He wasn't responsible for his actions. That rested with me.

I had to put what happened behind us and start afresh. For all our sakes.

———— ✦ ————

Midsummer arrived with a blaze of storms and cloying heat. All day long, folk had been passing through town atop carts laden with hay; the harvest was in full swing. It had been exhausting just seeing the men, women and children covered in bits of wheat, their sweaty clothes clinging to them, their arms weary from swinging a scythe or the backbreaking work of gleaning. Dear God, but I remembered how much I loathed doing that.

I was nursing my second goblet of wine. Alyson, never able to sit idle, was spinning. There was something so comforting about the steady pace, the way the thread appeared between her practiced fingers, the cloud of wool floating at the top of her distaff being transformed into something so fine and yet so hardy below. One of our cloths was draped over the back of her chair, and I couldn't help but marvel we were responsible for such beauty.

I began to stroke my kirtle, also a product of our labors. Outside, the day was slowly going to bed, the rosy clouds pale ribbons across the sky. Though it was far from being dark, we'd lit candles, enjoying the cozy feel they bestowed upon the room. Someone below us was playing a fiddle, joined by a pipe; the tune was merry and laughter as well as a song enveloped us. Some of my weavers had asked permission for their men to join them for a drink in the workshop after harvest.

Thus it was, as I was resting on my laurels, Jankin joined us. He entered the room, gave us his blessing, then poured himself wine, the servants having been dismissed. Milda and Oriel had gone to visit the sick daughter of one of the weavers, taking some medicants and fruit for her.

Jankin sank heavily into a chair, released a long sigh, and patted the sheaf of pages in his lap.

"Is that your work on Ovid?" I wanted to include him in my benevolent mood. Dark rings circled his eyes and his cheeks were gaunt but very flushed. He'd been working ceaselessly on this project. I'd known him since he was a lad and felt a responsibility beyond that of wife. One can't help how one feels, nor the maternal instinct even when one has not borne children.

"Nay, wife," said Jankin slowly. "This is not my work on Ovid, but something much, much more important."

The air between us crackled. Alyson cast an anxious look.

"Oh, I didn't realize you'd ceased work on your translation. What's it about?" I pointed at the bundle.

Jankin untied the pages and stroked the first one with great affection. "You once told me, wife, that your friend Geoffrey wrote a book about good women?"

"It was incomplete last I heard, but he read portions of it to me. It was quite . . . challenging."

Jankin nodded as I spoke.

"Excellent work should stretch the mind."

What I didn't mention was the argument Geoffrey and I had

about it. I told him the title was misleading, as for a book purporting to be about "good" women, he spent far too much time praising men. "What's all of myth and history if not paeans to bloody men?" I'd said. I'd held my ground. After all, if women couldn't be celebrated in a poem whose very title suggested that purpose, what hope did we have?

"I'm writing it in order to set the scales in balance," said Jankin, interrupting my recollection. "To offer a counter to your Geoffrey's words—"

Since when was he *my* Geoffrey?

"I've been collecting stories which prove, beyond doubt, the wickedness of women."

Alyson put down the distaff. I choked on my drink, striking my chest a few times to help me swallow. Memories I'd worked hard to banish batted the edges of my mind.

Jankin waited to see if I'd comment. His hand clenched and unclenched. I kept silent.

"I would you listen to what I've written, wife. You too, Alyson."

My heart was a bell in a tower, clanging, clanging. A trickle of sweat coursed down the side of my face. My seat, so comfortable before, became a bed of thorns.

At that very moment, Jankin scared me. Nay, he terrified me.

"Very well," I said, clearing my throat. "Please, husband, proceed."

With a lopsided grin, he detached the topmost page and held it close to a candle.

From before vespers until almost compline, Alyson and I listened to stories about a range of women who all, without fail, betrayed their husbands. The first was Eriphyle, a woman who, for the price of a gold necklace, persuaded her husband to fight in a battle she knew would end in his death. Eriphyle was later murdered by her son. Then there was Xantippe, the wife of Socrates, a shrew who poured a piss-pot over his head. Next there was Lucilia, who hated her man and murdered him in cold blood. All the women were punished for their sins.

As Jankin read, my mind raced. Was this a warning? Were these tales to alert me that Simon would be avenged? That I would pay for it? That would only work if the killer knew the hopes I'd so wickedly expressed. Who but my own Jankin did? Who but my own Jankin could enact vengeance?

My nails dug into my palms. I fixed my gaze upon my husband and smiled. I would not let him see the impact his stories were having, even though every part of me longed to shout at him to stop. I began to imagine taking the wool from the top of Alyson's distaff and shoving it down his throat.

Next, he told the story of Clytemnestra. I could have wrested the parchment from him and told it myself, I had heard it so often, Alyson too—the tragic story of Agamemnon. Always, the men spoke of his wife's treachery, how she dared to take a lover during her husband's long absence, and then lure him into a bath and slay him when he finally returned to her. Not once did anyone speak for Clytemnestra. I knew her story—Geoffrey made sure of that. She was not just a murdering queen, but a grieving mother whose youngest daughter had been slain by this same husband (Agamemnon, who sarded another woman the entire time he was away—ten bloody years) in order that his fleet of ships might sail to a futile war. He tricked his wife into sending their youngest daughter to him, saying she was to be wed to a great hero. When Agamemnon finally returned with his pregnant mistress in tow (Cassandra, another wronged woman), what did he expect his wife to do? Forgive his many sins? Bah! He was a murderer of children; all she did was swive another man—and seek revenge for the death of her daughter. Does she get understanding? Nay. She's remembered as a fornicator and murderer for men to judge.

Well, I judge her remarkable.

All this was running through my mind as Jankin read. His face was puffed with pride at this catalogue of female sins.

How dull. How tiresome.

Just as I was wondering how many more tales I'd have to listen to, he finished.

"That's all for tonight," he said, and replaced the pages he'd read. He'd barely made an impression upon them. My heart sank.

"What do you think?"

I should have guarded my tongue. "I think you would do well to address the men in these stories if it's balance you're seeking. Make a sport of their faults as well."

One minute Jankin was in his chair, the next, he'd hurtled out of it and struck me hard across the face. I sat, stunned. Not certain what had happened, Alyson began to rise. I waved her to remain seated.

"You hit me," I said quietly, my hand against my hot cheek.

He boxed the other side of my face. "There, now your color is even."

I leaped to my feet and, before he could duck, punched him as hard as I could in the mouth. Unprepared, he staggered back a step or two then found his footing. He was about to level another blow, when Alyson shouted.

"Stop! Stop, both of you. For the love of God, stop."

My eyes were brimming with tears—not of sadness, but fury.

Jankin touched his mouth. My ring had torn his lip. He licked the blood. "If I'd known you could hit so hard, wife, I might have been more cautious."

"Well, now you do, sir. Have it on advice." My breath came in spurts, my breasts heaved. I was ready to swing again. He eyed me warily, raised his fists.

Just when I thought he was about to clobber me, he swooped and crushed me in an embrace, fastening his lips onto mine.

I resisted at first, fury and confusion warring within me until my body took over. My insides melted and my knees grew weak. When he pulled away, I could taste his blood, coppery and sharp.

"I love you, my fiery wife, my flame-haired beauty," Jankin murmured. "That was quite the haymaker you leveled."

I wanted both to pull away and to cleave to him. Uncertain, more than a little unnerved, I went limp in his arms.

"Tomorrow, or mayhap the next night, I'll read some more." He dared me to protest.

I stifled a moan.

He grinned. His teeth were stained with blood. "I wrote it for you. For both of you." He forced me to stand by myself. "It's taken months, but now I understand what God intends. As a man, as a husband, it's my duty to teach you women, to tame and shape your weak, feeble minds. For too long, I've allowed you mastery, Eleanor—this isn't right. It defies the natural order. From hereon, I will take my rightful place as head of this household, and you will take yours as my helpmeet and subordinate. While you, Alyson, will simply be subordinate. Whatever happens, my women will obey *me*. Am I clear?"

Believe me when I say I wanted to slap his smug young face, even while I understood he was trying on his manhood.

"If it pleases you, husband," I said, my eyes urging Alyson to agree. She nodded.

"Come, wife, we'll away to bed. God give you good evening, cousin," he said to Alyson, who still hadn't moved. His arms about me, Jankin led me from the room.

It took many more months for my burning anger at his foolish pride to explode and when it did, it was no match for his.

As it turned out, none of us were.

THIRTY

❖

Bath
The Year of Our Lord 1386
In the ninth year of the reign of Richard II

*T*here was great rejoicing when Geoffrey Chaucer arrived at Slynge House. It was an icy, snowbound St. Valentine's Day. He came on horseback, a young squire in tow upon a mule, laden with luggage. Forgetting all propriety, I ran from the house and flung my arms around him. I hadn't known I'd be so overcome. My heart swelled, and tears banked as I held him in a tight embrace, showering kisses upon his cold, bristly cheeks. As if nothing had caused a chasm in our friendship, he apologized for not coming sooner.

Delighted by my evident affection, he placed an arm around my waist. It was all I could do not to wince as together, Alyson bobbing by his side, having also given him a loving welcome, we entered the house. Jankin was at the Abbey visiting Father Alistair. They shared drafts of works in progress and, I was convinced, encouraged each other to uncover more and more female vices. As you can imagine, I didn't hold Father Alistair in very high esteem.

Geoffrey, however, was another matter and, as we walked through the house, servants and workers who'd known the man almost as long as I had offered greetings.

When we finally made it to the solar, Geoffrey was all smiles. Standing before the hearth, holding his hands out to the flames, he shifted his weight from foot to foot.

"Ah, Eleanor, how wonderful it is to see so many familiar faces. You've always been one to ensure your workers are looked after—not just in coin, but in the ways that count."

I nodded at Milda, who was holding up a jug with a question on her face. Time to celebrate.

As she offered around brimming goblets, I took the opportunity to study Geoffrey. The time we'd been apart had not been kind. Pouches hung heavily under his eyes and the lines between his brows had deepened. What remained of his hair was as much white as the burned umber I remembered. Still, his eyes twinkled merrily and I'd no doubt he didn't miss a thing, including the fading marks and scars upon my own, older face.

If I wondered what he saw when he looked at me, I didn't have to wait long to find out.

"You're fading away, Eleanor. Is that the price you pay for wedding a younger man? You struggle to keep apace?"

"Not in the bedroom," I grinned, hoping to embarrass him. But this was Geoffrey I was talking to, the poet who made *amore* his subject.

Geoffrey laughed heartily, while Alyson rolled her eyes. "I note," he continued, "that age hasn't been kind to either of us, my dear. You look . . . troubled, as if whimsy is your master."

I flashed a warning look at Alyson. "Not whimsy—" How could I explain that Mars and Venus fought for mastery in this house? Sadly, what I was slowly learning was where Mars rises, Venus doesn't just fall, she leaves. I may have loved bedding my husband, but I was no longer persuaded I loved him. "No more than usual, Geoffrey. Winter is a season of woes. Like the grand old trees and fragrant flowers, I burst into bloom come spring."

"But not as you once did."

"Isn't that the truth," I chuckled and raised my goblet. Were my problems really so evident? In preparation for Geoffrey's arrival, I'd donned my scarlet, a deep crimson kirtle with emerald tunic and hose. Milda and Oriel had helped style my hair, and my veil was of the finest fabric. Alyson looked splendid as well in blue scarlet and a gold tunic. In contrast, Geoffrey's breeches and paltock bore signs of the road—muddy clothes that had been damp and dried, the hair peeking beneath his cap stringy and in need of a comb. Not that I cared about any of that. My friend was here. With me.

It was as if nothing had changed.

Except everything had.

We sat by the hearth in the solar, the light coming through the window behind me dim as snow sighed against the thick glass. Milda propped herself in a corner, ready to serve if needed, but also keen for Geoffrey's news, which we didn't have to wait long to hear.

He regaled us with stories of his life in London, which, ever since the revolt of a few years earlier and the Good Parliament, had settled into a mixture of feasts, celebrations, plays, and pageantry, all of it, he said, serving to disguise (but not hide) the dirt, death, deceit, and barbarism of some or the discontent at the King's profligate ways. In this regard I had the distinct feeling he didn't just mean the commons.

He went on, moaning about the Wool Customs and the undue pressures being brought to bear upon him by leading London merchants such as Nicholas Brembe and John Northampton, both of whom had been known to Mervyn and to Simon.

"I should let you know, dear Eleanor, that I finally took your wise advice."

Lost in thoughts about these powerful men with whom my Poet dealt daily, I took a moment to respond. "*My* advice?" *Wise.* Dear Lord but I wished my husband was around to hear him.

"You might recall, some years back, you said that instead of writing about knights and damsels and folk from myth all the time, I should write about real people."

I sat up, interested and flattered. Alyson gave me a look of approval.

"When I wrote *Troilus and Criseyde*—I've a copy here somewhere for you—" he patted his satchel, "I set it in the famed city of Troy, which was also a thinly disguised London. Too thinly, I fear. It made me think. You were right and it was time to leave the mythic past behind and explore the types who swirl about me, for I have to tell you, living in Aldgate, so close to the Tower, and being at the Customs House, I see my fair share of the commons. The kind of people who, as you said, are often overlooked when it comes to stories. I intend to change that."

"Stories? There'll be more than one?"

He nodded.

"Have you started?"

"I have. I'm using the idea of a pilgrimage to tie the tales together."

I slapped my thigh in delight. "I've been on many of those!"

"Aye, and your letters have been most entertaining. Inspirational too. 'Twas you who gave me that idea as well. As you've so often noted, a pilgrimage brings together all manner of people in a shared adventure."

"Where are your pilgrims venturing?"

"I'm thinking Canterbury. Why the face?" asked Geoffrey.

"It's so . . . so . . . ordinary. There are far more interesting places you could have them go—Santiago, Rome, Normandy."

"Aye, there is. But sending them there defeats the point."

"Which is?"

"I want my pilgrims to venture somewhere those who read my poem might also have been, or one day visit themselves. I want it to be an English story."

"But isn't going on a pilgrimage an English thing to do?"

"Not entirely."

I thought of those I'd encountered on my travels. He was right. "And who are these pilgrims you're sending to Canterbury?"

"Ah." Geoffrey took a long drink. Quick as a starling, Milda was up and replenishing his goblet. "Thus far, I have a knight—"

I pulled a face.

"And his squire. There's a prioress, a nun, manciple, cook, miller, and . . . I cannot recall. All I know is that there'll be a large party who, on their way to Canterbury must relate one tale and, on the return journey, another. The best will be voted upon by their host, another ordinary chap who happens to be a Southwark innkeep I know."

"What about a wife?" asked Alyson. "You need a wife."

I gave her a gratified smile. "I'm not sure how many women are upon this imaginative journey apart from those who call themselves Christ's brides. But on every pilgrimage we've undertaken, there's been at least one wife." I thumped my breast. "Me. If you want to be authentic, speak to the everyman, then you need an everywoman."

"Funny you should say that," said Geoffrey. The twinkle was back in his eye. "That's what my friend John Brynchele says as well."

I smiled. "I'll look forward to hearing this tale one day. Or should I say tales?"

"You should."

"Well, here's to your pilgrim poem, may it amuse and bemuse." I clinked my goblet against his and drank.

After that, we spoke of the young King and his wife, how John of Gaunt was putting together an army to go to Spain and claim the throne of Castile. We discussed the price of wool, the weather, what we'd deny ourselves come Lent and so many other things besides. Below us, the rhythmic noise of the looms continued unabated. Horsemen rode past outside, slow in the growing drifts of snow. Voices penetrated the walls, as did a loud whistle and the ever-tolling bells. Someone must have died, I thought, as they made the house quiver.

We broke briefly for a meal before I took Geoffrey on a tour of the workshop. We paused to speak to the workers and he admired their craft and asked so many questions, I wondered if he intended to include a weaver in his story. I hoped so. We even braved the cold so Alyson might show him where she lived, pausing to enjoy a mulled wine.

The bells for none rang. The day was growing darker when we returned to the warmth of the solar. I was so enjoying having Geoffrey about. We sat in companionable silence, drowsy after our efforts and our many, many cups of ale and wine.

When Jankin entered a short time later, I was startled. I'd quite forgotten my husband, lost as I was in reminiscing and the joys of reuniting with my oldest friend. He barreled in the door, his cap sodden, his boots too. Oriel had managed to take his cloak or I'm sure he would have still had that on.

"Master Geoffrey!" he declared and strode to the chair, hoisting Geoffrey to his feet and clasping his hand in greeting. "May God give you good day, sir. You're a treat for sore eyes and heart."

"Sore heart?" said Geoffrey, returning the welcome, taken aback by Jankin's boisterousness (for certes he was like a puppy bounding into a pack of elderly hounds) but smiling all the same. "Must be because it's so full of love for your lady wife."

Jankin appeared to notice me for the first time. "Quite," he said unconvincingly. Oh dear, we had a guest, someone he'd always been keen to host, and he wasn't even trying.

Discommoded for a moment, Jankin threw his arm around Geoffrey. "Come, sir, let's leave these old gossips to themselves and retire to my study. I'm working on something I'm very keen to share with you—"

"Jankin, dear—" I began, half-rising out of my chair. "Geoffrey has had a long ride and a busy day, mayhap it would be better if—"

"I said—" Jankin's eyes flashed. I knew the signs, the warning. I quickly sat back down. Geoffrey's brows knitted. "I've work I wish to share and I know Geoffrey will want to see it." Jankin bestowed a brilliant smile upon my friend. "Is it too much to ask that you attend me, sir?"

Geoffrey looked from Jankin to me. I fixed a smile and gave the barest of nods. Then, he looked to Alyson, whose face was not yet guarded. "Nay, sir," he said with great jollity. "'Tis not. Lead on, please. May God give you good evening, ladies." He leaned over and brushed his lips against my cheek. "We'll talk anon," he whispered.

We waited until the door shut and their footsteps retreated as Jankin gave orders for Oriel to bring wine. Another door opened then clicked closed.

"What do you suppose Geoffrey will think of Jankin's Woes?" asked Alyson, reaching for her distaff. That's what we'd taken to calling his work. It went some way to softening the impact it was having on our lives.

"Knowing Geoffrey," I said, nursing my wine, "he'll either love it or use it for fodder in one of his poems. It's what Jankin's work deserves."

Alyson bit her lip. "Aye. One man in the house preaching women's sins is enough of a cross for us to bear, don't you think, sister?"

"Amen to that," I said.

THIRTY-ONE

Bath
The Year of Our Lord 1386
In the tenth year of the reign of Richard II

*T*he next morning Geoffrey suggested we go for a walk. Alyson and I donned cloaks, boots, gloves, and all manner of protection, for it was bitterly cold and a light snow was falling. Geoffrey was determined to leave the house, so we obliged, taking the hounds. Jankin had not yet risen; no doubt he had worked until dawn again.

Once outside the walls, we trudged along the verge of the River Avon, admiring the ducks floating upon its slow-moving surface, waving to the few bargemen poling their goods to distant towns. Only when we drew parallel to Bathwick Mill did Geoffrey ask how I found my new husband. There were not many who would ask such a bold question and even less to whom I would give an answer. But this was Geoffrey.

I spared him the worst details, but admitted there'd been difficult times. Very difficult. Though Alyson didn't say much, just gave little splutters and sighs to punctuate my responses, they served to put across her points clearly enough.

"Does he beat you often, Eleanor?" asked Geoffrey after a while.

I sucked the icy air in hard. "As often as I deserve it—or not."

"He's a man."

"Does that excuse or explain it?" I posed the question I oft asked myself.

"It's enough."

"He's hardly a man, Geoffrey, as you have pointed out. A choleric man-child more like."

"Though he's within his rights to maintain order in his household—" he halted, plucking a twig from a bush and twirling it in his fingers, "the sacrament does not permit him to be cruel."

"He does not strike me through cruelty."

Geoffrey glanced at me. "Why then? Do you not pay the conjugal debt?"

I gave a lopsided grin. "Frequently."

He studied the ground, lost in thought. "He cannot love you if he strikes so hard he damages you, Eleanor. I can see from the marks upon your face, the way you hold your middle, and from your limp that you have sustained much injury to your person. Alyson too."

She touched her nose.

"It is because he loves me that he does this, sir," I said.

"Loves you? How do you know this?"

"Because if he didn't, he would not strike me." God's bones! Why was I defending my husband? Because I had to defend my poor choice.

Alyson harrumphed.

Geoffrey shook his head sorrowfully. "This is not what I wished for you, Eleanor."

It's not what I wished either.

We walked in silence a while. The snow had ceased to fall, leaving the countryside blanketed in a glistening, pristine caul. Siren and Hera rolled and played in the freshly fallen snow, Rhea and Bountiful watching disdainfully. A lone child sat in a tree observing. Her bright cap and ruddy cheeks stood out in the bleak landscape. Up ahead, the monks' fulling mill loomed. There were a few novices working, some common folk as well. Inside the open doors, we could see the cloth being stretched on the tenters, straining at the hooks. Others pounded the wool, eliminating the dirt and grease. They were so focused on their work, they failed to see us drifting past.

"I know in law and, indeed, in God's eyes," said Geoffrey once we were out of earshot, "a man may beat his wife providing the instrument of his punishment is not too big, but I think there are better ways to exact cooperation and, for certes, better ways to demonstrate love."

Alyson made a small sound of agreement. I'd no reply. He was right. But what was I to do? I didn't know how to stop Jankin, nor how to stop myself. It was as if, as Alyson once said, he appealed to a darkness within me.

Geoffrey and I had no more conversations about Jankin that day, though I suspected he and Alyson did. Invited to join her for supper that night, he begged pardon and left me and Jankin alone. Jankin wasted no time and retreated to his study. I spun for a short while, then, dismissing Oriel and asking her to take the weary dogs back to Wy, allowed Milda to ready me for bed.

———◆———

The following night Jankin, who no doubt felt he'd showed great restraint previously, brought his work to the solar. We'd had a busy day. Geoffrey had spent it writing, while Alyson and I returned to the looms. We'd large orders to fill and were keen to get them done before the merchants from Brabant and Ypres returned once the winter storms receded. Jankin had given over his study to Geoffrey and gone to the Abbey.

The evening began well with many wines and Geoffrey regaling us about an incident at his local tavern involving himself and his friend John Gower.

We all laughed heartily before, with a dramatic clearing of his throat, Jankin begged our ears. I signaled for Milda to pour more drinks. God knew, we'd need them. My heart began to skip and my throat grew tight. Alyson picked up her spinning. Geoffrey appeared relaxed until you looked at his intertwined hands. His knuckles were white.

Jankin began with the story of a man named Latumius who owned an orchard. In that orchard grew a tree from which three of his wives had hanged themselves. His friend, a scoundrel named Arrius, instead of expressing sorrow or lamenting the man's grief (assuming he felt any) asked for a cutting, so he could grow a like tree in order that his wife might meet the same fate.

Geoffrey laughed politely. I couldn't even summon a smile.

Jankin then regaled us with stories of wives who, having killed their husbands as they slept, swived their lovers all night long, some beside their husbands' corpses.

"A pretty woman who sards men is akin to a pig with a golden ring in its snout—she's still a sow, no matter how she decorates herself," he said smugly. "Imagine what an ugly old one must be like."

I gripped the arms of my chair. Geoffrey gestured to Milda to top up his goblet, believing the recital over.

My husband wasn't finished. Next, he gave a roll call of bad women—disloyal, deceitful murderesses, those who made cuckolds of their men. He declared wives made a deliberate effort to hate what their husbands liked, just to make their lives a misery.

"Why, look to mine as an exemplar. Eleanor loathes my work, don't you, love? Yet it's my duty to both educate and tame her, is it not?"

I begged Geoffrey not to respond. He coughed, which Jankin, thank God, took as agreement.

But when he started on that damn story of Clytemnestra again, something happened. White-hot indignation filled my head, made me clench my fists, clouded my vision. When he reached the part about her stabbing Agamemnon in the bath, I swear, a Lilith-sent imp possessed me. I leaped from the chair. Alyson lunged, but I tore my tunic from her hands.

I grabbed Jankin's book and swiftly tore three pages from its midst. He called out in fury and shock. I pulled back my fist and punched him hard in the side of the face.

"That's for Clytemnestra and all the other women you wrong with your poisonous words!" I screamed.

Holding the pages I'd removed out of reach, as he reeled from my blow, I ripped them into shreds then tossed them in the air. They fell, a poor parody of the flurries tumbling from the heavens outside.

There was silence. The fire crackled. Dancing shadows filled the room. I stared with wild eyes, my breasts heaving, my face a furnace. Jankin's cheek was red where my knuckles had connected. It was beginning to swell.

My entire focus was upon him, daring him to act. It was as if no one else was in the room.

With a strangled yell, he propelled himself out of the chair, lifted his book high and brought it down with such force upon my head, I fell to the floor and rolled toward the fire.

Bright sparks exploded. My ears rang. I was vaguely aware of movement to my right.

Like a wild tiger, Alyson leaped on Jankin, her hands transforming into claws and raking his face. "You cowardly bastard!" she shrieked. "You've killed her. You've killed my Eleanor." She grabbed him by the ears, bit his cheek. Blood spurted and Jankin's legs buckled, bringing her down on top of him. She'd twined her fingers through his hair and began to beat his head repeatedly against the floor.

Geoffrey tried to pull her away. There were cries of pain, anger. I struggled to rise, the room moving in peculiar waves. Milda rushed to my side, desperate to help. Less than an arm's reach away, Alyson fought Jankin. Astride him, she determined to punish him. Not just for this night, but for every word, every blow he'd ever inflicted. For the agony he'd caused me and in doing that, caused her too.

There was an unnatural flash.

Milda gave a piercing scream.

"No!" shouted Geoffrey, springing over us, just as Jankin plunged a knife deep into Alyson's neck.

Blood spurted from where the blade jutted, spraying Jankin, Geoffrey, Milda, and me. Terrible gurgling noises issued from Alyson's throat; her eyes were wide, disbelieving. She whimpered, her hands rushing to the hilt as she looked to me to undo what had happened.

I managed to get onto my hands and knees. Milda fell back on her heels in horror. I crawled to Alyson, who'd gone white as fallen snow, her hands trapped birds fluttering near the wound. I drew her off Jankin, who just lay staring, covered in blood.

Alyson's face was a peculiar shade—stained with blood, yet so pale beneath it. Her eyes filled with terror as I dragged her onto my lap. Blood, hot and plentiful, pumped down her neck, over her breasts, pooling on my kirtle. Geoffrey knelt beside us. "No, dear God, no."

I wanted to draw the knife out, but was afraid. "Alyson, Alyson, my love, my love," I whispered, trying not to stare at the obscenity protruding from her neck, focusing on her eyes, those beautiful, spring day eyes, and smoothing the hair from her face.

Milda made a feeble attempt to stanch the blood with her apron. I pushed her gently away.

"What do I do?" I whispered to Geoffrey.

He was a picture of sorrow. Carmine spattered one cheek, his beard. It was everywhere. He tried to push against Alyson's neck, around the blade, to stop the life flowing from her. It was hopeless.

Alyson tried to speak, her voice barely a sigh. Her eyelids were heavy. I pushed my good ear close to her mouth, but all I could hear was soft susurrations that resembled my name.

Eleanor . . .

"I'm here, my love, I'm here." Sobs were stealing my voice. I forced them back. "I'm here." I smiled at her through unseeing eyes, my tears dripping on her cheek. "It will be alright. We'll fetch the doctor, he'll tend your wound. Don't worry."

Alyson found my hand and gripped it weakly.

Her face was a palette of gray. Her lips had taken on a violet hue.

I bent closer. My nose streamed. My mouth was full, my heart overflowing. "Don't leave me, Alyson. Please, God, don't let her leave me," I moaned.

Ever so gently, I pressed my lips to hers, uncaring of the blood escaping her mouth.

A great shiver racked her body. She gazed at me with a love so fierce and hot, it reduced my soul to ash. Then, my beautiful, patient, wise Alyson, my Godsib and most beloved, was gone.

Geoffrey was weeping. He closed Alyson's unseeing eyes and caressed her soft cheek. "Sweet, loyal lady."

Beside us, my husband groaned and stirred.

He killed her. Brutally took the person I loved more than anyone else on this cold, hard, thankless earth.

He raised himself on one elbow and, leaning close, studied his handiwork. "Is she dead?" There was no remorse, no guilt. "One less wicked woman for men to abide."

There was a beat.

With a yowl of rage and grief, I pulled the knife from Alyson's neck and plunged it into Jankin's eye.

"Now you need never see our wickedness again."

THIRTY-TWO

Bath
The Year of Our Lord 1386
In the tenth year of the reign of Richard II

I was Diana. I was Venus. I was Mars.

As Jankin lay senseless beside me, the knife's hilt casting a long shadow across his face, I felt nothing. Empty. A hollow vessel. I looked from him to Alyson and back again, waiting for the rage that had spurred me to such violence to return; for overwhelming sorrow to overtake me.

Around me chaos erupted.

Geoffrey first dragged Alyson off me, then clambered to his feet and, placing his hands beneath my arms, heaved me to a standing position. Milda calmly took my place and, ignoring the pools of blood and gore, wiped the stains from Alyson's face and neck. Dear God, Milda had borne witness to this horror. Geoffrey checked Jankin and, first removing the knife, covered his face with a kerchief, then used a piece of fabric draped over a stool to wipe the blade. The ringing in my ears was so loud, I couldn't hear what Geoffrey was saying. Milda stopped her attentions and stared. He forced me to face him and shook me hard.

"You must leave," he said. His hands left bloody marks on my kirtle.

I blinked. "Leave?" I gazed at Alyson.

Gone. She was gone.

"Aye, get away. Now. Wash off the blood, change your clothes, don a cloak. Go. Go to Alyson's house and wait. Milda and I will tend to this. Do you understand?"

I did, but I wasn't sure I could do it. Leave? Leave Alyson?

"Is she really dead?" Her upturned face, the pool of blood about her head, were my answer.

Geoffrey shoved me in the back. "Don't think. Do as I say. Go."

In a daze, I stepped over Jankin's body and, without looking back, went to my room, washed, threw out the bloody water (I had the sense to make sure it landed on the gravel, not the snow where it would arouse suspicion), and changed my clothes. An acrid metallic odor filled my nostrils.

Outside, the dogs began to bark, as if they knew something evil had occurred.

That bastard killed my Alyson. But I felled him. Surely, surely, that went some way to putting things aright? Why then did everything feel so wrong? Why did I?

I passed by the door of the solar, but could hear nothing within. Like a spirit, I moved through the passages of the house, out the front door and into the street. The cold didn't touch me. I felt as if nothing could anymore. Obediently, I went to Alyson's. The fire still blazed, the table held plates and a loaf with two slices cut. A distaff leaned in one corner, a basket of wool waiting to be spun in another. There were signs of life, of Alyson, everywhere. Her scent, roses and violet. Further back in the house were faint giggles. The two young maids who lived with Alyson sounded as if they were entertaining. It was hard to shut out their joy, or the dogs' incessant barking, but I did. I sank into Alyson's old chair and, lifting the distaff away from the wall and picking up the spindle, continued where she'd left off.

I kept replaying the moment Jankin plunged the knife into Alyson's throat. How easily it had glided in; how long it seemed to take for us all to react, as if we were in a daze. Mayhap, we were.

One thing I knew with sickening clarity was that I no longer doubted Jankin had killed Simon.

And, just as I'd been the cause of that murder, I'd caused Alyson's.

Dear God, I should have taken her away or, better still, thrown Jankin out on his tight rump the moment he first laid a hand on me . . . on us.

Jankin's hand may have driven the blade, but through my refusal to admit what he was, what he was capable of, I'd created the conditions for this tragedy to unfold.

The fire had guttered by the time Geoffrey found me. The wool had long since been turned into thread, unlike my thoughts, which had unspooled about my feet. Church bells had marked the passing of many hours—or was that the noise of my crazed mind?

First pouring a drink for me and then himself, Geoffrey forced the mazer into my hands and pulled up a chair. Our knees almost touched, he sat so close.

"Listen to me very carefully, Eleanor."

I could barely hear him. Something was wrong with my ears. The ringing I'd thought was endless echoes of the church bells wouldn't cease. I shook my head, tipped it to one side.

Geoffrey held my hand. "What's amiss?"

"I can scarce hear. The blow Jankin gave me. It's caused a ringing in my head."

"Can you hear me now?" Geoffrey said more loudly, one eye upon the door lest someone come through.

"Just," I said. "But it's as if you're talking to me from far away."

"You'll need to see a doctor."

"I need to see a sergeant," I said grimly. "Tell him what has happened. Confess to my part."

"And what's that?" asked Geoffrey, his hold tightening. There was blood on his shirt.

"I killed my husband."

"No, you defended your friend."

An image of Alyson's lifeless body appeared before me. The tears

I'd denied myself spilled. "Oh, dear God, Geoffrey. She's gone, she's dead. That bastard. That devil-sent beast. This, this is my doing. All of it." My words were jumbled, garbled. I drew a deep, shuddering breath. "I'll hang for this. But it's no more than I deserve."

"Listen to me," said Geoffrey forcefully, shaking my shoulders. "You deserve nothing. Jankin deserved everything he got and more."

I shook my head. "I should have made her stay away. Stay here, in her cottage where she was safe. She shouldn't have been there. If only I'd known she loathed that story as much as I did—"

"It wasn't the story she hated; it was what he did to you. What he's been doing for months. She told me as much in this very room." His voice was so stern, so authoritative, I ceased to cry and sniffed. "And that's why you'll do everything I say."

"Since when have I ever listened to you?"

"Never. But this time, your life depends on it. Milda's and mine as well."

I paid attention.

In harsh whispers, tolerating my interruptions, Geoffrey spoke into my least afflicted ear, and outlined a plan.

Alyson's and Jankin's bodies had already been removed from the house. Forced to get help, Milda had fetched those she trusted above anyone else: Arnold, Sweteman, and Oriel.

I gasped. Now they too were party to our crime—my crime.

Between them, Arnold and Sweteman had loaded a cart and taken the bodies far out into the countryside where the snow was deepest. There, they'd bury them.

"But what about the sacrament? What about Alyson's soul?" I gripped Geoffrey's hands, lifting them in anguish. "You must get Father Elias. She must have prayers said. She is unshriven. Her soul can't rest—"

"Hush, hush," he said, pressing his fingers to my lips to stop me talking. "If we summon Elias, we may as well summon the authorities. It's bad enough your servants are involved. But if we include anyone else, especially a man of God, you risk being hauled away to prison and thence to the King's bench to face charges of murder. And then, Eleanor Binder, you will hang."

"But you said I wouldn't, that it would be understood as self-defense."

Geoffrey regarded me with a look I knew all too well. "I said that to make you feel better. To make you listen. The truth is, you will be facing men, Eleanor. They'll be entrusted with your story, your sentence. Do you think they'll care about what you've endured? About justice? No? Neither do I. Hiding the bodies is the sensible thing, the only thing to do—for now. It gives you time to get away but, more importantly, it gives *us* time to invent a story."

"Get away? You mean, leave Bath?"

"I do."

Then the remainder of what Geoffrey said hit me. "Why do I have to invent a story?"

"Because, and this is the hard part, you can no longer be you."

"But, if I'm not me, Eleanor, wife of Bath, then who am I?"

"From hereon, Eleanor, *you* will be Alyson. Your names are very close, it won't be hard." He didn't sound convincing.

I gasped. "Why?" Then I shook my head furiously. "I can't be her. It's wrong. It's evil, it's—"

"It's the only thing that will keep you safe. Until we come up with something else."

I began to have trouble breathing. Geoffrey wrapped an arm around me, and spoke softly, rubbing my back, waiting for me to calm. When my breathing settled, he reached for a drink and brought it to my mouth.

"Now, don't interrupt."

Geoffrey's plan was that I leave Bath immediately, tonight. Milda would accompany me. Along with Sweteman, Arnold, and Oriel, he would put about a story that Jankin and I had gone on a pilgrimage to Santiago de Compostela.

"But no one would believe we'd be so foolish as to go in the middle of winter," I objected.

"I've already thought of that. Wy and some of the others may doubt it, but they won't counter it. Especially if we say you've gone to Dover to await a ship to take you across the channel. You're remaining in Paris until such time as it's safe to make the passage through the Pyrenees. Everyone knows you've wanted to do that pilgrimage for years. We'll say Jankin arranged it as a surprise for you."

"I . . . I . . ." I didn't know what to say. "What about the . . . bodies?" My eyes began to fill again at the thought of Alyson lying there in the snow, freezing, unabsolved.

"No one will find them until the snow melts and then everyone will believe what we tell them."

I looked at him questioningly.

"That tragically, Jankin and his wife, Eleanor, must have been set upon by brigands and killed on their way to the coast."

"Eleanor? You mean for people to think Alyson is *me*? No one will mistake Alyson for—" I began, then recalled not only how many people had spoken of the resemblance between us, but by the time she was found, it was unlikely she'd bear any semblance to the woman she . . . *was*. I began to cry. "Oh, Geoffrey, Geoffrey. I cannot do this, I cannot leave Alyson. Alone, without the sacrament said for her soul."

"The sacrament will be said . . . eventually." He took both my hands in his. "Do you really believe that God wouldn't take a soul like Alyson's to His side? Do you really believe she's not looking down upon you this very minute and telling you to do as I say? Urging you to flee? Would she want you to be held responsible for her death? No. She would want you to take revenge for her murder in the best way possible."

"I thought I had. I killed the bastard."

"There's a better way." His voice was so kind.

"What's that?" I asked through swimming eyes.

"By becoming Alyson yourself and being a stronger and better woman than anyone, especially Jankin and men like him, thought possible."

I pondered his words, studied the ink-stained hands clasping my own. He continued. "You can no longer think of yourself as Eleanor.

She died in that room tonight." He pointed toward my house. "As of now, you are Alyson—Alyson Bigod, or whatever you choose to call yourself. But never again must you be Eleanor Binder. You must humble yourself, Ele— *Alyson*. Take what you can, but leave everything else behind. Your clothes, your fripperies, your old life. Add her years to yours. Do you have a will?"

"Of sorts," I said through tears. "Master Le Lene in London holds a copy. There's another in my bedroom. Oriel knows where. I left everything to—" I burst into fresh tears.

"Who?"

"In the event of Jankin's death? Alyson."

"Good, good," muttered Geoffrey. I could tell by the look on his face, he was thinking ahead. "I want you to go to Canterbury, pay penance to the Lord, and seek indulgences on behalf of your mistress. You must wear a veil. Pretend to be ill; do what you can to avoid company. You must remain ignorant of your mistress's death until such time the news is delivered."

"But where will I go after Canterbury?"

"You'll come to me in London. From there, we'll work out what to do. But again, you come to me as Alyson, not Eleanor. Your life will depend on you maintaining a disguise. This is not something temporary, you're not a mummer in a play. The role you don tonight will be for the rest of your life."

"Must I be her, though? Even for a short time? I feel as if I'm dishonoring her memory . . . what she was to me . . ."

"On the contrary," said Geoffrey. "You can show no greater love." He rose. "And, if you don't, then you put others at risk, others who have been drawn into this horror."

I raised my tear-streaked face. Of course. Geoffrey, Milda, and now Sweteman, Arnold, and Oriel, were party to murder, to terrible deceit. This was no longer just about me or Alyson, but about protecting those who couldn't protect themselves . . . Because of my actions. Because of my husband's actions.

I took a deep breath, stoppered up my tears, and stood. Shaky at first, I found a strength I didn't know I possessed. Not my strength. Alyson's.

"What about the others? Wy? Peter? Aggy, Rag? The weavers, the maids?"

"They must believe you dead too. When *Eleanor's* body is found, we'll tell them Alyson couldn't bear to return here; that it was too much for her. She has made a new life elsewhere." I began to protest. "Do not worry, I will look to their well-being. Sweteman will help me."

"I don't want them to suffer for my sins, not in any way."

"I assure you, they won't. Now, wait here. When Milda has finished collecting what you need and you're suitably dressed, I'll send for the horses and you'll be on your way. It will be as if none of this happened, do you understand? You are Mistress Alyson, off to visit the shrine of Thomas à Becket while your Godsib and new husband go on a grand adventure."

"I'd never—*she'd* never leave without me—Eleanor would never go without Alyson."

Geoffrey gave me a sad smile. "No, she would not. And you must think of how you, Alyson, feel about that too."

Milda appeared a short time later and gave me Alyson's clothes to change into. While I dressed, Geoffrey turned his back to protect my modesty. The modesty of a murderer. Or was I the one murdered now?

None of my clothes were in the burlap Milda had packed. They were all Alyson's.

I dressed slowly, savoring her smell on every garment, trying not to burst into tears. The linen underdress, her hose, kirtle, tunic, and cloak. My boots were my own, the hat was hers, as was the pilgrim's cloak and staff. She'd never really liked wearing all the badges that adorned mine, shunning their display as a vanity that undermined the whole purpose of the pilgrimage. I missed my badges and made a promise I would buy some more. For me, for her.

After all, that's what I was now, not quite Eleanor nor quite Alyson, but as I smoothed the front of my dress, her dress, and felt a wave of sadness swamp me, I knew I was both.

I swallowed, aware of Geoffrey and Milda, whose face was swollen from crying, watching me.

Outside, the sky had lightened to a dull pewter. Heavy clouds sat low, threatening rain and possibly snow later. Good, it would hide our tracks, bury the bodies deeper.

The bodies . . . I choked back a sob.

Before we left, there was one last thing I had to do. I begged Geoffrey to fetch the book and all the quires Jankin had filled. Without questioning, he did. I held them briefly, shocked by the weight of all those pages, pages which listed the sins of womenkind: our sins according to men.

With a grunt, I hurled them into the fire and watched with great satisfaction as they began to burn.

"Make haste," said Geoffrey.

A short time later, Milda and I mounted the mules. There was only Geoffrey and Oriel to bid us farewell. And the hounds. I buried my face in their fur. Tried to settle their whines, but it was as if they knew life would never be the same again and mourned for what they'd already lost.

I took Oriel in my arms and held her tight. Her body shook with the effort not to weep. I cupped her face in my hands and kissed her forehead, wiped away her falling tears with my thumbs.

"God be with you, dear, dear Oriel."

"And you, mistress," she whispered. "And you."

Geoffrey gripped my hand tightly, the pressure of his fingers telling me what he couldn't say. I didn't want to let him go, but I must. For all our sakes.

Hunched in a cloak, I pulled a thin black veil over my face and looked at the world through a dark barrier. That's how the future would seem to me from hereon in. One colored in the meanest of hues.

"God bless you and keep you, Mistress Alyson," said Geoffrey, his voice raised in case anyone heard. "Be sure to write and let me and Eleanor know how you fare."

Was it too late to tell Geoffrey that unlike me, Alyson had never really taken to her lessons and remained illiterate? It no longer mattered and mayhap, that was the one gift I could give my beloved.

Not only the joy of words, but of writing a new life—as Geoffrey said, a better life for her, for us, no longer here in Bath, but in London.

And so, Eleanor, formerly the Wife of Bath, both murdered and murderess, began a different kind of pilgrimage.

This time, into an unknown future.

PILGRIMAGE TO CANTERBURY

———◆———

A letter to
Master Geoffrey Chaucer
from
Mistress Alyson Bigod,
in the year of our Lord 1386

After many and most dutiful commendations, I beg for your blessing as humbly as I can, dear Geoffrey. God knows, I need it.

Many months have passed since I last corresponded with you and then from the Tabard Inn in Southwark on our way here to Canterbury. I've been in receipt of your letters, the first which reached me at the Tabard Inn, the rest once we reached our lodgings in Canterbury. If not for the presence of Milda and, latterly, Arnold (who joined us, at your request—I offer thanks for that), I would have been rendered senseless as the reality of what has happened only struck me when my pilgrimage was complete and I stood once more in the mighty Canterbury Cathedral.

Before the shrine of Thomas à Becket, I couldn't help wondering whether, had I remained in Bath, the outcome would have been different. If I'd listened to you when you cautioned another marriage. Would my beloved ~~Alyso~~ Eleanor still be alive?

I know what your response would be, my friend. All the same, I cannot help but ask, especially of the saint himself, but neither he nor God Almighty saw fit to answer my question.

It pains me sorely to understand I've lost not simply a member of my family, but a woman who was all.

Nevertheless, I can no longer remain in stasis. I have to forge ahead. Eleanor would want me to. This is the reason I'm writing, Geoffrey: it's time to quit this place.

In preparation, I've a boon to ask and I do beg your forgiveness in advance as I'm aware that matters of state, the business with the Lords Appellant, the King's own mischief, and the dreadful battles must be preoccupying your every waking moment. That, and the fact you've been forced to relocate. I pray you find Kent and being a member of parliament more convivial than Customs. Mayhap, the Lord has been guarding your back, for I've no doubt if you were still in your previous position and among those who now find themselves branded criminals, you might also be facing heinous charges.

All this aside, I do most humbly ask if you would please seek out some suitable accommodation for me. I'm uncertain exactly how I'll occupy myself once I reach London since I cannot associate myself with Slynge House and benefit from its reputation as fine weavers. As you've reminded me many a time, I must invent a new past. But, since spinning and weaving are unlikely to be associated with Bath alone, I feel I can safely establish a fledgling business in London.

I'm hoping you'll use the connections you made while Comptroller of Wool etc. to aid me, even if your former colleagues are, from what we hear, most unpopular at present. The property I seek would need to have room for a couple of weavers to work in comfort, lodging for servants, as well as storage for wool and cloth and room for a cart to deliver and pick up same.

Other than considering how to start weaving and spinning again, I've done little. I've walked the streets of this benighted town. The journey here was one of the most somber I've had to endure. The confusion and sadness of past follies, of recent loss, made it impossible to enjoy.

If not for the affability and discretion of your friend the innkeep at the Tabard in Southwark, Master Harry Bailly, from whence our pilgrimage embarked, I might have changed my mind about going to Canterbury altogether, such was my misery. Master Harry gave me and Milda his best room, and shared many a fine story. He made it his purpose to shuck off my melancholy and provided us with excellent repasts, quality ale and wine, and ensured we weren't disturbed. According to Master Harry, he received a note from you not only revealing the truth of my situation but a set of strict instructions, which he did naught but follow. While I understood he would likely recognize me as Eleanor from previous pilgrimages, I was greatly alarmed by your decision to reveal why both my name and cir-cumstances were so drastically altered. Unnecessarily, it turns out, as you judged well, Geoffrey. Master Harry was the soul of circumspection. I'm once more in your debt.

I remained beneath the Tabard Inn's roof for over a month while we awaited the arrival of the rest of the pilgrims. I wish you could have seen them, Geoffrey. A more motley bunch you're unlikely to encounter.

Unlike last time, when I threw myself among my fellow travellers, I remained remote, observing them through a veil.

We reached the walls of Canterbury in late April and Milda and I, after bidding the pilgrims adieu, made for our lodgings in Longmarket. From where we reside, I can count more spires than pricks. You were ever determined to set my mind upon higher things, weren't you? Still, the beldame from whom we rent the rooms is inclined to leave us alone, and the place is clean, if not as quiet as I would have preferred. Our mules are stabled and Arnold's horse as well. Convenient considering we've been here a goodly while.

By my count, it's five months. Summer is spent and autumn has arrived, the season best known as the harbinger of death. Even so, I've heard naught of my beloved mistress. I pray you have news to share?

Death was something we were all fortunate to avoid when the imminent invasion by the French failed, praise be to God. We heard that in London, bastions were flung up against the city walls. While Canterbury didn't go to those extremes, men were recruited to increase the size of the garrison and protect the walls. Everyone was afeared there would be war and the French would smite us in our beds.

It's all moot now anyway. Praise be to God the winds proved contrary to the enemy fleet. The Lord was on our side, as the bishop said at mass a few weeks later. I think when he says "our" he means "men's." For there's little to show in my experience that God takes the part of women.

You've always felt there's much to love about this cathedral town, and there was a time I might have agreed with you. But not now. Everywhere I turn, I see Jankin Binder—Eleanor's monster of a husband. The man who sought to persuade us that all women were wicked, yet was the embodiment of sin himself. A devil-sent Cupid.

When I'm not seeing Jankin in the faces of scholars, drunks stumbling out of an alehouse, or an argumentative merchant, I'm seeing her . . .

This is why I must go. It's time for me to shuck off my cocoon of grief. Before winter sets in, I intend to hunker down in a new place. Make preparations so I might emerge the following spring renewed and ready to embrace life. Do you recall what you said to me, that dreadful night so long ago? You said that the best revenge was to become a better and stronger woman than anyone (including myself) thought possible. I've been weak; beholden to the specters of the past and the doldrums that trail in their wake. No more. I'm convinced of the wisdom of your words. For certes, living as I do does more harm than I would have reckoned. Reliving the what-ifs, the might-have-beens, tiny words with a mighty heft, is no way to exist. I would come to London and a fresh beginning. Something you've long urged and that I'm ready to act upon.

So, Geoffrey, expect me within the next few weeks. If you do not have room to accommodate us as we pass through on our way to the city, then I ask that you direct me to a suitable lodging until such time as I may move into my new premises.

May peace find you; God knows, it continues to elude me.

Written on the Feast of St. Jerome.

Yours, Alyson.

PART TWO

Feme Sole

1387 to 1401
There is no real difference at all
Between a lady-wife of high degree
Dishonest of her body, if she be,
And some poor wench, no difference but this:
That if so be they both should go amiss—
That since the gentlewoman ranks above
She therefore will be called his "lady-love,"
Whereas that other woman, being poor
Will be referred to as his wench or whore.

—The Manciple, *The Canterbury Tales* by Geoffrey Chaucer,
translated by Neville Coghill

Weaving a New Life

1387 to 1391
Advice is no commandment in my view.
He left it in our judgment what to do.

—The Wife of Bath's Prologue, *The Canterbury Tales* by Geoffrey
Chaucer, translated by Neville Coghill

THIRTY-THREE

Honey Lane, London
The Year of Our Lord 1388
In the twelfth year of the reign of Richard II

*M*uch had happened in the year or so since I came to London that cold wet day in November, taking up residence in a rather dilapidated house in Honey Lane, Cheap Ward.

Despite its pretty name, Honey Lane, located toward the center of the city, was a dark mish-mash of run-down buildings with jettied upper stories in such a state of disrepair, they resembled a moldy loaf of bread. The lane was narrow, with lifted cobbles and a shallow ditch down the center that tended to overflow. The home of beekeepers and honey sellers as well as some chandlers, the lane also housed a carpenter, a scrivener, an ordinary, a tavern, a cordwainer, a lacemaker, and, most recently, a small illicit spinning and weaving business. The church of All Hallows squatted at one end; Cheapside markets were just around the corner. There were, I'm reliably told, worse places to live. Not that I thought so the day we arrived. Not when we saw the state of the house. No wonder the lease had been affordable.

The moment we were settled, I'd written to Oriel and Sweteman, notifying them of our change of abode, and asking them to send

Drew (who, unlike Hob—may God assoil him—returned safe from the war) with the hounds. Drew had been entrusted with my deadly secret—*our* deadly secret—and was promised that as soon as we shifted to the city, he'd be reunited with Arnold. He just had to be patient and maintain a facade of grief and ignorance until then. As I anticipated, Drew has proven his loyalty. I keep asking myself, what have I done to deserve this?

While I'd once imagined I could magnanimously invite all my workers to come and spin and weave for me, that wasn't going to be possible. If any of my former workers saw me, the ruse would be up. There'd be uncomfortable questions. I had to let the past go in more ways than one—including not only Oriel and Sweteman, who remained in Bath to ensure the story we put about was believed, but also any chance of benefiting from my will.

As Geoffrey said, I had to face facts: coming forward to claim the proceeds of my will was as good as admitting to murder. Unless I wanted to hang by the neck, then I had to accept my wealth was lost to me. Even if there were those who would swear I was Alyson, they'd be committing perjury and I wouldn't ask anyone to do that.

I determined to live off my wits and earn a living by setting up a spinning and weaving business. Geoffrey warned me that unless I was married or claimed widowhood, I'd struggle to be allowed to trade as a feme sole, especially since I wasn't a citizen of London. The very idea of marrying again was an anathema to me. I'd railed at Geoffrey at the mere suggestion and swore I'd prove him wrong.

And priests might sprout angels' wings.

Less than two weeks after I sent the letter to Bath, Drew joined us. I'd half-expected Wy to accompany him and been concerned how we'd explain my presence and his need to maintain the deception. Drew brought not only Siren and Hera (Bountiful and Rhea remained in Bath—they were getting on in years) and some household items I'd asked for, but terrible news. Before the harvest had been brought in, Wy was killed when a laden cart rolled over him, crushing his thin chest. I held Drew, Arnold, and Milda tightly, crying softly against their shoulders.

Hera and Siren provided some solace. They bowled into the

house, throwing themselves at me and Milda before snuffling into every flea-ridden corner, burrowing among the filthy rushes in the rooms we hadn't yet cleared, dislodging rats and other vermin. Out in the garden, they'd left no stone or weed unturned, squatting and marking their territory.

Together, Milda, Arnold, Drew, and I rolled up our sleeves and, begging, borrowing, and even, on two occasions, stealing buckets and besoms, and tearing our oldest shifts into rags, set to and cleaned the place top to bottom. All three stories were in dire need not just of thorough washing and sweeping, but repairs. I'd some coin remaining, and acquired the services of a glazer, a mason, and a thatcher. We whitewashed the walls ourselves and Drew and Arnold dealt with the other repairs.

If there was one thing I learned over those months, it was that a shared secret, especially a terrible one, bonded people in ways that blood, marriage vows, and other kinds of agreements could not. The four of us became a family, united by shocking loss but also a dark knowledge that, if revealed, would unravel more than our tight-knit union. With one exception, my eternally missed Godsib, never before had I felt so trusted or able to depend on others. It was a revelation in so many ways.

I was rather careless with money in the beginning, adopting a devil-may-care approach. Apart from repairs, we'd often order food from the local ordinary. Ale we had aplenty as every second house had a woman brewing. Not that they were able to hang a shingle, or the usual broom to let passersby know a beverage was ready. London's Mystery of Brewers had strict laws about who could brew, where and when, and unless women were married to a brewer or their man paid his guild dues, she was forbidden to trade. The women sold ale regardless, whether in their own houses or on the street. Many a time you'd find a bailiff or overzealous ale-conner tipping out what had been fermented to the shouts and insults of neighbors.

It was these women who inspired me to defy the rules and spin and weave. I was yet to learn the power of the London guilds and how they could make or break a business; make or break a woman, too, if you let them.

In that regard, once again Geoffrey had been right.

Curious about the new residents in Honey Lane, where they were from and what they were doing, our neighbors asked questions, so I swiftly invented a story. I was from Canterbury—which was true. The story became embellished over the weeks—there were dead sisters and missing brothers (I thought of Alyson and Theo and Beton), uncles (Fulk and Mervyn), unscrupulous merchants and priests who, recognizing my talents, sought to profit from them by forcing me into marriage. I fled. Women mumbled empathetically, if a little disapprovingly, that I would defy nature and refuse wedlock; men would appraise me as if to ascertain my worth. Always careful, Milda, Arnold, Drew, and I told the same tale. It would be easy to believe we'd wiped the events of the recent past from our memories, but the nightmares that woke me said otherwise. I would lie tangled in damp sheets, drenched in sweat, seeing images of Alyson bloodied and pliant in my arms. The sensation of driving the knife into Jankin's eye and watching him keel over dead would wrench me from sleep.

I kept seeing them—Alyson and Jankin. Crowds swirling about the Poultry or Cheapside would be reduced to one woman with auburn hair and dimples. My breath would catch in my throat and I'd freeze on the spot, to the curses of the shoppers milling around me. At other times, I swore I saw Jankin's profile, those long limbs, that walk. Then he'd merge with the mob and I'd persuade myself it was all in my head.

For all that our street was filthy and stank night and day, it was friendly enough. We'd oft share an ale or two with the Bordwrygt family opposite. On one side of us were two beldames and their scribe grandson, a thin hunchbacked man who blinked like an owl whenever he was outside. They mostly kept to themselves, while on the other side was a beekeeper and his family—the Pollits. Regular churchgoers, they adhered to all the feast days and were strict about Lent, but also willing to lend a hand if we ever needed it. They also supplied us with sweet-scented rushlights and candles.

It was so different from living in Bath or Canterbury. There was so much noise, so much dirt and smoke.

When I'd first come to London at the age of sixteen, I'd been overwhelmed by its size, by the bustle and endless crowds. When I arrived from Canterbury, it had been with a different purpose and, therefore, with a different and older set of eyes. The grand houses of the nobles still made my mouth drop, none more so than the house of Geoffrey's patron, John of Gaunt—the Savoy—burned by the rebels, a ghost of its former self. But over time, the various sights scarce raised a brow, whether it was a juggler defying reason by tossing numerous balls into the air or a bearded, reedy man issuing dire warnings to all sinners as he stood precariously atop a box on a corner or women with low-cut tunics and red pouting mouths beckoning callow youths and finely dressed gents into the shadows. Shouts, songs, bells, curses—many in alien languages—fights, embraces, arrests, cutpurses fleeing constables, weapons drawn, dead bodies rotting in ditches—I'd seen it all. Priests, lawyers, knights in armor, drunken sailors staggering from the docks, dark-skinned Moors, they'd all turned my head once and yet, now I lived here, they were commonplace. The only thing I hadn't grown accustomed to was Geoffrey's absence. I'd always thought, hoped, that if ever I came to London, Geoffrey would be my guide to this ever-changing city. But he had moved to Kent. Not long after, his wife had died, removing another reason for him to visit the city.

London was now mine. It was Alyson's.

Only, it wasn't really, just as I wasn't really Alyson.

But I was someone who needed to work, even if what I'd chosen to do was proving hard to sustain. While the house Geoffrey found was exactly what I requested in terms of size and location, his warnings regarding trading had proved prescient. It's one thing to know how to operate a business and quite another to be allowed to do it. My efforts to sell what we made were swiftly quashed.

Within a week of trading, the Guild of Weavers and Fullers sent two of their men to inspect my operation and close it.

While both agreed upon the fine quality of the wool, thread, and the small sample of cloth I gave them, it wasn't enough. As Geoffrey had made clear, since I was neither the wife nor widow of a guild member, I was ordered to sell the looms and desist trading immediately.

"All I want is to be able to conduct honest business," I objected.

The older of the men, a Master le Brune, looked me up and down, a sneer forming. "Women aren't put on this earth to conduct business, madam," he said haughtily, "but to help men with *their* work. As the good book says, 'suffer not a woman to teach, nor to use authority over the man: but to be in silence.'"

Furious he dared quote the sermon of the dumpy little priest from All Hallows last Sunday, I nevertheless bit my tongue.

"As such," he continued, "you'll be allowed to spin, but nothing more. Sell your thread to those who know what to do with it."

"I'll scarce make enough to put food on the table."

"That's hardly our problem," said Master le Brune, indicating for his colleague to precede him to the door. "This is your one and only warning, Mistress Bookbinder. Next time, there'll be fines if not worse."

I guess I should explain the name I chose to go by. Geoffrey had urged me to think upon a name by which I'd be known in London. I'd thought long and hard about what to call myself. I chose "Book" firstly to honor the learning I'd been given—not by bloody Jankin, but his dear father and the books he'd introduced me to that I relished. That learning enabled me to manage my own affairs. But I also chose to keep both Alyson and Binder so I'd never forget what and who had brought me here.

Most of all, I chose it to pay tribute to the beloved woman who died for me and to whom I was irrevocably bound.

When I told Geoffrey, much to my relief, he approved.

While I publicly made a show of seeking out spinsters and doing what the guild told me, I made other plans. Damned if I'd allow those men to dictate terms.

It took a few weeks, but I managed to hire three girls and two men. I would have loved more, but the space was too small, we only had two looms, and I needed to be discreet.

The first was Rose, a young thing who'd come from Essex way, escaping a bullying older brother. I'd found her begging on Cornhill, not too far from the conduit. Two strumpets, whose occupation was evident by their lack of aprons as well as their shorn heads—indicating someone in authority had ensured they were publicly punished—were talking to her, trying to convince her to go with them. From the expression on her face, she was none too keen.

Part of me thought, walk away, fool, while another voice (and I swear it sounded like my Alyson's) whispered, "Come on, hen, if anyone can help this chick, it's you."

I went up to the girl, grabbed her wrist, and hauled her upright, almost pushing the two women over in my eagerness. "Been looking for you!" I said loudly. Afraid the girl would deny me or, worse, cry for help, I dragged her away, talking over the top of any protests. My performance must have been convincing because the women didn't stop me; nor did anyone else. As soon as we'd put some distance between us, I pulled her close. "Now, I'm going to get you one of those hot pies, and then we're going to find somewhere to sit, mayhap the churchyard—" I pointed to St. Thomas of Acon, "and you can tell me your story."

It was both sad and familiar. I mentioned I was looking for maids, spinsters, and dyers.

"I can spin," she said, her entire face lighting up, crumbs from the pie dotting her lips. "Oh, mistress, I can spin real well. And as for maiding, I'll be the best you ever had."

"Well, Rose," I smiled at her enthusiasm, "providing it's not a tale you're spinning, then I think you best come home with me."

And that was how Rose joined the household.

The second was Donnet. I found her one evening close to Yuletide, hunkering down for the night in a small, neglected alley off Russia Row, the street behind us. I'd been hovering outside the Mercer's Hall, hoping to find an alien merchant or two who might be interested in buying the ells of cloth I'd made, with no success. I'd cut through the back alleys to avoid the crush on Cheap Street.

Huddled beneath a pile of rags, Donnet was filthy and so very hungry. It was also evident she hadn't long given birth. Her stomach was still swollen, her breasts as well. Barely able to summon words, she allowed me and Milda to bring her back to Honey Lane. After a bath, a cup of steeped herbs, some watery pottage, and bread, she told us her tale. She'd come to London from Deptford, desperate to

escape a brutal husband who, when their child was born dead—a
son—had taken to her with fists and boots. It was only when he fell
over drunk and struck his head that she was able to get away.

"God must have been looking out for me, mistress," she said.
"Otherwise, like my little boy, I'd be dead too."

I kept my opinion about God to myself and, quashing the painful
memories her story evoked, offered her a place. Room, board, and a
small wage for helping with chores and spinning. Over the weeks,
with decent food and without fear to chase away sleep, Donnet
transformed from a grubby, emaciated woman who could have been
someone's grandmother, into a person who turned heads in church
or even wandering through the markets. She had rich brown hair
and large pale eyes fringed with dark lashes and, when she smiled,
dimples impressed her cheeks. I confess, her smile undid me, it was
so like Alyson's.

Donnet and Rose were great investments. Donnet especially, who
could both spin and dye the thread.

My third girl was brought to me by one of the women who'd been
trying to persuade Rose to become a bawd. A banging on the door
early one morning roused us. It was snowing heavily and the air was
so cold, you could have cut it with a knife. Outside stood an older
woman and a greasy-haired young girl with bony wrists and the largest, softest brown eyes I'd ever seen. Her name was Lowdy. The bawd
was Megge.

I brought them straight inside lest a constable pass and think
I was a house of procurement. As I was rapidly learning, a feme
sole couldn't be too careful. Before a crackling fire in the kitchen,
Megge, who despite her bruised cheeks and the sward of hair
growing back, had eyes that sparked defiance and courage, told
us Lowdy's tale.

Lowdy's mother, a harlot, had been beaten to death outside a tavern in Soper Lane. Her pimp had sent her to two soldiers, men who'd
been knocking down all the houses, shanties, and tumbledown shops
without the walls. This destruction had been ordered by parliament
in case the French fleet that was gathering around Sluys invaded, and

many souls had been brutally displaced, making the soldiers deeply unpopular. Of course, the French never came; the houses and shops were never rebuilt either. These so-called brave men at arms took out their anger and frustration at the way the now-homeless locals treated them on a whore.

Wrapped in a shawl, Megge risked her life bringing Lowdy to Honey Lane—not just because an officious constable might shave her head again or put her in the stocks for being out of her parish, or because the murderous soldiers might track her down, but because someone had to replace the dead mother. Didn't matter Lowdy was seven years old. As far as the pimp was concerned, he'd waited long enough. She was his whore's get and therefore his property.

"Take her, mistress, please," Megge said. "Her mother, may God assoil her, never wanted a maudlyn's life. We saw you take those other women; mayhap you'll do the same for Lowdy."

Women had so few choices; this kind even less. How could I refuse? And so, Lowdy began by helping Milda keep house and spinning. One day, I promised, I would teach her to weave.

An old Flemish weaver named Pieter, who had bent shoulders and a mellow, singsong voice, and a young fellow from Cornwall way named Conal, also joined us. Only Conal lived with us and I made him Pieter's apprentice.

Before long, I sold some cloth to Hanse merchants who, being detested in London because they received special treatment (less excise and fees) from the King, were my only option. At least I was dealing in alien markets. There was something about the Hanse men. Mayhap, it was their direct way of speaking—if they cared they were dealing with a woman, it didn't show. More likely it was their brawny arms and broad chests and their appreciation of large-breasted wenches with gap-teeth.

Whispers soon spread that there was a weaver in Cheap Ward whose prices were better than guild members. Careful only to fill a few private orders, sniffing out those the guild sent to spy on me, I'd enough business to get by. Just.

But if I didn't find a proper buyer for my cloth, and soon, I'd not only have to reduce the household (which would break my heart), but think of another way to make money.

———— ◆ ————

A sharp rap on the door broke my reverie. There were voices. Dear Lord, but I'd let the morning slip away. Geoffrey was coming for a much-anticipated visit, a scrawled note delivered by his flustered squire only the day before all the notice I'd been given. I'd been busy cleaning, ensuring the house looked its best. I quickly untied my apron and shoved the rag in a corner, smoothed my tunic, tucked my hair beneath my hood. Footsteps resounded on the stairs, then the door swung open.

The smile that had formed quickly faded as I saw the expression on Geoffrey's face. He'd not been the same since his former colleagues, Nicholas Brembre among them, had been put to death earlier that year. For a while, the city had gone mad, the King and the Lords Appellant accusing each other of treason and recruiting armies to their causes. But that had all been settled, hadn't it?

"What is it?" I moved toward him, hands before me. He placed his within mine, squeezing tight. His kiss lacked its usual warmth.

"Alyson, I must speak with you, in private."

"Anything you have to say can be said before Milda, Geoffrey, you know that."

He inhaled sharply. "Very well, but shut the door." He led me to a chair as Milda did as he ordered, a frown furrowing her brow.

"You're scaring me," I said, sinking onto the seat.

"Good," he said, sitting opposite. "Because what I'm about to tell you is terrifying."

Without letting go of my hands, he drew himself so close, our knees touched. "I've learned something most unsettling."

My heart gave a flutter. "What?"

"The heir to Eleanor's fortune is still alive."

I gave a bark of laughter and extracted my hands, crossing them over my heart. "Dear Lord but you scared me! Of course she is. She's sitting right in front of you."

"This is no laughing matter, Alyson. I'm not referring to you."

I blinked. "Who then?"

He took my hands again and locked eyes, willing me to understand.

Slowly, what he was trying to tell me dawned. "Nay—" My shoulders began to shake, my knees too. I glanced at Milda, whose mouth had fallen open. I tried to withdraw from Geoffrey's grip. "It cannot be—"

"I'm afraid it is." He drew in a breath. "Against all odds, Jankin Binder lives."

THIRTY-FOUR

———— • ————

Honey Lane, London
The Year of Our Lord 1388
In the twelfth year of the reign of Richard II

*J*udas's balls in a vice. Just like the blessed Savior, Jankin Bastard Binder had come back to life.

I'd been so caught up in my own sin, the horror of Alyson's death, and protecting my sorry ass by taking on her identity, I never thought to check Jankin was actually dead. We had dumped his body (and Alyson's) and run.

"Do you understand what this means?" said Geoffrey, studying me with concern.

"Oh, I understand alright. That stinking piece of cow shit has got away with killing my most beloved friend and now the buzzard's cock will get to live off my wealth as well."

I heaved myself out of the chair and went to the window. Across the way, Master Bordwrygt was shutting his workshop. Upon seeing me, he waved. I think I responded. Curls of wood shavings tumbled about, pushed by invisible stirrings of air until the rain quashed them. A mottled cat sitting on a window sill watched with half-closed eyes. Already, the lane was growing dark. The thin band of sky above was slate, heavy. Just like me. I closed the shutter, making the room suddenly darker. It seemed apt.

I spun around and saw Milda's arms wrapped around her middle. I folded her in a tight embrace.

We stood clutching each other like twins in a womb. "How did he survive?" I asked over the top of Milda's head. "I mean . . ." Jankin's cruel, blood-spattered face swam before me as he gloated over Alyson's death. "I drove the knife in so hard . . . He was dead, I swear. Sweteman, Arnold, they took him into the fields, buried him . . ."

Had they lied? Nay, nay. They would never do that. Would they?

"And what of Alyson?" My lips started to tremble. "Is it possible she too . . . ?"

Geoffrey was swift to douse my hope. "She's dead, my dear. That's beyond doubt. They found her body—what remained of it." He paused, swallowed, and rested his forehead on the tips of his fingers and sighed. It was weary, long. How pale he was. His tunic and coat were stained, he looked disheveled, as if he were wearing his thoughts. I wasn't the only one turned inside out by this news. No wonder. Was not Geoffrey complicit in the crime? Milda? Dear God: Arnold, Oriel, Sweteman—even Drew. Hadn't we all sought to hide the truth?

Even Harry Bailly . . .

On the upside, I was no longer a murderer. Just a woman living under a false identity who'd covered up a brutal crime. Covered up for that piece of pus, Jankin.

What do we do now? The stinking arse-wisp lived and as long as he did, we were all in danger.

"Where is he?" I asked finally. "What's he doing? Is he in Bath? I mean, he can't very well go to the sheriff, can he? Report what happened . . ."

"I don't know everything . . . yet," said Geoffrey. "But you're right. If he makes mention of your attack on *him*, then his part would be revealed. There are too many witnesses." He removed his cap and raked what remained of his hair with his fingers. "I received a brief note from Sweteman over a week ago, telling me Jankin had returned to Slynge House, bold as you like. I could scarce countenance it."

"You and me both."

"Me neither," said Milda softly.

I led her to a stool and returned to my own seat. I didn't think my legs would hold me any longer.

"I set out from Kent immediately," said Geoffrey, his cap dangled between his knees.

"You've come here from Bath then?" He nodded. That explained the hasty note. "Why didn't you tell me as soon as you heard?"

"I wanted to see for myself. There was no point alarming you otherwise."

There was both sense and kindness in his gesture.

"Well, I'm alarmed now." I waited. "And? What did you find?"

"Jankin was there, at the house. I made sure he didn't see me. I managed to have a quick exchange with Sweteman, Oriel too. Before you ask, they're both fine. Shaken, but fine. But before I could ask anything further, they were summoned. Didn't matter, I learned what I needed just by walking the streets. Jankin's been parading around town like the prodigal son returned, him and that monk friend of his."

"Father Alistair." I'd never liked that holy mumbler.

"He wears a patch over one eye, but you can see a terrible scar spilling from the edges. A beard mostly hides the bite on his cheek." Good. Alyson had left her mark.

I shook my head. "I don't understand how he survived." Once more, I felt the knife entering his flesh, the slight resistance before it gave way. The dreadful sucking sound, the blood, the viscous fluids.

"I've seen it before," said Geoffrey, looking inward as he spoke. "In battle. Ghastly wounds that you'd think would force a soul to flee a body, only the man lives. I think Jankin was unconscious, not dead, when he was buried. The snow must have slowed the bleeding, even stanched it . . ." He shrugged. "Matters not the how, only that he is alive. His speech is slightly slurred, he bears reminders of that night—" He touched his face. "But otherwise, he's in rude health. So much so, he's enjoying the attentions of local women, keen to look after the injured widower . . ."

"The *wealthy* widower, you mean. From poor scholar to gentleman of modest means in one fell swoop . . ."

Or knife thrust. *Dear God, why didn't you direct my hand to drive the blade further?*

I rested my elbows on my knees, cupped my chin, and brooded. Women swooning over him. Of course they would, a one-eyed Adonis in their midst. My heart was doing somersaults, my thoughts scrabbling like chickens' claws in dirt. I had to stay calm.

I sat up. "Why has he taken so long to reappear?"

"Ah," said Geoffrey, throwing his cap on the table. "That part I can answer. The story is on everyone's lips."

"Wait," I said. "Milda, do you think you can fetch some wine for me and Master Geoffrey? The one Meneer Mendelsohn brought." I turned to Geoffrey. "A Hanse merchant gifted us the wine." I didn't explain it was after we'd spent a very pleasurable night together. "Bring a goblet for yourself as well, Milda. And not a word of this to anyone."

Milda shuffled out of the room.

As soon as she was out of hearing, I swung back to Geoffrey. "Are we in danger? I mean, is Jankin a threat? To me? To us?" My gesture encompassed him and the entire house.

Geoffrey tugged his beard. "I'm not sure. For certes, he's a threat to who you are now—" He jerked his chin in my direction. "After all, he knows you're not Alyson."

"Surely it's in his best interests not to expose me? The truth would out."

Dear God, the thought of being returned to Jankin as his wife . . . I might be able to reclaim my wealth but . . .

It occurred to me then that had we known Jankin survived, I would never have had to become Alyson, a woman with an invented past and uncertain future. We could have called the sheriff, had Jankin arrested and put on trial for murder. Not only would my actions be understood as self-defense, but with so many witnesses, surely, the King's Bench would have seen him hanged.

By seeking to cover up *my* crime, all I'd done—we'd done—was cover up his, turning ourselves into felons in the process. In effect, we'd become his accomplices. If I exposed him now, then my role—not in attacking him, but in not reporting what he'd done—would see me hang too. Mayhap, all of us.

I would never allow that to happen. Damn Jankin. Damn his putrid soul.

The room became close, stuffy. Sickened to the core, I jumped up and threw open a shutter, leaning on the sill and gulping the air like a fish brought to land.

A warm hand began tracing circles on my back. I kept my head bowed, enjoying the comfort of Geoffrey's touch.

"I gather you've worked out why we have to tread with great caution. If we expose him, we're all at risk."

I nodded.

"Any thoughts of revenge, of confronting him, must be put aside," urged Geoffrey. "It's better he thinks you gone, out of reach."

"Only, I'm not."

"*Eleanor* is," said Geoffrey firmly. "He will have been told what happened to his wife, the story everyone believes. Of course, he knows it's not true. But, should he counter it, then his own role will come to light. He cannot afford that, not if he wants to remain in Slynge House. He must play the role of widower, wherever it takes him, whatever it gives him. Including your wealth. And, *Alyson*—" he bent so his lips were near my ear, "you must allow him to. As much as it offends your sense of justice and mine. We all must."

I dry retched. Geoffrey held my shoulders as my body lurched and spasmed.

Once more I'd had my hard work flung in my face, and the work of everyone who'd put their faith in me, including Alyson—and by the man who murdered her. Tears burned in my throat, behind my eyes.

I would not cry, I would not.

God in Heaven, why do you punish me so?

The door behind us opened. Milda. I took a goblet, downed the contents swiftly, almost bringing them straight up again. Geoffrey watched, eyes filled with disquiet.

"Do we know why Jankin took so long to reveal himself?" I asked, finally, watching as Milda lit some candles.

"A little of it. Again, there are rumors and stories aplenty. From what I gleaned, he was found not long after he was . . . buried. Taken by a hunter to the friars at Laycock who cared for him. They didn't expect him to live."

I scratched my cheek. "Why wait until now to return?"

"Apart from needing to heal?" asked Geoffrey. "Because, initially, he'd no memory of who he was. Conveniently, that meant he also didn't remember he was married either. He remained at Laycock until a priest visiting from Bath recognized him, and the moment he heard his name, everything miraculously came back."

"So he says . . ." I didn't believe it for a second. Neither did Geoffrey.

"Aye. He was asked what happened to his wife, since she was missing. He claimed ignorance, of course. The sheriff ordered men to return to where Jankin was found—thus, Alyson's body was recovered. By that time, though the snows had long melted—" he hesitated.

"Go on," I said thickly.

"Well, it was difficult to recognize who or what she'd been. The animals, you understand."

I did. One didn't grow up on the land, let alone make a living from sheep, without knowing how swiftly creatures and the weather transformed a corpse into something else. How pleased Jankin must have been to discover any evidence of his crime was, like Alyson . . . spoiled.

Geoffrey continued. "For now, he's holding to what Sweteman and the others say—that you and he were set upon by brutal bandits en route to the coast. He organized your burial, has spoken with Father Elias, paid respects to your grave, had mass said for you—for Eleanor."

"Christ's prick on a cross." I sank back into the chair. I was literally dead and buried. "This changes everything, Geoffrey. Everything."

"I know," he said, resuming his seat.

Below us there was a burst of laughter. Hera gave a volley of barks and Lowdy squealed in delight.

"I'll have to tell the others," I said.

"Why, mistress?" said Milda.

My brows rose.

"Well, forgive me, madam, sir." Milda sat straight-backed, her fine-featured face serious. "But I don't see the point in alarming everyone. We've worked hard to set up a new life, put what happened behind us. If you tell the boys that Jankin's alive, what will it do but make them fret? As you said yourself, they've been hiding a crime. The last thing you want is for them to be looking over their shoulders lest Master Jankin come knocking to shut them up or wanting justice." She laced her hands together. "I think you'd best do what you told me, keep this to yourself. Between the good master here and me. That way, you can still be Mistress Alyson who's training weavers . . . I mean spinners—" she flashed a weak smile, "and doing her best to make ends meet."

Trust Milda to offer a solution that smacked of common sense. When had she not?

Geoffrey nodded, all smiles.

I rose and kissed her soundly on both cheeks. When I had good folk like this in my corner, what did I have to worry about? She was right. We must continue on as we were and pray that Jankin didn't seek us out. But it was in his best interests to leave us in the past.

What choice was there?

Once Milda finished her drink and refilled ours, she left to attend to the tasks of the day. As the sound of her footsteps receded on the stairs, I turned back to Geoffrey, my face expectant.

Geoffrey heaved himself out of the chair. "Alyson, Eleanor." He knelt before me. "I know that look. If you have ever valued our friendship, ever held me in esteem, then listen when I say: let this be. I know you'd like nothing better than to make Jankin pay for what he did, what he's still doing. Remember, revenge is mine, sayeth the Lord." He put a finger under my chin, forcing me to look at him. "Promise me, you won't do anything rash."

I took a deep breath, wrestling with my desire to set things right. "I promise," I said finally.

We kissed farewell. Geoffrey assured me he'd be in touch soon. He had to return to Kent, but would keep an eye on what was happening in Bath. "We can discuss this matter further, once time and distance have allowed you to see this as the blessing it is rather than a curse."

"Blessing?" I stared at him in disbelief. "How can you say that?"

"Because, unless you choose to return to Jankin—"

"No house or coin is worth that," I said hastily.

"Exactly. Well, then, you're a free woman once more—albeit poorer." He looked about the room. "At least you no longer have murder on your conscience."

I didn't want to tell him it never had been.

I accompanied him to the door. "Remember your promise, my friend," he said. "Revenge is a destructive way of grieving."

I kissed him by way of an answer and waved as he set off down the lane. Drew and Arnold accompanied him to the river lest a footpad or cutpurse lurked. I watched their retreating backs, noting Geoffrey's was more bowed than I remembered, his gait slower. Drew and Arnold matched their pace to his.

Noise from a nearby alehouse surged. The creaking wheels of a cart that came to a sudden halt, lodged between the cobbles, caught my attention. Two lads ran to help the poor man free it, holding out their hands for recompense, hurling abuse, then shit, when the man revealed an empty purse. A pig squealed, a goose honked loudly. Master Bordwrygt hailed me as he exited his house, carrying something under his arm. Sleet began to fall, landing on backs, coating upturned barrels, the laneway, and a broken shovel abandoned outside the scribe's house. Cold as it was, I waited until Geoffrey and the lads rounded the corner, then shut the door and leaned against it.

I intended to keep my promise to Geoffrey, even though he was wrong. Revenge wasn't a destructive form of grief.

It was the only way to give it meaning.

Though it went against all my instincts, I would follow Geoffrey's course. There were others involved, others I cared about and who cared enough about me to keep my deadly secret. And what would happen to Rose, Donnet, Conal, Pieter, and dear, sweet Lowdy if I satisfied my desires? They relied on me to protect them too.

God's bones, I would do that, whatever it took—even letting go of what I wanted more than anything else on heaven or earth.

To see Jankin Binder in his grave. A grave he would never crawl out of again.

THIRTY-FIVE

Honey Lane, London
The Years of Our Lord 1388 to 1389
In the twelfth and thirteenth years of the reign of Richard II

The looms thumped and clinked. Distaffs twirled, spindles spun, and thread rained from the clouds of wool hovering over thin shoulders. The spinsters had joined me at the back of the house for company so we only needed to light one fire. Quiet chatter hovered like butterflies about the room, flitting here, alighting there. There was something soothing about the repetitious movements and quiet chorus.

Lowdy was sitting beside Donnet, learning how to repair a broken thread. Conal and Pieter were finishing off a piece of cloth. Rose had just sat down after completing the chores Milda had given her.

Outside, near the shed, I could hear Arnold whistling as he mucked out straw, the dogs rumbling under his feet. Drew was chopping wood so we'd have fuel for the fires. Milda was near the gate bartering with someone selling eels *and* ribbons. I must remind her to watch our coin—and wash the ribbons.

We'd been lavish over Yuletide as, distressed by Geoffrey's news,

I'd thrown caution to the wind, needing to take my mind off both Jankin and how to shore up a viable future in London.

Geoffrey sent a brief note mid-January apologizing for not returning yet, but he was busy. As it was, I'd much to keep me distracted.

What had once seemed a grand notion, weaving and then selling our cloth, was revealed for what it was—a woman's folly. After buying a few ells, the Germans, either deterred by dealing with a woman or because they too were afraid of drawing the wrath of the Guildhall, ceased to buy. Meneer Mendelsohn too. Seems my charms weren't so . . . charming after all. We still had a few private orders here and there but the truth was our tiny workshop would never keep me and Milda, let alone the rest of us.

Anytime I attempted to approach a merchant, offering a sample of our cloth and allowing the quality to speak for itself, the first thing I was asked was could they speak to my husband or the man in charge. When I explained there wasn't one, just me, their interest evaporated faster than snow on hot coals. Others assumed I was a widow. Damn my pride if I wouldn't allow that assumption to continue—not then.

Gradually, my savings dwindled, our debts increased, and we were forced to do what the guild demanded—spin and sell thread to scrape together enough to pay the lease and purchase staples. Relegated to a lavish pastime, weaving all but ceased. Our clothes became patched and worn, unbecoming in someone who wished to make a living from weaving. I used cloth we couldn't sell to make new clothes for first Lowdy, then whoever else needed them most. I could tolerate my own falling into a state of disrepair, but to see that dear child running around with her wrists and thin ankles on display in a threadbare tunic and patched kirtle was more than I could bear.

I could hardly ask Geoffrey for a loan. Dear God, if things weren't bad enough for him, his former friend, John Churchman, was threatening to sue him for debt. How Geoffrey managed to get himself into so much financial trouble defeated me. Clearly, losing Philippa's annuity upon her death must have cost him more than I'd realized. He'd made it clear I wasn't welcome to ask, so I hadn't. Instead, I'd written to him about my plight and, swallowing pride, admitted he'd been right in his fears and asked if he'd any remaining contacts or advice that might help me overcome the insurmountable barrier of the guild. A barrier my sex created and compounded.

The irony was, if I'd access to my monies, I could have helped him, as well as myself. I'd promised as much once upon a time. Aye, I'd been free with promises, hadn't I? Promises aplenty when I thought, mayhap, I could keep them. Resentment toward Jankin burned and some nights, when I lay awake trying to work out how to pay for the wool we bought, the food for our table, the general upkeep of the place, it was all I could do not to shake my fists at the heavens. At God the bloody Father, someone else seeking to undermine my efforts to achieve liberty and peace of mind.

They were all the same, weren't they? Men. God or mortal, they took what they wanted when they wanted, and watch out if a mere woman stood in their way. The guild ensured I couldn't sell my cloth in London, except to a few folk whose patronage wasn't wanted, and then for prices that barely made a profit.

The shuttle fell from my fingers and clanked on the floor. None of the others missed a beat, God love them. I bent and picked it up, shaking my hand. What sort of fool was I to ever think I could best a system where men profited while women paid?

Winter didn't so much melt into spring as give over grudgingly. Snow retreated in sulking stages, buds shyly blossomed on the once-barren trees, and people swarmed into the city as the sun punched its way through the heavy firmament, spreading a bit of much-needed warmth.

We continued to spin thread and make small amounts of cloth for less reputable seamstresses and tailors. It wasn't enough. The thread was all that kept us from starving. I made the difficult decision to devote more time to spinning. It didn't upset the guild, on the contrary, we were encouraged. The profit was minimal, but that was because of the quantity we were producing. I needed to increase our output—but how to do that without it costing us more?

It wasn't until the day Lowdy refused to accompany me to market that a solution presented itself.

Throughout winter, Lowdy had made a point of joining me on market excursions. Rugged up, she would remain close, her cheeks pink, her eyes shining. As she slid her gloved hand into mine, I took pride in her burgeoning confidence, the way she was slowly filling out as a consequence of food and a safe roof to sleep under. She'd peer into various barrows piled with pots, pans or vegetables, or gaze into buckets of squirming eels, before she'd barter with the best for a hot pie or heel of bread. Together, we'd enter warm shops and she'd twirl about, touching the wares on display in wonder, whether it was leather for shoe-making, mounds of spices and herbs for medicinal purposes or cooking, lace and ribbons, or parchments and inks. When I'd occasionally order replacement parts for a loom, she'd sit by the smithy, watching wide-eyed as the blacksmith hammered a nail just so, or sit quietly next to Master Bordwrygt as he lathed a peg or made a fresh rod.

Folk went about their business, whether couriers, criers, pardoners with their indulgences, beggars, or those just released from the pillory with their painfully crooked backs or missing limbs and empty bowls. Dogs scampered around barking, cats slinked, and pigs snuffled through the snow and filthy ditches. On occasion, I would catch Lowdy waving shyly toward a shadowy doorway or the entrance to a lane. Afterward she would cower in my skirts, peeping out. I didn't think too much of it at the time.

It wasn't until the weather grew warmer, and people started to pause for a chat, exchanging news, studying what everyone was wearing, eating, buying, gossiping, that Lowdy began to make excuses not to accompany me.

It was Rose who told me why.

"She's afeared she'll see the man who hurt her mother, the one who controls all the bawds in that ward. He's a nasty piece of work who used to beat Lowdy. She's afeared if he sees her, he'll snatch her back and there'll be naught you can do to stop him."

"Sweet Mother Mary." I was filled with righteous anger. Nobody would harm my Lowdy—or anyone else in my care for that matter.

Without wasting time, I told Rose to see to Lowdy, grabbed my cloak and hood, made Drew and Arnold carry knives and look as smart and fierce as they were able. Milda and Donnet practically ran out of the house after me, baskets swinging. I strode past vendors I'd normally engage with, set on a mission.

Drew and Arnold marched either side, clearing a path like scythes through wheat.

Milda and Donnet urged me not to do anything imprudent. But my plan was simply to let the maudlyns of Gropecunt, Soper, Bordehawe, and Puppekirty Lanes and any others plying their trade in the parishes of St. Pancras, St. Mary Colechurch and the Cheap, know that if ever a hair on Lowdy's head was touched, there'd be hell to pay. That message would get back to whoever dared to frighten my girl. She was but a child. I never thought about the consequences. I just wanted Lowdy safe. I wanted them all safe.

Gropecunt was dank and filled with shadows and the lingering smells of misery and urgency. Even the sunlight stayed away. Stains that might have been blood, but could have been tossed from a jordan, splayed the slimy cobbles and the sides of a closed alehouse. Animal pens contained sorry-looking hens, two flea-ridden kids bleating painfully, and broken barrels, a rusted wagon wheel, a trampled cloak, and a torn boot. A cracked shingle swung in the breeze. I banged on the door of Lowdy's old house, a sorry place with bowed shutters, filth on the doorstep, and an overflowing ditch. Mold grew all over the facade, its smell cloying. It reminded me of never-ending nights filled with terrible dreams. That she ever lived here squeezed my heart.

Impatient, I nodded to Drew to rap on the door again.

"You'll not find anyone," said a voice. "We're over here. It's warmer."

Across the way three women were huddled in a doorway, a small fire burning in a brazier at their feet.

In the flickering light, they could have been beldames, so buried beneath shawls and swathes of fabric were they; the flames cast their faces into a series of deep planes and angles.

They were the Fates manifest.

I crossed, fiddling with my purse, wincing as I thought of the cheese we'd forgo, the ale, and signaling for Drew and Arnold to remain where they were. The last thing I needed was to intimidate these women. A few houses away, a group of men broke apart to study us, whispering and nudging each other. Was Lowdy's pimp among them? I glared in their direction.

A forlorn child with a nest of fine hair stared through an open shutter in the house next door; I couldn't tell if it was a boy or girl. A small kitten was tucked beneath a grimy arm. Weary voices could be heard through thin walls. The wail of a baby, the chitter of women. The deep bass of a man singing a ditty. Somewhere, glass broke. A scream rent the air; it was swiftly cut off then replaced by sobbing.

"God give you good day, ladies," I said, trying not to shudder.

They murmured a return blessing, hands floating before the weak fire.

"I've a message to deliver—" I began, coins ready in my fist, when one of the women straightened.

"You're that woman what took Lowdy," she said.

Taken aback, I regarded her closely. It was Megge. The maudlyn with the defiant eyes who had brought Lowdy to Honey Lane.

"I am."

With a cry, the women leaped to their feet and threw their arms around me, showering me with kisses, speaking at once.

"God bless you, mistress!"

"Sweet Jesu, you be an angel on earth."

"We seen Lowdy. Catch her eye sometimes. Why! She's a different girl 'cause of you, mistress."

I gripped hands, accepted blessings, gazing at them in astonishment as they came out of the shadows and into the street, their hoods falling back, their shawls askew. Why, these weren't old women. They were young, just worn, tired, bruised, and weary.

A piece of my heart broke. I forced the coins into their fists.

"Nay, mistress, we can't take this," said Megge. "Not when you already done so much."

The others agreed, and fought to close my fingers, trying to give me back the money. If it hadn't been so sad, it would have been funny, these ragged, lovely women returning my poor attempt at largesse.

"Do you have room for more?" A tall woman stood in the doorway behind the trio. It had been so dark, I hadn't noticed the door open. Her belly arrived before she did, swollen with child. Long golden hair tumbled down her shoulders. Her proud nugs sat heavy atop the arm she'd slid under them—whether to support her breasts or shield her stomach, it was hard to tell. Her sullen eyes regarded me, a sneer twisting her lips. All the same, even covered in dirt, she was one of the most beautiful women I'd ever seen.

"I . . . I don't know what you mean . . ." I began.

"I mean," she said slowly, as if my mind was bent, "since you're so generous, would you take this when it's born?" There was no mistaking her meaning as she rubbed her belly in wide circles.

"Take your child? I . . . I can't do that."

"See," she said to the other women, throwing her arm up dismissively. "They're all the same, these do-gooders. These grand beldames who strut the streets, offering nothing but words and prayers. They don't mean nothing. Nor does her coin. Why—" she peered at the pennies in Megge's palm, "I can earn that in a minute sucking some cove's prick. More on me back." She slapped Megge's hand, the money striking the cobbles. Out of nowhere, an urchin scrambled for the coins, disappearing in the wink of an eye.

"You make out she's some saint," hissed the golden-tressed bawd. It was clear who had power here. "The only reason she took Lowdy was 'cause she got herself cheap help. You think she cares 'bout that girl? More like, she cares the child can scrub a hearth. Bah. She's no more a saint than Widow Gardy over there." She spat in the direction of a shriveled woman who sat at another open window staring out into the street, a distaff slung across her shoulder and a great cloud of wool atop it.

Widow Gardy's face split into a wide, gummy grin.

"You don't mean that, Leda," said Megge.

One side of her face was horribly swollen. The other women bore a variety of injuries—cut lips, blue and purple bruises on their wrists. Even Leda had red raw marks around her neck.

Unaware of their wounds or accustomed to them, the three continued to plead with Leda.

"God forgive you, you can't ask her to take your babe."

"He wouldn't allow it."

"He'll see you dead . . ."

I was vaguely aware of their imploring, the one called Leda cursing them, me, Donnet stiffening in protest, Milda plucking at my sleeve. The steady spinning of the crone sent my mind into a whirl.

"Wait," I said loudly as Leda went to disappear into the house.

"What?" she said with such venom, I stepped back.

"Can you spin?" I asked.

"*What?*" Whatever Leda was expecting to be asked, it wasn't that. I'd a brief advantage and, by God, I took it.

The women parted as I closed the distance. "I asked, can you spin? It's not a difficult question."

"Mistress, no!" said Milda.

"I can," said Megge, pushing to stand beside Leda. "I can spin."

"We all can," said Leda, giving Megge a shove, cutting off the others, wresting back control. "What's it to you?"

A slip of a woman sidled next to Megge, her eyes flicking to my face before settling on her boots. Her hair had been shorn badly. Her cap had slipped, revealing patches of pale scalp, some cuts. One eye bore an old bruise.

"What's your name?" I asked softly.

"Yolande." Sweet Jesu, she was so young. Soon, I had all their names. Leda, Yolande, Megge, and Bianca.

They stood expectantly in a semicircle around me.

"What would you say if I asked you to come and spin for me?"

"Mistress! Alyson!" Milda tried to force me to look at her. "Are you mad?"

Donnet tugged at my sleeve. "Mistress, we need to go."

I shook them both off.

"Well? What do you say? Will you leave this . . ." I looked about. "Come work for me? I can't promise much, but you'll have a bed, food, and, mayhap, some wages. Not as much as you might make with a cock in your mouth or spreading your legs." I dared Leda to defy me. She remained tight-lipped. "But you'd be safe. Just like Lowdy. I can promise you that."

Could I? Could I really?

The weight of Milda's consternation hung in the air. I pushed aside my doubts, the alarum screaming in my mind.

The women were stunned into silence.

"Don't have much to say for yourself anymore," I said to Leda. Her eyes narrowed. "What do you say, ladies?"

Megge turned, her hands clasped in an attitude of prayer.

"She's full of shit," said Leda, arms crossed.

"Nay." Milda barged between us and stood before Leda. Forced to tilt her head to look up at the taller woman, her fists were balled, her face red. "She's not. She never has been and don't you dare say so. You don't know her. How can you? You think because she makes an offer the likes your kind never had, she's a swindler? A crook? That she doesn't know what it's like to yearn, to hope, to bleed? To be poor? To cry and wish to God in Heaven things were different?" She pointed at me. "I've been with this woman since she was just a wee bit older than Lowdy. She's been through more than you can imagine and, guess what? It's never stopped her trying, nor giving folk a chance. She never says anything she doesn't mean and she certainly wouldn't be making offers if they weren't genuine. You should be down on your knees thanking Mother Mary and all the saints that this woman, Alyson Bookbinder, came down this lane today and offered you decent work instead of insulting her, you foolish slut."

Leda stared at Milda, who was puce in the face and puffing. While she spoke, the men further up the alley had joined us. They stood a few feet away, wary of Drew and Arnold, who'd drawn their knives.

Bianca shot a timid glance in their direction.

"Well, I believe her," Megge said to Leda. "When would you want us, mistress?" she whispered, wringing her hands.

The sun rose in my chest, warming me from the toes of my boots to my neck. "Now," I said. Before I could change my mind. "Gather your belongings and come this very minute." I glanced at Leda. "Those of you who want to."

Megge and Yolande went to cross the lane, stopping only when the men barred their way. Bianca remained where she was, looking from me to the men and back again.

"These women are coming with me," I said, coldly. "If any of you prevent them, I'll have the beadle and sheriff down here faster than you can lace your breeches, understand? I'll tell them you're holding these women against their will."

For all that the law didn't favor whores, the one thing it wouldn't tolerate was women being held forcibly.

"Those women belong to Ordric Fleshewer, bitch," said the oldest of the men. "You can't just come here and take 'em. They're his property."

Ordric Fleshewer. The man responsible for the death of Lowdy's mother, who believed he owned the daughter as well.

"They're nobody's property, churl," I said. "These women have no contracts, no apprenticeship." I gave a coarse laugh. "They've no guild. Fleshewer doesn't own them any more than I do." The men didn't respond. "They're now hired workers. You tell Master Fleshewer they've found other employ and are leaving his service. Today. Here—" I said, and thrust what remained in my purse into his hand. "Tell him this is for rent owed." I nodded toward the shambles that passed for a house Megge and Yolande had gone into. "I've a feeling he won't have much trouble finding more tenants, even if it's not fit for a river-rat."

One of the men whispered to a lad. He looked me up and down, gave a sharp nod, then took off in the direction of St. Olave's.

I swept past the remaining men with a confidence I didn't feel. Grateful Drew and Arnold were there, bravely defiant, staring down these men who didn't know how to handle a bold woman or recalcitrant whores. Bless Milda and Donnet, they glared as well, brazen as you like, even as concern at my impulsive action warred within them.

Moments later, the maudlyns joined us, burlaps slung over shoulders, nervous grins upon their faces. The only exception was Bianca, who ignored their entreaties; after a few fearful glances at the men and looks of longing at me and the girls, she scurried into the house.

While my heart ached for her, I couldn't force her. Yet . . .

Megge saw my ambivalence. "Bianca won't come. The man with the crooked nose is her husband. She'll never leave him."

I tried not to look shocked. *Her husband.* The turd-cured coward. Bianca wasn't his wife, she was his purse. Still, I couldn't save everyone. I had to respect her choice, even if it arose out of . . . what? Fear? Fear and some misguided notion of obligation. I shot the man a look that would have felled a raven mid-flight. He laughed and spat.

I made Megge and Yolande go ahead, Drew leading the way, Arnold bringing up the rear. The men muttered grimly but didn't try and stop us. As we reached the wider thoroughfare of Old Jewry, one of the men called out: "We know who you are, Alyson Bookbinder. We'll find you."

Damn. In defending me to Leda, Milda had revealed my name. She groaned. I turned to comfort her, only to see Leda, a burlap bumping on her back, running to join us.

Just then, I didn't care about the men, their threat, or that Bianca had rejected my offer. I'd just employed three women, one with a babe due, I couldn't afford. Joy filled with reckless pluck made my heart soar, my feet fly. I turned around, walking backward and shouted, "Aye, that's my name, fellows. And don't you forget it."

They didn't.

THIRTY-SIX

Honey Lane, London
The Year of Our Lord 1389
In the thirteenth year of the reign of Richard II

$\mathcal{M}$y plans to set the girls to work the following day were rudely curtailed. Just before lauds, I was awoken by a gentle touch on my shoulder. It was Yolande.

"You must come, mistress," she said. "Leda needs you."

Milda stirred on the pallet beside my bed. We threw shawls over our shifts and, first setting Lowdy to boil water, flew upstairs.

Leda was pacing the small, slope-ceilinged room before a chalk-faced audience. Her face was slick with sweat, a frown of pain furrowed her brow. One hand rested on her stomach, as if to prevent it from bursting, the other was screwed into a fist and pressed against her mouth. Upon seeing us, she groaned and stumbled.

Milda ran to her side, Yolande on her heels, but she sent them away with a growl. From the look on Megge's chastened face, it wasn't the first time offers of help had been so crudely rejected.

I'd been in a few birthing chambers over the years, and I'd learned that the temperament of the woman was no indication of how she'd behave when about to bring a child into the world. The most placid could turn into a snarling lion, or fling curses like a toothless beldame. Those you'd expect to moan and make a passion play of the hours would sometimes whimper softly and apologize for causing inconvenience. Inconvenience? Aye, that's one way to describe an ornery mound of flesh forcing its way out of your queynte. Bloody inconvenient in every regard.

Without so much as a by-your-leave, I took charge. Far from being the woman of the world she pretended to be, Leda was a mere chit of fifteen. A donkey's cousin could see the girl was terrified and snapping at all and sundry because she felt unsafe. I led her to the pallet, which thanks to Megge had a clean sheet atop to soak up the fluids, and pushed her onto it.

"Yolande. Go fetch the midwife, Mistress Ibbot. Drew knows where she lives. Take him with you. For Godsakes," I snapped over my shoulder, "the rest of you, stoke the fire, open the shutters, and get some fresh air in here. Smells worse than a barn. Bring the lass some ale, fast, you hear, some for me and Milda too." Megge shot through the door, leaving it open as was proper during childbirth, anything to aid the womb in releasing its burden. Rose and Donnet, woken by the commotion, came upstairs and did what they could. Donnet even threw some rose petals in the water when Lowdy hauled it in. Whether or not it would help, it made the room smell sweeter.

I dipped a cloth in the hot liquid, gave it a quick wring, and dabbed Leda's brow. "Squeeze my hand as tight as you like," I urged. "The midwife is on her way. In the meantime, shout if you must, cry and curse or praise God, the angels, Holy Mother Mary, whatever your choice, we'll not judge."

She shot me a look of utter disbelief as if about to level some of those curses at me when pain gripped her. She doubled over, pink fluid gushing between her thighs. At the same time, the ale arrived. Before offering Leda any, I took a great swig myself.

The hand I'd offered was now numb and Leda scarce loosened her hold when she was finally able to gulp at the mazer.

"How long have you been like this?" I asked.

"Too long," she said.

"She started getting ratty after matins," said Rose helpfully.

"She's always ratty," added Megge.

Leda would have retorted, but another spasm took hold and she gritted her teeth, rising to her knees as the urge to move overtook her.

I held her upright, then helped her up off the pallet as she sought the floor. It seemed an age before the midwife, Mistress Ibbot, followed by half the gossips in the bloody lane, arrived. Mistress Ibbot brought salt and honey to dry up the baby's humors and bind Leda's womb when all was over. The other women, including the two crones next door and Mistress Bordwrygt, put down the stools they'd carried, along with the jugs of ale and mazers. Crammed around the sides of the room, they began praying to St. Margaret, conversing, and one even started spinning (I took note, a young wench I hadn't seen before). The midwife pressed a jasper stone into Leda's palm and bade her squeeze it. Grateful for her foresight, I took back my hand and massaged life into it.

The next few hours were a blur of cries, blood, bodily fluids, and Leda's oaths and screams, which rang about the house. Chatter rose and fell, advice was kindly given and bluntly spurned. Day dawned, wet and cool, the rain steady upon the roof, some coming in through the window. When Yolande leaped up to close the shutters, Mistress Ibbot shouted at her to leave them open.

"You want this baby to come, don't you?"

The entire time Mistress Ibbot remained with Leda, ignoring her threats, the foul language spilling from her mouth. She rubbed a fragrant oil into Leda's back, her legs, pressed her ear to her stomach, and ordered me about as if I were her servant. She kept up a stream of words.

"These men who say bawds can't get pregnant because their queyntes are slippery with too much seed, or clogged with the dirt of sin, need to be silenced. No doubt you thought you were free to swive whoever you pleased. Foolish girl. Look at the price you're payin'." She tut-tutted. "It's always the woman; never the man, ain't it? Even though Adam took the apple of his own free will. Eve didn't force-feed it to him, did she? I'll bet the bastard relished every mouthful, knowing he'd never be held to account."

I liked this woman.

Finally, when all color had fled from Leda's face and a sizeable crowd was gathered both in the room and in the lane below, the babe made its entrance.

Squatting over some rushes, Leda pushed and pushed, as if she had the worst dose of squits. The babe's head crowned, a slow emergence that was greeted with a cheer from the women and a river of words that don't bear repeating from Leda (but impressed me mightily). Wrapped in a thick caul of white, it hung suspended above the floor before, as Leda's stomach rippled again, the child escaped in a spurt of blood and fluid. Mistress Ibbot caught it before it hit the rushes. I held onto Leda, whose knees gave way.

The caul was torn from the baby's face, the midwife pushed her finger into its mouth then put her lips over its tiny ones and sucked. She turned and spat.

All at once, a welcome cry followed. Timid at first, like a young rooster learning to crow, it soon filled the room. There was laughter, tears, and more curses (that might have been me).

With experienced hands, Mistress Ibbot tied the cord, leaving a small nub. She washed away the blood then rubbed the babe's body with salt and honey. Then she swaddled it tightly, muttering the words every layperson attending births was trained to say lest the babe die before it was baptized.

"*Ego te baptizo—*" She looked at Leda. "What's his name?"

"He? I have a son?"

The midwife gave her a curious look. "Dear God, girl, I'd have thought you'd held enough pricks in your life to recognize what was hanging between his legs. Aye, you have a beautiful boy."

Leda choked back a sob and her eyes filled. She turned to where I sat on the edge of the pallet, sweat dripping as if I'd just given birth myself. Impatient to have a hold, Milda came and whisked the baby from the midwife, all the other women gathering about her, cooing like a dovecote in the gloaming.

"What shall I call him?" asked Leda, one eye on the child.

The question took me unawares. "Can you name him after the father?"

Her eyes narrowed. "I'll not name him after that bastard."

"What about your father?"

"Nor him," she said, her eyes growing harder than flint. "He was not . . . a good man." She regarded me strangely. "Was your father?"

I hadn't thought of Papa in so long. "He wasn't bad, I guess." He worked hard, was loyal to a fault. By all accounts, he'd loved Mama and I'd loved him.

"What was *his* name?" Leda asked.

"Wace. His name was Wace," I said, recalling the last time I saw him, standing with a group of broggers, enjoying an ale, throwing his head back to laugh at something one of them had said. A wave of sorrow swept me.

"Wace," said Leda, glancing at her baby who was being held by a delighted Lowdy. He began to mewl. "His name is Wace."

I gasped. My heart swelled. "You can't—" I began, even while an inner voice was shouting at me to be silent. "Why—?"

"I can call him whatever I want," snapped Leda. "I like your father's name. I like you."

Suddenly, the babe was thrust into my arms, as if I knew how to soothe his plaintive whimpers. I looked down at his little bunched face, his wrinkled, downy skin, the way the gray light from the window sat like an aura about him. His darkling eyes stared at me, or so I liked to believe.

God had denied me the joy of motherhood and, until this moment, I thought myself reconciled to that. If ever I felt the pinch of sadness that all my husbands and swiving had led to naught, I'd remember the babe I saw born on a ceaseless tide of crimson, draining his mother of life, or the one born with no face, one arm, and twisted like a sailor's knot. Those cut from a womb or born violet and cold, not breathing. And now here was this sweet little creature. A boy who would bear my father's name. A yearning rose in me, followed by a glow, as if I was a blacksmith's furnace kindled for the day's labor. Only, this fire would never be doused.

"Aye. It's a strong name," I whispered. I stroked his downy cheek as his screwed-up pinkened face swam before me. I sniffed. "A good name."

In that moment I knew I would do anything to protect him. I

dropped the lightest of kisses upon his rosy brow, inhaled his scent, which came not from this stinking earth but from the abode of angels.

"Wace—" continued Mistress Ibbot as if my world hadn't just expanded. "*In Nomine Patris, et Filii, et Spiritus Sancti, Amen.*"

"Amen," we repeated.

Strictly speaking, she didn't need to baptize the babe—it should only be done when there was a chance of imminent death. One had only to look at Wace's sturdy feet, hear his lusty cries, to know he was secure in this world. Still, we women had so few opportunities to assert our authority—especially over the church.

Then we set to welcoming the baby as one should—with ale, song and much cheer.

My joy in little Wace was, however, short-lived. Among those outside waiting to hear the result of the birth was Wace's father—none other than Ordric Fleshewer.

THIRTY-SEVEN

———◆———

Honey Lane, London
The Year of Our Lord 1389
In the thirteenth year of the reign of Richard II

*W*ace was baptized eight days after his birth, and to my great pleasure, I was named godmother. The lad was mine twice over now. Because Leda knew so few decent men, and Wace needed two as godparents, she asked our weavers Pieter and Conal to step in.

When Leda was churched weeks later, in mid-November, it was a merry procession that went to All Hallows, bedecked in our Sunday finery, chattering and laughing as if it were Yuletide Eve. Followed by those in Honey Lane who could tear themselves away from work, as well as some curious passersby, we wended our way. Leda, carrying Wace, looked particularly lovely in a pale apricot kirtle and bronze tunic, her hair carelessly gathered under a cap, most tumbling down her back in golden cascades. Lowdy skipped beside her, reaching up to stroke Wace's cheek. Directly behind us were Milda, Arnold, Drew, Pieter, and Conal, smiling and waving like they were part of a royal procession. Megge, Yolande, Rose, and Donnet brought up the rear; their joy and lively chatter made my heart sing.

To think, only a couple of months earlier they'd been selling their bodies. Now, they worked for me. They were all adept spinners and, as the amount of thread we produced increased and the range of colors used in the dying grew, we sold more. We weren't making a fortune, but we were more than covering costs and able to feed ourselves. The girls looked so much better for eating regularly and not living with the constant fear of being beaten by violent customers or their pimp. I even managed to weave some cloth so the girls could make new tunics and Wace had fresh swaddling.

The sun struck our heads and made the rapidly drying pools of water on the cobbles shine, adding to the notion that God was sending His beneficence our way. Distracted by my pleasant thoughts, I narrowly dodged two shrieking hens running away from a stalking cat, almost colliding with a maid leading a donkey. I sang out an apology. Nothing would spoil this glorious day.

We crammed into the church. Father William invited us to light candles and place them before the altar of Our Lady. Once that was done and we assembled for him to say mass, we became impatient for the prayers and blessings to end as a great feast awaited us back at the house. Hips were nudged, arms pinched. Arnold reached over Leda's shoulder to tweak the baby's chin. Padre was a tolerant man and as keen to indulge in fine ale, Rhenish, the roast goose and eel pies, sweetmeats, and other delicacies as we were, so rushed the mass— nobody complained.

Filled with a pervading sense of goodwill, we spilled out of All Hallows, pausing to accept tokens for Leda and the child, stopping at the nearest tavern to enjoy a drink. I insisted on carrying Wace, holding him tightly. Careful not to overindulge (there was time for that), I was pleased to see Leda relishing being in the community she was yet to discover, and the other girls not only enjoying themselves after all their hard work of the last few weeks, but being accepted by locals. I'd been concerned about how folk on Honey Lane would feel about having former bawds living among them. It wasn't as if we could keep it a secret. Seems one couldn't fart in this place without someone smelling it. But so far, apart from one or two beldames lifting their noses and crossing themselves, and a few men knocking on the door, pennies in fists, seeking comfort, there'd been naught to concern me.

The general air of jollity wrapped us in its arms like the rare sunshine, so it took a moment to notice that not far past the tavern, our way was blocked.

A wall of backs brought us to a halt. Gradually, the laughter and general chitter died. It was replaced by the sharp crack of wood breaking, the ring of crockery smashing, and the wet sounds of something tender striking something hard.

'Twas then I heard Milda and my heart lurched. Along with Lowdy, the old woman had gone ahead to ensure the feast was ready.

"Nay! Nay! Not the yarn!"

I passed Wace to Leda and began to push through the bodies, then they suddenly gave way, parting like stalks before the plough.

On the road before our house was what was left of the looms. They'd been hewn with an axe. Huge, broken splinters, shards really, reached to the heavens, like the fingers of a dying man. The warp threads were separated from each other, drowning in shallow pools of filth in the central ditch. But it was the sight of all the thread and beautiful woven cloth that almost broke me. Torn from the loom, severed from the lower beam, it had been trampled into the muck. Yards and yards of thread were scattered, a field of scythed wheat that no one would ever gather.

Beside me, a child held a shuttle in his hand, still twined with yarn. I resisted the urge to tear it from him and fling it at the thugs who, even as I watched, were throwing our belongings onto the street—jugs, mazers, decorative plate, bedding, a tapestry that had disguised a damp stain on a wall in the solar. Our clothes, shoes, pattens. Trays of food lovingly prepared by Milda and the girls were hoisted out the door. Ribbed dogs darted forward to grab a haunch of meat and run, pigs snuffled their way forward, ignoring what flew overhead or landed with dull thuds about them.

People whispered, others shouted.

At our appearance, and our evident distress, the mood shifted. Some began encouraging the men, raising their fists, pointing at me and the girls.

"Whores, they are. Not spinsters."

"Sinners, the lot of them."

"You should be ashamed to stand with them, Father," shouted a burly man from the other side of the debris. "They are bawds and maudlyns, devil-spawn." To his credit, Father William put an arm about my shoulders. I couldn't speak. I feared if I did, it would unleash the rage burning in my breast and only cause more damage.

Folk began to dart forward and take whatever wasn't completely destroyed. The goose carcass was swiftly removed, a swathe of cloth only partly dirtied in the ditch. A lone boot. The torn curtain from my bed. The goblets brought from Slynge House had already been pocketed by the men. Held back by Father William and Master Bordwrygt, Pieter and Conal, who knew better than to try and stop the brutes, nevertheless struggled against their captors. The girls began to weep.

Geoffrey had warned me something like this could happen. That as a feme sole who was neither widow nor wife, I would pay a hefty price for attempting to do business, for taking in women deemed sinners. I'd ignored him, thinking I knew better. I'd be inconsequential, I said, overlooked. What I didn't reckon with was that my good intentions and small illegal business would be mistaken for another kind.

Once more, I'd gambled and lost.

My knees gave way and I slowly sank to the cobbles. Not even Father William could support my weight. Milda squatted beside me, her arms enfolding me. On the other side, Lowdy wrapped her thin arms around my neck, weeping. More bodies pressed against me. Leda, Rose, Donnet, Yolande, and Megge.

When someone struck a flint and threw smoking tinder onto what was now a pyre, I cried out. The men laughed, some cheered. Folk folded their arms and shook their heads. Whether at me or the wreckage, I couldn't tell.

The men behind the demolition of my household poked the fire, pushing everything that was left into the flames.

"Who are these men?" I asked.

I couldn't be heard above the crowd, the crackle of the fire. The heat was fierce, my cheeks burned.

"Why are you doing this?" I shouted at the nearest fellow.

"Isn't it obvious, Alyson?" murmured Milda. "They are the guild, or sent by them."

I struggled to my feet. "Nay. Nay," I said, shaking off Milda's arm as she tried to prevent me getting closer—not just to the growing conflagration, which would soon prove dangerous to the surrounding houses, but the invaders.

My fingers latched onto an arm. "Who sent you?" I demanded. A pimply lad with broad shoulders spun at my touch. In his hand was a rake—Drew's by the look of it. "Are you from the guild?"

The lad's eyes were small, hard, like river stones. He looked me up and down and sneered. "The guild? No, but they know what we're doing. Done with their blessing."

"Then who sent you?"

He pursed his lips and shook his head, but not before I saw the look he cast into the crowd at a tall, bald man with a scar running across his cheek and over his chin. A man, who, when he knew I'd seen him, saluted and threw back his head and laughed.

It didn't need Leda's gasp or to see Lowdy, Megge, and Yolande cowering for me to know who it was. Ordric Fleshewer. Behind him stood Bianca's husband, his face triumphant. Blood marred his cheeks.

Fury washed with sorrow swept over me. Before I could do or say anything more, Ordric signaled his men. The youth before me threw the rake in the fire. Men turned and vanished into the crowd. Already people began to back away as the flames rose higher, threatening the house and its broken shutters, from which so much had been thrown to the ground.

Dismay changed to cries of fear as tongues of flame came too close to the thatch.

The call went up. "Fire!"

Master Bordwrygt, bearing a great hook, shoved his way forward. From the opposite direction, folk appeared with sloshing buckets of water.

What was first a spectacle involving the destruction of a wanton's property became a matter of life and death. The crowd swiftly dispersed, but most returned with hooks, blankets, besoms, anything to beat the flames. More buckets appeared, a line was formed and wound all the way out to the conduit on Cheapside.

The joy of the morning was forgotten. My wits returned and I ordered Leda and the other girls back to the church, entrusting their care to Father William.

"But, Wace's crib, his swaddling—" began Leda, her eyes larger than ever, her beautiful skin covered in smuts.

"It's too late for that. Go. Go," I demanded, pushing her in the back. "Make sure Wace is safe. Lowdy too."

"What about you?" she asked. "You cannot mean to stay."

"Not for long," I said, determined to salvage something, anything. Already flames were licking the lower window, crawling up the front of the house to tease the shutters.

I studied the house, wondering if it was possible they'd overlooked something, that they hadn't destroyed everything.

It was only then, God forgive me, that I thought about Drew, Arnold, and the hounds. Why, the boys had returned with Milda and Lowdy, promising to untie the dogs. We'd secured them before going to church.

"Milda." I grabbed her hand. "Where are Arnold and Drew? Hera and Siren?"

Her eyes shifted to the rear lane. "I haven't seen them since we got here—"

I flew from her side, pushing through the line of buckets, past the men using their hooks to grapple down the thatch of the surrounding houses and ours. The dull thuds as huge sections struck the cobbles was both reassuring and sickening. Already the bonfire was a smoldering mess. It was the house that posed the greatest danger—to the entire lane.

Smoke obscured my vision, tears filled my eyes as I coughed my way inside, holding my apron over my mouth. The rear gate was open. I rushed through. The fire hadn't taken here . . . yet. In fact, apart from the dense smoke and the noise of the flames and shouting men, it would be easy to believe it was someone else's problem, that fire was a distant threat.

"Arnold! Drew!" I cried and then doubled over coughing.

"Hera, Siren!" Their empty ropes were still tied to the shed. That gave me hope, even as the ominous silence signaled doom. The door to the shed was ajar, a black chasm that beckoned me forward. I hesitated.

It took a moment to become accustomed to the darkness, the thin slats of light that severed the black. Smoke swirled, surrounding me. I was an apparition.

It was the smell that caught me first. Sharp, metallic. Afraid what I'd find, but knowing I must search, I continued forward, arms outstretched. It was my toes that discovered them. My boots struck something soft. I bent ever so slowly, a mole finding its way. My fingers landed on Arnold, then Drew, before they slid in blood.

So much blood.

Suddenly, the blood I'd seen on Bianca's husband made a dreadful sense.

I lifted my hands until a thin ribbon of light illuminated them. Ripped from my aching throat, the scream was like no sound I'd ever made before.

Some time later, when the fire was extinguished and the neighborhood engulfed in a pall of reeking gray smoke, I sat before Father William's hearth wrapped in a shawl, a mazer of ale in my shaking hands.

Upon finding Arnold and Drew in the yard, about to release the hounds, the men struck the boys with the hilts of their knives, their fists and boots, before they cut the dogs free. Scared, the dogs had bolted. Or that's what one of Ordric's men claimed in a tavern later that afternoon. Under no circumstances would the dogs have fled. They'd have fought to the death to protect Arnold and Drew. In my heart, I feared Houndsditch had two more bodies in its clogged waterway. As for Drew and Arnold, the blessed nonces had fought back, unarmed. There were scores to be settled. Had not Arnold and Drew, two servants, drawn knives on these same men weeks back when the girls left to join us? Arnold had taken a killing blow to the chest. In and up the knife had gone. He'd died quickly. Drew had sustained a wound to his shoulder and slashes, abrasions, bruises from boots and fists, and the greater pain of loss.

Upstairs in Father William's bedroom, he was being tended by a physician who could be relied upon to be discreet. The same physician had sent to an apothecary for unguents to treat Pieter, Conal, and Milda's burns. My hurts were not visible, but I knew they would never, ever heal. Like the wound of Alyson's death, they would scar my soul.

There'd been some talk of raising a hue and cry, but what was the point? I was afraid if we involved the law there'd be too many questions. Didn't matter that a pimp and his rascals had caused untold damage and death. Nothing would come of opening up an investigation, not when I'd so much to hide. Anyone who thought otherwise was a fool.

I said as much.

When Milda, Leda, and the others tried to disagree, it was Father William who stood by me.

"Mistress Alyson is right. 'Tis best to let sleeping dogs lie." He looked at me meaningfully and I knew what he meant. No amount of seeking justice would prevent those able to administer it from turning against me and my illegal weaving trade.

Instead, I asked for pen and parchment and wrote to Geoffrey. Aye, I know what you're thinking and don't for a moment believe I didn't think the same thing. He'd warned me that starting a venture as a feme sole, unmarried, not even claiming the status of a widow, would be a problem. When I boasted about rescuing the girls and how I was a godmother, he'd offered more cautions, saying my actions could be misread. My pride meant I ignored him. And look where that led.

I glanced around at what remained of my household. A few pallets had been erected in the sacristy. Lowdy was curled up beside Milda,

Yolande shared another with Megge, while Rose, Leda, and Wace lay under covers on a third. Donnet was upstairs, sharing Drew's care with me and Milda. We were a sorry-looking lot. The earlier gaiety was like a distant dream. The clothes on our backs and the few objects I'd managed to salvage were all we had left, those and the few coins I'd donated for Leda's churching, which Father William generously refunded. He and his elderly housekeeper, Mistress Glenford, also fed us—not the fine fare we'd been anticipating, but a tasty pottage with maslin. I was beyond grateful.

Conal offered to take my letter directly to Geoffrey. Pressing the river fare into his palm, I bade him take care. Mistress Glenford bundled leftover maslin and some cold coney into a kerchief for him.

"If you find Master Chaucer," I said, "I've asked him to accompany you back. If he's not home, then return and we'll seek him elsewhere."

I prayed he'd be in Kent. Parliament wasn't sitting, and while he'd made no mention of traveling, who knew where his role as a member took him.

Before the city gates closed that night, Conal was gone; Pieter went with him as far as the river.

It was a long time before sleep claimed me, and then it was brief, broken by Drew's cries and my own nightmares. Once again, someone had lost their life through my wilful blindness.

And then there were the hounds . . .

I swore then and there it would never, ever happen again. In the flickering light of the candle, the huddled shapes of my girls, of Milda, Lowdy, and little Wace, were like monuments to my failures. Failures that were, if I was honest, mostly my fault, but also facilitated by men who couldn't face a woman treading on what they perceived as their ground.

One day, I swore, I would find a place—a home, a business—for us all. I would build something that was mine and mine alone. Where we would all be safe and which could never be torn down by the spiteful actions of bitter men.

The irony that I turned to a man in my time of need was not lost on me; but I could no longer depend on my own judgment. Anyway,

Geoffrey was hardly a man, not in the way others were to me. Did he not say he was foremost a poet?

Well, I was relying on those skills now, for, as a poet, he was capable of great feats of imagination. God knew, if I was to survive this city with my household intact, that was exactly what I needed.

PILGRIMAGE TO ST. MARTIN'S LE GRAND

———◆———

A letter to
Master Geoffrey Chaucer
from
Alyson Bookbinder, feme sole

I send my greetings from London, Geoffrey, and God's and all the saints' blessings, and mine, and that of my grateful household.

While I know the brief journey to St. Martin's Le Grand hardly counts as a pilgrimage, being as it's in London, it's the best I can do for now. This sanctuary within a city renowned for its sinners and churches—a mighty contradiction if ever there was one—has proved to be a blessing indeed. When you first suggested I move here, while we were still camped in All Hallows, telling me it was not only exempt from the usual laws governing London but offered a haven for felons and those with a reason to hide, I wondered why you were telling me this. What reason could I have for not rebuilding Honey Lane? Why would I want to live like an exile in the city I wished to call home? (Apart from the obvious, but we'll remain mute about that.) I was a victim of thuggery and criminals, not a perpetrator. I didn't set fire to my own house or destroy my own property.

Unlike you, what I hadn't counted on was the resentment and anger directed toward us by the parish. Whereas once I could have reckoned many of the residents of Honey Lane, and within the church, as friends, less than a month after the fire we'd become pariahs, as likely to be abused and shunned as greeted. Oh, Geoffrey, it was difficult to hold my tongue and not let forth. You'd be proud of me. Only once did I call Widow Carter a leper's get with nugs not even Satan's brood would suckle. And while I may have punched Master Godfrey, the cordwainer, in the jaw for putting his hand up Leda's skirt, the next time he did it, I restrained myself so well, I only twisted his balls. The cry he issued did, however, cause Anthony Dun's mule to kick Sergeant Fenkirk in the chin, dislodging two teeth. It was hardly my fault the man had squatted behind the beast to have a shit. If he hadn't been so lazy and had bothered to stick his ass over the Fleet, well, none of it would have happened.

But I digress . . .

When Father William showed me the petition to have us evicted from his church, accusing me of inviting danger, disturbing the peace, and bringing the parish into disrepute by procuring, I was speechless. When folk threatened to bring the authorities down upon us, I was left with little choice but to follow your advice.

And so here we are, relocated to St. Martin's Le Grand, this town within a city. Even though I've lived in London a while, I'd no idea this place existed. Yet, here it is, abutting Grayfriars to the west, Aldersgate to the north, and Faster's Lane and a great many cordwainers' properties to the east. We entered from the south, the stink and noise of the Shambles escorting us the entire way.

As you'd be well aware, cousin, within the walls are not only many people, but churches, canons' houses, a college, and all the other places and spaces one would expect in a religious precinct, including a nunnery. There's a huge courtyard as you enter, filled with stalls, shops, a couple of rowdy taverns, and two- and three-storey houses with tenants from all walks of life. This astonished me the most, for living here, side by side with the clergy, are so many cutpurses, thieves, brigands, and felons, all escaping the law within St. Martin's dun-colored walls, I doubted Newgate (which isn't far away) held more. There are also bawds, though most of them seemed to be without pimps and looked a darn sight happier for having shed that costly burden.

Before the Dean, your friend, and the Commissary—a lugubrious man with the largest chin I've ever seen—and a ruddy-faced scribe, I explained the reason I was seeking sanctuary (I had to swear it wasn't due to treason—not even St. Martin's can save a soul from that), and promise that my household would uphold the rules governing this place. It was explained the gates shut at compline and opened at matins. The Dean said something about ensuring anything brought into St. Martin's belonged to us lawfully. Then there were numerous regulations about not committing crimes within the precinct or bringing in stolen goods. By now I wasn't really listening. I was looking around the room and thinking that from the amount of gold and silver—whether it was candlesticks, plate, goblets, and even a small hammer and block, not to mention the huge fire that was such a welcome respite from the freezing weather—the priests here did very well from the crooks they housed. No wonder they all looked well fed.

I also had to divest myself of weapons. When I explained I needed my tongue and wouldn't be handing it over, no one laughed. Well, they were warned.

After that, I signed my name (I could see they were impressed I knew how to wield a quill and make more than a mark). Then I was assigned a house. Now, here is where I'm sure I owe you extra thanks. Not only did you smooth my passage into this place, but the lodgings we were given, and for such a reasonable sum, are more than adequate.

A novice named Malcolm ushered us back into the large square, which, despite the snow falling thickly, was filled with vendors. People milled about and molten sparks danced from burning braziers. There were children playing, animals squawking, bleating, and honking.

Leda confessed she thought the place "bloody marvelous" and I think that sums up the general feeling quite well.

The novice led us across the square toward a row of rather ramshackle two-story houses. Dark-eyed women sat on the stoop of one, peeling vegetables and throwing the scraps into a bucket. A couple of men were playing a game of dice on another and stopped to watch us pass. There was no hostility, which we were expecting, just curiosity and appraisal. A barrel filled with water sat outside one house, a lone glove languished at the bottom of a step. Someone called a name and a large black dog ran past, its tail wagging.

Malcolm stopped outside the seventh house. Our new home.

It's small, Geoffrey, and there were holes in the thatch and slats missing on a couple of the shutters. Nevertheless, the area outside had been swept clean and was in reasonably good condition—at least until a few houses along, where it deteriorated into a cesspit.

The house tilted against its neighbor like a drunken friend. I found this reassuring.

By the time the sun was setting that first day, casting filaments of pale rose and violet clouds about a golden sky, I sat with everyone in an upstairs room, entertaining our first visitors. The curious neighbors had invited themselves over. They weren't empty-handed either, bringing food and ale to share. As you can imagine, they were most welcome.

Chatter washed over me and I enjoyed the way the light entered, highlighting the worn wooden mantel over the hearth and making the whitewashed walls glow, soot-stained as they were, with their rusty sconces and melting candles.

I couldn't relish it too long, Geoffrey. In the faces around me, in Milda's and Lowdy's especially, the reason for this change of abode was all too apparent. Arnold dead and buried and Drew still with Father William until he's well enough to join us. Not even the angry parish could persuade the priest to release him, bless.

As for the hounds . . . my beautiful dogs, I don't want to think about them. It hurts more than I can bear.

I'm not writing to pour out my sorrow, though I confess it does help and beg you'll forgive my indulgence, but to let you know that, despite what's happened, the upheaval, despair, and grief, and the ongoing worry about coin, it hasn't taken us long to settle. The house was partly furnished when we took it over, with a long, narrow table in the kitchen, a few stools, as well as some pallet beds and pillows. At the novice Malcolm's insistence, and with a note to give to the proprietor, Conal, Lowdy, and Yolande went to a secondhand dealer in the square to borrow blankets and other necessaries. They were given more than they asked for and I was touched by the generosity, though I suspect there will come a time we'll be asked to repay.

We've managed to purchase some wool, so most of our days are spent spinning, and we sell what we've made in the markets at St. Martin's, or barter it for food and ale. In the evenings we tell each other stories and I find yours are much in demand. I know I don't do them justice, but when I share your wonderful tales, I feel you close to me.

The favorite one at the moment is the two knights who loved the same woman and fought to the death for her. It's such a sad, beguiling story of the fragility of life, how the cost of victory often far outweighs the spoils. And yet, every time I tell it, I'm struck by the fact these men sacrificed their mutual love, their friendship, to win a woman. Surely true love isn't a competition, a sport in which one emerges the victor and the other the loser? It's a shared intimacy that grows over time. Passion comes in all forms. The love I bear my Godsib is an example. So is the love I bear my household. And the love I bear for you.

You asked about my plans for the future. Spinning is a way forward but it's a mighty slow one. Eventually, I hope, we'll make enough coin to contract the services of a carpenter to either restore or build a loom. If we can do that, then, mayhap, I can weave again, Milda too. Sadly, Pieter has left us. Who can blame him? He has a young family and cannot wait for our fortunes to recover. I can scarce wait myself. It will be much easier to operate as a weaver from within these walls, where those deemed felons by the authorities, whatever the reason, are at liberty to at least try and make a life for themselves.

You'll be pleased to know that I've also taken your advice not to correct folk when they assume I'm a widow. At least that way I won't be continually asked for my husband's or employer's approval when striking deals. Thus far, it's worked.

So, Geoffrey, this is how things stand. We're poor, and hungry most of the time. Drew is healing, Wace is growing, Lowdy too—I'm teaching her to read and write, and when Wace is old enough, I'll give him lessons. We spin, talk, eat, laugh, sometimes weep, and shiver in our damp little house. But we're safe.

What I've come to realize in the short few months we've been here is that if thieves, counterfeiters, forgers, strumpets, pimps, and so many other men and women (and too many children) have fallen so far they're left with no choice but to flee city justice and make a new life here—from all accounts, a good one—then what's stopping me?

May peace be with you.

Written on the Feast of St. Patrick.

Yours, Alyson.

Spinning the Bawd's Tale

1390 to 1401
And so I tell this tale to every man,
"It's all for sale and let him win who can."

—The Wife of Bath's Prologue, *The Canterbury Tales* by
Geoffrey Chaucer, translated by Neville Coghill

———◆———

Go a pilgrim, return a whore.

—Common saying in the Middle Ages

THIRTY-EIGHT

—◆—

St. Martin's Le Grand, London
The Year of Our Lord 1390
In the fourteenth year of the reign of Richard II

We hadn't been living within St. Martin's' stony embrace long before we realized that just about all the rules I'd agreed to obey were more to reassure those living outside the walls than to be followed within. Curfew was regularly broken, fences were kept busy buying and selling stolen goods, forgers were conspicuous, their work snuck out in the coats and paltocks of knaves and knights. Gambling was rife, as was counterfeiting. Likewise, bawds earned good coin operating inside St. Martin's and in the streets beyond. We'd see them each day, either leaving the confines to ply their trade or openly soliciting men and priests, beckoning them into the shadows between buildings or even the nave and aisles of the churches.

The months flew by, folding into each other like ells of cloth. Our second winter was far worse than the first, which, though bad, had at least been shored up by some coin Father William had given us. It came early, fierce, and bitter and grew worse as the new year rolled on. Sleet-filled winds lashed the house and heavy snow coated the grounds, driving folk out of doors to sweep the square so vendors could still function and others conduct their mainly illicit affairs. Most of our days were spent spinning the little wool we'd been able to purchase, mainly through altering the secondhand clothes we'd been so generously given, washing, then selling them outside the walls. Down to our last kirtles and tunics, they were difficult to keep clean, especially since the aprons we wore—often simply to keep warm— were so patched and thin anything spilled upon them seeped straight through. No one complained—not about their clothes, the lack of food or warmth—to my face at any rate. What I couldn't credit was that everyone remained. I didn't know what I'd done to deserve such loyalty. It shattered my heart into little shards but kept it whole as well. I was like a riven vase, full of cracks and threads pasted back together, threatening to break at the least prompting.

It pained me to see Lowdy's face so pinched, her puny wrists jutting out the sleeves of a kirtle she'd long outgrown. Or her bony ankles peeking below her frayed hem. Milda had aged since we'd arrived, Donnet too. Always slender, Rose now had a gray pallor, as if she'd been kept in a dark cupboard her entire life. She'd also developed a moist cough. I liked it not, but we didn't have enough money for medicants. Instead, we did what we could to restore her humors, but feared we were failing. Megge and Yolande had lost the weight they'd gained when they first came to me, though not their joy. Leda, bless her, while losing flesh, was still as bonny as ever, as was Wace, who fed greedily and grew. Up and running about, he needed more than his mother's milk. He required bread and some meat in his broth. We all did. Drew, who had returned to us at Easter the year before, needed the odd caudle. The watery pottages we'd grown accustomed to were not enough—as Conal was forever reminding us. St. Thomas's foreskin in a purse, but that lad had two stomachs, I swear.

As it was, though we spun what we could, when we could, mended clothing for any who needed it, sold whatever of our be- longings were worth selling, we'd barely enough to buy milk, let alone pigeon or eels.

Not only hungry, we were freezing.

Firewood was salvaged from the woodpile in the corner of the

Dean's garden. We weren't the only ones breaking the rules and climbing the fence at night and taking what we could.

Beyond the walls, life went on. Gossip was rife within St. Martin's and news spread faster than Greek fire. What we didn't hear we could rely on Geoffrey to tell us; his letters were frequent, his visits not so much, but his accounts always had a particular frisson as he'd borne witness to events himself or knew someone who had.

I didn't pay all that much attention to what Geoffrey wrote, what the criers announced or the rumors, not really. Made not a whit of difference who was on the Papal throne or ours for that matter.

It's funny how, outside the walls of St. Martin's, outside London— whether it was Westminster, the other royal palaces, or Scotland and abroad—men were arguing, beating their chests, shaking their pikes, drawing their swords, claiming and losing power, fighting and dying, and for what? A ruler's pride. Meanwhile, within the city, we ate, shat, argued, loved, traded, grew sick, lived, and died.

Aye, we died. And worried endlessly about where our next penny was coming from; how we could purchase wool, wood, and food.

Preoccupied with earning more and keeping my household alive, Geoffrey's woes and those of the gentles seemed trivial to me. My girls needed purpose, Wace and Lowdy more than pottage, bread, and stories by a weak fire. Drew had to regain his confidence and we all needed to create a future worth striving for. A future, that, despite Geoffrey's optimism and the girls' refusal to be crushed by our circumstances, looked bleak.

———◆———

Just when it appeared as if our fortunes might turn the corner, the Botch returned. It struck London with the force of an autumn gale, sweeping aside not only the elderly and infirm, but our youth. At first it was just vague rumors from the river. Talk spread that ships were leaving port even while the last of the winter seas heaved. Always a bad sign, in this instance it signaled the worst. One mad priest, who stood atop a box on the Cheap most days, raining doom and gloom upon all who passed by, began to shout about deaths outside the walls. How apprentice tanners and fullers and those near Moorfield and Smithfield were dying in vast numbers. It wasn't until the whispers became the wails of the grieving, and the city's usual smoke and stench reduced, that people began to listen. Crowds began to thin. Shopkeepers shut up, carts and barrows became scarce, as did produce. People began to buy in greater quantities, hoarding what they could as memories of the last Great Sickness returned. Back then, many who hadn't fallen ill had starved. It wouldn't happen again, folk muttered, using the last of their coin to buy flour, beans, fruit, and meat to preserve as best they could. Those who couldn't afford to come by supplies honestly, stole them.

Who could blame them?

Then the Botch came to St. Martin's. Two novices at the church of St. Nicolas fell ill, quickly followed by some lay nuns at St. Agnes. Our neighbor's lad, a twelve-year-old cutpurse, was hale and hearty one day, bedridden the next, and in the ground the day after.

A letter arrived from Geoffrey. This time, I paid attention. It was true—all the chatter, the gossip. The countryside was rife with pestilence and while his tiny hamlet in Kent had so far been spared, he warned that London would not be and to act lest the sickness come to us. Little did he know, his warning came too late.

Already, Westminster was closed to outsiders; nobles were fleeing to their country estates. The rivers were empty of craft and the roads given over to cattle and sheep. Weeds began to choke the cobbles, so few people braved the streets. Unlike the pestilence of years gone by, this one was plucking the bloom of youth, boys especially. Geoffrey urged me to protect our garden lest the reaper swing his scythe and cut my flowers.

I began to fear for Wace, Conal, Lowdy, Rose, Megge, and Yolande. I remembered when the Botch came to Bigod Farm, how swiftly even the most robust became sick and how quickly and painfully they'd died. The thought of any of my babes, Wace and Lowdy especially, falling victim to its cruel pain was like demons gnawing at my soul. I couldn't sleep, I could scarce eat.

I refused to let anyone leave the house, sent callers away, even those begging for aid. We stoppered up our ears to the cries of the sick and frightened lest we too catch their illness.

Day after day, we sat in the kitchen, the solar, lay upon our pallet beds, staring at each other, the walls, out the window, listless, bored, hungry, and always afraid. Not even spinning the little wool we had distracted us from our woes. The weeks passed and the weather grew warm then stifling hot. Stories were soon exhausted, card and dice games too. We grew sick of the sight of each other, uncaring of our clothes, not washing, dreaming of food. It was not a good time. The usual sounds of St. Martin's and life beyond the walls grew quiet then ceased altogether as others sought refuge within their own homes. Only the most foolhardy, desperate, or brave ventured out, and then not to sell food, which was scarce, but either to steal it or candles, knives, nets, fishing equipment, and all manner of tools so they might catch food and maintain light.

Bells broke the silence, ringing out over London, earthly reminders of why we were hiding. From the window in the bedroom I shared with Milda, I would listen as a town crier, no doubt paid a pretty sum for the risk, stood in the empty square and announced the death toll. Not a morning went past that the number didn't grow. The Grim Reaper reigned in London and, while we tried to wait him out, our supplies diminished, as did our resistance to the lure of the outside world. Left with no choice, I finally gave Donnet and Conal permission to search for sustenance. They took the last of our groats and went to the Cheap.

They returned with weevil-ridden flour, sprouting beans, sour milk, days-old fish, and some stringy coneys that Conal had managed to catch outside Aldersgate himself.

We feasted like kings that night, careful to keep aside enough to last a few days.

But when the pottage became little more than gray water, the milk churned into butter was exhausted, and Wace's cries and Conal's griping were intolerable, and all Lowdy wanted to do was sleep, her long black hair falling out in strands, her skin tight against her skull, I allowed Conal, Yolande, Rose, and Donnet to go in search of more food. Summer was almost over. Where was its abundance?

Nuts were found, berries too, as well as a pigeon, coneys, and even some eggs Conal uncovered in abandoned nests. No doubt the mothers had filled empty pots. When Conal admitted he'd given some eggs and a coney to the women next door, I couldn't object. I would have done the same and, anyway, hadn't they suffered enough?

But when, the very next day, Conal didn't rise from his bed, his act of generosity became one of sheer folly.

Unable to wake him, scared of the marks she'd found upon his chest and under his arms, Yolande found me upstairs, still abed.

"Mistress," she said.

"What is it?" I asked, rolling over. Sleep had eluded me. When I saw the expression on her face, I sat up.

"Who?"

"Conal . . ." she began, then started to cry.

I was so caught up with Conal's condition, keeping the others, especially Wace, Leda, Rose, and Lowdy away, I didn't notice how pale and slow Donnet was. Yolande too. By the time I did, it was too late for Donnet.

Conal and Donnet died within two days of each other. Milda and I nursed them and, putting Megge in charge, sent the others upstairs.

As I bathed Donnet's and Yolande's hot bodies, listened to their hoarse and terrified whispers, I silently railed at God.

This was meant to take boys! Our youth. Conal is seventeen, a man. Yolande nineteen and Donnet a woman of twenty-three. How dare you, sir. How dare you.

I bargained with the Almighty. Promised that if He would save them, I would reform my ways. I would admit who I was, own my part in Alyson's death and Jankin's injury and ensure justice was served. I would take whatever punishment He meted out and the authorities as well. I even swore, after Conal died in my arms, crying for his mother, his sandy hair matted to his forehead, his eyes sunk into his head, spewing and choking on whatever malign fluid was filling his chest, that I would give my life to Him. If only He would spare those I loved.

For I knew, as I cradled these dear, sweet souls who trusted me as if I was indeed their mother, that they were the family I'd always wished for. They were my children, as if I'd carried them myself. Had I not helped shape them into the men and women they were becoming?

Aye, and through my weakness, my inability to heed sound advice, I'd sent them to their deaths as surely as if I'd brought the Botch to the door and invited it in.

When Donnet, the last to die, drew her final breaths, I looked into those bloodshot gray eyes filled with the knowledge of her impending death, and stroked her hot cheek.

"Mistress," she whispered. "I want to thank you."

"What for?" I asked softly. A slow tear rolled down my cheek and splashed onto hers.

"For saving me from what might have been. For the happiness."

I choked. Saving her? Why, I'd sent her straight into that devil-molded Reaper's arms. I began to shake my head, struggling not to weep, to beg her not to leave me. I'd no right. Not anymore.

Pressing my lips against her fevered face, I whispered, "Rest in peace, my lovely, and know you'll soon be with your wee son. Then you'll know happiness."

"My boy," she whimpered and tried to smile.

She closed her eyes, coughed once or twice, then was gone.

I don't know how long I cried, only that at some stage, Milda came and lifted me to my feet.

"We have to prepare her, Alyson. We cannot leave her. It is too dangerous. Come, love, come. Help me."

I did as I was bid. Already, Conal had been bathed and wrapped in his sheet, which we used as a shroud. Together, Milda and I said the last rites, having heard them often enough to know what to say even if the exact meaning eluded us. If midwives could do it for babies, then surely the Lord, if not the Dean, would forgive us this presumption.

Milda and I remained downstairs with the bodies that night, calling up the stairs to let the others know what had happened. Beneath this roof, the Botch was host. A song of sorrow serenaded us throughout the night. The next day, Conal and Donnet were taken from the house and buried in the churchyard. I wondered when Milda and I would become ill.

Determined not to let any more of my soldiers fall in this one-sided battle, we remained in the small room downstairs for the next few weeks, placing food on the bottom stair, water and milk and even ale as well. We didn't allow any to share a room with us until we were certain the threat was no more.

Mayhap, the Lord answered my prayers—in part at least. Much to my astonishment and delight, Yolande recovered.

When we finally emerged, all of us sallow-faced, gaunt, and blinking, into the early autumn heat and iron-heavy skies, we were somber, yet also determined to let the deaths mean something. To work harder than ever to reclaim our lives and business. To succeed this time and never, ever endure another season like the last, no matter what it took.

⬥

They say one's loss is another's gain. I assume that excludes lives taken—or I sincerely hope so, even as I suspect heaven keeps a tally. God has to be a businessman, doesn't He? There must be an advantage to the suffering He metes out—for Him at least. Else it makes no sense. A growth in church numbers, more sons and daughters sacrificed to holy vocations. Additional pennies in the coffers, spent to glorify His name. Otherwise, how can one account for the sorrow and hardship?

Just as our fortunes fell and required rebuilding, so Geoffrey's rose. I guess I should have been thankful for that—and I was—praise be to God. The political business that had never really interested me involving the former (and now very dead) Lord Mayor, Nicholas Brembre, and the Lord Appellants, was well and truly over. When the King had come into his majority and assumed power the year before, casting off his self-appointed advisors and rewarding those he felt had been faithful to his cause, Geoffrey was among them. I don't think anyone was more surprised than Geoffrey himself.

Not only was he appointed Clerk of the King's Works and given a decent salary to accompany such a grand title, but was sent across the counties to inspect and supervise His Majesty's building projects. John of Gaunt returned from Spain, having failed to secure whatever it was he went there for, but upon settling back home, renewed his patronage of Geoffrey, which meant that, between projects, my poet could pursue his writing.

Once the Botch passed, Geoffrey made a point of calling whenever he could, sharing his time between us, the Dean of St. Martin's, his friend John Gower, and Westminster. It was from Geoffrey we heard more about the ongoing rivalries between the two Popes—now Boniface IX in Rome and Clement VII in Avignon. The latter was generally referred to as the Antipope. A church with two heads—like one of those oddities you paid a penny to see at county fairs. All I could think was that if God, the cardinals, and the Pope couldn't agree who was the prince of the church, the Lord's emissary on earth, how were we supposed to? Surely, it couldn't continue like that, with its great flock divided so. Geoffrey said I should keep those thoughts to myself and not share them with the Dean or Father Malcolm.

Aye, the young novice who saw us settled in at St. Martin's and through the Botch and beyond, became both a priest and a good friend. Responsible for burying Conal and Donnet and administering last rites to Yolande (I insisted he retract them when she survived, but he explained that wasn't necessary), he'd organized for mass to be said once we were able to assemble again, and even supplied some lovely beeswax candles. Geoffrey came to the service, gathering me in a tight embrace the moment he saw me.

"You're half the woman you used to be," he said, holding me at arm's length, his eyes raking my admittedly much thinner body.

"Only on the surface," I said, kissing him soundly.

"I'm relieved to hear it."

While I'd wasted away, along with the household, Geoffrey had increased his girth and the quality of his robes. I guess having a royal position, even a minor one, called for decent cloth. I wished I'd the means to make it for him, and said so.

It was then Geoffrey placed a small purse in my hands and, refusing to take no for an answer, insisted I keep it.

"When next I come up from Kent," he said, "I'll bring more. Don't argue, Alyson. Consider this an investment. When your business is flush, you can return my coin with interest."

"So, it's a loan then?" I asked.

"If that's what it takes for you to accept it, aye."

—————◆—————

Remember what I said about fortunes rising and falling? Fortuna must have decided she'd worked in Geoffrey's favor long enough, for the additional money never materialised. Geoffrey was set upon by brigands and robbed—not once, but twice. The first time was on the road between Kent and London, on his way to Eltham Palace.

"The second was at Fowle Oak," he said, examining with dismay the tear in his lovely green woollen robe. "What's so bloody funny?" he grumbled, downing a mazer as he sat in the kitchen.

"It wasn't Fragrant or Fair Oak?" I asked.

"There are no such places." He fixed me with a withering look.

"Exactly," I chuckled. "Which just goes to prove God has a sense of humor."

"Aye," he agreed wryly. "A very twisted one."

THIRTY-NINE

St. Martin's Le Grand, London
The Years of Our Lord 1391 to 1394
From the fourteenth to the seventeenth years of the reign of Richard II

We limped through the reminder of the year, grateful that the winter wasn't as benighted as the last. Even so, Yuletide was a sorry affair as the spaces around the table reminded us of those who were no longer with us. We gave half-hearted wassails, any cheer feeling like an insult to the others' memories.

Late the following year, we lost more of the household. Just before the snows fell in mid-December, Megge surprised me by announcing she was to be wed. When all we'd known for so long was sorrow and penny-pinching, hard work for poor returns, unbeknownst to me she'd been stepping out with a baker, a man in his twenties named Jon Brown. Jon came to St. Martin's in spring because his master forced him to add chalk to the bread. When that was uncovered, the master blamed his journeyman and promptly sent him to the pillory.

"After they released me, I fled here to avoid paying the fine, mistress," he admitted, cap in hand, eyes on the floor. He was confessing all his sins before asking permission for Megge's hand. I'd no intention of withholding it. I was overjoyed for her—for them—for all of us that we'd finally something to celebrate.

"I also reckon the master would have had me done for if I'd shown me face again. Everyone knew he'd put me up to adding chalk, but the authorities took his word I acted alone."

"Took your master's coin more like," added Megge loyally.

Jon nodded. I'd no doubt.

"He was forced to leave the city," said Jon. "Take his business elsewhere."

I liked this slight man with clear blue eyes and a toothy grin. It was clear he adored Megge; her past made not a whit of difference to him.

"Far as I be concerned, mistress," he said to me earnestly, over a few ales, "and I told this to my Megge," he patted her leg as she sat beside him, her cheeks not quite so thin, her eyes shining with love, not defiance, "what happens outside the walls of St. Martin's stays out there. Ain't that right?"

It wasn't strictly true; still, I wasn't going to argue.

The marriage was performed by Father Malcolm on the kalends of December 1391, at the church door of St. Agnes.

Jon and Megge shared a house around the corner with an alien mercer, his wife, and their two small children. Jon had been living there since he arrived and had built an oven in the outdoor kitchen so he could bake bread. He was one of the more popular bakers in the precinct, but by no means the only one.

From that day forth, bread was something we rarely paid for, which made life a bit easier. When it came to other necessities, we traded where we could, offering if not cloth or thread, then our mending services. Milda, Yolande, and Leda were the neatest seamstresses around and both Rose and Lowdy could manage to alter or patch a tunic or shirt to make it respectable again. We also turned our hands to dyeing tunics, shirts, breeches, and kirtles, Milda taking charge and imposing a small fee to breathe new life into old garments. It went down a treat with the bawds.

From being a household where both sexes dwelled, we'd become a house of mainly women—Drew and Wace excepted. Though, with his golden curls, chubby cheeks, and rosebud mouth, Wace could be mistaken for a chit as he ran about and demanded attention. Whereas Drew, weakened by the attack on him, then lack of food and sunshine, never fully recovered. He carried scars both external—the knife wound, but also a deep ridge along his jaw and an eyelid that drooped—and internal. It was a trial for him to chop wood, though he was able to collect scraps, answer the door, and deliver messages. I taught him to spin to help pass the time.

It's understandable that newcomers to the precinct—and there were admissions all the time, as well as people leaving the safety of its walls—mistook us for a house of ill repute. Upon seeing Drew, the men who called would start negotiating while looking the rest of us over, as if we were apples brought from the country and ripe for tasting. It would have been amusing had it not been dangerous. I knew soliciting was ignored within St. Martin's, but that was because the women either left the grounds or conducted their affairs swiftly and privately. There was no house dedicated to whoring. Not that I knew of, at any rate. Having been accused once of tarnishing the reputation of an entire parish by simply trying to run an honest business with mainly women workers, it was no surprise. Women weren't regarded as serious craftsmen or capable of trading unless it was on their backs. When it was explained we sold thread and cloth, not our queyntes, many offered more coin. Especially when they caught sight of Leda or Rose. We turned away disappointed men (and a couple of women seeking work). The fortune we could have made didn't bear thinking about.

———————

By the time summer arrived in 1394, we were making ends meet. If we didn't manage to earn more so we could buy extra wool to make more thread, then even the small bits of cloth I managed to weave on the ancient loom the nuns had given us wouldn't be sufficient. But without the cloth to make the coin to buy the wool, we'd no thread. It was a perplexing circular problem, a serpent digesting its tail, and I could see no way out of it.

Whenever Geoffrey visited, he would bring what he could spare from his own larder and purchase firewood and other provisions for us. He was unable to loan money as his own situation was again dire (don't ask me why or how—I didn't know then). It was never enough. Not with seven mouths to feed.

Milda began to work miracles making the provisions we did have stretch as summer bowed to autumn. Suddenly, there was some meat in the pottage and the fire was more often lit in the solar as well as the kitchen. Salt and other spices, usually a luxury, began to flavor the food (as well as preserve it). I thanked God for that woman's talents.

Memories of the previous winters and the one when the Botch struck, were still vivid, wounds that hadn't quite healed. Though we conserved what coin we could, and began to preserve and stockpile food and wood in preparation for the cold months ahead, it wasn't going to be easy. Even with our reduced numbers.

Something had to change—and soon.

Just before the first snows fell, Leda and Yolande came to see me in the solar.

I was sitting beneath some thin blankets, almost on top of the fire, trying to work the distaff and thread with stiff, frozen fingers. I couldn't bear to sit in the kitchen anymore and listen to the others, their refusal to succumb to the misery of our safe but beggarly existence. To think this is where five marriages had led.

To think Jankin Binder was likely warm, well-fed, and enjoying the cumulative spoils of them. If I dwelled on that subject for too long, I would unravel.

As was her habit, Milda sat with me, spinning. She knew when to speak and when to remain silent.

"What is it you want, girls?" I asked, concentrating on making the spindle turn.

They didn't answer at first, but came forward and placed some coins on the small table where a pile of wool rested.

"What's this?" I asked, looking suspiciously at the money, halting the spindle and lowering the distaff.

Milda remained focused on her thread.

"What it looks like, mistress," said Leda. "Some coin so you can buy what we need." She folded her arms defiantly.

"There's more where that came from," said Yolande.

I put the equipment down and leaned forward, one finger shifting the coins apart. It had been a long time since I'd seen so many pennies, let alone a few shillings.

"Where did you get these?" My heart felt heavy, an anchor holding me to the floor.

Yolande nudged Leda. "Before you say anything, mistress," said Leda, clearly the spokeswoman, "we only did it with priests. They're cleaner than the others and, as you can see, they pay well."

"We didn't do it where anyone could see us either, but went to their cells," Yolande added.

"And inside the church," added Leda helpfully.

Dear God.

I fixed my eyes on the coins, which began to shimmer and lose shape as my thoughts flew in a thousand different directions at once, gulls fleeing a storm. What had possessed them? I hadn't taken these girls in to put them back on the street. Hadn't freed them from a ruthless master to take his place.

Outside, bells began to ring. There was a cheer from somewhere and the faint bellow of a cow. Below, I could hear laughter followed by a shriek of joy.

"That'd be Lowdy," said Yolande. "She's found the haunch of meat we brought."

"You *bought* meat?" My head flew up.

"Nay, mistress," said Yolande. "Father Runcible gave it to me. As a token of his . . . what'd he say? Appriestiation."

I swallowed a smile. "I see." I didn't correct her. The term was apt.

There was silence. Yolande shifted uncomfortably.

"Others do it," said Leda, finally. "Why shouldn't we? It's what we're used to and, frankly, mistress, we bring in more swiving than we do spinning."

Words flew from my mouth. "This isn't about money—" Panic, a need to tell them I didn't want them to do this, made my voice shrill.

"Well, what's it about then?" demanded Leda. "Don't tell me *you* disapprove? You, who's been wed more times than John of Gaunt, and swives who you fancy beneath our noses." Her face hardened. She thought I was angry with them. I wasn't. How could I be? It's just that this was never how it was supposed to be—the women supporting me, using their queyntes to keep us solvent, fed, and warm. Disappointment in myself swamped me.

They were so proud. Their chins raised defiantly, their eyes glittering. They'd done what I'd failed to do.

"Milda? You're remarkably quiet." I faced her.

Milda colored and then gave a shrug.

"You knew about this." All of a sudden, the recent improvements in our larder made terrible sense.

"*Knew* might be too strong a word," she said. "Guessed. How do you think we came by the extra food? Through prayer?" She brushed her silver hair out of her face.

Leda stepped forward. "You didn't force us out there, mistress. You didn't beat us or take our wages."

I flicked my hand at the coins. "And I won't start now."

"They've *given* those to you," said Milda, raising her voice. "You can't reject them."

The expression on her face was hard to read. A mixture of pride in the girls, relief we wouldn't starve or freeze, but also guilt. Moses in a basket, I knew that feeling.

"If you're so worried about what we're doing," said Leda, "then set rules. Make it we can only swive, suck, or tug priests. God knows, there's plenty of them prepared to pay. From the day we got here, they've been begging for it and offering plenty if we would. Until a few weeks back, we refused."

"There's no shame in doing what's needed so we might have food in our stomachs, clothes on our backs, and a few faggots for the kitchen hearth," said Yolande. "Drew feels the cold mighty bad and I didn't want him sickening again—nor the children."

A bolt of shame sent me back against my chair. "I'm so sorry—" I began. Sorry that they were reduced to this, that my attempt to save them from that life had failed. I buried my face in my hands.

"Sorry?" scoffed Leda. "What for? We wouldn't have done it if we didn't want to. If we didn't think it worth it."

I raised my head.

"We know you look out for us, mistress, that you wouldn't see us come to harm. We just thought it was about time we looked out for you."

The back of my eyes began to itch.

I stared at the coins. They were dull, scratched, used. Just like the girls had once been. If I took them, I was no better than Judas, betraying all I stood for, all I wanted to give these women.

"Nay!" I leaped to my feet. "Nay. I'll not have it."

Yolande stepped back, hands flying up to protect herself. The action shocked me. I'd never strike the girls, never. I moved to reassure her at the same time as Leda moved between us.

"*You'll* not have it?" she hissed, thrusting her face into mine. "You once promised you'd never tell us what we could and couldn't do." Her eyes narrowed. "Just 'cause you don't like it, don't give you the right to tell us nay. If we've learned anything from you after all these years, it's that. You've plied your trade despite the men who try and stop you; why shouldn't we ply ours? God knows, yours, the spinning and cloth-makin' you trained us to, isn't getting us anywhere."

I sank back into the seat. My stomach roiled. The urge to be sick was strong. Muddy images swirled like an overflowing ditch in my mind. Leda was right. I had said those things. Told them I'd never seek to control them . . . not allowing them to be whores—it wasn't control, but protection . . . Wasn't it?

I studied the women. Leda was twenty now, Yolande older. They'd regained a little of the weight they'd lost during the Botch year, but were still slender. By God, they were beauties. Leda's was the obvious kind—golden tresses, pink cheeks, and ruby lips with those large pale blue eyes. Yolande's was more subtle—the dark ringlets, the deeply-hooded hazel eyes, and thin mouth that could break into a wide smile without warning. They weren't girls, but women grown. Leda was a mother. Yolande had seen death, survived it beneath this very roof. Made choices that changed her life. Why did it matter so much to me that she was making one more? Leda too? Was it because I hadn't made it for them?

I wasn't like that, was I? I didn't want authority over these girls. Just over *my* life. But if I wanted it, I who'd had husbands, wealth, and opportunity, why shouldn't these girls want it too? To take control of their destiny, spin Fortuna's wheel as they wanted? If it was a poor choice, so be it. At least I would be there to set it to rights again.

If that is what *they* wanted.

"This isn't what I wanted . . ." I said softly.

"What did you want, mistress?" asked Yolande.

"For you to have better lives."

Leda dropped to her knees before me. "And that's what we have, you old goose." She gave me one of her beautiful smiles. "Our lives, hard as they've been lately, are also the best they've ever been. One has only to look at Wace and Lowdy to see that. How can you not?" She put a tentative hand on my knee. "Just because we choose to do something you don't like, doesn't make it wrong. It just makes it our responsibility."

I choked back a sob; placed my hand over Leda's. A memory came to me—the story of Fulk's sister, Loveday Bigod. How she too had come to London, a feme sole with grand ideas. Look where that had led. I couldn't let this happen to my girls. To me.

Leda squeezed my knee. I rubbed my face, staring at the coins, at what they meant. What we could do with them . . . with more. It didn't bear consideration, did it? If the girls were willing, if it's what they wanted and were safe, was it so bad? It was their first trade; one they knew how to ply. They weren't innocent virgins being sacrificed to male desire and brutality.

This was their choice. Chosen because it helped me. Helped us all. There was no shame, no regret. The expression on Yolande's face said so much. She wanted my approval—they both did. What would it make me if I gave it?

It need only be for a little while, until we had enough to mayhap weave again.

But how could I ask them to do this? Only, I wasn't asking, was I?

"Mistress," said Leda, as if she were a prognosticator, reading my mind. "We'll do it whether you wish it or no."

I rose slowly, uncertain if my knees would hold. I glanced at Milda. She trusted me to make the right decision. God bless her.

What if I were to offer my queynte as well? Would that salve my conscience? Would that lessen the pain of allowing the girls to sell theirs?

What if no one wanted it? I was almost two score years. It didn't bear thinking about.

"If this is what you choose to do," I said, finally, "then do it. You'll get no objections from me. Not today at any rate."

Leda flew into my arms, Yolande gave a whoop of joy. Rose chose that moment to enter, or so I thought.

"Then you'll have no objection if I do the same," said Rose.

"Now, wait a minute," I said. "Allowing Leda and Yolande to return to their old profession is very different from asking you to enter it."

"Enter it? Ha! Have you forgotten where you found me, mistress?" asked Rose. That shut me up. "Anyhow, I heard what you said. It's my choice. I choose to do this. I'm also a woman, lest you haven't noticed."

I hadn't. Why, slight as Rose was, she was buxom, with long, lithe legs, and pert breasts. She'd be over twenty. How had I failed to see these changes—without and within?

I had to sit down again. The girls gathered around me, chittering like robins in excitement. Milda found my hand and held it tightly.

How had my desire to be in charge of my own life, to be my own master, come back to bite me on the rump so viciously? Well, it was hard to miss, being a generous arse and all. There'd be a price to pay for condoning this—I felt it in my aging bones.

But another part saw the right of it too. What I'd desired for these women, good marriages, the promise of a life away from poverty, from debt and brutal men, hadn't eventuated as I'd hoped. While Megge had found happiness with Jon, it was within a precinct where felons sought refuge. At least if the girls did trade their bodies, I could oversee it, ensure they came to no harm; that they were paid fairly for what they offered. Unlike Loveday, these girls, *my* girls, wouldn't be left to fend for themselves, to give up their children. The girls had me. Me and Milda.

If it went well, and I prayed it would, trying not to consider Ordric and his kind, and we continued to spin and weave a little, we could slowly rebuild our original business. Better still, I could hire someone to protect the girls. Beneath this roof, I could look to their well-being, but beyond . . . well, I needed someone who could keep them from harm.

If we earned enough, I could shore up an education for Wace. I'd already spoken to Geoffrey about securing an apprenticeship for him when the time came. At thirteen, it was also time to seriously consider what to do with Lowdy. Though I'd taught her to read and write, I'd been negligent. There was no reason she couldn't have an apprenticeship as well. That nun from St. Agnes, the apothecary, was very fond of her . . .

Summoned by my thoughts, the children appeared in the doorway.

"What are you all giddy about?" Lowdy asked no one in particular, wiping one hand on her apron while Wace clutched the other, thumb in his mouth. I looked at Lowdy. Tall, with fine features, her dark hair was braided, her wide, brown eyes narrowed with mock suspicion as she regarded us fondly. Smart, quick, and kind, that girl would succeed at whatever she tried.

The women fell quiet, shooting guilty glances at each other.

"What else, Lowdy," I came to their rescue, standing and taking both children's hands, leading them to the hearth, "but trade."

"Trade? What kind?" she asked.

Leda choked back a cough as I guided her son's hand to hers and she straightened his little shirt, smoothed his nest of curls.

"The fair kind," I said solemnly. "One where women make the rules and men obey."

"Hear, hear," said Leda and Yolande. Rose whooped.

"I think it's time we celebrate, don't you?" said Milda, standing. "It's not every day you get bested by your own words, mistress." She winked and, taking Yolande with her, disappeared before the cushion I threw hit her.

Laughing, Lowdy fetched it and returned it to its seat. Then she came and draped her arms around me, nuzzling my cheek. She smelled so sweet; like home. Violets and wood smoke mixed with cinnamon and sage, the promise of spring or autumn.

I returned her embrace, enjoying the closeness, the dizzy excitement of the girls; an excitement I feared wouldn't last long.

Whether this was right or wrong, I swore to myself then and there as the ale was poured and mazers passed around, Drew joining us, it was a choice Lowdy would never, ever have to consider.

"Here's to being bawds," I said, raising my drink.

"Bored?" asked Lowdy, frowning. "Why would you ever want to be *that*?"

FORTY

St. Martin's Le Grand, London, and Southwark
The Year of Our Lord 1396
In the twentieth year of the reign of Richard II

*F*rom that day forward, the household became one whose primary business was queynte. Reluctant though I'd been to become what I most loathed, someone who profited from a woman's body, when the role was thrust upon me, I not only enjoyed the privilege, but was damn good at it too.

Whoring was illegal in London and yet, as was the way with anything men desired, the authorities turned a blind eye, excusing it with prayers and pardons. Naturally, it thrived. Each Sunday, the priests and bishops would rail against the wickedness of women and their whoring ways and then seek them out for just that purpose the moment they left church. Yet, when punishment was meted out, even though it took two to commit the act, it was the women who suffered.

So it is for now and for evermore, amen.

Apart from a few churls who thought it was within their rights to beat the girls as well as swive them, and one young lordling who convinced himself he was in love with Leda and attempted to kidnap her, Leda, Rose, and Yolande ventured out into the city most days and returned with shillings and pennies.

In no time, our fortunes turned. Decent quantities of food graced the table; throughout the following winters we were warm. Soon, we were able to afford enough wool to make good quantities of thread. I began to weave again—not that it was necessary.

Instead, spinning and weaving became the legitimate cover for our real trade.

When the girls came home, always together as instructed in those early days, then waiting until the children were abed, I'd ask them about their day. Gathered around the kitchen table, the yellow hoods that whores were required by law to wear cast aside, they'd chat about who sought their services and where. Some of the men were young, others old, some wealthy, many just able to afford them. They'd laugh, wink, and make light of what they were doing, even the occasional bruises or grazes. I watched carefully for any signs of unhappiness, but, God be praised, there were none. What they most complained about were men whose breath smelled like onions and stale ale, were covered in lice and treated soap and water like a leper—best avoided lest they catch something. When I understood they were still accommodating these hog's entrails, I was horrified.

"Don't you understand? You don't need to go with just anyone. Ordric may demand that, but I don't. If the men stink like the Fleet, tell them to piss off."

"Some already have," said Rose, screwing up her nose. "Pissed, that is."

"Then tell them to find someone prepared to tolerate their filth. You won't."

The girls stared in disbelief.

"But they have coin—" began Yolande.

"So? Doesn't mean you have to take it."

"But—" said Leda, looking at Yolande and Rose.

"But what?" I said. "God's balls, ladies! The whole point of me agreeing to this was to give *you* control. If you don't respect your bodies, how can you expect anyone else to?"

My thoughts flew to Jankin. I hadn't respected mine, allowing him to use it ill. The shame was still raw, and I pushed it aside. "Order them to wash, present themselves accordingly. Just because the men have coin, doesn't give them rights. It's *you* who has the authority in this transaction. Use it. Oh—" I added, as the women shook their heads in wonder, "and then raise your price."

"We can't do that!" protested Rose. "Making them wash is bad enough. We'll lose custom."

"Nay, you won't. Anyway, since you're offering a discount to the priests here, we need to make up the shortfall."

Not only did the majority of men agree to make themselves more presentable, but as the months flew by, word got around my girls were fussy. This made men more inclined to hire them, believing it reduced the chance of the pox or some other disease. While that worked in our favor a while, it made the other bawds and pimps angry. We were stealing customers. Careful never to frequent Gropecunt, Puppekirty, or Cock Lane and upset the likes of Ordric and his maudlyns, soon we were hard-pressed to find anywhere we were welcome.

Sometimes, the girls would seek my advice regarding men—how to ensure the cleaner and better-quality customers returned.

"Encourage them to talk about themselves," I said. "Men love to be listened to. Ask about their wives, if they have one, then prepare to hear them moan." My experience was showing. "Get them to tell you about their sweethearts. If they're sailors, the ports they've visited. If they have a trade, liken their pricks to tools and tell them they must be good at what they do, because they wield their instrument so well."

The girls would fall about laughing. Later, they'd report my advice worked, depositing a few extra coins as proof.

"If only we could lease our ears along with our queyntes," said Leda. "We'd double our money."

I'd make a businesswoman of her yet.

More than once the girls were threatened and chased away from popular meeting places like St. Paul's, the land up near Smithfield, or Aldgate. Customers were never brought into St. Martin's Le Grand (the priests being the only exception), so it was becoming difficult to find suitable places to offer services—after all, we still had to avoid the law. It wasn't until a sympathetic customer told Leda the alleys around St. Katherine's were more accepting of the trade than others that we operated securely there a while. But after a year and a half, even that became untenable as more and more women were also drawn to a place where pimps wouldn't coerce them or other whores attack them.

It was a crowded market and no one traded well in those.

Then I heard some maudlyns were making trips across the river into Southwark during the day. The Bishop of Winchester's Liberty on the south side of the river had different laws from London. Over there, the oldest profession in the world flourished. Bankside was dominated by a colony of Flemish people who'd settled there years earlier, and many of the places along the waterfront had been turned into bathhouses. Over near the fishponds owned by the bishop, the area became known as the "Stews."

Time to see what it was like. If this was a place the girls could ply their trade safely.

In the October of 1396, I finally crossed the river. Along with Milda and Drew, who I'd coaxed out of the precinct, I left as the bells sounded prime. The wicker gates had just opened, yet the city was bustling. Vendors parked their carts and wagons along the Cheap, barrow-boys too. The grind of wheels and hooves on cobbles was matched by the grunts of swine, baying of cattle, and bleating of sheep being herded with crops and sticks along the main thorough-fare toward the markets and the blood-soaked lanes of the Shambles. Bakers and milkmaids cried out in singsong voices, the shutters of shops flew open. Trestle tables were swiftly erected and goods carried outside. A stiff wind made awnings flap and pennants crackle as frost was blown away. Above us was the promise of weak sunshine. Women wrapped in shawls, baskets over their arms, chins tucked into chests, walked toward the conduit or paused to purchase candles, fur, nails, rushes, woad, leather, or stockfish—everything was for sale. The ring of hammers almost drowned the faint strains of a keen lute player. Men in livery, satchels slapping their hips as they darted between folk, their faces grim, refused to be distracted by the temptations around them.

We walked through St. Paul's, ignoring the urgent beckoning of merchants who invited us to buy their ink, books, oranges, spices, and all manner of other goods. One old man with a scrappy white beard delivered warnings atop a barrel. Another held a star chart in his hand, promising he'd forecast futures for a mere shilling. One young maid held up handfuls of ribbons, claiming they were the finest in all the world and not to be found anywhere else.

"Poppycock," grumbled Milda. "I saw the same ones just yesterday in Master Hall's shop."

Distracted, Drew kept pausing to consider a barrow filled with cabbages or a milkmaid's brimming jug and doe-eyed cow. His limp slowed us as well, and I tried to be patient. I laced my arm through his and kept him close, pointing out the man tossing swords or the cat suckling its kitties beneath a costermonger's cart, all the while moving forward.

We headed to Powle's Wharf near Baynard's Castle. The smell of the river was strong and the number of carts and buckets filled with fish, oysters, and eels being pushed uphill increased with every step we took down. When we reached the water stairs, a boatman who'd just deposited some passengers was happy to take us back across the choppy brown waters.

"What you reckon 'bout his lordship, eh?" he asked, steering us toward the middle of the river, hailing neighboring wherries and boats.

He was referring to John of Gaunt, who'd recently wedded his former mistress, Katherine Swynford. It just so happened, she was the sister of Geoffrey's late wife. I'd been stunned when Geoffrey told me—he was now related to royalty, albeit in a roundabout manner. It was like a fairytale, a prince marrying a commoner; a man as rich as Croesus plighting troth with a pauper. It was the talk of the town and set women's hearts racing as suddenly the stuff of dreams became a reality. Fools. I knew the stuff those kinds of dreams were made upon. Marriage was no elevation for a woman but a slow descent into ignominy and slavery, all in the name of God.

Much better to be a whore and be beholden to neither God nor one man.

When Geoffrey first told me, I'd asked, "Why does the Duke wed her now?"

"Likely so his children won't be bastards anymore."

Together, John of Gaunt and Katherine had four children.

"You don't think he marries for love?" I asked, certain of my own thoughts on the matter.

Geoffrey shrugged. "Who does?"

It was on the tip of my tongue to say I had once and look where that led, but stayed silent. I caught the wistful look on his face. Had Geoffrey ever loved? Was he even capable? He loved his children— at least, I think he did, even though he rarely spoke of them. I knew Elizabeth was still at Barking Abbey. I didn't know much about his eldest son, Thomas, except he'd made a good marriage recently. Of Lewis, Geoffrey scarce made mention, though when he did, his entire face lit up.

Mayhap, the Duke had wed for his progeny. There were worse reasons, and if it benefited the woman who birthed them, then that was the least she was owed.

While the boatman discussed Gaunt and his new wife, declaring her a whore who'd pay for her sins if not on earth then in the hell where she belonged, I thought about pushing him overboard, but how would we finish our crossing? Instead, I shut out his carping and focused on the approaching bank and the houses set back from it.

Clouds of smoke squatted above the buildings, the familiar stench of tanning and fulling apparent as we drew closer. On the muddy foreshore, there were some horses and carts, as well as thin dogs, skulking cats, and hens with their feathers fluffed up against the cold. People milled about, working on the wharves, unloading boats and wherries. Goods were stacked in crates to one side, while people queued to board swaying vessels on the other, baskets and burlaps empty, purses no doubt full. There were shouts to move aside, chatter and the general din of industry. Church steeples cut through the haze, signs that the godly also dwelled in a place with a reputation for vice and sin. Well, they'd ever been comfortable bedfellows.

As we paid the boatman and came ashore, I was struck by the poor efforts of those nearby not to stare at us. It would have been laughable if it wasn't also reassuring: after a cursory glance, they turned away. We didn't warrant a second look. A good sign.

We hadn't walked very far when the door of a rather large two-storey house with a mews opened. A fading shingle depicted a large bird. A big woman stood, her cap askew, her puffy face blotchy as she shook a rug then proceeded to beat it with a stick, uncaring that the dust flew in our faces and back inside the open door. Over her shoulder she called out in another language. Flemish. I looked again at the house. It was in a dire state. So was the one next to it, the sign so dirty it was hard to discern—a cross and key? The shingle on the next house appeared to depict a pointed edifice.

The frontage was strewn with rubbish and stank of shit and piss. A couple of men came out of another place, again Flemish from the sound of them. I steered Drew and Milda away and back toward the water where, even though the shore was littered with the innards of fish and other animals and a dead dog's carcass, it was cleaner.

"Big houses," said Milda, nodding toward them.

"Bathhouses."

Drew twisted his head to study them. "What? You have baths in 'em?"

"I think once upon a time, you did, but now they're just bawdy houses."

"Like what we are?" he asked.

"Sort of. Only our girls can't swive indoors."

"Not yet," said Milda.

"Not ever, not in St. Martin's," I reminded her. "If they do, that will be the end of us."

"Will that necessarily be a bad thing?" She fixed her eyes on my face. Ever present was the worry the girls would be harmed. Every week, news reached us about this or that maudlyn being beaten bloody or having her throat cut and found in a ditch.

"Nay, it wouldn't. But as the girls remind me daily, no job is without risk." I drew her close. "There'll come a time, Milda, I promise, when we won't make a living in this manner." I nodded toward a woman in the window of one of the whorehouses. Her kirtle had slipped over one shoulder, exposing the swell of her bosom. Her long, mahogany hair was unbound. She sat eating an apple in a manner I'm certain most priests imagined when discussing Eve. "For now—" I jerked my chin toward another large establishment as two young girls without aprons emerged from a doorway beneath a shingle bearing a crane, "we'll see if we can ply trade around here. Mayhap, not *here* exactly. That'll get everyone offside, Flemish or not. Let's see where the girls can work, shall we?"

We followed the maudlyns toward the High Street, meandering in and out of the various alleys, past a cordwainer's, a butcher, at least two mercers, taverns, a bookseller, a goldsmith, a scrivener's, and a lawyer's. Barrows and carts filled with vegetables, fruits, fish, and all sorts of tempting vittles as well as hay, planks, coal, wine, and laths lined the street. Hucksters with jugs of ale wandered about, so did bakers with trays of steaming bread. Every so often, we'd see a woman leaning against a doorway or just standing idly on a street corner. Not too far away was a man or boy, his face alert, one hand hovering over a weapon strapped to his hip. When a customer approached the woman, the man or boy would step forward, there'd be some discussion, the coin would be taken, and the woman led her client into the shadows. It happened right beneath people's noses; no one turned a hair. Was it really so simple?

We paused, watching a while, pretending to be interested in some fragrant oils a Moor was selling. I purchased some rose oil and, when there was a lull in business, approached two women. Even though they didn't wear the yellow hood, they were from London. None too happy to talk at first, when I pressed a few pennies in their hands, they admitted it was fairly easy to get custom, provided you didn't venture into the next liberty.

"Stay this side of the street and don't go any further than St. Margaret's Hill, up by the Tabard, then you're alright. But take one step over there—" the older of the two, possibly the mother of the

other, nodded toward the opposite side of the road where a tavern
stood with a sign bearing an angel standing on a hoop, as if its halo
had slipped to the ground, "and the cocksucking bailiff'll be onto
you. He's a nasty piece of work—Lewis Fynk. Likes to pinch you
if he thinks you ain't listening to 'im." She pushed up her sleeve to
display a series of livid bruises.

"That's the least of what he does," said the younger girl, rubbing
her jaw.

Milda sucked in her breath. Drew frowned. My heart began to
beat strangely. I resisted the urge to put my arm about her. Bastard.

"You thinkin' of doin' some business, are you?" said the older
woman. She looked me up and down. "You be a looker for an old
doxy. There be some like 'em buxom and with age on the bones—and
cunt," she cackled. "Experience." She rotated her hips suggestively.
Abruptly, her demeanour changed. "But don't tread on our turf, you
hear?" She shook a fist in my face, then unfurled her fingers. Her
nails were long and filthy. "If you do, I'll mark you like I've others."

I said I'd keep that in mind, and dragged Milda and Drew away.

We strolled a bit further up the High Street, into the part known
as Long Southwark, pausing to buy eel pies. While we ate, I studied
the area. Most of the street corners were claimed. Upon reaching the
tavern with a White Hart on its shingle, I suggested we return. There
had to be somewhere suitable closer to the bridge, surely.

We spent the next few hours talking to any of the women willing
to share their stories. So many had run away from untenable homes,
marriages, the brutality of brothers, uncles, men, sometimes their
own mothers, grandmothers, or sisters. Some fled just so they could
choose their own fate. Others had been lured to London with promises of a ring, love and wealth, only to find once they'd sacrificed
the thing all females should hold precious (oh, how I sound like the
women of Noke Manor), they were abandoned—too often with a
babe in their bellies.

There were women not beholden to a bawd or a pimp, and those
who came from the bathhouses. We chatted to a well-dressed trio
who cautiously admitted their degree of well-being depended on who
ran the business. Protected from the worst ravages of the profession,

though not always from the violence and drunken expectations of men, they'd decent food, a roof over their heads, and freedom to do what they wanted when they weren't flat on their backs.

"Better than slaving for a bastard husband who ruts like a pig and smells worse," said one.

"Better than being in service to a man who thinks he's entitled to your titties and queynte for nothin'," said another.

"Better than being at the mercy of the Fathers at the priory," said yet another.

And on it went.

Not all were so fortunate. Bathhouse owners were mostly considered tyrants—especially the Flemish, and by their own.

The way I saw it, there wasn't much difference between these women and me. To them, their queyntes were a commodity they sold. What was marriage but an exchange of queynte and title: that of wife. Only, once the ring was on a woman's finger and she gained respectability and, if she was fortunate, a home and possessions, 'twas the men had the best of the deal. A woman had not only to surrender her queynte but her entire body, will, mind, right to make decisions. Even her children were not considered hers, but her husband's. She was like a piece of property, traded on the marriage market for a man's profit; to ensure his name continued and his lineage was secured. The moment a woman married, her past was erased—even her name. All she'd been was forgotten when she became a wife. Mistress Husband, more like. Wives had as much value as a beast—less if they couldn't breed.

Whores had the right of it. Charge a man for use of their cunts and then tell him to piss off. There might be danger in such a profession, but wasn't marriage also dangerous? Look at mine. And that's before childbirth was considered. My arm fell across my soft stomach. Would I ever feel my womb quicken? I doubted it, not now. I was two score year and four or thereabouts (what did it matter?) and no babe had quickened inside me. Not from want of trying. A picture of Fulk rose, followed by the rest of my husbands—Turbet, and his unimpressive pole, Mervyn who used his for other purposes, and then Simon, named after his, which dominated his life and mine.

Then there was Jankin. What a lover he'd been, gentle, passionate—yet also violent: hating, punching, and bruising . . .

No good dwelling on him. No good dwelling on any of them.

"Isn't the Tabard just ahead?" asked Milda, interrupting my thoughts. She gestured toward Harry Bailly's place, from where I'd undertaken at least three pilgrimages—two with Milda. Harry, the man who was also privy to my secret.

"Aye."

"Why don't we call on him?" She began to steer me toward it. "He's right fond of you. He knows the area. Could give us advice."

"I've learned all I need." I resisted her efforts to turn me around.

Milda regarded me curiously. Truth was, I didn't want Harry to see me as I was—dressed in old scarlet, trawling Southwark for places *my* maudlyns could operate. I didn't want him to see how I'd been reduced. Or Milda. As for Drew, he was like a returned soldier, injured from fighting my battles. The next time I met Harry, I wanted it to be because I'd succeeded. Because if I did, then we all did.

"Anyhow," I said, heading back toward to the river, "I want to check what's down this end of Southwark."

Just before the pillory, which was in the middle of the High Street, directly in line with the entrance to the bridge so those being punished could consider the heads of traitors rotting on the poles above them, the perfect spot presented itself. Just after Mart Place was the courthouse. Not one strumpet or suspicious-looking person dared loiter there. It was crowded with regular folk—traders, lawyers, knights, shoppers, as well as farmers, travelers, diplomats, and all sorts going to the city from Kent, the countryside, and beyond. Why, I'd trod this very road en route to Canterbury. If the girls stood outside the church, they'd catch traffic from the main road *and* the courthouse. A wide alleyway running along the back of the courthouse was the ideal place to take customers. Cleaner than most, only two doors faced onto it. There were even trees and what appeared to be a bench. A beldame sat there feeding a coven of cats. Here was a situation where the law, such as it was, might work in our favor.

"I've seen enough," I said suddenly, striding back to the High Street. "The girls can start as soon as I've organized one last thing."

"What's that, mistress?" asked Drew.

I hesitated. I didn't want what I was about to say to make Drew feel unworthy or think that I didn't value him.

"I need to hire someone to accompany the girls; look out for their welfare when they walk the streets. I've been remiss not organizing it sooner. It's clear many here have protection. Mine will have no less."

Drew stopped suddenly, doubling over and clutching his knees, forcing the crowd to go around him. There were curses and some dark looks. A man in black robes stumbled.

"Are you alright, sweetling?" I bent over, one hand on his back.

He slowly straightened, sucking in the air. "Oh, mistress. For a while there, I was afraid you were going to order me to do it! I've been afeared since we got here."

I hid a small smile. "Oh. Well. Who'd look to our welfare in St. Martin's if you were over here?"

Drew squared his shoulders. "Exactly. That's my job."

"Damn right," I said, cuffing his shoulder.

The entire trip home, Drew couldn't stop grinning. We discussed the right sort of person needed to safeguard the girls and look out for us in Southwark. Whoever we chose would need to live with us, so would have to be accustomed to being in a small tight-knit household and play his part. He'd have to have good instincts, be discreet, not be swayed by a heavy purse and, above all, able to take orders from a woman.

Where on God's good earth were we going to find that kind of man?

As luck would have it, he found me.

FORTY-ONE

St. Martin's Le Grand, London, and the banks of the River Thames
The Year of Our Lord 1396
In the twentieth year of the reign of Richard II

A month later, we still hadn't found anyone suitable to escort the girls to Southwark and watch over them. In the meantime, they continued to work where they could in London, avoiding not just overzealous constables and bailiffs, but also the wrath of other maudlyns and their pimps. Milda and I put aside spinning and weaving and took to accompanying the girls. It didn't stop them or us getting abused, bitten, scratched, shoved to the ground, and kicked occasionally, but it did prevent the violence escalating—and not just because the other whores were up for a fight. My girls, bless 'em, were prepared to defend themselves. Milda and I carried big sticks. They worked as both a deterrent and defense, that is, when you knew the attack was coming. There were days we returned with swollen eyes, sore ribs and grazed knuckles. We all lost some hair, ripped from our scalps. Yolande even lost two teeth after being punched.

On the ides of November, after seeing Wace safe with his tutor and Lowdy to the nunnery where she was newly apprenticed to the apothecary, Sister Cecilia, Leda, Rose, Yolande, Milda, and I decided to venture further afield, out toward Moorgate. A fair was being held that not only attracted locals, but travelers as well. There should be enough customers to satisfy even the lustiest of whores and the most demanding of pimps. Drew remained, looking after the house and spinning to ensure we had enough of the thread we intended to sell at the little stall we'd leased in the Cheap. We had to keep up appearances, after all.

We were heading up Coleman Street, mingling with the crowds going to the fair, when I was knocked to the ground. By the time I found my feet, I'd not only lost my stick, but couldn't find the girls or Milda. Heartsick, I searched for them, pulling on shoulders, pushing men, women, and even children aside. I tripped on a barrow, brushed aside the pleading hands of a beggar woman, all the while shouting for Milda, Leda, Yolande, and Rose. Heads turned, but not the faces I wanted to see.

I paused at the sign of the crocodile, an apothecary's shop, trying to get my bearings. My knees had been hurt in the fall, my damned pride as well. Though I stood on tiptoe, there was no sign of the girls, or where they'd gone. How was I supposed to find them among so many people? Had they been snatched? Who'd take them? Why? Where? I turned back in the direction I'd come, my eyes narrowing.

Of course! I plunged into the crowd, forcing my way against the tide of flesh. I ducked into the first alleyway, Trystrams. It was quieter here, gloomy with shadows. It was then I heard a scream, followed by shouting.

"Leda!" I picked up my skirts and ran, leaping over a foul-smelling ditch, dashing past a bundle of rags tucked against a door that stirred as I flew by.

Around the corner, trapped in a doorway were Leda, Yolande, and Rose. Leda had a swollen, torn lip, and a cut beneath one half-closed eye. Yolande's cap was missing, her hair had come undone, and her shift was torn. Rose had a swelling on the side of her face and blood trickling out one ear. Milda was nowhere to be seen. Surrounding them were Ordric and his men. As I reached them, Ordric drew back his fist and punched Leda in the stomach.

She doubled over, gagging and retching. Rose and Yolande went to help, but Ordric thrust a knife in their direction. The other two men laughed.

Fury ignited within me. "How dare you," I bellowed.

Ordric spun around, his wicked dagger aloft. Upon seeing who it was, and that I was alone, he began to smirk. His men leered.

I marched toward him. "You sorry excuse for a hound's prick, you shriveled piece of monkey turd, human excrement dressed in a knave's coat. Leave my girls alone."

"So, the Whore of Honey Lane dares to show her face after I told her what I'd do if she set up shop again. Worse, she brings my missus—"

"I ain't your wife, Ordric, and you know it." Leda spat blood.

"Shut up, bitch." He lashed out, the back of his hand striking her so hard, she stumbled. Rose caught her.

"You leave her alone, leave us all alone, or else—" I kept one wary eye on the knife.

"Or else what?" muttered one of the other men and sniggered.

That was it. "Don't you speak to me, you hedge-born, flea-bitten bastards. You should be ashamed of yourselves, doing the bidding of this levereter whose sole purpose is to harm women. Why? Because he's afraid. And you know what that means?" Without thinking, I stepped right up to the first man and pushed my face into his.

"Nay, mistress," he squeaked.

"You are too." I slapped him hard across the cheek.

"Oy," said the other. I turned and struck him. By God, my palm burned worse than hellfire, but I didn't let them see that. A demon possessed me, a female demon with horns, sharp teeth, giant nugs, and cruel fingers.

They stared in shock, uncertain how to respond.

Before Ordric could react, I knocked the knife from his hand. "As for you, you lily-livered scum-eater, why don't you go back to the cesspit you crawled from. The only reason you pick on us, and bring extra *men*—" the word meant something else on my lips, "is because you don't have the balls to fight us. That's not a pair of hairy turnips you're keeping in your breeches, but a hairless queynte, you coward."

By now, the shouts and insults had attracted a small crowd. Shutters flew open, doors were cracked so eyes could spy what was going on. More spilled from nearby alleys and lanes, congregating behind and beside us. Damn, but they were blocking my intended escape route. I'd no choice but to brazen this out. A pisspot was emptied, the stinking contents narrowly missing the girls. I gestured. They ran to me. I pushed them behind me.

A chant was taken up. "Cowardly queynte, cowardly queynte." I began to laugh. Ordric's face grew red, his eyes colder than the Queen's jewels. He gathered up his knife, his shoulders heaving.

"You stupid old gabbing bitch. Don't you ever get tired of hearing yourself? You think your words can hurt me?"

"Nay, Ordric. I don't. You don't possess the sense to understand them."

"Then why bother, you pus-filled slut?"

"Because they make me and those who do understand—" I gestured to the crowd, "feel better. They give us a laugh . . . at you."

There was an appreciative roar. Caught up in the applause, I took a bow, taking my eyes off Ordric. It was enough. With one solid punch, he felled me.

Bright lights flashed as a sharp pain lanced my temple and shot out my right eye. My ears rang. There was a swell of voices, like those you hear when you dunk your head in a basinful of water, deep, distorted, uncanny. Another pain exploded on my side. I opened my eyes as Ordric's boot descended for a second kick. I threw my arms up over my head.

The boot never connected. I moved my hands in time to see a huge man with enormous shoulders and even larger arms lift Ordric off his feet and, with a mighty bellow, fling him against a wall.

Ordric hit the ground like a tinker's rag doll. He didn't move.

Once again, a huge cheer rose and the colossus lumbered toward me, the people parting like the sea before Moses to let him through. Beside him was Milda, her face red and damp with tears. She crouched beside me.

"Oh, Alyson. What's he done to you?"

The girls brushed off my hair and skirts, gently touching where

Ordric had struck, dabbing at the blood. Looming over them, keeping the onlookers at bay, was the giant.

"I'm alright," I said, sweeping their hands and kerchiefs from my face. "Take more than that streak of dog shit to hurt me," I lied. "But," I winced, blinking at the enormous shadow above, "who is it I have to thank for coming to our aid?"

The giant bent over and with astonishing gentleness, helped me rise. "The name's Stephen atte Place, mistress." His voice rumbled like a laden cart upon stones. "At your service."

Forced to tilt my head, he was older than me by a few years, and had the grizzled look of a world-weary sailor: the weathered skin, the callused hands and scars that came with running the rigging. If that wasn't enough, he wore an earring in one lobe. Not his Grace's navy then, but a merchant's ship. Mayhap, even a pirate's.

The ringing in my ears that oft defeated me commenced again. "What did you say? What's your name?"

"I said—" He leaned closer. He smelled of salt, sweat, smoke, and wild spices. "My name is Stephen atte Place, and I am at your service."

I cocked an eyebrow at Milda, looked at the girls, then back at Master atte Place with a wide grin. "Good. You can start immediately."

———•———

Master Stephen settled in well and was more than happy not only to work under a woman, so to speak, but to protect the girls as they went about their business.

"My mother always said, a man who has to strike a woman is no man at all."

I liked the sound of Stephen's mother; a woman of sense who raised a fine fellow. Not even the work we did perturbed him. "If you knew what I've seen, mistress, let alone done," he'd say, a mazer of ale and huge trencher of meat before him as he sat at the kitchen table, Wace, Drew, and the girls drinking in his every word (he was a man of few, so gained an audience when he did speak), "you'd know I've no right to judge. That's for God and Him alone."

With Stephen escorting the girls to Southwark, finding a biddable innkeeper to allow him to pass the time in his premises, I thought I'd be able to focus more on the spinning and weaving side of the business.

But as Fortuna would have it, something else occurred that caused a great distraction and turned my life upside down again.

It was Geoffrey's fault. Him and his damn scribbles.

FORTY-TWO

St. Martin's Le Grand, London
The Year of Our Lord 1396
In the twentieth year of the reign of Richard II

I recall clearly the first time I heard mention of a wondrous poem written by a gentleman of Kent who had the patronage of John of Gaunt. Like half the city, I'd made my way to London Bridge in the hope of catching a glimpse of the new Queen, King Richard's child bride, Isabella of France. The poor chit was only six or seven, barely out of the nursery, but her parents saw fit to send her to a foreign country and give her over to a man who, by all accounts, was still grieving his last wife. Needs must, I guess, especially when the weight of the kingdom sits upon your shoulders—or, more accurately, the child-queen's womb.

The girls and Master Stephen had departed for Southwark before dawn. The day promised good takings with so many coming to the city. Whereas at first I'd thought lining up on the bridge would be a fine thing, the moment I saw the number of people pressing to cross, squeezed like fish in a barrow, I whispered to Drew and we adjusted course, Milda complaining as she was jostled and bumped. Lowdy and I kept firm hold of Wace. Like Lowdy, he'd been given the day off schooling.

We wended our way to Heywharf near the Stilliard in the hope of catching a wherry and watching the Queen's arrival from the river.

Alas, others had the same idea, so, instead of watching from the water, we were forced to witness the momentous occasion from the shore. As it turned out, this was a sensible move. Unable to see the tiny Queen, we nonetheless caught the moment the royal procession reached the bridge and began to cross. Pennants flapped, the silver buckles, shining weapons, and glistening armor of the knights astride their liveried horses stood out. The procession was slow, the cheering raucous. Along the banks, folk clapped, jumped, and cried out blessings along with those atop the bridge. From the river, people stood in boats, barges, and wherries, some using instruments to trumpet their approval, waving ribbons and expressing their joy.

I'd hoisted Wace into my arms so he might see over the two esquires in front of us, nicely dressed men who nevertheless refused to cede their places. Angry at their selfishness, I moved as close to them as possible, uncaring that Wace's toes occasionally struck their velvet paltocks and coats, ignoring their pointed looks.

Their conversation was loud, deliberately so, as they spoke of those they recognized—esteem by association—and pointed to spots on the bridge that not even an eagle could have distinguished. It was both tiresome and amusing. But it wasn't until I heard them discussing the wondrous poems of the gentleman from Kent that my attention was seized.

"They're all the court talk about," said one with a large, flat cap and trim red beard.

"Over in Tower Ward it's the same, let me tell you," said his smooth-cheeked companion. "Why, when I dined with Lord Lumpton the other night, he'd a bard recite some."

A rush of pride and pleasure washed over me. I knew exactly who they spoke of, though I wasn't aware Geoffrey had finished any new poems. Why, this was cause for celebration. But he hadn't made any mention of it.

"I found the Man of Law's Tale very amusing," said Red Beard.

Smooth Cheeks laughed and slapped his friend on the back, uncaring that this action almost caused me to topple. "You would, considering your profession. Though I enjoyed all the pilgrims' stories. The Miller's Tale stood out. I don't think I've laughed so hard in a long time. Noah's Ark, the lusty wife, the farting scholar." He began to chuckle.

The pilgrims' stories. These must be the Canterbury poems Geoffrey spoke about so long ago. I cocked my ears. "And what'd you think of the Wife's part?" asked Red Beard.

At first, I thought he was referring to the Miller's bride.

"The brazen Alyson and her insatiable cunt?" clarified Smooth Cheeks.

Hoarfrost spread throughout my body before it was melted by a blaze of heat so fierce, I broke out in a sweat. Wace twisted, frowning at me. I brushed the hair out of his eyes and gave him a reassuring kiss. He turned back to the river.

"Quite vulgar, really," said Red Beard. "And too much to say for herself. Experience gives her authority? Bah! Is it any wonder men seek pleasure away from their wives when they're scolds like that?"

"Indeed. Boasting about lying to her husbands, scorning them. Five? I doubt she had one, the deceiving, garrulous wretch. Who'd marry her kind?"

"Those without the will to live."

They both shared a laugh.

I wanted to cry.

"The only course is to take a woman like that in hand," said Smooth Cheeks, driving his fist into the palm of his other hand. "Show her who's master. Surely that's what Chaucer's saying. For all the Wife claims a man ceding control to a woman is what makes a good marriage, the lesson there is the opposite is true."

I couldn't bear to hear any more and determined to leave, when a shrill scream rent the air. It was drowned by a roar, followed by shouts.

Our heads turned toward the bridge. There, the masses were being impossibly compressed. As we watched, there was a great surge; people were forced against the wooden railings. The crowd bulged like a canker about to burst. There were more screams, cries of utter distress. A bonneted man, lanky and bearded, was pressed hard against the side of the bridge. There was a sharp crack. The railing broke and he overbalanced. With a hoarse cry, echoed in the shrieks of witnesses, he plummeted toward the rapids below, arms circling wildly. Blood exploded as he struck the great footings, then rolled into the white waters.

A boatman tried to steer toward where the body disappeared, his passengers yelling and pointing as the craft rocked wildly. Above them came more bellows and wails as people fought not to fall, clutching anything in desperation. A woman was hauled back onto the bridge, a child as well. Two more fell. Wails filled the air— human and animal.

In the center of the bridge, the royal party crawled to a halt.

It was only later, as we walked subdued back to St. Martin's, we learned what had happened. In the excitement to glimpse the Queen, people had rushed forward. There'd been no room and many had been crushed to death. On both sides of the bridge, people had fallen to their deaths. Others had been trampled by horses, donkeys, panicked boots. Dozens died for their little Queen. An ignominious beginning to her reign. Already people were muttering about bad omens on what should have been a celebration.

It was a terrible tragedy. All the same, I couldn't stop thinking about what I'd heard, what those men had said about Geoffrey's poem. What they said about me. It was evident who the five-times-married wife from Bath was. He'd even given her my name.

Worse. Alyson's name.

But why were the men so harsh? What exactly had Geoffrey written? I had to get hold of a copy. For good or ill, I had to see for myself.

Less than a week later, Father Malcom tracked down a copy of the tentatively titled *The Canterbury Tales*. There were a few quires doing the rounds, but not one contained the entire poem. Among what Father Malcolm found were the General Prologue, The Miller's Tale (with which I was already familiar), the Knight's and Pardoner's tales, and then what was called The Wife of Bath's Tale. This was in two parts: an introduction or prologue, followed by a story. Eager to discover what Geoffrey had written, I locked myself away and read first the General Prologue to the entire poem, in which a detailed description of the Wife is given, before reading the preamble she gives to her own tale.

By the time I'd finished these, I'd no appetite for more. The Wife's actual tale I set aside, unread. My cheeks burned, I felt hollow, empty. While the wind roared outside, shaking the house and making even the thatch whine, I stared into the fire burning in the hearth, doing my best not to weep. I was alone. I'd sent Milda and the others to bed. I'd been wise not to share Geoffrey's words, the shame they aroused. The blistering hurt.

How could he portray me so? For certes, this Wife was everything Red Beard said with her scarlet and finery, her bold gap-toothed grin and wide hips. Geoffrey got those right. Dear God, he even had her boasting of her many husbands—five of them.

And what of the Wife's expressed desire for mastery? Over the years, we'd talked so much about authority, about a woman's part in marriage—a man's as well. I'd oft complained to him, poured out my heart, my secret longings.

This is how he repays my trust? Misrepresenting what I confessed in moments of despair, of triumph or grief? Making a mockery of my youthful desires?

Surely Geoffrey, of all people, knew my views had modified somewhat over the years. Oh, I still wanted the right to bed and wed whomever I wanted, to make my own choices, that hadn't changed. The fact that mastery eluded me wasn't due to lack of ability or a poor mind, but simply because of my sex. Denied access to learning, to knowledge, and treated like children at best, property at worst, women were deemed weak and incapable. It still caused me great consternation. As I'd said to Geoffrey, if we females could but exercise our minds as we did our bodies, then we could give birth not just to babes, but ideas, and be valued for more than our queyntes and our wombs.

Did he write that? Nay.

I wanted authority, aye, but not over my husbands. That made me no better than them. What I really wanted, what I'd learned through experience, was authority over myself. I wanted respect. I thought Geoffrey understood. I thought he approved.

But, if he did, why make me such a bold figure of reproach and mockery? Why make me so damn crude?

My head dropped into my hands.

Even Jankin made an appearance. My Alyson too, albeit as an Alice.

Is that all our friendship was to him? Was my life simply fodder for his quill? Then why not write about murder, deceit, sorrow, and guilt?

Why write about any of it?

Or is that what writers did? Sacrifice their friends, make public their secrets and desires, their innermost fears, all for personal gain?

And I'd encouraged him . . .

My breath was loud in my ears; my heartbeat a war drum that made pain flare in my chest. I was numb, a statue, unable to move. I was a feather, about to twirl and float into the heavens. I was a giant wave, about to crash and dissolve upon a boundless shore.

I stared at the offensive quire. Is this how he really saw me? Clever, loquacious, lying, deceitful? Funny, oh aye, his Wife was all that and more. But did we laugh with her or at her? Or both?

Was she—was I—an object of scorn, not to be taken seriously? Or were folk meant to regard his Wife's recollections of marriage, the experience she claimed (as I did) as giving her the right to speak as she asserts? Was it wisdom or foolishness that guided her tongue?

Dear Lord, my mind was spinning in circles. My concerns, my hurt, had to be voiced. He'd risked our entire friendship by writing this and not warning me.

Worse, he'd forsaken all there was between us.

I was betrayed. Wounded by a quill and parchment. In writing me in such a way, Geoffrey had killed the real Eleanor/Alyson and given birth to his own creation. Geoffrey had murdered me. Again.

What if I was recognized? I'd be a laughing stock, a pariah. And after I'd worked so hard to shed my old self and establish a new life.

But then, if those who read the tales thought that the Wife was a real person, they'd have to think all the characters were real, wouldn't they? While Harry Bailly appears in the Prologue to the entire poem, and Geoffrey himself, people wouldn't seek out a real parson or knight to match them to the fictitious ones he'd invented, would they?

Mayhap, no one would know. No one except me.

The thought did naught to ease my pain.

I don't know how long I sat there, tears drying before falling afresh. The fire guttered, the light outside, cold and still, began to grow gray as dawn approached.

Whatever else I thought, I knew one thing to be true. This was not the work of a friend. I'd no room for someone like that in my life—not anymore.

It didn't take me long to find parchment and quill. Before I could change my mind, I wrote.

Authority, eh? Mastery, eh? If that's what he thought I wanted then, by God, I'd show him mine.

And I did. I wrote I never wanted to see such a false friend, a wayward, wicked wordsmith who both deceived me and abused my trust, ever, ever again.

Amen.

FORTY-THREE

St. Martin's Le Grand, London, and Southwark
The Years of Our Lord 1397 to 1398
In the twentieth and twenty-first years of the reign of Richard II

*W*ith Stephen to take care of the girls and ensure the likes of Ordric Fleshewer and his men kept their distance and angry maud-lyns sheathed their claws, we managed to establish a presence in Southwark and make good coin. On top of what the girls earned whoring, Milda and I made extra spinning and weaving. Together, we slowly rebuilt our lives, not just in terms of material comforts, but pride. Aye, I felt proud of what we were doing, for it was our labor, our choices; we were beholden to no one.

Not even Geoffrey; not anymore.

Ever since he'd received my letter, he'd made numerous attempts to see me. First, there were messages (which I ignored), then came long missives which I burned unopened. Finally, he came to the house, begging Milda, Yolande, and Drew to admit him, even speaking to Lowdy and Wace—to no avail. He asked the Dean of St. Michael's to intercede. That didn't work either. Nor did sending Father Malcolm with a copy of both The Wife of Bath's Prologue and Tale for me to keep. Though I didn't burn them, I didn't read them either. I stowed the quire in a chest, swearing to God, the Virgin, and all the saints they'd never see the light of day.

One evening, he stood beneath my window and shouted, telling me and all the neighbors how sorry he was, and if he could just explain, I'd cast aside my anger and admit him once more.

"Tell him," I instructed Milda, when his voice had grown hoarse and the folk next door had shouted for him to cease, "Satan would have a better chance of ascending to the Kingdom of Heaven than he has of being admitted to my house."

He left shortly after, sending my faithful Milda upstairs with a message of his own.

"Don't you think you're being a bit harsh, Alyson?" she asked. Whenever she used my first name, she was appealing to our years together, the bond that cleaved us.

I lowered the distaff. "Not as harsh as his words, Milda." I'd summarised what I'd read of the poem for her not long after it arrived. Milda had been shocked.

"He says it's not *you*; not exactly. His Wife is meant to be everywoman, an example of what foolish men think women are."

"Mayhap, but he didn't need to base his design so particularly on me, did he?"

Milda had no argument with that.

Next, he deployed innocent Lowdy in his campaign.

"But, Aunty Alyson, think on this," said Lowdy, her brow puckered, her eyes serious. "In his other poems, and in the one that features the Wife, he has all these crusty old scholars being quoted, men who can't even put their own learning into good moral practice. His point is, if they cannot, why should women have to?"

"Since when do you parrot others' words, Lowdy?" I said coldly.

I could be stubborn.

Whereas once I might have given in, I was afraid to. What if Geoffrey's explanation didn't satisfy me? Hurt had poured into the cracks his words had created. I was scared that if there was more to come, I'd be torn asunder. I couldn't risk it.

Unable to help myself, I kept an ear to the ground for any discussion of the poems. Mayhap, I was as vain as Geoffrey's Wife after all; I liked to hear what other people thought—or didn't, as was more often the case.

If I raised the subject, someone always offered an opinion—mostly about the Wife, who folk either loved or loathed.

"Why, there was a minstrel in here the other night," said the ruddy-faced owner of the White Hart, "he recited a piece. Had the whole place enraptured."

"Shows wives up for what they are," said one ancient drinker with two teeth in his head, scratching his crotch. "They talk too much, fail to obey their masters, suffer the sin of pride, and deceive."

"Aye, the Wife proves what men have always known," said a constable who'd popped in for a quick ale.

"What's that?" I asked in a tone that should have told him he'd be wise not to answer.

"Men who surrender mastery to their women do so at great peril to their souls." He drained his mazer, smacking his lips noisily. "And their cocks." There was merriment. "Women are but children, should be seen and not heard. They be good for one thing and one thing only. Nay, two things." He made a crude gesture with his hands then smacked his swollen belly.

When Lowdy raised the matter with me again, as by now she'd read the tales, I sat very still, thinking. Possessed of a quick mind and kind heart, Lowdy was considerate, weighing her words carefully.

"I know you think he's modeled his Wife on you, Aunty Alyson. There's no doubt, she carries your name and certainly bears a striking physical resemblance. And while she's also very clever—" Lowdy wasn't above flattery, "there's many points of difference. For a start, she's from Bath. He even calls her the Wife of Bath. You're from Canterbury."

Milda cleared her throat.

"Furthermore, while I know you don't discuss your past, we know you've been married before. But five husbands *is* excessive, don't you think?"

Milda coughed. I found my spindle very interesting all of a sudden.

"I mean," continued Lowdy, "Master Geoffrey is being preposterous simply to make his points."

"I'll concede five is excessive, aye." Bless her ignorance. This wasn't her fault. I cast a warning look in Milda's direction and modified my tone. "But his Wife could have arisen from the Dead Sea or tumbled from the heavens, and I'd still recognize her—as he no doubt intends."

Lowdy sighed. "But surely, it's not all bad? Have you ever thought that maybe, just maybe, Master Geoffrey's defending our sex? After all, the men in the Wife's story come off looking very poorly. She leads them about as if they're swine with rings in their noses. Even Jankin—"

The mention of his name caused me to stiffen. Milda stopped what she was doing.

". . . is so contrite after he beats her, he surrenders everything—gives her full control."

"Not every husband is so . . . willing, Lowdy," I said, as steadily as I could. "One could also argue that the Wife condemns herself out of her own mouth by demanding mastery, by eventually controlling . . . her last husband. She's everything she accuses men of being, if not worse."

"Which is what makes it so funny, Aunty Alyson." Lowdy smiled and then shrugged. "I know this is important to you, that you feel Master Geoffrey has betrayed you, but is that really the case? He says the Wife is an everywoman, just as the manciple is not one particular manciple, nor the parson anyone of his acquaintance." Lowdy leaned forward on her stool. "What if he's defending you and all women by making the Wife so ridiculously bold and more than able to defend herself?"

"Did Geoffrey tell you to say that also?"

Lowdy lowered her chin. "He might have . . ."

Amusement flickered. The man didn't give up. I watched as the pink in Lowdy's cheeks deepened. Dear Lord but she was a sweet one. Seventeen and a lovely young woman who'd earned the admiration of the nuns of St. Agnes. Her mother couldn't have been any prouder than I was.

"Come here," I said and put my arms about her.

"I hate that you and Master Geoffrey are at odds," she said softly, leaning into my embrace.

"So do I, Lowdy, so do I."

She pulled away slightly so she could see my face. "Then, why don't you make up?"

"Because that's for him to initiate."

"But, he's tried, Aunty Alyson. Over and over, many times."

"Not enough."

Lowdy kissed me, and extracted herself from my hold, rising. "What I don't understand is why it has to be one way or the other." She looked down at me, hands on her slender hips. "Can the Wife not be criticizing men while also being criticized? Nobody's perfect. If you consider it that way, then it might make it a bit easier for you to forgive him . . . till the next time."

We both laughed.

Her footsteps retreated. A door closed. There was the low hum of chatter.

I picked up the spinning and contemplated her words, clever chit. Nevertheless, regardless of what Geoffrey intended, it still affected me deeply.

Thus far, no one had associated me with the brash-mouthed woman searching for yet another husband to rule over. To many, I was nothing more than a widow, an old woman who happened to be a bawd, preoccupied, like everyone else, with a poet's entertaining words. Even to Lowdy.

Unbeknownst to them, I was also grieving a friendship. I found a kerchief and dabbed my eyes. Dear Lord, I was the living embodiment of that old proverb: "God made women to weep, talk, and spin."

Suddenly, Geoffrey's version of the Wife of Bath didn't seem so unappealing.

Even with Master Stephen to protect them, there were times the girls were beaten. Men would wait until they'd lured them far enough away from Stephen before hurting them, usually because they refused to oblige a strange request or were simply furious at all women. Cut lips, black eyes, hanks of hair torn out, and, once, a cut from a swung dagger (that man had his jaw broken by Master Stephen and a dunking in the Thames for his pains). Anger always filled me when they came home hurt, trying not to make a fuss as I daubed and strapped their wounds, Master Stephen offering apologies. But it wasn't his fault. This was the work of brutish, weak men.

No matter where they were or who was there, the girls were in danger on the street. Mayhap, it was time to leave St. Martin's and find a place of my own, a place like those over in Southwark, where I could dictate who entered the premises, how long they stayed, and where Master Stephen could linger outside a door, ready to render assistance. A place where, if the men couldn't adjust their vicious ways, they'd be shown out and banned from ever entering again. See how they liked having their movements controlled by a woman.

That made me smile.

In order to be more than a fool's dream, we needed to save enough to pay for a lease and the overheads on a bathhouse. Unless I could find somewhere with furniture, there'd be that to think of too. A bawdy house had to look and feel a particular way to invite custom, as did the girls, for that matter. There'd be clothes to consider, bedding, perfumes, soaps. I began to imagine what it would be like, what shape my very own bawdy house would take. How I'd decorate the entrance, the rooms. The rules I'd set, how I'd care for the girls. As I sat in the solar and did the sums one night, I realized we were still an impossibly long way from being able to afford that sort of freedom. Disappointment engulfed me.

Nevertheless, things started to improve slowly. Not only were my girls much sought after in Southwark, but orders for cloth from the Flemish at Bankside, who had noticed the lovely fabrics Leda, Rose, and Yolande wore, grew.

The house wasn't kept nearly as well as I would have liked. Between us, Lowdy, Milda, and I did what we could, but if the rushes weren't changed as often and meals were bought from the local ordinary more than I would have liked, at least the spinning and weaving was becoming a little profitable. If I wanted it to remain that way, I'd have to consider hiring a housekeeper and even another maid to free me to spin more, Milda as well.

Once more, Fortuna turned her wheel in our direction. Before summer finished her annual dance, our household increased by two and a half.

First came someone I'd oft thought about but never dared to openly approach.

She arrived on the doorstep one miserable afternoon. The rain was relentless and everything was leaking and dripping. The girls and Master Stephen had come home early, Lowdy was busy with the nuns, making and distributing medic to monks who'd fallen ill due to the damp. Yolande had gone to fetch Wace from his tutor. We were sitting in the kitchen listening to the water dripping through the holes in the thatch, enjoying some ale and the warmth of the fire, discussing the death of John of Gaunt a few months before, when there was a resounding knock on the door.

"Who could that be?" asked Milda, half-rising.

"An inmate of Bethlehem, if the weather's anything to go by," I said, shooing her back into her seat. "Stay. I'll answer."

There was another knock. Louder. "By St. Cuthbert's hairy legs, I'm coming!" I shouted.

"I'll go with you," said Master Stephen, raising his bulk from the stool where he was whittling an old stick he'd found.

Together we ascended the few stairs to the hall and wrenched open the door. I couldn't believe my eyes. Time contracted. Once again, I was a woman in my prime, agreeing to marry Mervyn Slynge and being welcomed into his beautiful home. Then, I was the silly, lust-filled widow, delighted the handsome knave Simon de la Pole had asked me to be his bride. Finally, I was the giddy older woman, smitten in every way with her young lover. And through these men and marriages, the secrets, pain, and blood, had been this woman.

"Oriel," I said, and drew her into my arms.

"Oh, mistress." She burst into tears.

Hours later, after Lowdy, Wace, Drew, and the girls had gone to bed, and it was just me, Milda, and Master Stephen (who wouldn't leave my side except to take the girls to Southwark), Oriel revealed what had brought her, after all these years and my endless hints via Geoffrey, to London.

"There's two reasons. The first is Master Sweteman." She glanced at her hands. "He's dead, mistress." She gave me and Milda a sorrowful smile.

"How?" I asked softly, my hand covering hers. Dear Sweteman. He'd been old when I left. It was no shock, but it was very sad tidings. He'd been like a father to Oriel. To many of the servants. It would hit Drew hard. I'd be sure to tell him first thing in the morning.

"He'd been ill a long time," said Oriel, gazing at the window. One of the shutters was broken, refused to close, so we'd left it wide open. Rain still fell, thick drops that splashed on the sill. "Though he lost a great deal of weight, his stomach swelled like a woman's with child. In his final days, he stopped drinking and was unable to use the jordan. It was a blessing when he passed away." A great tear swam down her cheek. I wiped it away gently, lifting her hand to my mouth and kissing it.

"What's your other reason, Oriel?" I asked softly. "Before you answer, know my home is yours."

"Thank you, mistress." She took a deep shuddering breath, the tension she'd carried loosening. "The other reason I'm here is Master Jankin."

The room expanded then contracted to a tiny dark spot. I blinked, rubbed the back of my hand across my forehead, and everything, except my heart, returned to normal. Even after so much had happened, his name still had the power to disrupt me.

"Why?" I asked carefully. Milda's eyes sought mine. I could feel my ribs tightening, a cord about my middle sucking the air from my body.

Oriel glanced at Master Stephen.

"You may speak freely." Long ago, I'd revealed to him what brought me to London. He had my complete trust.

"He's married again."

"Oh." I waited to feel pain, anger, jealousy. I felt nothing except the cold hard satisfaction that comes with knowing that though he might have plighted his troth to another woman at the church door, I was still his wife in God's eyes. "Who's the . . . bride?"

"Sabyn Horsewhyre."

"Sir Horsewhyre's eldest?" My. Jankin had set his sights higher than I'd have thought possible for a scholar's son. Then again, he was a widower—and a wealthy one.

"Mistress Horsewhyre—I mean, Binder—had no need of me any longer. At least, that's what Master Jankin said. I think the real reason he dismissed me was he was frightened I'd say something to his new wife about . . . about . . . what he did."

I released her hands and stood. "Nay, Oriel, I think he could worm his way out of that. What he was really afraid of was you'd make mention of *me*. His living, breathing wife."

Her mouth formed a perfect O.

"Never mind," I said quickly. "You're here now, where you belong."

I went to the sideboard and poured some ale. When I'd passed the mazers around, I returned to the hearth and studied Oriel.

In the years we'd been apart, she hadn't changed much. She was thinner, willowy, and tall, her hair the rich brown it had always been. Yet there was a heaviness about her, a seriousness I didn't recall. It was no wonder, with the secrets I'd begged her to keep. It was a great burden for anyone. Jankin's return must have been such a shock—a shock and relief.

I thought about the sacrifices she'd made, Sweteman too, all for me. For me and Alyson. I owed this woman so much. Through Oriel, I learned the fates of those I'd left behind—how Peter had gone to the monks at Bath Abbey and become a novice. Aggy and her family had moved north after her husband inherited a farm and was doing very well. As for Rag, she'd married Hugh Strongbow, who'd been courting her back in my day, and they'd a brood of children. Father Elias was yet preaching at St. Michael's Without, older, frailer, but still in possession of a sharp mind and a big heart. I'd thought about them all so often, it warmed my soul to know they'd thrived; that my actions had not hurt them.

Naturally, Oriel took on the role of housekeeper, delighted she'd real duties to keep her occupied. If she was appalled to learn how we earned a living, it never showed. After all, this was the woman who'd managed the house of a sodomite for years, keeping his secrets and then mine. The girls loved her and Master Stephen worshipped her, falling over himself to do her bidding.

By the time autumn's chill made the mornings brisk, another person joined our household—well, another person and her son.

Her name was Letitia Frowyk. She'd been a bawd in the Cardinal's Hatte on Bankside—the house I thought had a sign that looked like a tower. She'd worked for a Flemish couple there for five years. But when they learned about her son, Harry, they threw her out on the streets.

"'Twasn't their fault," said Letitia, her first night with us. We were in the kitchen watching as she and Harry, a lad of about three, gulped down a rich pottage and some maslin. "Whores aren't meant to have children, let alone keep 'em. If the bailiff, Master Fynk, found out—" she ruffled Harry's hair, "they'd cop a huge fine, which would have fallen to me. I'm better off gone. They weren't good people, not really. And I'd kept my son hidden for so long. He needs to find his place in the world."

Wace was delighted to have a smaller boy to play with, and Lowdy another child to boss around. I heard her teaching Harry his letters before a rushlight had even burned. Wace was correcting him, smart fellow. It made me chuckle. When I was speaking to Geoffrey again,

I must ask him if he'd talked to Gower about an apprenticeship for Wace. We'd been discussing finding the boy a position, even with Geoffrey's scrivener, Adam Pinkhurst.

For certes, the future was looking bright for my Lowdy and Wace. There was no reason it couldn't for little Harry Frowyk as well. I fluffed his unruly cap of dark hair and was rewarded with a happy grin.

I smiled and sat beside him.

The child pushed a fingertip into my mouth, resting it against my front teeth. "You got a big hole there," he said, staring in wonder at the gap.

I tickled his finger with the tip of my tongue. He squealed and pulled his finger away, laughing.

His mother rose and gave him a clap across the ear. "Mistress, I'm sorry. You rude little beggar! You say sorry, y'hear?"

"It's alright, Letitia. The boy only speaks true."

"But, Ma," said Harry, his eyes drowning as they filled. "The old lady has teeth like mine." He indicated where a front tooth was missing.

"Less of the old, thanks, Harry," I said. "Or next time it'll be me clipping your ears."

"So much for speaking true," murmured Milda.

After we'd put Letitia and Harry to bed, Leda, Rose, Yolande, and Master Stephen told me they'd found Letitia and Harry hunkered down in the alley adjacent to where they worked, Foule's Lane, being picked upon by a group of youths. One had broken a jug and was threatening to tear out Harry's throat if Letitia didn't comply with his demands.

"Oh?"

Leda's eyes slid to Master Stephen, who coughed. "Wanted his cock sucked," said Master Stephen. "I offered to do it for him, but explained that with my careless ways and big teeth, I was more likely to bite it off." He gnashed a row of great gray tombstones. "Needless to say, the lad didn't accept my offer. Neither did his friends."

I couldn't have loved him more in that moment if I'd tried.

"We couldn't leave her there," said Rose.

"Nor the lad," added Leda.

"Of course not," I said, reaching over and patting their hands. "Anyhow, timing couldn't be better." I tried not to think of the expense of extra mouths. "Someone needs to help Oriel. I'll invite Letitia and Harry to stay in the morning."

The girls leaped from their chairs and threw their arms around me. Master Stephen hoisted himself off the stool and with a grunt added his embrace to theirs. Once more, my eyes felt hot and my throat developed a terrible tickle. Dear Lord but my family had the capacity to make my body do the most peculiar things.

As it was, Letitia didn't become a maid but willingly replaced Rose when, a fortnight later, the latter accepted a marriage proposal from a farmer, Tom Adams, out Essex way.

It was a day of mixed blessings when we witnessed her being wed to her brown-bearded man who smelled of horses, the country, and fresh air. Tom was a widower with four young children and willing to overlook how he'd met Rose and just make, as he put it, a goodwife of her.

"Work's work, ain't it?" he said when he asked for her hand. "Whether or not it's honest is in the eye of the doer, it's not up to others, except the Lord to judge. And how can He judge my Rose except by what's in my heart?"

Where did my girls find these men? They were worth their weight in a Florentine merchant's gold. Rose left us not only with her saved earnings, but a small dowry.

So, while Letitia worked in Southwark, I took charge of young Harry. What a handful he proved to be. Smart as well. Constantly dashing across the square when we delivered Wace to his tutor, he'd disappear into open doors only to emerge moments later with a slice of bread, an apple, or a burning hot ear. Few could resist him. He asked endless questions, was keen to help with the spinning or weaving, insisting on being shown what to do. His little fingers were deft, but also prone to getting threads tangled or snapping the wool, and his ability to stay focused on a task was worse than a puppy's. Each day he'd come to the markets in St. Martin's or, when they weren't being held, venture out into the streets, gawping at all the people and the stalls. Gradually, the vendors came to know him and would pass a ripe pear, a hot pastry, or give him a vegetable to feed their soft-eared donkey. The lad had more charisma than a royal child, and would hold court whether we were in Cheapside, the Shambles, or down by the river.

When he turned four, just a couple of weeks after he'd arrived, I begged Father Malcolm to find a place for him with Wace's tutor—all that inquisitiveness, that desire to soak up knowledge, it needed training. And, God knew, I needed a break.

Letitia couldn't believe her good fortune when I told her Harry was to get lessons at the college.

"Bless you, mistress," she said, dropping to her knees and taking my hands. "I don't know what I done to deserve you—and the girls, and Master atte Place and Mistresses Milda and Oriel and Master Drew, but I must have done something good somewhere, sometime, for He is looking out for me and my son." I pulled her to her feet and she held me tightly, weeping for joy. Damn it, if those eyes and throat of mine didn't become all scratchy again.

I swear I was sickening or something.

Alas, it wasn't me who was sickening.

FORTY-FOUR

St. Martin's Le Grand, London, and Southwark
The Year of Our Lord 1399
In the twenty-second year of the reign of Richard II

Mayhap, it was living in the streets for the few weeks before Rose, Leda, Yolande, and Master Stephen found her and Harry that caused Letitia's illness. Mayhap, it was the fact that any bread or small ale she found or was able to purchase, she gave to Harry. Within a few weeks of coming to St. Martin's, just as the mornings became bitterly cold, the windows limned with frost, and the house damper than a Thames privy, Letitia developed a wet, racking cough. Her body, already so slender, began to shrink. Her cheeks, once rosy from exerting herself hurrying up the hill from the river so she might see Harry before he went to bed, became fiery, her eyes unnaturally bright.

When I found her one morning, unable to rise from her pallet, her body burning with fever and blood staining her pillow, I first checked for any signs of tokens, then ordered Lowdy to take Wace and Harry to the college, and swiftly sent Drew for the doctor. Lowdy returned immediately with the nun she worked with, Sister Cecilia, in tow. Together they prepared a warm caudle for Letitia, spooning it between her dried lips.

No one went to Southwark that day.

When the doctor arrived, he sat with Letitia a long time. I watched as he read her star charts, tested her urine, examined her chest, studied her translucent skin, and looked into her eyes and mouth. He whispered quietly with Sister Cecelia and Lowdy. A strange mix of pride and fear mingled as I watched Lowdy being treated as someone with knowledge. Before long, she would leave us. The thought made me melancholy. Had I not wished this for her? Ensured that everything we did was to give the children a future? Aye, and Lowdy would be the first to reap what we'd sown; proof that what we did, for all the sinning, was for a greater good.

"Is it the pestilence?" I asked quietly, when they eventually left Letitia to sleep.

"Not the kind that visited a few years ago, mistress," said Doctor Thomas. "This is phthisis."

"Phthisis?"

"The white plague," explained Lowdy, her eyes downcast. Consumption.

Letitia lay there, unaware of her death sentence. Her hair tumbled over the pillow, her lips and cheeks so red, her skin so pale. She was like a damsel from one of Geoffrey's tales. My breast ached.

"Can nothing be done?"

The doctor didn't deign to answer, but began to pull out pouches of herbs. He was a kindly man who, for a small fee, looked to those less fortunate within the precinct. Rumor had it he'd once been a monk, but left the order when he fell in love. I don't know if he ever married, or even if his love was requited, but I know Doctor Thomas Hendy did everything he could for my girl—that day and for the next two weeks.

That's what, in a short time, Letitia and her little lad had become: mine.

Letitia's cough grew worse, her breathing labored. Doctor Thomas came each day and ordered us to move her bed into the solar and do all in our power to keep the cold air at bay. Night after night either Milda or I sat with her, stoking the fire, tying the broken shutter closed, ensuring she drank the preparations the apothecary made, mopping her brow. Afraid the girls might catch something, I ordered them to keep away. Harry, Lowdy, and Wace as well.

When it was evident Letitia was not long for the world, Father Malcom was summoned. He spoke to the doctor, then went to Letitia's side. Bending over, he asked her a number of questions, took confession, then administered extreme unction. I could see her soul was fretting to be freed. The rest of the day, members of the household paraded through the solar saying their farewells, some bearing crucifixes, others candles. Neighbors also arrived, as did vendors and priests. Stories from the Bible were told, a psalm was sung. Afterward people congregated in the kitchen, drinking ale and eating whatever Oriel and Milda prepared.

Only when the sun began to set did I allow Harry to see his mother. I stood by his side, hands on his shoulders as she whispered to him and, between coughs, told him how proud she was, how much she loved him. I kept my face averted lest she see how much the loving beauty of her words moved me.

Harry, God bless him, crawled onto the bed beside her, resting his plump cheek against her hollow one.

"I love you too, Mamma," he said. "But you must go to God now, so He can make you better. I'll be fine. I've Mistress Alyson to look out for me."

I stumbled out of the room.

When I returned, Letitia was in a deep sleep. She woke just before lauds. The house was quiet. The sky had begun to lighten, silver shafts squeezing through the cracks in the shutters to reveal the hulking silhouettes of the furniture, of the pallet bed upon which she lay.

"Mistress?" she said hoarsely.

I scrambled from where I sat, dropping to my knees by her side. Milda stirred in the chair.

"I'm here, Letitia," I said, taking her hand. It was dry, light as an eider duck's feather. "What can I do?"

She smiled. I could see her teeth in the dim light, a sheen in her eyes. "You have done so much, so much. But—" Her throat made a peculiar growling sound, a cough was building. I tried to help her sit up, but she shook her head. Her chest rattled. She found her kerchief and spat into it. The red was vivid, even in the poor light.

She crushed it into her hand.

"But—?" I urged.

"I would ask you to take care of Harry when I'm . . . gone."

"Oh, there's no need for me to do that. You're not going anywhere—" I began, then saw the look in her eyes, the hurt that I would pretend.

"Oh, sweetling," I said, my words half-formed. I drew nearer to her, stroking her forehead with my other hand, careful to avoid the oily mark where Father Malcolm had imprinted God's blessing. I could smell the sickness, the treacly, palling odor. "Forgive me. I didn't say that to prevent you talking any more, but to give myself false hope."

"The time for that has passed," she said, with a wisdom that belied her years. "You will look to him, mistress? Keep him safe? See that he learns his manners, keeps with his words and scribbles?"

"I will."

"You'll see him become what I know he can—"

"What's that, sweetling?" I was having trouble speaking, seeing.

"A good man."

I couldn't wipe away my tears as I didn't want to cease holding her. They fell upon Letitia's face. She didn't seem to notice.

She twisted her hand beneath mine until she held it. There was no strength in her fingers. "Thank you. Bless you, mistress. I thank God the day you found me." It was the girls and Stephen who did that, but I didn't correct her.

"I thank Him too." I did, with all my hurting heart.

Before I could say more, Letitia shut her eyes and drew one long last shaky breath as the bells tolled.

By the time prime was announced, Milda and I had washed and dressed her and brought Harry to see his mother. He stood by the bed, his face and hands clean, his eyes shining with unshed tears. I wasn't sure at first if he understood. But then he crossed himself, and said a short prayer Lowdy had taught him. Along with the others, he placed a kiss upon her smooth brow, and with his head bowed, allowed himself to be led away, Lowdy on one side, Wace on the other.

In the kitchen a few hours later, I watched as the little boy, usually so full of vigor and energy, traced patterns in the flour on the table. Oriel didn't chide him as she usually did, nor did Lowdy. Father Malcolm and the doctor had already been and gone. Letitia, now wrapped in a shroud Milda and Oriel had made, would be buried on the morrow, in the graveyard of St. Agnes. Bless Father Malcolm.

Unable to settle, I looked at the children. Of the three, two were orphans—and if you didn't count Ordric Fleshewer, and I certainly didn't, the other only had a mother. Wace sat fidgeting on Leda's lap, but he wasn't the one who needed comfort.

Lowdy's eyes were swollen, her lips trembled slightly as her gaze focused inward instead of on what was around her. I wondered if Letitia's death made her think of her own mother. God knew, she'd been taken brutally.

I wiped my eyes, rubbed my face. God give me the strength and knowledge to do justice to their faith and give these women, these heaven-sent children, a decent life.

I tipped my head back and stared at the ceiling. Smoke-stained, patterned with mold, it was quite dark, even with the firelight. Mayhap, Lowdy's mother could see her, Harry's too—well, they could if the damn ceiling wasn't so grubby, the room so smoky. I needed to get them out of here.

"Come on," I said, slapping my thigh and rising to my feet. "Who wants to come to Cheapside? See who's in the pillory and if we can find some sweetbreads or honey apples? The rain's stopped and there's no wind."

Harry, Wace, and Lowdy's heads shot up. Harry began to climb off his stool. Lowdy looked from me to Milda and back again.

"Do you think it's right, Alyson?" asked Milda. "We're in mourning."

"Aye. But there's no rule says we can't mourn while walking about or eating, is there? And I need to breathe some air that isn't tainted with death and candles."

In the end, only Master Stephen, Leda, Yolande, Lowdy, Wace, and Harry came with me. Between us, Lowdy and I held Harry's hands, accepting the blessings and sympathy of all we encountered as we ventured out.

All too soon, we were in the thick of Cheapside. It was bright, noisy, and smelly, and the pie and honey-apples purchased were delicious. Even Harry smiled.

We'd veered out of the stream of people, pausing on a corner near the White Bear. We were just opposite the entrance to Honey Lane. It wasn't deliberate, it just happened. Harry was nagging me to keep going as he wanted to see who was in the pillory—Wace adding his arguments. A great crowd had gathered near the conduit where a preacher was warning about end of days as the New Year approached, telling us that Satan was nigh if we didn't mend our ways. Leda and Yolande giggled and rolled their eyes. Aye, it was a bit late for the likes of us. I winked at them. I was about to suggest we move when the preacher finished and the mob began to disperse. At that moment, a group of mounted knights ploughed through, uncaring of the mass of people who scattered before them.

It was just as well we were off the main thoroughfare, otherwise we might have been trampled. There were shouts, shaking fists, stones, and clods of earth were thrown. They exploded on the back of the knights' armor, on the caparisoned horses. Harry was pointing excitedly at the markings on one of the shields, asking me why the horse had a horn coming out of its forehead. I was about to explain when I became aware I was being watched.

Isn't it strange how that can happen, even in a crowded space? The feeling of eyes upon you, as if ghostly fingers stroked your flesh. I twisted my neck slowly.

Separated from us by a few people and at least two levels, a man and woman were perched on a sill, looking down upon the street. I'd never seen the woman before, but the man . . . My breath caught. My heart seized.

It was Jankin Binder.

His golden hair curled about a face that was older, but more handsome with some age upon it. He'd a neatly trimmed beard that served to partly bury a puckering on his cheek and frame his sensuous mouth. As our eyes met, the one not hidden behind a dark patch widened and his face paled. I shifted Harry onto my other hip, looking boldly in his direction, then at the woman squeezed next to him.

Pretty, she had dark hair swept up in a fashionable do, a cap perched atop her head. Her nose was straight, her complexion darker than her husband's. One hand was pressed to the side of her face. No doubt, she was shocked by the behavior below. Aware he wasn't paying attention to the fracas, she followed his gaze and saw me.

Her hand slipped away to reveal a terrible dark bruise. It filled the entire side of her face; one eye was swollen shut.

Jankin pushed his wife back inside their room and disappeared, closing the shutters.

"What are you looking at, mistress?" asked Leda as Wace and Harry began to get restless. "Are you alright?"

I remembered to breathe. "Me? I'm fine. Just thinking about marriage—well, husbands to be exact."

Leda took Wace's hand firmly, and nodded for Yolande to take the other. Lowdy extracted Harry from my hip. I indicated that Master Stephen should lead the way. "You're not thinking of making an honest woman of yourself, are you?" Leda asked, nudging Yolande, who laughed.

"What, me? I've only ever been honest, girls. It's men who make us dishonest." I glanced back at the shutters. "Trust me."

Without another word, I followed Master Stephen east along Cheapside and granted the boys' wish to visit the pillory.

Much to their disappointment, it was empty.

———◆———

Unable to sleep that night, I rose and pushed open the shutters to stare out beyond the walls of the precinct and into the city. Somewhere out there was Jankin—Jankin and his new, young, and obviously thrashed wife. What had she done to earn his wrath? Probably nothing more than to look askance. Had he continued with that book of his? Poor woman. Sabyn Horsewhyre had not the wiles nor experience to know how to handle Jankin. Lord knew, I hadn't and I'd been much older.

The moonlight cast pools of silvery light over the square. Residual smoke lingered in the air as well as the mawkish smell of rancid meat. A cat was slinking past a nearby house. A lone bird rose into the air, its outline stark against the pewter sky. It released a plaintive cry and, as it was answered, veered in the direction of its mate. Was it to seek solace or fight? Sweet Jesu, I wanted to fight. Drive a knife into Jankin's other eye and finish what I'd started all those years ago. At least if he was blind, he would never see me again; he couldn't be so swift with those bloody fists of his either.

My shoulders slumped as I recognized my bold reckonings for the fantasies they were. Geoffrey had the right of it when he advised me to forget Jankin—and, mostly, I had. What I hadn't expected was that he'd appear on my doorstep with his new wife—a wife who reminded me of the misery he'd inflicted upon me and all those I loved.

Oh, Alyson.

How was I supposed to push him to the back of my mind now? But I'd made a promise to Letitia—Letitia, who we'd be burying in a few hours. I owed it to her and Harry, not to mention the rest of my makeshift family, to do the right thing.

If only I could take them away from here, from Jankin. What was he doing in London? Was it a visit? Or had he moved to the city?

How I wished I'd my own place, a house of ill repute away from London, where I could retreat until the man was gone. But that needed more money than I was able to make; more than I'd a right to expect of the girls. I ground my knuckles into my stomach. Money I'd once had, which that bastard now flaunted. Him and his wife . . .

His *wife*.

I let go of the sill, rubbing the stiffness out of my fingers.

But *I* was his wife. *I* was Jankin's lawful wedded wife. Which meant Sabyn Horsewhyre was not. In fact, she may believe she was married, but I was living proof she was no better than a whore.

A smile tugged the corner of my mouth.

How much might a proud man like Jankin, a gentlewoman like Sabyn with a family name to protect, pay to stop that information escaping?

My mind began to race. The tiredness and anger that had weighed me down all day sloughed away.

My guess was they'd pay a great deal.

FORTY-FIVE

—◆—

St. Martin's Le Grand, London
The Year of Our Lord 1399
In the twenty-second year of the reign of Richard II

*I*t was still early when Lowdy returned, walking as fast as she could through the mud, waving to neighbors and vendors who were just setting up their carts and opening their shops. I closed the shutters, ignoring the broken one when it refused to latch, smoothed my apron, and went downstairs to meet her.

Only Milda and Oriel were home, the girls and Master Stephen having left for Southwark at first light. Drew had taken Wace and Harry to the college for their lessons soon after.

It was easy to sneak past the kitchen to the front door. Milda and Oriel were thick in conversation, discussing Letitia's funeral, how kind Father Malcolm had been and how generous the neighbors, who'd arrived on our doorstep afterward with ale, wine, and all manner of vittles to share. Letitia had only been with us a few weeks, but with her ready smile and gratitude, she'd won hearts. Lord knows, she'd captured mine—as had her little boy.

It was for them and the rest of my household I was taking this next step. A step I'd recruited Lowdy to help me make.

Before she reached the door, I had it open, stepping into the cold so we wouldn't be overheard.

"Well?" I asked.

She brushed a stray lock from her face. Her eyes were disturbed, her wide mouth downturned. "I gave it to him as you asked, Aunty Alyson."

"And—what did he say?"

"I thought at first he was going to strike me—"

"*What?*"

"No, no," she flapped her arms to calm me. "It's alright. He didn't. But he did ball his fists and his face turned crimson. Then he shut the door of the room I'd been asked to wait in and told me to tell you he'd be here before the bells sounded sext—just as you asked."

I inhaled sharply. It was done. There was no turning back.

"Who is he, mistress? How do you know him?"

I stared, but without seeing her. How did I explain Jankin? I'd asked Lowdy to deliver the note for the simple reason she didn't know who he was to me. That, and if I'd sent one of the girls, or even Master Stephen, they likely wouldn't have been admitted. Oriel would have refused and Milda, well, she would have had me committed to Bethlehem.

Lowdy continued to regard me, a little frown puckering her otherwise smooth brow. When had she grown so tall? Tall and willowy like her mother, according to Leda. Megge had said the same when she saw her at the funeral. Unlike her mother, she would have a respectable trade and be able to marry well. Already, the apothecary's son in Panyer Alley, whose father did a roaring business, being so close to the Doctors' Commons and St. Paul's, had expressed interest in her. He was a fine lad, had been up to Oxford for a time.

"He was someone I knew a long time ago," I said.

She was silent a moment. "Did Master Geoffrey know him too?"

I started. "Why do you ask?"

"There's a Jankin in the Wife's Tale he wrote." She shrugged.

Told you she was clever.

Lowdy shuffled her feet. "He's married, you know."

"Oh, I know."

"I saw his wife. She was very . . . timid. He said she was unwell, but no disease I know causes bruises on a face and neck like hers."

"Aye. It's a particular sickness that some men carry, sweetling. They pass it to their wives."

"Is there a name for it?"

"Cowardice," I said. "Comes from living in a state of constant fear."

"Of what?" said Lowdy. "He's a big man, that Master Jankin. What's he got to be afraid of?"

"That we women might get the better of him."

Lowdy waited.

"Better go to Sister Cecilia, sweetling. Blame me for your tardiness. I'll see you this evening, hopefully with some good news." I kissed her brow.

To my surprise, she threw her arms around me, her face burrowed in my neck. "Be careful, Aunty Alyson, won't you? There was something about him . . . I cannot put my finger on it. I don't care how Master Geoffrey described him, but he reminded me of Ordric Fleshewer."

She never called him father.

I inhaled the perfume of her—cinnamon, violets, and a little musk—before pulling away. "I'll be careful, Lowdy, never you fear. I know these types of men well. And I know how to handle them."

I waited as she ducked down the side alley that would lead her to St. Agnes. Sleet started to fall, fast and thick, covering the indentations her boots made. It would be a cold day for a cold reckoning. Even so, my blood felt hot, choler rising as I thought about what I had to say and do.

With a long sigh, I went back indoors to the kitchen. Time to make sure the house was empty when Jankin arrived.

———◆———

As soon as Milda, Oriel, Stephen, and Drew left—Milda and Oriel sent to Pander Lane to pick up a particular powder that aided megrims, which I'd declared I was suffering, while the other two visited the tavern—I went to my room and changed. It had been a long time since I paid so much attention to my dress. I put on my best kirtle, a tunic Lowdy had embroidered with butterflies and bees around the neckline and a fine leather belt. I attached my eating knife, a new purse, and then tidied my hair. It had a few more silver threads, making its former russet paler.

Vain, I knew I wasn't the woman Jankin had wed, fed on a fine diet, with the best clothes and shoes, able to purchase whatever she pleased. I'd endured grief, hardship, and hunger, worried endlessly about how to pay rent, put food on the table, and the welfare of my girls, boys, men, and women. What had Jankin to think about but himself? Still, though my face was tracked with the journeys I'd taken over the years, it wasn't a bad-looking one. I'd only to recall the offers I still received from men to know that.

Appearing more confident than I felt, I waited in the solar, looking out through the ever-present gap in the shutters. The fire was stoked, the room warm. A jug of Rhenish and my best mazers sat on a tray on the armoire.

Lost in reflections, wondering how my marriage to a young, intelligent lad who'd doted on me had ended in such violence and betrayal, I almost missed Jankin crossing the square. He was wearing a hooded cloak and it was pulled so far over his head it obscured his features. Bent over, and not just against the wind, it was only his limp that gave him away—a legacy of the night he was left for dead in the snow in the middle of winter. Geoffrey had made a point of mentioning it and I'd never forgotten. It was the least of what he deserved.

Before he could knock, I opened the door. He entered without a word, mounting the stairs when I gestured, hesitating briefly on the threshold of the solar.

I went to close the door, but remembered there was no one to hear or see us.

The first thing I did was pour wine. As I brought over the cups, he threw back his hood. Though I'd invited him into my house, believing it was an advantage to meet in my territory, like a soldier choosing where to make the last stand, I may have been in error.

Far from claiming the higher ground, I'd admitted the fox to the henhouse.

My hand shook as I passed a mazer to him. When he took it, he placed his hands over mine. Damn if my body didn't shiver in response. I prayed he hadn't sensed it, though the curl of his lip suggested otherwise.

"So, Eleanor, we meet again." Without removing his cloak, he tipped the drink into his mouth.

I watched him drain it. Dear God, he might be many things, this man I'd wed, but he was still bloody handsome. Wealth aside, no wonder the poor chit he married thought she'd struck a fine deal. No doubt they'd make pretty children.

Without asking, he refilled his goblet. I sat by the window, not too far from the hearth. The cold draught coming through the gap kept me alert, even while the fire warmed me.

Jankin threw himself into the chair opposite. "Your note said you needed to see me urgently—"

I nodded and went to speak.

"It also threatened me. Me and my wife."

"*I'm* your wife." Mother Mary and all the saints. What did I blurt that for? I was planning to build up to that point, to present my case until it was irrefutable and Jankin had to concede to my demands. He'd thrown me off-kilter with his candor.

His eyes narrowed. He took a couple of gulps of wine and put the cup down on the small table between us. I still hadn't drunk a drop.

"Ah. I see. That's the way of it, is it? You intend to claim *you're* my wife."

"But I am."

He threw back his head and laughed. Forced as it was, it was still charming. I remember how much we used to amuse each other. Our trip to Jerusalem, how we'd make fun of the Saracens and the Jews and their peculiar ways. How we'd mock our own when we thought no one could hear. What had happened to that easy camaraderie?

Death. That's what happened. Simon. Alyson.

"You cannot come back from the dead, Eleanor—or, what do you call yourself now? Alyson?"

That he could utter her name and not bat an eyelid.

"Why not?" I said, refusing to be goaded. "You did."

"That was God's will, Eleanor. Whereas your resurrection, this is *your* will."

His gaze was unnerving me. It was a combination of disdain and something else, like a hungry animal.

"It could be my will, Jankin. It doesn't have to be."

"Ah. Straight to the heart of the matter." He reached for his drink and finished it, looking over his shoulder at the jug, deciding whether or not to refill once more. He decided against it. "What will it take for you to remain dead? That's the real reason you asked me here, isn't it? To extort money from me."

"Well, Jankin, since we're getting to the bones of it, let's pick that one clean. It's actually *my* money."

Jankin's eyes narrowed and he grinned like a rabid dog sizing up a coney. "*Your* money? How can it be, *Alyson*? What I inherited was within my rights as a husband—it was Eleanor's wealth, not yours."

I could no longer sit. Rising to my feet, I stepped away from the hearth, away from him, and stood in front of the shutters. "*My* wealth, Jankin. Let's not forget, though years have passed, there are still many who would remember me—some of them dwell beneath this very roof. One word from Father Elias would confirm my identity."

"The man is in his dotage. No one would credit what he says."

"There are others in Bath. Not that much time has passed. Why, I'm sure your wife's father, Sir Robert Horsewhyre, would recall me. I remember him very well." I gave a saucy smile so he was in no doubt of what I meant.

He leaped to his feet, knocking his mazer to the floor. In two strides, he'd closed the distance between us and grabbed me by the shoulders.

"You wouldn't dare."

"Wouldn't I?"

We stared into each other's eyes as he pressed his fingers into my flesh. I'd forgotten how very blue his eye was. The other, hidden behind the patch, had once been that color too. Now, pale pink, puckered skin surrounded the cloth. The imperfection simply enhanced his looks, made him appear so very dangerous.

He was, I thought, as his fingers crawled upward, circling my neck.

"I could stop all this now," he whispered, pressing his forehead to mine. Our noses touched. His mouth hovered over my lips. "I loved you, you know. Really loved you. So much, I would have done anything. I did."

"You killed Simon," I gasped.

"No, my love. I did not. You did that. Like everything else that happened, everything I did—to him, to you, to her. *You* made me do it. Simon, your pale shadow, Alyson. They were *your* doing. Even when I strike my lovely new wife, I hear your voice; see your face. It's you, Eleanor, my beldame, even after all this time, it's you who force me to act against my better self. You always have."

He began to increase his hold, pressing tight, digging his thumbs into the hollow at the base of my throat. I began to struggle. He pushed me against the sill, leaning against me with his entire body. The shutters protested, began swinging open. He lifted me from there and slammed me against the wall. I tried to pull his hands away, gouge his eyes, but he ducked and dodged, laughed in my face as he stared into it.

"I don't know what it is about you, Eleanor—God knows, you're no beauty, and you were old even when I wed you. But you have— had—something I wanted. Vitality, boldness, the courage of your beliefs, your cleverness. I thought if I could win your heart, then you'd give some of that to me. Even after I committed the greatest of sins for you, all you did was make a mockery of me, my manhood. You refused to cast aside thoughts of your former husband, ridiculed my learning, my writing, and in doing so, you derided all men. I couldn't have that."

My throat grew thick, my eyes began to water, tears flowed down my cheeks. Lights danced. Jankin's face, his flushed cheeks, his bloodshot eye circled and doubled before becoming one. Dear God, he was going to kill me.

"You'll not get one groat, you hear? This time, you *will* die. Sabyn is my wife, my only wife. You're just a swiving old whore, a witch, who doesn't know better than to stay dead."

The jug shattered as it connected with Jankin's head and his knees buckled. He collapsed and fell backward, blood streaming. Standing there, the handle in her grip, was Lowdy. Behind her stood Oriel and Milda. Their eyes were round, their faces ashen.

"Aunty Alyson," cried Lowdy, and casting aside the handle, threw herself into my arms. Just as swiftly, she pulled away and began checking my throat, my face, my lips. I'd bitten my tongue and it had swollen and filled my mouth with blood, making it difficult to speak.

I needn't have worried. Ignoring Jankin's bleeding form collapsed on the floor behind her, Lowdy chattered as she found a kerchief and, leading me to the window, she pushed the shutters ajar so she could use the light. She dipped the fabric in the wine spilled on the table and began to dab my face.

"I didn't trust him, Aunty Alyson, God forgive me. When I left you, I pleaded sickness and came back home. I hid in the kitchen. When I saw him enter, I knew he was up to no good. I ran as fast as I could and got Milda and Oriel."

I looked at the two women. Milda's face had folded into gray creases as she looked from Jankin to me and back again. Oriel was picking up pieces of the jug and putting them on the table. No one tended to Jankin.

"Where's Master Stephen? Drew?" My voice was croaky.

"Still at the White Hart. The last thing we needed was for Drew to find Jankin here," said Milda. She came to my side, held my hand.

"Or Master Stephen," said Oriel.

They were so concerned with my state, relieved at my timely rescue, none of us paid attention to Jankin. Part of me hoped he was dead.

Alas, he wasn't.

With what must have been the last of his strength, he rose unsteadily to his feet. With a cry like a raven, he lunged.

I couldn't scream, my throat was so torn, but my mouth opened, my eyes widened.

"Get out of my way, you little bitch!"

He grabbed Lowdy, lifting her off her feet. Then, he threw her at the window. She struck the edge of the sill, forcing the shutters wide apart, then tilted backward. For one brief moment she was frozen in the opening, her eyes stark in terror. Off-balance, her arms wheeled. Too late, she'd nothing to hold her in the room, not my reaching hands, my twisting body, not my will which escaped in a shrill scream; not Jankin's coat which she desperately tried to clutch.

Her cry as she tumbled out the window was a sound that haunts me still. A hoarse sigh of utter disbelief.

There was a dull thud.

I pushed Jankin aside as I almost hurled myself after Lowdy. Only Milda's arms prevented me from following. Limbs akimbo on the ground below lay my beautiful girl, her dark hair spread like a fan about her sweet face, blood pooling around her head.

"Lowdy!" I screamed. Folk flew from their houses, ran from the square, slowing in disbelief as they reached her twisted frame. They looked from me to her and back again, confused, shocked.

Lowdy's eyes locked onto mine. Her mouth opened and closed a few times; one arm flailed uselessly by her side.

I spun, desperate to reach her, when there was a shout below. Jankin staggered out the front door. He paused, and upon seeing Lowdy and the people crouching over her, trying to stanch the blood, offer comfort, he tried to run.

"Stop him!" I bellowed, pointing. "That bastard pushed Lowdy."

There was an almighty growl from the gathering crowd as they came running to block Jankin's escape. Some thrust tools and other makeshift weapons at him.

Milda followed as I ran downstairs. Of Oriel, there was no sign.

Assured Jankin wouldn't get away, I dropped next to Lowdy, pushing people aside. Milda kept them away. Uncertain what to do, I gazed upon Lowdy, willing her to wake, to look at me. Her eyes fluttered open. There was so much blood, blood and something else.

"Nay," I croaked.

It was Alyson all over again.

I stroked her hair back from her face, blood painting her forehead, her cheeks. "Oh, Lowdy, Lowdy." My voice cracked. "It should've been me . . ." I began to sob, great tearing cries that resembled howls.

"No, Aunty Alyson," she whispered. "It's not your time."

"It's not yours either, chick," I wept. "Sweetling, sweetling, stay with me. Look at me, oh, my darling, clever girl. I'm not worthy—" I pressed my lips to her cheek. She sucked in her breath.

"Not worthy?" she gasped. "You're worth more than you know." Her teeth were stained red. Her eyes rolled and began to lose focus. "I heard what he said, Jankin." She struggled to breathe. "He's wrong. You *are* a good woman. The best." Her voice was a mere sigh, a fading whisper. "Master Geoffrey says you are, a good wife too . . ."

"Lowdy." I slapped her face gently. "Lowdy. Please, God, don't let her die. Don't you dare take her. Don't you dare . . . Not my chick. Not my chick . . ."

But God, as was His wont, didn't listen.

I like to think the last thing Lowdy felt, that she saw, was the love bursting from my torn heart, flowing from my drowning eyes, from Milda's too, as we lamented this woman-child, this beautiful soul who was so cruelly ripped from our lives.

It wasn't until Jankin shouted that I remembered him. When Oriel ran, she'd gone to fetch the authorities. With a sergeant on the scene, the neighbors, who were ready to commit murder, were ordered to lower their weapons and tie up Jankin. The plan was to hold him until the sheriff and his men arrived. Thank goodness for Oriel. She'd done what neither Milda nor I in our distress thought to do—ensure that this time, at least, justice would be served.

FORTY-SIX

St. Martin's Le Grand, London
The Year of Our Lord 1399
In the first year of the reign of Henry IV

News that King Richard had been overthrown by his cousin Henry Bolingbroke barely caused a stir within the household. While part of London celebrated, we were wreathed in sorrow. The days since Lowdy's terrible death passed in a fugue. We drifted about the place, barely talking, eating little. If not for Wace and Harry, I would have scarce stirred from my room. Routine was all that kept us from falling into despair; the girls' insistence on going to Southwark, bringing in coin, the counting of it when they returned before curfew, meals, and sleep.

When the sheriff arrived that bleak, dark day, and saw that young Lowdy Fleshewer, daughter of Ordric, had been brutally murdered, he had Jankin arrested. Though Jankin protested it was an accident, there were witnesses to swear to the contrary. For once, his wealth and the fact his father-in-law was titled mattered not a whit. Ordric, rightly or wrongly, wielded great influence in parts of London. For once, our interests aligned.

Ordric came to visit in the days after Lowdy's death, dragging along a coroner, demanding a full recount of what happened. We obliged, Milda and Oriel adding their statements, as did the neighbors. After that, Ordric ensured Jankin received no privileges from the turnkeys at the jail.

No doubt, money exchanged hands to make Jankin's life a misery; no doubt he paid, futilely, to try to improve his conditions as well—a windfall for the jailers. I thought of it as money he should, by rights, have paid me. Though it would have meant liberty from London, from walking the streets of Southwark and putting my girls in danger, I was glad of any coin spent ensuring his torment. Danger hadn't come from the streets as I'd feared, but risen up snarling from my past to destroy us.

Destroy Lowdy.

Guilt ate my soul, gnawed my bones. After Ordric explained that nothing and no one could save Jankin, that even the coroner had stated the trial was just a formality, it was as if my life force dimmed. Was it relief? Was it the realization it really didn't matter anymore? None of it, the trial, the punishment. Not even the fact that with Jankin's death, I could claim what was rightfully mine— Slynge House, the lands and flock. I was his lawful wife, after all, and with the proceeds from the sale, I could finally lease a place in Southwark, start afresh. I didn't care. It wouldn't bring Lowdy back, just as nothing had brought Alyson back, either. Oh, I went to the funeral, comforted the boys, Milda, Oriel, Drew, and the girls, and then crawled into bed. I said nothing of the land and property in Bath.

Geoffrey came in the immediate aftermath of Lowdy's death; of course he did. I refused to see him. By then, his poem was inconsequential. I refused to see anyone—Father Malcolm, Sister Cecilia, both of whom were crushed by Lowdy's death, as we all were. I didn't see it at the time, but grief can make one selfish. Forced to stay with John Gower, Geoffrey nonetheless called a few times a day in the hope I'd change my mind.

Then, I was summoned, along with Milda and Oriel, to give evidence at Jankin's trial. A courier came to the house and said we were to present ourselves at Westminster in seven days. He left an official document. I couldn't bring myself to read it.

He also explained that Jankin's trial had been delayed because the judges who were part of the Court of the King's Bench were traveling throughout the country to try other criminal cases. In the meantime, the perpetrator had been moved, locked away in the King's Bench Prison, a miserable establishment in Southwark. In a street called Angel Place. The irony didn't escape me.

I sank into a melancholy as dark as the endless rain-filled nights. I didn't want to go. I didn't want to speak. Judas's balls, I didn't want to relive those bloody moments or see Jankin again.

I remained beneath my covers, unwashed, unkempt, staring at the official letter ordering me to take part without reading it. Until, four days before I was due in court, I forced myself. The words blurred, then reformed. There was my name, the names of the others who'd borne witness, and Jankin's. Then, in bold letters, was the crime he was accused of committing:

That Jankin Binder did murther one Lowdy Fleshewer in a cruel and unjust manner, ending her life without care or thought.

Unjust. Cruel. Without care or thought. Jankin Binder.

It's hard to describe what came over me at that precise moment. Mayhap, it was seeing what he'd done set out in bold brown script. Memories coalesced, emotions too. All the anger I'd harbored, the need for revenge that had roiled in me ever since Alyson's death, stilled. All the wrath, blame, guilt, and self-loathing, calmed. The feelings were there, but they weren't frothing and bubbling.

Heat coursed through my veins, galloping up my chest and into my throat. I opened my mouth and roared. The sound struck the ceiling, bounced off the walls, and traveled through all the gaps and cracks in the room, the shutters, through the floor. One long, plaintive sound that went on and on, until like a spinning top, it gradually ceased.

The silence that followed was deafening. Slowly, I became aware of other sounds. Labored breathing and a heaving chest. My heartbeat thudding in my ears. Rain coursing down the thatch and striking the puddles below. Chairs scraping, a babble of voices, then the slam of boots on the stairs.

I climbed out of bed, smoothed my shift. The door burst open and there they were: Leda, followed by Yolande, then Milda and Oriel. The boys squeezed past, stopped and stared. Last was Master Stephen, a great brooding hulk standing over them. They looked upon me with wide, frightened eyes.

"Are you alright, Alyson?" asked Milda, approaching uncertainly, her voice quavering.

"Should we call Sister Cecilia or Doctor Thomas?" asked Oriel.

"Should we call a priest?" asked Wace in his tiny voice, staring back at his mother.

"Whatever for, lad?" I asked.

"To cast the devil out."

"Oh dear Lord." I gave a grim laugh. "The lad has been spending too much time at the college." I came forward and stroked his hair, pulled him, then Harry, into my arms. "I've no need of a priest." I sniffed. "Only a bath. Milda? Oriel? Can you see to it?" No one moved. "I'm fine. Truly. I'm sorry I was cause for such concern, but I won't be any longer. I've a duty to Lowdy, to my Godsib, to you all, to see justice served and I can't very well do that from my bed, can I?"

Milda and Oriel exchanged wary smiles.

Leda folded her arms. "Well, thank the Lord you're back among us, mistress. Forget a priest, I thought we'd have to put you in Bethlehem, and I'm not the only one."

Master Stephen lowered his head. Yolande scraped the floor with her toes a few times.

"I'll see to that bath, shall I?" she said, tugging Stephen's shirt.

Milda remained while I washed, the others returning to the kitchen to discuss the miracle of my return, no doubt.

Was it a heavenly intervention? God speaking to me with his burning breath? Was it the power of words to stir the soul, make even the most unlikely or unpalatable of truths real? From that moment on, I was filled with purpose. Purpose and courage.

"I blamed myself," I told Milda as she poured more hot water into the tub.

Milda said nothing. She didn't have to.

"It wasn't until I saw Jankin's crimes written down in ink that I understood—none of this was my fault. It doesn't matter what Jankin said, what I know he'll tell the court. He chose to kill, to wield the knife that ended Alyson's life and to hurl Lowdy out the window. Just as he chose to beat me and his new wife and God knows who else. It wasn't God's will that made him do it. It wasn't mine or anything I said or did—nor Alyson, nor Lowdy. It was *his*. His will, his choice, his actions. And, as God is my bloody witness, I'll see him pay."

The spiraling cloth was as soothing as Milda's presence. The water changed color as days of grime sloughed off my skin. My flesh was rosy in the firelight; like me, renewed.

"If I continued to burden myself with guilt, then Jankin wins— they all do."

"Who, mistress?" she asked quietly.

"The men who continue to make us women pay for their sins; who have done so since Eve offered the apple to Adam. But—" I twisted around in the tub so I could look Milda in the face. "Remember Mistress Ibbot? Wace's midwife? She said—and I've always thought—Eve didn't *make* him eat the bloody fruit. She offered Adam a choice and he made one. So whose sin is it really? Who is really responsible for the Fall of mankind? Is it her or him? Or are they both equally culpable?"

Milda smiled. Pushing the cloth into my hand, she dropped a kiss on my wet head and, groaning, rose to her feet.

"You don't need me to answer that."

"Nay," I smiled. It had been so long since I last did that. "I don't."

———————

Four days later, after short testimonies from me, Milda, Oriel, and even a few more people whose names I didn't know but who spoke eloquently about Jankin's propensity for violence—toward their daughters, maids, tavern wenches, and maudlyns—he was charged with Lowdy's murder.

The scribes sat at their big table, the rolls upon which they recorded the names of witnesses and their statements unspooling. Their quills quivered as they wrote at speed, ink splattering. Filled with a sense of rightness that Jankin's brutal acts would be recorded for posterity, but also sadness for the clever lad he once was, I sat quietly. Would that things had been different. But as I said to Milda, it's the choices we make that define us. Words—written or spoken—can inspire, wound, fill us with passion or despair, but it's what we do that will determine how we are judged. How we are remembered.

This is something Geoffrey knew and it was why he expended so much effort writing and rewriting. I needed to revisit his words and soon. To think about how I would act upon them.

In the end, despite Jankin's spit-filled denials and accusations—at me, his wife, at Alyson (the court understandably confused her with me), and what were interpreted as the ravings of a madman as he declared his dead wife was sitting among us—he was led away. Sir Horsewhyre, who'd attended in lieu of his daughter, spied me among the crowd, his eyes widening. When he sought me out in the immediate aftermath of Jankin's sentencing, I was unprepared as he steered me into an alcove just outside the courtroom.

Before I could open my mouth, he hissed in my ear. "I know who and what you are. If you dare to come forward as Binder's wife, I'll destroy you and all you hold dear." He looked back to where Milda, Oriel, and the girls stood, his meaning clear.

His grip on my arm grew tighter.

"My daughter will not be classed a whore for the sake of one, do you understand? She *is* that man's lawful wife and I won't allow anything else to be said—not even a whisper. Slynge House is hers. The land, the sheep. You forwent it a long time ago, *Eleanor*. I can guess why. Leave it that way, or else."

With one last rough shake and a look that would have struck a knight's steed dead, Sir Horsewhyre strode away. Part of me raged that he dared to threaten me, while another part knew it was the guilt he felt for allowing his daughter's marriage, and his likely encouragement of it, that prompted him to deprive me of what was rightfully mine. Yet another, calmer, part, honed by experience, understood this was meant to be. With my new identity, new life, and the passing years, I'd waived my rights. Sabyn didn't deserve to suffer for Jankin's actions, nor mine.

At least one of us would gain materially. With a deep, deep sigh of resentment, but mostly, I like to think, acceptance, I went and joined the others. My advantage would have to take other forms.

Though I'd seen enough death and bloodshed to last me into eternity and the hell I'd no doubt was awaiting me (and Satan better watch his sorry arse when I get there), I owed it to Alyson, Lowdy, and my girls to watch the bastard hang. I owed it to Sabyn and all wives who'd been forced to endure their husbands' insults, fists, and worse.

Jankin was led to the scaffold in sackcloth, accompanied by two priests. A group of soldiers and constables surrounded the cart carrying him as a large crowd, keen to see any felon hang, became a noisy procession. Rope was tied loosely about his wrists and neck, and he stared at his bare feet, shutting out those baying for his blood. I'd insisted Wace and Harry remain at home. A kindly neighbor stayed with them. Everyone else had been with me in court and were by my side as we were jostled across the bridge and through the city to Tyburn Tree. With every step, we were joined by more and more people. Shops and barrows were abandoned as folk became part of the throng ready to see the man foolish enough to kill Ordric Fleshewer's daughter hang. Every time Lowdy's name was uttered, I would add "and Alyson" under my breath.

Rather than feeling jubilant, when we paused so an innkeeper might offer the condemned man refreshment, I felt ambivalent. At first, Jankin refused the drinks, but as the crowd grew larger and louder, he took what was offered and before long was swaying from their effects.

It took over three hours to reach Tyburn. Ordric and his men led us to the front of the scaffold, a large triangle that could accommodate at least eight condemned on each side. Beneath the Tree, I had second thoughts. Did I really want to be here, glorying in death? Nay, but I did want to see justice served. To let Jankin, God up above, Alyson, and Lowdy know that I had seen it as well. I sent a swift prayer heavenward for strength. It's quite one thing to imagine you can witness a hanging and another to actually be there.

There were thirteen more condemned men joining Jankin that day. There was no one exceptional, just felons being punished for their crimes.

One by one, they were brought to the noose, offered the chance to confess and beg forgiveness. Most did. As they performed the last jig they'd ever dance, the stink of piss and shit filled the air. I covered my nose and mouth with a perfumed kerchief and blessed Yolande for her forethought.

"He's up next," Ordric leaned down to tell me. Lowdy's death had made strange bedfellows. While I grieved, I wasn't sure what Ordric felt. He'd barely known his daughter. Mayhap, his outrage was based on a sense of ownership. Jankin had destroyed his property and must pay the price. Whatever, I was grateful for his presence, and what he'd done to ensure Jankin got to this point.

Or I thought I was.

Up until the moment the noose was placed around his neck, Jankin hadn't uttered a word. He'd refused prayers and the opportunity to ask forgiveness. In his silence, he condemned himself further. The executioner put a sack over his head.

"Leave it off," shouted Ordric. "I want to see the bastard die. So does she." He gestured to me beside him.

Only then did Jankin spy me. He had seen me in court, of course, which had prompted a fit as his eyes bulged and he began to scream and spit. The executioner obeyed Ordric, stepping back, ready to heave Jankin heavenward and break his neck.

Just before he did, Jankin finally spoke. He leveled his gaze at me. "This is all your fault, you whoring bitch."

Without hesitation, I shouted back, "And don't you forget it, you Satan-cursed lump of camel-dung."

Before he could say anything more, his feet left the ground. Jankin squirmed and twisted, his bound ankles jerked, his face grew red, then a mottled blue. His eyes bulged, his cheeks appeared to swell. Then his body merely swung back and forth, back and forth, a huge pendulum on an unforgiving rope.

It was a while before anyone could persuade me to leave. The crowds began to disperse. Milda, Oriel, and the others found a vendor selling ale and hot pies and, with Ordric and his men, sought sustenance. The wind picked up, bitter and cruel, biting my hands and face. I barely felt it.

Instead, I stared at Jankin's shit-stained corpse, wondering how such a lovely boy had grown into such a cruel and dangerous man. More dangerous than most because he appeared to be the opposite. He lulled folk, women in particular, into a false sense of reliability. He was like those animals that make fake burrows to lure weaker creatures inside. He only revealed his true nature once the trap was sprung.

With a huge sigh, I left as the sky was darkening, thick purple clouds casting a doom-laden light on the hill. Scavengers appeared, searching the area for anything of value. There were coins, some mementos, not much to show for fourteen lives.

As we made our way back to St. Martin's, Ordric's men providing a welcome escort, I was quiet, listening to the conversation around me. It was Ordric who finally drew me aside. "So, mistress, I hear you're wanting to move," he said. "Over Southwark way."

I glanced at him in astonishment. "How do you know?"

He tapped the side of his nose. "One hears things. Nah," he smiled, showing his half-rotten teeth, "your friend Chaucer's been asking around on your behalf. Word got back."

Not surprised that Ordric's network extended over the river, I was quietly pleased Geoffrey had involved himself. We still hadn't spoken, not directly, though he'd written many letters, which I'd read—anything to distract me from my misery. I would thank him for that. If nothing else, the last few days had taught me it was time to forgive my oldest friend. As soon as I reached home, I would invite him over. From his missives, I knew King Henry had been demanding his time of late, going so far as to double Geoffrey's annuity—and that after the previous king had been so mercurial in his patronage. He'd offered to come to Jankin's trial, but I'd all the support I needed. Anyway, a trial wasn't something you'd attend unless you had no choice. I prayed I'd never have to go to one again, or bear witness to someone's death, even if you believed they deserved it. There was something barbaric about it; it stripped both felon and witnesses of humanity. Of dignity. I shuddered.

"Are you cold, mistress?" asked Ordric.

"It's just—" I waved my hand in the direction we'd come. "You know. The day."

"Aye." Ordric looked over his shoulder. In the gathering gloom, he was even more sinister than in daylight. "Makes me want to down a few ales and find a lusty bawd to share my glee with." He eyed me up and down. "Whatcha reckon, mistress?"

I almost tripped over. Dear God, the man was serious. How things had changed. I would no more swive him than the pig I could see snuffling among the refuse outside an ordinary. "You flatter me, sir. But back to Southwark. Aye, I'm looking to move. Why? Do you have objections?"

"On the contrary. I wanted to say, I can put in a word for you, if you like?" He nudged me and winked, jerking his chin in the direction of his men, leaving me in no doubt what form his "word" would take.

It was the last thing I needed. Even so, someone like me took friends where we could. "Thank you, Ordric, that's very decent of you. If I have need, I'll let you know."

"Make sure you do," he said, taking my arm as we neared the gate of St. Martin's. He gave a bark of laughter. "No one's called me decent in a long time. Fact is, there's nothing decent 'bout me offer. I don't want you here, taking business from my girls."

I laughed and extracted my arm. "Why, Ordric, if I didn't know better, I'd say you're paying me a compliment."

"I recognize competition when I see it."

"Aye. And me as well."

Just outside St. Martin's, he stopped. "I also know a decent person when I see one."

I arched a brow.

He lowered his voice. "You gave my Lowdy a proper life." He

cleared his throat, turned his face away. "And you're good to my son, to Wace."

I was speechless as we parted.

The bells had rung compline before the house settled. Wace and Harry, with the typical ghoulishness of the young, wanted to know the details of what we'd seen. When they learned that Lowdy's killer had been hanged, they cheered. After that, we downed some ales, had something to eat, and determined, as we bid each other goodnight, that Jankin's death marked the close of a chapter.

"Tomorrow, we'll return to the usual, won't we, mistress?" asked Leda, speaking on behalf of the others as was her wont.

I looked at their expectant faces, the sleepy ones of the boys. "Aye. Back to work, school, and planning our future."

"And where's that gonna be, mistress?" asked Yolande, stifling a yawn.

"One day, it will be over there." I nodded toward the Thames. "On the other side of that great river. One day, we'll have a house of our own and a thriving business where every maudlyn will want to work."

Leda pushed back her stool. "Wouldn't that be nice." She deposited a kiss on my cheek. "But methinks you've been hanging around that poet friend of yours too much. You're having an attack of imagination."

As I sat by my window that night, watching the early snow fall, I wondered if Leda was right.

Not about Geoffrey, but if what I was planning—to be my own woman—was nothing but an unrealistic dream.

FORTY-SEVEN

———◆———

St. Martin's Le Grand, London
The Years of Our Lord 1399 to 1400
In the first year of the reign of Henry IV

Geoffrey, that's marvelous news!"

It was not long after sext on Christmas Eve and, in answer to my invitation, Geoffrey had arrived not only with a goose, some lamprey, and venison, but jugs of fine wine. Better still, he brought with him a copy of the lease agreement he'd just signed, which would make him a neighbor once more.

That very day, he'd moved into a tenement in the beautiful garden of the Lady Chapel in Westminster.

In honor of his relocation, we were enjoying wine in the solar. The fire roared, casting welcome warmth. Milda was spinning, her once-steady hands not quite so quick now her swollen fingers found it hard to twist the thread. Her eyesight was also beginning to fade. I'd told her over and over she didn't have to keep working, but she insisted.

"What else would I do?"

"Look after me."

"I don't even do that anymore," she grumbled. "You look after yourself."

"Then love me."

"Can't do more of what I already do in abundance," she said with a gentle smile.

Oriel was cooking, Yolande helping. Drew was at the market. He'd become keen on the widow of a former cutpurse who was living with the butcher and his family. Emily was her name. It was hard to keep him indoors these days, which was a boon. Wace and Harry were at lessons. In the New Year, Wace would leave us to go and live in Master Adam Pinkhurst's house and become his factotum— a general help when it came to scribing and researching. Geoffrey had arranged it. He would have taken Wace on himself, but said he couldn't afford to. Again, I couldn't conceive of how he lacked coin when King Henry had been so generous. Mayhap, I thought, it was because of this new lease. Fifty-three years he'd taken the place in Westminster. Who did he think he was? Methuselah? The girls and Master Stephen were, as always, over in Southwark, though I expected them home at any moment. The weather was terrible and while there'd always be men keen for a sard before Christmas, the snow would likely keep them beside their own hearths.

"From here on, I'll be able to concentrate on my writing," said Geoffrey, interrupting my thoughts. "Finish that damn poem."

I regarded him over the top of the goblet. "I thought we agreed not to mention it anymore."

Geoffrey shifted uncomfortably. "I only mention it because what you read was unfinished."

"So, you're rewriting?"

Geoffrey had the grace to color. "Parts, aye. Mainly the Wife's Tale."

"I didn't read that part. Only her Prologue—the bit that tells *my* story."

"It's not exactly *your* story, Alyson."

I flapped a hand to silence him. "So you've said, over and over. It's close enough for discomfort."

He gave a sad smile. "It was never my intention to cause you distress."

"But you did. You used me, Geoffrey. Used my life, plundered it, unearthed my soul, my dreams, and what for? To entertain your cronies."

"Nay, not *just* entertain. You make it sound trivial. I wrote it to bring ordinary people's stories to the fore, the commons' lives—"

I held up my palm. "Stop. Please. I don't want to talk about it anymore. Not today at any rate. Mayhap, one day I'll be ready. Mayhap . . ."

He opened his mouth then, thinking better of it, closed it again.

Determined to change the subject, I lifted my mazer in Geoffrey's direction. "You'll enjoy being back in London. In the thick of things again," I said. "In the beating heart of the court."

Geoffrey nodded. He was paler than last time I saw him, his eyes lacked their usual luster. "Moreso because I've no official role. I can merely observe. Observe and write." His hand shook as he drank.

It was easy to forget he was old. What remained of his hair was mostly gray and white, his beard had grown bushy and long. Lines crossed his cheeks and forehead, crowded the corners of his eyes. It was his quick wit and warm voice that belied his age. No warble or stuttering for him. He was as sharp as ever.

We feasted that night with Geoffrey, and though it wasn't officially Christmas, we wassailed, sang carols, and burned the Yule Log. In all the time I'd known Geoffrey, we'd never spent Christmas together, and though we didn't exchange presents, having him there was gift enough for me. I said so after a few wines as well.

"Ah, but you'll see plenty of me now you've forgiven me."

"Forgiven might be overreaching—" I smiled to soften the sting.

Geoffrey ignored me. "Because I'm so much closer, I'm hoping you'll come to visit me as well."

As the words were spoken, a shiver racked my body, as if a demon had walked over my grave. I hid my concern by drinking more, laughing louder, and making extravagant promises to Geoffrey, Wace, Harry, Master Stephen, and my girls.

Yet, as Geoffrey staggered out into the evening, Master Stephen taking a lantern to escort him to John Gower's house, Wace scrambling for his coat and hat so he might accompany them, I was left with the heavy feeling that I'd never see Geoffrey again.

Dear Lord, but wine makes maudlin fools of us, doesn't it? The man had just moved closer and here I was, predicting the end of our friendship.

I should have also known, *in vino veritas*. Truth glimpsed while drunk may seem like sentimental rubbish, but it's still truth.

———◆———

The New Year was clear and cold. Before the month was complete, Wace went to live in Adam Pinkhurst's household, and within weeks they were singing his praises. Leda was bursting with pride and there wasn't a day went past she didn't mention her clever son—to passersby, customers, other maudlyns, barrow-boys, and milk-maids, the custodians at London Bridge or the boatmen who ferried her, Yolande, and Master Stephen across the river daily. She kept mispronouncing factotum, turning it into a variety of words that had people asking her if a living could be made from farting and if so, we'd all be rich.

Milda and I spun and wove, the thread we sold barely covering the cost of the wool. Likewise, my slow-growing ells, beautifully made as they were, brought little. Sometimes, when I accompanied the girls to Southwark, I also took on clients. Don't judge. I could scarce ask the others to do what I wasn't prepared to do myself. I'd not had the heart to seek other whores to join my girls and none sought me out—not then; I suspected Ordric had a hand in that. The men I took had to be clean, well-spoken, and pay for the privilege. I'd standards, you know. Sad thing, I made more sucking or tugging than I did weaving, and me an old woman and all. Albeit a lusty one with Venus in my veins.

My dream of moving to Southwark and opening a bathhouse re-treated into a fog-bound distance. I didn't let it go, it was just be-coming harder to see. When Leda was knocked out by a brute of a sailor and Yolande lost another tooth and had her nose broken, and Master Stephen almost killed the rogues responsible, I had to use my acquaintance with Ordric to escape the worst penalties. Some hours in the pillory and a small fine sufficed, praise be to God (and Ordric).

Even so, I'll not forget the humiliation, the pain of being shackled by wrists and ankles for hours in a public place. Nor will I forget those who threw their rotten fruit at me—and that was the best of what was flung. Dung, eggs, mud, water, stones—and from some scarce old enough to wield them, the chuckling little bastards. As I cursed and rained threats upon those who stepped forward to administer their brand of punishment, growing dirtier, colder, and more covered in shit than I'd been since I wrestled with Alyson all those years ago, my only consolation was that my shame spared the girls. Anyhow, it was nothing a good wash wouldn't take care of.

"The sooner you get those girls off the streets and into that bawdy house you're wanting, the better," said Ordric, who happened along as I was freed, helping me stand as my aching limbs tried to work again.

If pigs were pigeons, it'd be raining bacon.

We marked the year after Lowdy's death by casting off our mourning and spending the first part of the day in chapel saying prayers and lighting candles. I lit some for Alyson, too, and asked that both women forgive me that still, after all this time, I hadn't managed to fulfill my silent promise to both of them, not really. I may have authority over my household, but my life and livelihood were still reliant on the monks of St. Michael's and the customers who used our services. We could be evicted for the slightest infringement and every day the girls and I walked through the city and were rowed to Southwark was dangerous, and that was before we sidled off into the shadows and rented rooms to please men.

Then, one day in November, everything changed.

———— ◆ ————

I wish I could say Geoffrey's death was sudden, only it wasn't. I'd known it was coming late last year. I should have made more of an effort; taken up his invitation to visit, insisted when he declined my invitations that he tear himself away from his wretched poems.

But I didn't. And he stayed in his beloved apartment and garden, dreaming, receiving visitors who interrupted his work, and writing. He wrote to me often, that's why I knew not to visit. That's why, I like to think, I felt him ever-close. Geoffrey had always been a man who communicated better with the written word than the spoken. Often underestimated in person, mistaken for a buffoon or a weak man of shallow thought, the opposite was true. Read any one of his works and you are given entrée to a mind that observed closely, remembered faultlessly and was possessed of an acerbic and generous wit.

I didn't find out Geoffrey had died until a week afterward. By then, he was already buried and hymns sung for his soul. But the moment I saw Harry Bailly on my doorstep, the innkeep from the Tabard Inn in Southwark, I knew something was amiss.

"May I come in, mistress?" said Harry, studying my face curiously, as if trying to assess the changes the years had wrought since we'd last spoken.

"Forgive me, Harry, of course."

Once we were settled in the solar, ale in hand before the fire, Harry told me what brought him here.

I swear, I didn't hear another word for a long time. All I could perceive was the sound of regret and grief pounding in my head, each pulse of my heart an ache against my ribs. I imagined it growing bigger and bigger until it would explode. My life with Geoffrey flashed before me, from the time he caught me with that young priest, Layamon. Holy Mary and all the saints, his name had been prescient, had it not? If I'd done anything in my life, it was lay with a man many times. All except Geoffrey. Yet, he'd not only been the first man to care for me, but he'd been the only constant one in my life.

My friend, my cousin, my confidant, my mentor, and my conscience.

Dear God in Heaven—my beloved.

That's when the tears began. When I finally understood that Geoffrey was my one true love. Don't mistake me, I don't mean in the passionate way that he so oft wrote about. Nor do I mean in that heightened state of lust where a woman would risk her reputation, her very future, just to touch the man she desires. Nay. What I felt for Geoffrey was deeper, truer, than that. It was akin to the love I bore Alyson. It was a love that transcended the flesh and reached deep into the soul.

And now he was gone.

I buried my face in my hands and wept. Harry didn't know what to do, so sat clearing his throat again and again between sips of ale. Milda rose and wrapped her plump arms around me, making soft crooning noises as she once did to quiet Wace.

There was no quieting me, not for a time. It wasn't so much that Geoffrey was lost to me, because he wasn't. I had my memories and, God be praised, I had his words.

It was because I had never told him what he meant to me.

When I finally dried my eyes (only for them to well up again), Harry coughed loudly. "There's more, mistress."

"Oh," I said, raising a bleary, weary face. "You'll have to speak up, Harry. My ear." I tapped it lightly. "It's not good. When I shed tears, it's worse."

Harry shifted his chair closer, leaning forward. "That better?" he shouted.

"I'm not deaf, you know!"

Chagrined, Harry moderated his volume. Poor Harry, I could see he was battling to hold himself together. Geoffrey had been his friend, too. When he'd finished telling me whatever it was, then I'd suggest we get drunk. Roaring, mightily drunk.

"A few months ago," said Harry, reaching into the bulging satchel he'd brought with him, "Chaucer asked me to hold on to these." He extracted some thick quires and a roll of parchment with five wax seals hanging off it. "He said to me that if anything should ever happen to him, I was to give them to you." He passed them over.

The quires tumbled into my lap. The scroll of parchment wobbled on top and rolled onto the floor. Milda retrieved it.

Cautiously, I picked up the first quire and opened it. I immediately recognized the hand. It was Adam Pinkhurst, Wace's master and Geoffrey's favored scribe for copying out his poems and essays. My heart, so swollen and full, began to throb. Could it be? Aye, it was. It was his *Canterbury Tales*. Incomplete, but enough for anyone to understand what he wanted to achieve. I scanned the quire I'd plucked out swiftly. It was the one about the miller cuckolded by a young scholar. Dear Lord.

I read some lines aloud: *"He knew not Cato, for his wit was rude/ Who bade that man should wed his similitude."*

I'd forgotten the miller quotes Cato about men marrying their equal. The miller's wife was also called Alyson—a woman who, along with her young lover, deceives her husband. It wasn't hard to think where inspiration for that had come from. I only wish I'd enjoyed the success she had. I closed that quire and opened another, then another, until at last I found it. The Wife of Bath's Prologue and, in another thick quire, her Tale. The part that still remained unread by me.

No more.

For the first time, at Harry's encouragement, I read the Tale—aloud.

The Wife tells a story about a handsome young knight who rapes a woman. When he is apprehended and sent to court for punishment, the Queen and her women set him a task: to find out what women most desire. He learns much in the year he searches for an answer—they want flattery, jewels, riches, nice clothes. How shallow. Geoffrey was most certainly having a laugh—but at whom? Women, or those who believed such nonsense?

I continued. It's not until the knight is returning to court, defeated because his quest has failed, that he meets an ugly old woman. She promises to give him the answer he seeks—if he will do her a favor. He agrees and presents the answer she gives him to the court: women desire to have mastery over men.

I paused. *Oh, Geoffrey.* I returned to the tale.

When the old woman insists the knight marry her, he's appalled, but is bound by their agreement. On their wedding night, he turns from his ancient bride in disgust—she's physically repulsive, wrinkled, poor, and not of noble birth. She rebukes him for his manner, telling him nobility is not attained through birth, but through actions—through being a good person.

My eyes began to swim.

The old woman then reminds the knight that Christ was poor—poverty might bring misery, but it's also an incentive to work harder. True friends stand by you whether you're poor or rich. And, as for being ugly, well, ugly women are less likely to make cuckolds of their husbands.

I couldn't help it, my laughter burst forth, startling Harry and Milda, who were both lost in the tale.

Then, the old bride offers the knight something he's unlikely to refuse. Capable of magic, she can either be young and beautiful and unfaithful to him, or old, ugly, and constant. Which will it be? The knight considers her offer then, remorseful but also enlightened, puts the question back to her—he tells *her* to choose.

Judas's prick in a noose. Geoffrey gives the woman the right to make her own choice . . .

I pressed the quire to my chest and bowed my head.

Harry wiped his eyes, not understanding the source of my tears, my long silence. "I'm in there too and all, mistress. Not that wondrous tale, but in the journey part—with the pilgrims. He told me to tell you not to be angry. To remind you it's but a work of fiction, but one in which he granted you your heart's desire."

The authority to make my own decisions. Aye, well, his Wife of Bath did that, didn't she? As brash and bold as you like. But it was in her Tale, not her Prologue, that her real story is told. Mayhap, mine as well.

It wasn't quite what I'd have wished, but it would have to do.

"Thank you, Geoffrey," I whispered.

"What about this?" Milda passed over the scroll with the seals.

"Oh, aye," said Harry, wagging a finger at it. "He bade me deliver that into your hands as well."

Very carefully, I unrolled the parchment, weighing it down with a mazer at one end and a candlestick at the other.

The room spun. This could not be.

"What is it, mistress?" asked Milda.

My shoulders began to shake, my hands, my lips. Milda and Harry exchanged concerned looks. Harry swept up my mazer, the parchment curling over, and thrust it into my hands. I gulped a few times.

"Oh, Milda," I gasped. "Harry. Geoffrey, he . . . Geoffrey . . ."

"What's Chaucer done now?" asked Harry, slapping his forehead.

"Mistress?" Milda's voice was frail. Frail and scared.

I stood, the quires tumbling to the floor, and grasped her hands. "He's done what he's always done."

"What's that?" asked Milda, her faded eyes blinking as she gazed into mine.

I began to laugh. "Putting impossible dreams into words and making them a reality."

"I don't understand, mistress."

"He's bought a house, Milda. Goddamn Geoffrey Chaucer has bought us a home."

Milda's eyes widened. "Where?"

I stepped over the quires and pushed open the shutters. I pointed toward the river. "Over there. In Southwark." The opposite bank was veiled by a shroud of fog and smoke, but it was there all the same.

Just like our future. Because of Geoffrey.

Because of my damn, beloved poet.

FORTY-EIGHT

The Swanne, Southwark
The Year of Our Lord 1401
In the second year of the reign of Henry IV

The shingle swung in the breeze coming off the river, the sun striking the fresh paint and making it glow. One could almost believe the water bird depicted upon it was actually buoyant.

"The Swanne, eh?" called a singsong voice from the adjacent house. It was my Flemish neighbor, none too happy the former bathhouse owner had sold the premises to another bawd, a bawd with such a good reputation for looking after her girls that many of them had already left their current employers and sought work—and refuge—within her walls.

I welcomed all who would be part of my family, just as Geoffrey suggested. You see, the quires with his final but unfinished poem weren't all he gifted me, nor this run-down, wondrous house that, with Master Stephen and the girls, I would turn into a profitable enterprise. He'd also left a box. It came a month after we'd moved in, delivered in person by Adam Pinkhurst.

The scrivener made the excuse of bringing Wace to see his mother's new home, ignoring that Wace was already more than conversant with the site and had in fact helped the day we ferried our belongings across.

While Leda and Wace went to the High Street to buy something for nuncheon, Adam joined me in the room I'd decided to make my office, handing over a plain wooden box.

"This is for you, from Master Geoffrey."

Unwilling to open it before an audience, I chose instead to show Adam around. The house was the one I'd first clapped eyes on the day I crossed the river. Three stories with an attic and mews and an inner courtyard that could house carts and horses. It had been run-down and sorely in need of repair, but it was large. If ever I needed to keep a good store of supplies, it had a huge cellar that could hold everything from barrels of wine and ale to sacks of flour, wood, and so much more. I had both a bedroom and an office on the second floor. The girls entertained customers on this floor and in some of the rooms on the one above. Most of the third-floor rooms were private bedrooms. The lower floor had a large kitchen, buttery, a grand hall, and two smaller rooms, one of which I gave to Master Stephen. Within a month, we'd seven extra girls working, two more maids, and another burly man, chosen by Stephen, to help keep order about the place. Word got around I was a friend of Ordric Fleshewer, so, even though this was an exaggeration, and I was greeted with hostility by the Flemish and with warnings by the squint-eyed bailiff, Lewis Fynk, thus far no real trouble had occurred. But I knew it wouldn't be long. I was resented. I was a woman, alone. It didn't stop me declaring my widow status loud and long. But I was a legitimate businesswoman. The Bishop of Winchester (after some persuasion from Father Malcolm and the Dean of St. Michael's) had granted permission for me to run a bawdy house and taken my fees.

Adam seemed impressed with the house and could see the efforts we'd made to clean and improve it. As I outlined my plans, he nodded. "I can't say I understand Geoffrey's motives—he could have left what he had to his children. As it was, they received very little. Oh, don't worry, Mistress Alyson, they know nothing of this. Of you."

I didn't want to point out that his children had no need of coin, having done very well for themselves.

"Actually, Master Adam," I said, "I go by Goodwife Alyson these days. Goody, if you prefer." *Thank you, Lowdy, thank you, Geoffrey.*

"My apologies, Goody Alyson."

It also didn't do any harm for my neighbors and the authorities to know that I'd a man, albeit dead, at my back. If I had to use one to give me legitimacy, then by God (I smiled) I would. My choice.

I waited until Adam left, taking Wace with him, before opening this last gift. I was anxious about what it contained. What if, somehow, all this good fortune wasn't mine after all? What if it was some great cosmic joke that would be ripped away the moment I lifted the lid?

Before I opened it, I quickly checked on Milda, who, more and more, was taking to her bed. Just before we moved, she had been laid low with an illness. The doctor didn't know what it was, but the Bankside physician, a Moor named Marcian Vetazes, said with surprising frankness that it was unlikely she'd improve and to make her as comfortable as I was able. It was the least I could do.

Finally, closing the door of the office, I was alone. I lit a candle and, with a mixture of dread and excitement, opened the box. On top was a note addressed to me. Below it, tied in a huge bundle, was every single letter I'd ever written to Geoffrey. My early ones, written for me by Father Elias, my first clumsy attempts at writing to him myself, replete with blots and terrible errors and crossings out. Then the later ones, from Rome, Jerusalem, Canterbury, and everywhere else I used to travel.

I couldn't believe he'd kept my correspondence. But why not? I'd kept everything he'd ever sent me, or had, until much of it was destroyed in Honey Lane. I shook my head, determined not to cry. This was lovely. Beyond what I ever expected. Just like this house, I thought, looking about with wonder, as I oft did.

Finally, after some fortifying sips of ale, I was ready to read his final piece of correspondence.

Most humble and dutiful commendations to you, Alyson.

I hope you'll forgive my presumption in buying you a place in Southwark. I know you were determined to make your own way and not be controlled or have to bow to the authority of those who by chance of birth are granted it. I reasoned that with me dead, you have no one to answer to, no gratitude to express, and it's my dearest hope that you will take this in the spirit it was given, with my deepest affection to someone I'm proud to call both cousin and friend.

I had to stop and take a deep breath.

Knowing you as I do, I fear you'll be concerned that in giving you the house, in which I pray you are now comfortably ensconced, my children will be deprived.

I wasn't, but bless him for thinking that of me.

But my gift does not come without one request. Indeed, a couple. First, I ask that you look to my Lewis now and then. Lewis, in case you haven't already guessed, is my child by that woman you abhorred, Cecilia de Champain. While you were right to warn me about her, once I owned my part in Lewis's making, she dropped all the charges against me, provided I supported her and my son. Oft wanting coin myself as a consequence, I cannot regret Lewis, who is cut in my image and, I'm told, has my love of words and will make a good living using them. I pray it is so.

Well, I'll be damned . . .

Which leads me to the other children . . . I know you were always perplexed by my relationship with Philippa, wondering why I didn't try harder to be a good husband and father, oft hovering around the subject without asking directly. I feel I owe you an explanation. It's easier from beyond the grave where our only judge is God the Father, who, in my mind, I'd rather sit before than you, Alyson, the wife who once wished to rule her men.

The truth of the matter is, neither Thomas nor Helen are mine, at least, I don't believe they are. I'm certain they're Gaunt's spawn. The man loved de Roet women—his Katherine and her sister, my Philippa, though she never really was mine, was she?

So often men and even the fairer sex look to their children to carry their blood, their name and, if greatness should elude the parent in their lifetime, then they pray their children will achieve it on their behalf, make them immortal. I was never destined for greatness or, it appears, to have a family—a legitimate one at any rate. In that way, my dearest friend, we're more alike than not.

For years, you yearned for a family. I did too. But what I discovered in my dotage, and wish to share with you, is that it's not too late; it's never too late. If I learned one thing from you, dear heart, it's that families come in different guises. One has only to look at what you created with Alyson, with Mervyn Slynge and his household. What you built in London—first in Honey Lane and then at St. Martin's. You made the family you always longed for, and while it didn't come without terrible cost and grief, knowing you, it will continue to grow and thrive.

What I must also tell you, and it's my deepest regret that I never said this to you personally, is that, you, Eleanor, Alyson, have always been family to me. I didn't always appreciate that, but you embraced me in ways a man can only dream. You blessed me with your good heart and goodwill and trusted me with your secret hopes and fears. You're the wife of my soul—one to whom I could cede control and know it was in the best of hands.

It's my greatest hope you'll truly forgive me for using elements of your life, of yourself, in my poems. I ask that you recall you'd oft castigate me for not writing about real people. You were right, so I am honoring you by writing about one of the most real and magnificent people I've ever been blessed to know.

If ever I've caused you harm or hurt, or ever do, it's never been my intention. Go forward, dear heart, full of the courage and *spirit that bubbles forth within you. Be mighty and loud and let your bright light shine. The world will be dimmer if you don't. Find love—and love fully. Whoever is fortunate enough to earn that from you and give it to you is blessed indeed.*

I speak from my experience, the one of having known and loved you and, I know, been loved in return.

Written on the Feast of the Eleven Thousand Virgins. (Aye, I chose the day deliberately.)

Yours, in greatest affection and admiration now and forever more,

Geoffrey.

I sat until the room grew dark and cold. Awash with feelings, I was tossed on wave after wave of remembrance, moving through time like a traveller in a tale—from Bath-atte-Mere to Bigod Farm and beyond, until I finally drew to a halt, here in Geoffrey's most generous gift, The Swanne. Ugly now, I would ensure, like the hatchlings that burst forth from the egg, like the old bride in the Wife's Tale, it became beautiful, elegant, and soared over every other business on Bankside.

Finally, as the stars burst into the firmament and the noise from the nearby tavern began to carry, I rose, lit a fire and some candles. Yolande came and asked if I wanted anything to eat. When the door opened, I could hear laughter and the pleasant chitter of the girls and the deeper tones of Master Stephen and the new man, as well as the excited calls of Harry, who, it seemed, had found an owlet in the rafters.

"I'll be down shortly, Yolande. Don't wait."

With a warm smile, she shut the door.

I returned to my seat with a goblet of wine and read Geoffrey's letter again.

"Find love," I whispered. Easy for him to say. Oh, I could find a prick to plough me and transport me to heavenly delights and, now I was here, as often as I wished. The idea made me grin. But love? Real love?

Did I need it? Did I want it?

Aye, who didn't? Geoffrey knew that. He'd wanted it too, hadn't he? That's why he wrote about it the way he did. Oh, I'd read all his quires, all of his wondrous, funny, moving, spiritual, thoughtful, dramatic poems. There wasn't one tale that didn't talk about love in some form, marriage too, whether it was love for fellow man, woman, sprite, goddess, or God.

I rose after a few minutes and, looking through the window at the twinkling stars, raised my goblet.

"Here's to you, my love. May I become what you always intended. My own woman."

I drank, blew out the candles and, shutting the door, went downstairs to join my girls, my family in the kitchen, the heart of our home and business—the place that Geoffrey, through love—and mayhap a little guilt at stealing my life for his poem—bequeathed me.

'Twas a trade—his words about me for this. I'd call it a bargain.

It was also a great chance, an opportunity.

Geoffrey's balls in a vice, I'd seize it and turn all our dreams— mine, Alyson's, Lowdy's, Geoffrey's, the family I had, and the one still to come—into a damn fine reality.

One so bright with promise and love, words can scarce capture it.

———◆———

GLOSSARY

***

Alb: a vestment or robe, usually white, worn by priests and which fell to the ankles

Arras: a large tapestry or wall-hanging

Bawd: refers to either a prostitute or the madam of a brothel

Boon-work: the unpaid work a tenant would perform for the lord of the manor—often ploughing or harvesting but any kind of service could be asked—as part of the obligation a tenant owed for living on the land

Brogger: a broker

Burlap: both a rough fabric and a coarsely woven bag

Canonical hours: the medieval day (24 hours) was divided into eight periods, designed for monks and priests to devote themselves to prayers, etc., and ordinary folk followed these as well. Bells were rung at roughly three-hour intervals: matins (around 3 a.m.), lauds (dawn—this eventually melded with matins and started around sunrise), prime (6 a.m.-ish), terce (9 a.m.-ish), sext (noon), nones (mid-afternoon), vespers (sunset), and compline (9 p.m.-ish).

Cincture: type of belt—sometimes a rope—worn around the waist and over an alb

Coney: rabbit/hare

Distaff: the stick or spindle around which wool is wound in preparation for spinning

Draff: the spent grain left from making ale

Ell: a length of cloth—just over one metre

Foldcourses: portable hurdles used to enclose sheep

Froys: a dish made with beef or veal and eggs

Fuller: someone who cleanses and cleans cloth which involved, in medieval times, steeping it in urine. A very smelly occupation.

Godsib: God sibling. Someone close to you but not necessarily related. A good friend, etc.

Jordan: slang for a chamber pot

Kirtle: an outer tunic or gown worn by women

Levereter: a corrupt person; a "liver-eater'

Manicple: person who bought provisions for a monastery

Maslin: a coarse bread peasants ate

Mazer: a drinking bowl made from wood or metal

Mercer: someone who trades in cloth

Meretrix: whore

Mortrews: a sweetish meat dish (like a paté) made with chicken or fish and ground almonds

Murrain: disease afflicting sheep and cattle

Paltock: a man's tunic or doublet

Pottage: basically, a thick soup or stew. Sometimes described as being like porridge.

Queynte/quoniam: women's genitalia

Sard: colloquial expression meaning sexual intercourse

Scarlet: a type of fabric

Scrip: a leather purse or satchel that pilgrims often would wear

Solar: The word comes from the French *seul*, which means "alone." It was effectively a chamber (usually upstairs) where the master or mistress of the house could withdraw. It sometimes also contained his or her bed.

Stillage: rent

Swive: colloquial expression meaning sexual intercourse

The Botch: medieval term for the Black Death or plague

Wassail: both a mulled wine drunk over the Christmas period and the offering of cheers and carolling

Villeins: refers to the peasant class, the laborers and tenant-farmers who lived on manorial land and who were subject to their master's will but also had limited rights. Were often free men and women, but could also be serfs (servants).

LIST OF REAL PEOPLE IN THE NOVEL

———— ◆ ————

* Denotes a real person
** Denotes a character from *The Canterbury Tales*

**Eleanor/Alyson

*Melisine de Compton: Eleanor's
mother (dec.)

*/**Geoffrey Chaucer:
author of *The Canterbury
Tales* and many other
works

*Robert Chaucer: Geoffrey's
grandfather

*King Edward II

*King Edward III

*Isabella of France: Richard II's
second wife

*King Richard II

*Henry IV/Henry Bolingbroke

*Queen Philippa: Edward III's
wife

*Queen Anne (of Bohemia):
Richard II's first wife

*John of Gaunt/Prince John

*Blanche, Duchess of Lancaster:
Gaunt's first wife

*Princess Constanza: Gaunt's
second wife

*Prince Edward Woodstock/The
Black Prince

*Katherine (Roet) Swynford:
Gaunt's third wife

*Philippa (Roet) Chaucer:
Geoffrey's wife

*Thomas Chaucer: Geoffrey's
eldest son

*Elizabeth Chaucer: Geoffrey's
daughter

*Lewis Chaucer: Geoffrey's youngest son

*Cecily Champain: accused Chaucer of "raptus"

*Adam Pinkhurst: Chaucer's favored scribe

*John Gower: good friend of Chaucer's and writer

*Wat Tyler, also sometimes known as Jack Straw: leader of Peasants' Revolt

*Nicholas Brembre: infamous mayor of London

*William Walworth: Mayor of London

*John Harewell, Bishop of Bath and Wells

*Gregory XI, Pope, 1370–1378

*Urban VI, Pope, 1378–1389 (Rome)

*Clement VII, the Anti-Pope (Avignon), 1378–1394

*Boniface IX, Pope (Rome), 1389–1404

* Simon Sudbury, Archbishop of Canterbury and Chancellor

*John Ball: priest

*John Wycliffe: famous Lollard who translated parts of the Bible into English

*John Brynchele: friend of Chaucer who was given a very early copy of *The Canterbury Tales*

*William Langland: author of *Piers Plowman*

*John Churchman: (former) friend of Chaucer who attempted to sue him

*/**Harry Baily: host and tour guide

** Jankin/Jankyn (Binder): Alyson's fifth husband

**The various nuns, abbesses, priests, parsons, clerks, manciples, shipman, pardoners, etc. who feature are drawn from Chaucer's portraits in *The Canterbury Tales*.

AUTHOR'S NOTE

————◆————

*T*his book was probably one of the greatest challenges I've yet had as a writer. I thought my previous novel, *The Darkest Shore* (based on a true story about one of the last and most heinous of the Scottish witch hunts), was tough—that was, until I started writing *The Good Wife of Bath*. The reason for this is complicated and for no small reason because I chose, as my major source material for at least the first half of the book, Geoffrey Chaucer's *The Canterbury Tales* and, in particular, his Wife of Bath's Prologue and Tale. I've loved these since I was a teenager and studied them first at school and, later, at university.

As a consequence, I not only had to cover decades of a fictitious woman's life—as imagined by a medieval man—including a first marriage to a much older man at the age of twelve and all that entails, but I had to recreate a "real" life, an authentic one, for a woman invented over six hundred years ago. I thought that, using Chaucer's Alyson and her life as described in *The Canterbury Tales* as a template, I could portray a genuine woman of the Middle Ages who, though strong and desiring mastery, was also subject to the social, economic, sexual, gendered, cultural, and political forces of the day—ones that, in order to give the book veracity, I had to respect as well. What I didn't count on—apart from Covid-19 and the impact that would have on my family, community, country, and the world—was a few hard personal blows that I will share here.

First, there was my husband collapsing from a mystery illness and needing care, then my younger brother being diagnosed with Stage Four brain cancer and all the sadness and finality that entails. As you can imagine, these make writing both incredibly difficult but also a guilty avenue of escape into a world you can control. But that's the joy and bind of fiction for writers and readers—it's a form of escapism and pleasure, but also something that can and should give us pause and move us out of our comfort zones and generate some passionate and healthy discussions.

I know writing this book did that for me and, I suspect, if you've made it this far, it did for you too. Thus, I feel I must address the most obvious ways in which this book might have made you uneasy—including the fact that a twelve-year-old girl has sex with a sixty-one-year-old man.

As confronting as this is for a modern reader (and it should be), not only was this lifted from Chaucer's poem (though the ages of the Wife's first three husbands aren't specified, the implication is they are elderly and wizened), but it is true to what happened in that era. Girls were considered eligible for marriage at the age of twelve, boys fourteen. I call them "girls" and "boys" here, but in those times, and for many hundreds of years to come, they were deemed young women and men. Eleanor/Alyson marrying at such a young age is, as it had to be, integral to an understanding of who she is and how she develops in terms of the woman she becomes.

I have to say, as true as I wanted to be to the facts both as a writer of historical fiction and someone who researches the past closely, and to give an accurate portrayal of conditions and relationships, I struggled with this notion so much. For us, in contemporary times, the idea that a girl of twelve has sex is repugnant (even though, sadly, it still happens)—and can be both a terrible trigger and appall people. It *is* appalling. We should be horrified that this kind of thing happened and it's a demonstration of how far some societies have advanced that this kind of relationship is now criminal. In the Middle Ages it was relatively "normal."

I feel I have to reassure you, dear reader, that in no way do I condone or endorse underage sex, child sex abuse, or anything associated with something so heinous. I view what happens in the novel, which is accurate to its time and source material, as something quite separate, and I feel I'd be doing a grave injustice to all those girls who did endure and survive, and those who didn't, if I pretended this kind of thing didn't happen. I agonized over the writing of her first two marriages, really, and that's to understate it. But if I didn't include it or changed Eleanor's age to be more palatable for modern readers, then what was the point of writing historical fiction? Of using Chaucer's poem? I should also point out that *The Canterbury Tales* is still much admired and taught in schools and universities around the globe. "The Marriage Group" (the tales which specifically deal with marriage) in particular gets a great deal of attention—as it should, with its reflections and observations on marriage, gender, and sexual politics and relationships in a period we're still learning about. The Wife of Bath's Tale and Prologue is, arguably, the most popular with historians and literary scholars, all of whom accept Alyson's youthful marriage as something that occurred in that time—because they accept it, however, doesn't mean they approve of it. Likewise, for me. I hope you understand my intentions and the spirit and struggles (!) in which Eleanor/Alyson's story was written.

What we do know of Alyson from Chaucer's poem, apart from her five marriages, is mixed and complicated. To some scholars and readers, Alyson, the Wife of Bath, is a proto-feminist, railing against medieval strictures and the patriarchal society that governed women's behavior and blamed them for all ills. Something akin to the "all men are bastards" line. Yet the Wife doesn't come across as a very nice person either. Contrary to what was expected of women in her time, she boasts of her sexual conquests and how she achieves mastery in her various marriages (overturning the "natural" order) by withholding sexual favors, demanding them, lying, deceiving, and various other underhand methods. She's presented as vain, very aware of her rising social position, and enjoying the more material elements of her various pilgrimages as opposed to the spiritual. She also shows great learning by quoting philosophers, religious figures, and the Bible and then turning much of it on its head—pointing out that if men, who think so little of women, are charged with and responsible for recording history, laying down laws and religious guidelines, then of course women won't be featured in their best light. Men, she argues, will inevitably portray women as "wicked." However, she says, if women were allowed to tell their stories, imagine how different they might be. How might men fare then? Hence the famous line from Aesop's fables, "Who painted the lion?" (the title of the prologue in this book). Why, the person who slew it, of course. How different might the portrait be if the lion was given the chance to tell his story? What if women wrote history?

Other scholars understand the Wife as Geoffrey's raucous mouthpiece, who emphasizes every negative trait about women and then some—reinforcing the need for men to have mastery over their women. There's a sense in which the Wife's own eloquence condemns her and all other women she might speak for. Then, there are those who see both sides.

S. H. Rigby's essay "The Wife of Bath, Christine de Pizan and the Medieval Case for Women" in *The Chaucer Review* (Vol. 35 No. 2, 2000) sums them up well:

> *The debate [by scholars] thus comes down to the problem of who is speaking in the Wife of Bath's Prologue: is it "quite certain" that Alyson is the mouthpiece for Chaucer's own views, or is there a gap between the Wife's discourse and Chaucer's own voice, one which allows us to see the irony at work in her prolonged confession?*

Priscilla Martin in her fantastic book *Chaucer's Women* argues, "One could construct a feminist or a sexist Chaucer using essentially the same evidence from his writings."

This is so true.

I liked to think of Chaucer as someone who, despite his flaws, wrote to challenge the status quo, a writer who had his finger on the pulse of the everyday (as well as court and mercantile affairs), but who also used satire and learned discourse to hold a mirror up to men, women, marriage, and relationships overall—and not just in his *Canterbury Tales*, but in all his works. Certainly in having a woman contest accepted orthodoxy, he throws down a challenge.

Well, it was a challenge I couldn't resist—even if I have taken it up in a way I don't imagine Chaucer intended.

Like all writers of historical fiction, it's in history's gaps and omissions, in the deep and rich layers, that we uncover little nuggets we can turn into stories. So it is with Alyson, the Wife of Bath.

And, just as Chaucer did when he placed himself in his *Canterbury Tales*, I've inserted him into my story.

In this novel, I've made him an integral part of Eleanor/Alyson's life. I've also reversed what he did when he told her tale, by giving her the authoritative voice and allowing her to tell his story (the final letter aside). Even so, all mention of Chaucer throughout the novel—his various social, political, and familial roles, poems, movements, etc. are represented accurately. Unlike the Wife, he *was* a historical figure (some academics persist with the idea the Wife was based on Edward III's mistress, Alice Perrers; I'm not convinced—though Chaucer may have drawn on some of the woman's more colorful attributes, or how they were remembered by males of the period, in creating Alyson). I used a number of biographies of Chaucer to flesh out his character, and also his body of work—always with an eye to the fact that a writer's body of work is not indicative of who that person is.

Chaucer, while a mighty talent with an acute eye for detail and a gift for poetry and prose, was not above misbehaving (as charges of violence, his never-ending debt, and the accusation of *raptus*—which can mean rape or even kidnapping—attest). He began life as a middle-class London man, before becoming a page in Prince Lionel's house. Some believe he may have studied at the law courts when young (I borrowed that notion, as I did his missing years, having him work for a lawyer and visiting Lady Clarice and the Bath area often), before becoming an integral member of John of Gaunt's household. He had kings and princes as patrons (he was even ransomed for sixteen pounds when he was captured by the

French in 1360) and was a diplomat, an MP for Kent, a Surveyor of the King's Works, and, for many years, a Comptroller of the Wool Customs (among other goods). Likewise, a couple of scholars posed the question regarding his children and their paternity. I've used this and sought to offer an explanation—albeit in fiction, but not without solid reasoning behind it. So, every reference to Geoffrey, his travels, marriage, children, professional, and personal relationships, work, writing, the charge of *raptus*, Cecilia Champain (also called Champagne), doubts about the paternity of his children, everything apart from his interactions with Eleanor/Alyson, are based on known facts.

What about Alyson? For those of you interested in reading what Chaucer created, there are many wonderful editions of *The Canterbury Tales* in the original Middle English, including online. It takes a bit of getting used to, the old English, but eventually, if you read it aloud, it starts to make sense and has a beautiful singsong quality and flow. For those of you preferring a translation, Neville Coghill's really captures the spirit of the tales quite beautifully. When you read The Wife of Bath's Prologue and Tale, you'll get a sense of how it's woven through this novel.

What we know about Alyson from The Wife of Bath's Prologue, and *The Canterbury Tales* overall, is as follows: starting with her physical appearance, she was a solid woman, ruddy-cheeked, with large hips and well-dressed, who wore spurs on her boots and a broad-brimmed hat. She may have had red hair and had a great gap between her teeth and freckles/port-wine birthmark. She was married five times. The first time was at the age of twelve.

The Wife's first three husbands were really old and she was pretty awful to them (she admits this)—bribing them to attain mastery in the relationship, withholding sex (which she mostly enjoyed) to gain benefits that ranged from jewels to clothes. She was a magnificent weaver (in Chaucer's poem, she tells us all this—unashamedly, brashly, and magnificently). She also tells us she has a marvelous queynte and is a slave to her sexual passions—Venus being her ruler, though she was not above allowing Mars to rise as well.

Her fourth husband was unfaithful to her and caused her much pain. She met her fifth husband, the much younger Jankin (he is the only husband named in the poem) at her fourth husband's funeral and married him less than a month later. There was violence in the relationship, particularly because Jankin, a scholar, would quote endlessly about the wickedness of women until she was so fed up, she tore pages from his book, and he struck her so badly she lost her hearing in one ear and he thought her dead. After that, he gave her complete authority and they were happy.

Even so . . . it wasn't "ever after," for, as the poem makes clear, when we first meet Chaucer's Alyson in the General Prologue to *The Canterbury Tales*, she's on another pilgrimage and on the lookout for her next husband. One presumes then that Jankin is dead.

The poem also reveals that Alyson has a Godsib named Alison with whom she shares secrets, who lives next door. In Neville Coghill's translation of the Prologue, the Wife tells us:

> *My fifth (husband) and last—God keep his soul in health!*
> *The one I took for love and not for wealth,*
> *Had been at Oxford not so long before*
> *But had left school and gone to lodge next door,*
> *Yes, it was to my godmother's he'd gone.*
> *God bless her soul! Her name was Alison.*
> *She knew my heart and more of what I thought*
> *Than did the parish priest, and so she ought!*
> *She was my confidante, I told her all . . .*
> *And to my niece, because I loved her well,*
> *I'd have told everything there was to tell.*

There is also a Dame Alice mentioned—the niece? Regardless, I melded them into one person.

Alyson also tells us she's been on many pilgrimages. All the places my Eleanor/Alyson writes letters from in the novel are places Chaucer's Alyson visited (she also went to Spain, but I didn't include that except as an aside). The descriptions of those cities are as close as I could get to the period. What happened, how the pilgrims traveled, the places they stopped, modes of transport, etc.

are historically accurate. So too are the ampullae, badges, and various relics that were available for purchase on these trips, including those shaped like male and female genitalia. Apparently, there was a huge market in those!

(A quick aside: the "c" word is liberally used throughout the book, as are its variations, "queynte" and "quoniam." The words were not considered offensive in those times but merely nouns to very pragmatically describe a body part. They were used in daily parlance. No offense is intended in their use in the novel, just historical accuracy.)

While many people did undertake pilgrimages for spiritual reasons, it was also known that they offered adventure, liberty, and the opportunity to meet and get to "know"—in all senses—other people as well. Especially for women. The Wife and my Eleanor/Alyson are quite open about the fact they enjoy the secular side of the journey as much if not more than the spiritual. Medieval tourism was on the ascent at this time and for many commoners as well as the gentles, it was a form of exploration, liberation, and escapism, in addition to gaining knowledge of other people and cultures. The Wife was certainly at the forefront of this.

I should also add here that I've been so very fortunate in the last decade or more (pre-Covid) to have traveled to many of the places Eleanor/Alyson went. In Rome, I didn't visit all the shrines she did, but I did fall in love with the ancient city and threw coins in the Fountain of Trevi both times I was there—I sincerely hope that means I get to go a third time. I also spent a few days in Cologne and visited the magnificent Dom, as the Cathedral is known, and saw the casket that houses the Three Magi. It is as I describe, and apparently was then too.

I also went to Jerusalem. My mother is from Israel (Haifa—which I also visited) and a trip to that country would not be complete without going to the holiest of cities. Jerusalem is an amazing amalgam of faith, spirituality, seething violence, and cultural clashes. I adored it, but the entire time I was there, I felt not only the rich cultural and religious history and tensions, but the underbelly of hostility. This wasn't helped by the fact that not only is the old city divided into quarters (Christian, Jewish, Muslim), but the entry and exit points to these areas were guarded by armed soldiers who appeared wary and weary (probably of the young boys hurling rocks at them—truly!). But the sense of walking in the steps of history was awe-inspiring and emotional. The Church of the Holy Sepulchre was something I will never forget, nor my experience at the Wailing Wall. Oh, and my guide for that trip, Shalom (that was his name!), is honored in the novel as Eleanor's guide as well. He was wonderful—great sense of humor and incredible knowledge.

So, while I was familiar with some of the areas and places Alyson/Eleanor (and Geoffrey) journey to, I admit St. Martin's Le Grand was, until I began my research, unfamiliar to me. I've since discovered that, like other places, usually associated with religious houses (Whitefriars being another, later, example), it was considered a sort of "neutral zone" within the walls of London, a place of sanctuary where criminals could take refuge. Operated by religious men with a different set of laws, I've no doubt many sought to take great advantage of this fact, and not only those escaping justice—both fair and unfair.

Another point to make is regarding the laws governing prostitution—both in London and Southwark. All references in the novel to dress, punishments, fines, etc. are based on fact. While it was generally considered an illegal occupation and much maligned, and the women were sometimes brutally treated, it was mostly tolerated. Still, those who sold sex had to wear yellow hoods to stand out (which is strange when you think what they were doing was illegal). Within London, women who were apprehended were penalized, usually very publicly—even though authorities knew prostitutes were more likely to frequent certain areas. (All the streets I mention existed and their names refer to the trade conducted there—I mean, Gropecunt!) If they weren't thrown into prison for a time, their heads were shaved, they were placed in the pillory for hours or days and paraded through the streets with a sign around their neck for crowds to mock them and throw things at them.

However, in Southwark the laws were far more flexible. Here, on the south bank of the Thames, "bathhouses," mostly erected in the liberty of the Bishop of Winchester and run by the Flemish, flourished. They became known as "The Stews" and the women who plied their trade as "Winchester Geese." While the laws were laxer this side of the river, there were still rules by which the women had to abide. I can strongly recommend Martha Carlin's amazing and erudite book *Medieval Southwark* for details surrounding not just prostitution, but all trades and the way in which life there differed from that in London.

Before my Alyson became a bawd, however, she was known (as in the poem) for her talent with wool and weaving. All references to sheep, their husbandry, wool, the trade, the dependence on alien merchants, the Staple, and the way deals were done in those days are accurate. Likewise, the reluctance, if not downright refusal, of the guild to admit women, even experienced and talented ones. This was a rule that was by no means exclusive to the trades of weaving and fulling. One has only to read *The Brewer's Tale/The Lady Brewer of London* to know this as well—the book where Alyson, the bawd, first features.

All references to the plague, including the dates of outbreaks, are accurate. Known as the Botch or "the Great Sickness," the terms "Black Death" and even "plague" were applied much later. That I wrote many of those scenes while the world was in lockdown with Covid-19 added to the frisson. Likewise, weather patterns, crop failures, and famine, politics, wars, major figures such as mayors, nobility, rich merchants, etc. are all taken from history.

So too was the Peasant's Revolt, led by Wat Tyler, and what happened as a consequence of the "commons" marching on London Bridge and meeting with their young sovereign. The working classes were betrayed by their king and his nobles, quelled with false assurances. Their ability to rally and have a united voice must have worried the gentry. This peasant unity only came about because of the changes wrought by the Black Death of 1348–1350. History has recorded how so many deaths, of low- and high-born, changed the social landscape, bequeathing those who had no power a little, which they grasped and, slowly, turned to their advantage. Post the plague (and every subsequent outbreak, which was about every twenty years), there were more upheavals and changes to once rigid social structures. This gradually saw the end of the villeins and "boon-work" and better wages and overall conditions for poor freemen and others. The poem "Piers Plowman" by William Langland, mentioned in the novel, describes conditions. Likewise, the incident on London Bridge when the young Queen was welcomed to London really happened; a number of people were crushed, fell off the bridge, and lost their lives in their eagerness to see the King's new bride.

I should also add that those of you who've read *The Brewer's Tale/ The Lady Brewer of London* might recognize some characters who make an appearance in the latter half of the book—and not just Alyson. There's also Oriel, Leda, Yolande, Master Stephen atte Place, Marcian Vetazes, and young Harry. Harry Frowyk is based on a real person. According to records, Master Harry (Henry) Frowyk becomes Lord Mayor of London not once, but twice—from 1435–1436 and again in 1444–1445. So, from inauspicious beginnings, Harry finds success under Alyson's guidance (and Anneke's—but that's another story). Harry Bailly was also a real person as well as the innkeep of the Tabard in Southwark and a friend of Chaucer's.

I always enjoy placing women back into *his*tory, demonstrating, albeit through researched fiction, that while they may not be recorded or remembered in the same way as their male counterparts, they were there. *Her*story happened too. The omission of women from history doesn't mean they didn't live it, nor that they didn't influence it. But just as we forget that to our detriment, so too it's a mistake to think women fighting for their rights is exclusive to contemporary times. Many women have, over time, fought to be recognized as more than simply walking wombs, the "weaker vessel," good only for sating men's desires, "feeble-minded," penis-less poor copies of men, responsible for the Fall, men's inability to control their urges, and so much more. What's true about the past is that women didn't have the freedoms, education or ability to fight for their rights the way we continue to today. One has only to look at the evidence, whether it's Cleopatra, Boadicea, Joan of Arc, Mary Magdalene, Elizabeth the First, Margery Kemp, Chaucer's Alyson, to catch glimpses of those who knew they deserved better—if not authority, then at least respect and, one day, equality. These women—some powerful, but many not—would have striven in their own way, that is, used their wiles and more to achieve a degree of autonomy and a voice—one so loud and powerful, we still hear it today.

In order to write Eleanor/Alyson's story, I relied on a great many books, historical records, poems, articles by historians and scholars, past and current, contemporary sources wherever possible, and so much wonderful creative work too. Following are just some of those to whom I owe a debt of gratitude, and whose scholarship and insights I am in awe of.

First and foremost, I used *The Canterbury Tales* by Geoffrey Chaucer (both in Middle English and the fabulous translation by Neville Coghill); *The Wife of Bath's Prologue and Tale* edited by Valerie Allen and David Kirkham; *The Wife of Bath's Tale* edited by Steven Croft; *The Wife of Bath's Prologue and Tale: Notes* by J. A. Tasioulas.

In order to get a sense of women in the era, I read a range of books including *Chaucer's Women: Nuns, wives and Amazons* by Priscilla Martin; *Medieval Women: A social history of women in England 450–1500* by Henrietta Leyser; *The Ties that Bound* by Barbara Hanawalt; *Common Women: Prostitution and Sexuality in Medieval England* by Ruth Mazo Karras; *London: A Travel Guide Through Time* by Dr. Matthew Green; *London Life in the Fourteenth Century* by Charles Pendrill; John Stow's *A Survey of London* in two volumes.

Biographies of Chaucer included: *The Poet's Tale: Chaucer and the Year That Made The Canterbury Tales* by Paul Strohm; the magnificent *Chaucer: A European Life* by Marion Turner; and *Chaucer* by Peter Ackroyd.

To immerse myself in medieval London and England, I read: *London in the Age of Chaucer* by A. R. Myers; *Chaucer's People* by Liza Picard; *The Time Traveller's Guide to Medieval England* by Ian Mortimer; *Daily Life in Chaucer's England* by Jeffrey L. Forgeng and William McLean; *The Middle Ages Unlocked: A Guide to Life in Medieval England 1050–1300* by Gillian Polack and Katrin Kania; *Medieval Domesticity: Home, Housing and Household in Medieval England* edited by Maryanne Kowaleski and P. J. P. Goldberg; *Life in the Middle Ages* by Martyn Whitlock; *England in the Age of Chaucer* by William

Woods; *Everyday Life in Medieval Times* by Marjorie Rowling; *Everyday Life in the Middle Ages* by Sherrilyn Kenyon; *Medieval Southwark* by Martha Carlin; *Forensic Medicine and Death Investigation in Medieval England* by Sara M. Butler.

In order to portray what happened on medieval pilgrimages, I read the following: *Pilgrimages: The Great Adventure of the Middle Ages* by John Ure; *Pilgrimage in Medieval England* by Diana Webb; *The Pilgrim's Journey: A History of Pilgrimage in the Western World* by James Harpur.

Likewise, I watched countless documentaries, dramas, and read so many wonderful works of fiction set in this era—please see my website karenrbrooks.com for reviews.

Naturally, anything perceptive and clever is entirely due to these authors and creators' diligence and talent, and any mistakes, I humbly apologize for—they're my own. Either that, or I made them deliberately and cry "fiction." ☺

While the Wife of Bath's voice is granted to her by a man, it's no reason not to listen to what she has to say. It's also what makes her so interesting. As the scholars still argue—was she simply a ventriloquist's dummy? Or was Chaucer giving the women of his time a platform, offering something more than what folk of the Middle Ages expected from the female sex? Was he being ironic? Was it satire? And if so, who was he satirizing? Men? Women? Marriage? All of the above? Even the scholars the Wife quotes in the poem begin to look a little foolish when she applies her logic to their arguments. That would have been a bitter pill for many at the time to swallow, but it also caused a great deal of amusement, anger, and everything in between.

These questions have long fascinated me and I began thinking of what life might have been like for someone like the Wife of Bath—taking into account the major moments of the poem, but also placing her within lived history, respecting the strictures imposed by her age, sex, the liberties, or otherwise marriage may have granted her, and recreating an amazing, complicated life. I wondered, if she could tell her own story, what might she tell us? How might she tell it? And above all, what is *her* story?

I hope I've done her justice.

ACKNOWLEDGMENTS

I love writing this part: it's the bookend to a labor of love, to all the sweat, tears, agonizing over plotlines, sleepless nights and rotten days where the words just won't cooperate, or fabulous ones when they flow in torrents. This, even while I live in fear I'll leave someone important out. In case that happens, I'm commencing my acknowledgments with an apology. As I've said before, if I have left you out of these pages, you're not excluded from my heart.

Like all my other novels, this one couldn't have been written without the support, kindness, generosity, and love of so many people, many of them unaware of how much their encouragement, patience, occasional query about progress, texts, messages, invitations to dinner or drinks, and ability to help me shed my self-doubt mean. Even during the surreal isolation and slow restoration to a new "normal" that's been the aftermath of Covid-19, people still reached out to me and Stephen, my husband, and I love them for it. Now I've the chance to publicly thank you all.

First, I want to thank my wonderful Australian agent, Selwa Anthony, who from the moment I told her I wanted to write a sort of prequel to *The Brewer's Tale/The Lady Brewer of London* by writing about the brothel madam, Alyson, was on board. She encouraged me, as she always does, and even though she was going through some very dark times, she always made the effort to call or text and make sure I was creating and not sinking into a Covid-induced isolation inertia (and my heart goes out to all of those who found they did). Thank you, Selwa—you're my dearest friend as well as agent and I'm blessed you're in my life.

I also want to thank my US agents, Jim Frenkel and Catie Pfeifer, who, as always, have been as enthusiastic about this book as they have all my others—and during a fraught time for them as they experienced the double-whammy of Covid and the US 2020 election and its unprecedented aftermath in 2021. Thank you so very much, both of you—you are (my) champions! Jim, especially, would often write amazing emails full of information, humor, and blasts of encouragement.

Then, there's my gorgeous, clever publisher, Jo Mackay from HQ/HarperCollins. What can I say? When she phoned me up after reading an unedited version of this manuscript, bubbling with enthusiasm, laughing at some of my wife's antics, weeping at others, all the while appreciating and understanding what I was trying to accomplish, as well as entering into deep discussions about Eleanor's age, the historical context, and the events that occur and how it's important to be true to the women and the era, it meant the world. She raised my spirits—as you always do, Jo, and I cannot thank you enough for being you and for "getting" this book.

Likewise, my wonderful editor, Linda Funnell. Linda knows my work so well by now and what I'm seeking to say—not always successfully. Whether it's a word, a phrase, or a (contentious) plot point, Linda always knows how to put it the way I meant, to iron out the creases. She sees the holes that need filling and altogether makes my work so much smoother and thus better. I love working with you, I appreciate everything you do so much (and don't tell you enough), and thank you from the bottom of my heart.

Same to the joyous and talented Annabel Blay, my other editor who oversees everything and allays my fears, doubts, and anxieties (there were quite a few with this book!) and is so damn sensible, wise, and kind and just amazing. Thank you.

To the rest of the team at HQ/HarperCollins—especially Natika Palka, Eloise Plant, Jo Munroe, and Rejinder Sidhu—thank you. I also want to say a very special thank-you to the incredibly talented Michaela Alcaino for the absolutely gorgeous cover. The first time I saw it, I was utterly speechless. I could not have imagined a more perfect jacket for Eleanor/Alyson's story. I reckon even Chaucer would be delighted.

To my publishers in the US, UK, and Canada, William Morrow, especially, Rachel Kahan and the wonderful team in editing, design, and marketing, thank you for your faith in me and my work and for giving it such a great home.

Then there's my most cherished of friends, Kerry Doyle. When Kerry, her husband Peter Goddard, my husband Stephen, and I all traveled to the UK together in 2017, I dragged them to Bath. We'd just spent time in London and though Bath wasn't strictly where they wanted to go, they came anyway. I'd been there before back in 2014, but wanted to shore up a sense of the place where my Eleanor and Alyson would one day preside. Fortunately, they loved it as much as I did. While traces of medieval Bath are hard to find, they are there, but it was the overall ambience and magnificence of the place (that, and some great food and drinks in The Raven, which appears in the novel as The Corbie's Feet) that kept us content and in awe. Always tolerant and supportive of my digressions in order to research, there's no one I'd rather travel with than these fabulous, funny, clever, easy-to-get-along-with best buddies. Thank you.

Kerry is also one of my beta-readers. I've said this before, but I really mean it—it takes a very special person to be willing to undertake such a role. To read a work-in-progress and give feedback honestly to an (over)sensitive writer is a huge ask. Kerry is an experienced reader and a discerning one—we share our reading tastes and exchange books all the time, often sharing the same views about them. Yet, when it comes to my work, I trust her to be both brutally frank and kind when she reads. She is all that and so much more, which is a testimony to the wonderful woman she is and our longstanding friendship, which I value more than words can ever say. Thank you, Kerry, my lovely, my soul-sister.

Thanks to you too, Peter, for your love, friendship, and support and for being so much a part of this tale and the ones we're still creating together!

Thanks too, to my Hobart friends—you are always so supportive and interested in my work, even if it's feigned, and I love you for that too. Whether it's Stephen Bender, who, while he was stuck in Tassie during lockdown, became even more a part of our family than ever, and saw me having literary (as opposed to literal) meltdowns over the direction the book was taking and still loves me! Thanks too, to our beautiful neighbors, Bill, Lyn, and Jack Lark, for the many conversations, laughs, drinks, meals, and so much more. Also, thanks to Mark Nicholson and Robin Mclean for your unerring support. Then, there's someone else I share my love of reading with (and exchange "must reads"), the incomparable Luci (Lucinda) Wilkins and her gorgeous partner, Simon Thomson—thanks to both of you for the food, drinks, chats, laughs, and all else that comes with a great friendship—oh, and the puppy pics! Thanks too to Clinton and Rosie Steele, who always remember to ask what I'm writing and, when it's published, to read it too.

To the lovely Robbie (the Glaswegian Taswegian) and his beautiful wife and my friend, Emma Gilligan, and wee Harvey, thank you.

To my most special friends, with whom I share political diatribes (there were a few of those over the last couple of years, let me tell you), joy in images, poems, films, and books as well as celebrating each other's triumphs and mourning the setbacks, Professor Jim McKay, Dr. Helen Johnston, Dr. Liz Ferrier, Professor David Rowe, Professor Malcolm McLean, Professor Mike Emmison, Dr. Janine Mikosa (a superbly talented writer), and Linda Martello, thank you.

I also wish to thank (though they might not know it, they have been a great support and presence), Catherine Miller (my oldest buddy—as in, we've known each other since we were eleven and twelve), Dr. Frances Thiele, Grant Searle, Fletcher Austin, Dr. Lisa Hill, Sheryl Gwyther, Dannielle Miller, Mark Woodland, Mimi McIntyre, Gav

Jaeger, and Jason Greatbatch (who also kept me so entertained with their stories, beautiful pics, and wonderful company—and their furbies), Mick and Katri DuBois, Trevor Dale and Jeff Francombe, Professor Kim Wilkins, and my lovely stepmum, Moira Adams.

I also want to give a special—thanks is not the right word—acknowledgment to my brother, Peter Adams, who at the time of writing is still with us but, sadly, not for much longer. It's been a rocky road, an incredibly bumpy one for him and those who care about him. Sorry, for this, I just don't have the words.

I also want to thank the IASH at the University of Queensland where I am an honorary senior research consultant.

Thanks also to the talented Tony Mak and Sharn Hitchins for their wonderful music and friendship over the years and who, when they play at the brewstillery, give us and others such joy.

I also really want to thank my readers. Where would I be without you? I am so grateful to you for the shout-outs, reviews, the contact, and for picking up my books and telling others about them. Same with the booksellers and librarians, the custodians of stories—the matchmakers of the imagination—the gatekeepers of culture—thank you, each and every one of you wherever you are in this crazy, magnificent world.

Thank you as well to my gorgeous Facebook friends on my author page and on Goodreads, Twitter, and Instagram, as well as the podcasters and Facebook reading groups who also support books and writers, engage with us, review our works, discuss them passionately, and keep us motivated and feeling appreciated—you're beyond simply terrific.

Also, a huge thanks to the friends of Captain Bligh's Brewery and Distillery—Brewstillery now! Every time I see you, whether it's at our monthly bar nights or the markets or around town, you support what it is Stephen and I (and Adam) do—whether it be with beer, spirits, or books. Thank you so much. We love you guys.

I also want to thank my much-missed inspiration and cherished friend, Sara Douglass.

Now it's time for my last thanks—my family. Starting with my remarkable sister, Jenny Farrell, a nurse and my brother's main guardian. In a year that has tossed up more challenges than we ever anticipated, she's been a tower of strength, kindness, and the backbone of our family as we struggled with my brother's terminal cancer diagnosis and the aftermath of that. Even so, she has never relaxed her unerring support of me, her unshakeable belief in what I do. I love you, Jenny—and that lovely husband of yours, my dear brother-in-law, John Farrell.

To my furbies—my canine muses and beloved companions, Tallow, Dante, and Bounty—who sit with me day in and out as I write, act out scenes and accents (as their little heads twist one way then the other, reducing me to gales of laughter), I am so blessed you chose me as one of your humans. We're growing old together, but at least it's together. I so wish they could read this!

To my beautiful very adult children, Adam and Caragh—both incredible creators in their own unique ways—one with spirits, the other with words, computer code, and amazing artworks and ideas. They make me laugh, cry, frustrated, proud, cranky, and joyous and remind me every day that real life can be both as challenging and as crazily astonishing as the fictional ones I write. I love you both very much.

Finally, I have to thank my beloved husband, my partner in everything. Last year, for a few hours, I thought I was going to lose him. I cannot begin to tell you how that felt. Except, at some point in the long journey to be by his side where he was in a remote emergency room, it occurred to me that there was nothing I needed to say to him; I'd no regrets or things I wish we'd said or done—apart or together. How lucky am I? To have that realization that I shared my life with the right person, the only person I wanted to be with, was very powerful. As I traveled, I'd time to reflect on our life and partnership. There's been good and dreadful times, moments of unbelievable sorrow, yet also deep and joyous love, which always ends with gratitude for what we have. We often marvel. For me, I now marvel that I still have him. In terms of my professional life, he's always supported me—critiqued, read, been a wonderful sounding board. He loved Alyson from the moment I brought her voice to life and every step of the way since. If only she'd had a husband like him, then her life may have turned out very differently, even back then. But he's here, in this time, and he's my partner in everything and for that I'm beyond fortunate and beyond grateful. It's good to be his wife.

About the author

About the book

Read on

Insights,
Interviews
& More...

Meet Karen Brooks

Stephen Brooks

KAREN BROOKS is the author of fifteen books. She was an academic for over twenty years, a newspaper columnist, and a social commentator. She has a PhD in English/cultural studies and has published internationally on all things popular culture, education, and social psychology. An award-winning teacher, she has taught throughout Australia and in the Netherlands. Nowadays, she finds greatest contentment writing and studying history in Hobart, Tasmania. ✧

Reading Group Guide

1. Had you read *The Canterbury Tales* before reading this book? What was your impression, if any, of the Wife of Bath after reading Chaucer's story about her?

2. After being forced to accept a marriage to Fulk Bigod, Eleanor realizes to her surprise that "the man whom the villagers mocked and whispered about, who was said to be a bully at best and a murderer at worst, had shown me nothing but consideration and, for what it was worth, a welcome." How did her first marriage set up the rest of Eleanor's life?

3. When Fulk talks about his daughter, Alyson, with Eleanor he says, "You'll be good for her. And I know she'll be good for you." Was that true? Did it foreshadow what ultimately happened to Alyson and how it saved Eleanor?

4. What did you make of Eleanor's marriages of convenience to Turbet Gerrish and Mervyn Slynge? What did she gain from those marriages? How would you compare them to her later marriages, which were for love? ▶

5. What do Eleanor's letters to Geoffrey Chaucer about her travels reveal about her? Why do you think she chooses to write him?

6. When Eleanor has to flee to London, Geoffrey tells her to look on the bright side, exclaiming, "You're a free woman once more—albeit poorer." But is that truly a good thing? Would she have been better off staying and trying to fight for justice and to keep her wealth?

7. When Eleanor finds out that the girls she cares for have turned to prostitution, she thinks, "If the girls were willing, if it's what they wanted and were safe, was it so bad?" Do you agree? Does Eleanor truly feel this way, or do they simply have no other choice? What do you make of her later claim: "Reluctant though I'd been to become what I most loathed, someone who profited from a woman's body, when the role was thrust upon me, I not only enjoyed the privilege, but was damn good at it too"?

8. What did you think about Eleanor's final encounter with Jankin? Was she right not to reclaim her identity and wealth, and let Sabyn have it instead? In the end, was justice truly served?

9. Eleanor says of Chaucer, "Geoffrey was hardly a man, not in the way others were to me." Is this true? Was the relationship somehow more true because it wasn't sexual? What did you think of his deathbed letter, in which he writes to Eleanor, "You ... have always been family to me. . . . You're the wife of my soul"?

10. In The Wife of Bath's Tale in Chaucer's original, the moral of the story is that what women most want is control. Do you agree? How would that idea have resonated in medieval times versus modern times?

11. Karen Brooks subtitled this book "A (Mostly) True Story." What do you think she meant by that? Who decides what's true about Eleanor's story? ᥴᴗ

More by Karen Brooks

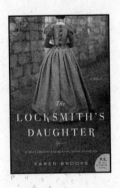

HAVE YOU ENJOYED THESE OTHER HISTORICAL NOVELS BY KAREN BROOKS?

The Lady Brewer of London

The Locksmith's Daughter

The Chocolate Maker's Wife

Discover great authors, exclusive offers, and more at hc.com.